ŪKO'S
LEGACY

ŪKO'S LEGACY

ROD PANOS

atmosphere press

SURVIVAL

CHAPTER 1
Pursuit

Alexandra lay back, letting the salty flavor erupt on her tongue. Behind closed eyes she savored the fish roe delicacy's rich, buttery texture, reminding herself that the first bite was always the most pleasurable. Her eyes opened to a sunlit scene of beachfront and blue water. Her ears bathed in the sibilant swoosh of waves washing ashore. A second bite had not yet completed the journey from plate to mouth when a loud blare jolted her arm, scattering the fork's burden across the dark wooden surface of her desktop. Had she forgotten to mute the comlink?

An interrupted lunch was a small breach of etiquette, but patience was not among Alexandra's more characteristic virtues. She sat upright and reached across the desk, nearly upsetting an ancient set of nested tea dolls as she passed a hand over the small activator beacon.

Beachfront beauty instantly dissolved, replaced by her first officer's overlarge solid image filling the far third of her stateroom. Alexandra looked directly at him, making no effort to soften the scowl on her face or the abrupt tone in her voice. "Yes? What is it?"

"Honorable Captain, I think you'll want to return to the bridge. We've just intercepted a data transmission."

Annoyance became anger. Was this a poor jest? Did she hear a joking tone beneath the comlink's distortion? *A data transmission! beliberda!* The unspoken expletive seemed more forceful when issued in the ancient language. Alexandra could still hear her patrician father's similar use of much stronger words.

Alexandra Ivanova Roshenkov enjoyed her reputation as one of the Astrocorps' more ambitious young captains. She paid little attention to rumors that her rank came more from family connections than from demonstrated skill and she was not in the habit of granting even the smallest latitude to junior officers. Aboard the interstellar vessel, Bright Victory II, no casual amusement would be conducted at her expense. The ship's general location, somewhere within the outer fringes of the Lesser Magellanic Cloud, placed more than 200,000 light-years between itself and any possible data transmission. None could be intercepted where none existed.

Pushing herself away from the desk, she buttoned her tunic as she rose. The elaborate garment impressed no one but her, but it was her own design and she saw nobility in its extraneous gold buttons. The door to her stateroom suite silently slid open and ushered her into the small, barren lift space that lowered her quickly to the nearby bridge. Alexandra entered to see her first officer's hand still touching the communication control. *Hah. Did I upset his little game?* "I'm in no mood for jokes, Commander!"

Commander Semgee Marlowe's barely whispered words reached unintended ears. "When are you ever?"

That Alexandra did not explode probably saved the bridge crew from an embarrassing scene. She and her first officer shared a somewhat distant relationship but, in her more lucid moments, she might allow that he occasionally performed his duties well. Yet, his attitude rankled. She'd heard the gossip. Semgee's assignment to Bright Victory, some said, came from Astrocorps Command's recognition of a need to balance the ship's leadership, a need for someone who might make up for the captain's abrupt ways. The fact that she had to look up to him when standing near did not help. One day soon she would simply have to find herself another first officer, one a bit more to her liking, a bit less defiant, and perhaps a little shorter.

Acting as though nothing had occurred, Commander Marlowe addressed her with his customary formality. "Honorable Captain, let me show you the signal we've received."

Alexandra accepted his formal manner as simply her due. She might have questioned its purpose had she known how he had never before found it necessary with any other ship's captain under whom he had served.

Under her silent scrutiny, Semgee touched a switch surface, unleashing into the whole of the bridge space a grating high-pitched buzz. Many hands moved to swiftly cover ears. Only Semgee remained fixed. "You're hearing a converted audio frequency version of what we just picked up. When analyzed further, we discovered data patterns. The signal contains some kind of code composed of limited characters."

Alexandra slowly lowered her hands, struck by the sincerity in her first officer's face. Her anger fled, leaving only numb shock in its wake. Feeling many eyes upon her, she hesitated, giving herself time to regain control. At length, she asked the only immediately pertinent question. "Where did it originate?"

Semgee nodded toward the three-dimensional display occupying the bridge area's central volume. "Somewhere very close to that star."

"Find the source. Now!"

Freed to do what he already knew he must, Semgee turned his full attention to the bridge crew. "Hansen, focus the visual display onto the best directional line you have for that transmission and filter out the strongest spectral bands from that red giant."

Yeoman Orango Hansen responded without a second's pause, eyes locked onto the instruments before him. "Done, sir."

In a blink, the display volume expanded and transformed the star's red dot into an orange ball floating above the center of the projector volume's waist-high enclosure. The striking red giant star had attracted Bright Victory to this small corner of the Lesser Magellanic Cloud in the first place. As the first starship from the League of Planets to ever travel outside the Milky Way, Bright Victory's exploratory mission would be well served by including in their growing catalogue a full workup of this spectacular star. The image seemed at first glance to occupy the display space in solitude. A closer look would reveal the presence of two tiny planetary companions, their relative images reduced to mere pinpoints by the star's sheer size.

A respectful nod joined Semgee's compliment. "Well done, yeoman." One had to admire the adept signalman's initiative, anticipating the order and preparing the display system to execute without delay.

"Now, start your search about a third of Victory's distance from our star and then slowly move closer along the radial line, increasing magnification as you go. I want to miss nothing as we move in."

Under Hansen's control, the spherical image slowly rotated as it descended toward the deck, growing larger until it filled the lowest portion of the projection enclosure with a shallow, nebulous, glowing dome. As the focus of the display moved yet closer to the star, the dome's gentle curve became more planar, settling into a low intensity, mottled orange background.

Intent on the changing image, Alexandra absently stepped closer. A moment later, she stood directly behind Yeoman Hansen, well in front of her first officer. She was not the only one staring. Every member of the bridge crew became intent on finding a source. Silence settled upon the bridge, softened only by a barely audible background hum rising from the heart of the ship. Nothing seemed to lie anywhere between Bright Victory and the giant star. Without thought, Alexandra usurped her first officer's duty. "Yeoman, repeat that process!"

Another several minutes passed before young Lieutenant Lee, ship's communications officer, pointed from his seat at one end of the long control console occupying a large portion of the circular periphery of the bridge. "There!"

So small and close to the star, the tiny planet's reflective glow lay hidden in the intense background. With everyone intent to find the elusive object, no one noticed Alexandra's uncharacteristic enthusiasm when she finally located it. "Yes!"

Resuming his normal role, Semgee issued another order as if his captain had not interrupted standard protocol. "Hansen, mark your coordinates and go directly to a high-mag on that small reflection."

No one but Yeoman Hansen moved a finger. The tiny image grew, rising to fill the projection volume with a sphere, glowing dull red over a gibbous lower portion of its surface. Lieutenant Lee seemed to be operating on autopilot, unmindful of decorum, expressing aloud what everyone was thinking. "That can't be the source. It's too close." Several heads nodded in agreement.

First to see the tiny shadow, Semgee spoke to no one in particular. "What is that? ... there! ... that reflection on the side."

Waiting for no instruction, Hansen enlarged the small spot and reoriented its image. Although the earlier radio transmission should have prepared them, Bright Victory's bridge crew sucked in a collective breath as the display settled onto the hemispheric shape of the huge heat shield and the orbiting station in its shadow. The implication of what they saw became shocking reality.

Alexandra turned to look at her first officer, finding his eyes trained upon her.

"Honorable Captain, I think we may have found the source of those transmissions. How would you have us proceed?"

The many eyes now focused in her direction gave Alexandra reason for caution. Unable to think, she retreated. "I wish to consider the matter further. Resume execution of mission directives, but maintain a zero-emission posture. Join me in my stateroom as soon as you can." Orders given, she turned and walked stiffly from the bridge.

An encounter like this must be planned.

When her first officer finally announced himself, his demeanor seemed to reflect the extraordinary circumstances. Speaking as soon as he entered her stateroom, Semgee displayed little formality. "The stealthiest thing we can do is to jump away again and approach from another direction."

Alexandra noted the off-hand manner. Perhaps her face betrayed some reaction for her first officer quickly recovered. "... but then I'm sure you've already concluded as much, Honorable Captain."

....

Bright Victory's repositioning jump and the braking dive that followed consumed the remainder of a maddeningly long day, exhausting everyone well before Semgee managed to maneuver his ship close to the small inner planet.

Some relief sounded in Semgee's voice when the com unit buzzed in Alexandra's cabin. "Honorable Captain, we're now in near approach to the planet."

"I assume we have not yet revealed our presence."

"Affirmative, Honorable Captain, we have been completely silent since our arrival."

"Very good, Commander. We should be very close before we announce ourselves."

Preoccupied with the implications of their discovery, Alexandra returned to the bridge biting her lower lip absentmindedly. She had heard stories but, to her knowledge, no ship in the League's fleet had ever encountered an alien civilization. She also thought of the Lost Independents. Historical records of those traitorous rebels contained no reference to the discovery of any sanctuary. Could they possibly have fled between galaxies? It mattered little. In either event, the discovery might even be worth a seat on the First Council.

She could not resist such thoughts even as she gave the order. "If they aren't already aware, we should let them know we're here. Broadcast our arrival, Commander." *This story will sound good when retold to Astrocorps Command.*

With a nod to his communications officer, Semgee put the order in motion. "As you wish, Honorable Captain."

Aboard League starships, standard procedures governed all action. One among them concerned new-contact communications. Following standard protocol, Bright Victory began transmitting a repeated series of pulse-coded messages, simultaneously broadcast in a dozen different narrow bands sweeping through a range of carrier frequencies from ultraviolet light down to low-frequency radio waves. Some form of communications equipment aboard that satellite would inevitably receive at least one of those transmitted messages and understand its significance.

No one uttered a word for several minutes, as everyone on the bridge watched the display screen filling the gentle curve of bulkhead above Lieutenant Lee's duty station. Split into several separate strips, the screen showed signal strength against the sweep of time in a number of different frequency bands. All eyes searched and waited. A dark blank display stared back.

Although he spoke softly, Semgee's order rang loud in the hanging silence. "Repeat the hail, Lieutenant."

After some minutes of repeated hailing, Alexandra's patience ran out. The occupants of the satellite either did not exist or did not wish to acknowledge Victory's presence. "Commander, it's time for more action. Keep up the com transmissions, but let's send an unmanned shuttle into a near standoff point, armed with interrogation instruments. Let's see if we can discover anything that way."

Hours later, the situation remained unchanged. "All right, Commander, perhaps it's time to go down there in person. Put together a small boarding party and let's get a good look at what's inside, if we can."

"Aye, Honorable Captain," Semgee acknowledged, picking up the com set.

Alexandra's thoughts flashed on the political ramifications of her order. A late addition to Bright Victory's crew, the presence of a small security force came as a result of considerable last-minute discussion between Corps Command and Security Command. That the presence of Security Forces aboard an exploratory mission might now prove useful would undoubtedly cause consternation between leaders of both commands. *They had better serve well.*

The sound of Semgee's voice brought Alexandra's focus back to the bridge. "Major, I need a boarding party assembled as soon as possible. Meet me in Lander Bay Eight in twenty minutes. I'll brief you when I see you." Allowing no reply, Semgee replaced the com set, turned and bowed curtly to his captain before leaving the bridge.

Hours passed before the manned shuttle managed to maneuver itself close to the orbiting station. The unmanned probe's revelation of sharp gravitational gradients had earned admiration for the station's builders. The builders' ability to stabilize the satellite with a static Riemann field represented technology rivaling the League's own. Forewarned, a close approach still required both care and caution. The station seemed to support a single access port, designed for a specific docking craft. Entry would present problems.

Meeting yet more silence from the orbiting station, Alexandra's impatience gained the upper hand. It seemed simple enough. "Board that station, Major!"

The first shots struck the landing craft with little more than the force of hand weapons. The station had not been fortified for military action. The landing craft's crew did not return fire, but returned to the ship, knowing that those shots had fundamentally changed the situation.

Alexandra's elation infected the bridge crew, filling them all with excitement over the importance of the historic encounter. The display of hostility gave her freedom to act. Real battle experience would look good on her service record. Glory lay before her. She need only grab it.

Gaining entry would not be difficult. She had the power to completely obliterate the station. Gaining entry without destroying the place required more finesse. She needed a carefully choreographed show of force. Her first shots were designed to put small holes in the station, something that would not destroy, would not kill. She felt pleased with the tactic.

The outpost's occupants were not, however, completely defenseless. Bright Victory's first shots found no target, deflected to leave a few small holes in the protective shroud. Alexandra's crew needed several tries and several minutes to reformulate tactics, finally projecting a dynamic Riemann space-time field ahead of each volley. Inevitably, one hit home.

Pulling on her bottom lip, Alexandra examined the apparent damage in the overhead display. "Perhaps now they'll talk."

The outpost responded with another hour of silence.

At the landing craft's second approach the satellite station remained quiet. No hostility greeted their arrival. Blasting open the entry port, the boarding party entered with hand weapons at the ready, finding nothing alive to meet their assault.

Aboard Victory disappointment replaced elation. Alexandra had hoped for more. Resigned to limited success, she retreated to her last hope. Perhaps the ruins held a clue. "Search every corner of that vessel, Major. I want to know everything that station can tell us. I want to know what they ate today."

Alexandra's disappointment eventually gave way to renewed excitement. Victory's exploratory mission had acquired new, more important purpose and the ship's holds still held weeks of supplies. All she needed was a clue, a hint to light the way. She might yet be able to find the aliens' home world.

The orbiting station tenaciously protected its secrets, revealing only begrudging hints of its inhabitants or of their origins. At the same time, every aspect of the station's design, from the size of crew quarters to the shape of control actuators, demonstrated that the occupants of the orbiting station were creatures in many ways similar to humans. Alexandra's impatience pushed her once again to forget normal procedure and answer the boarding party leader's hail herself. "Yes, Major. Have you found anything more?"

Perhaps surprised by the ship captain's voice, the major hesitated momentarily before answering. "Yes, Captain. We found a small device that seems to match a receptacle in one of the instrument consoles. It may be a data storage device. We found it under some loose debris in the station's control center. It struck me that the occupants may have overlooked it in their cleansing effort."

"And that's it? Nothing else?"

"I'm afraid not, Captain. The occupants of this station were very thorough. All instrumentation has been completely destroyed and we found only one small personal item: it may be a simple cloth towel."

"Get them both back here, Major. We'll feed the data

device into the ship's decryption module and that cloth might reveal something under analysis."

At the moment she issued that order it seemed innocent enough.

Hours after the boarding party's return, the message from System's Engineering seemed at first more annoying than anything else. Then she finished reading it. In carefully penned diplomatic language, the report described how Bright Victory had narrowly evaded a stealthy cyberattack. One could almost admire the attack's audacity. While Victory's crew had been focused on a physical assault on the station, their opponents had prepared a deadly mine with a delayed fuse. The thought made Alexandra shudder. *They nearly crippled my ship!*

Her thoughts shifted to the report she would eventually deliver to Astrocorps Command. How could she deflect blame for the incident? She had definitely issued the order to bring the data storage device on board for scrutiny. Perhaps she might couch the whole thing differently. After all, the ship had not been greatly harmed. She must remember to commend the alert yeoman who noticed extraneous activity in the progress monitor. He was under her command and his skill had likely prevented the parasitic code from escaping confinement in the decryption module. The fact that her magnificent ship might have been severely damaged could be understated. As it was, Victory could survive the remainder of its mission without decryption capability. *Yes, that would do it.*

Alexandra felt deflated. She would not, it seemed, be able to return with quite the triumph she had hoped. Perhaps that seat on the First Council would have to wait. She had nearly resigned herself to a more modest future when her first officer renewed her faith in a glorious destiny.

"Honorable Captain, we've intercepted another transmission. It seems this outpost has another visitor."

....

Almost a full day later, Alexandra lay prone on her bunk, staring at the ceiling. Semgee's announcement still reverberated in her ears. Now she could only wait; wait for her beautiful, powerful starship to emerge from the stellar dive that would swing it into position to surprise what she had to assume was another of the outpost's alien owners.

Success would depend on timing. Victory had withdrawn to wait behind the star's bulk. The new visitor would investigate the outpost's failure to respond. Victory must surprise her prey.

At the sound of the com hail, Alexandra nearly ran to her desk. "Yes, Commander?"

"Honorable Captain, we've just emerged from the star's atmosphere and sensor systems are beginning to pull reliable signals from the glare."

"Can you pinpoint them yet, Commander?"

"Yes, Honorable Captain, the newcomer would now seem to be settling into close approach near the orbiting station."

Feeling some pride in what she considered a good plan, Alexandra poured unnecessary words into what should have been a crisp command. "We'll wait until they have no time to withdraw. Keep Victory on a fast approach and monitor every signal from that vessel. We can hope they haven't yet observed the damage we caused."

Tension rose within the bridge company as Victory closed on her quarry, her great speed reduced to an apparent crawl by vast distance and their own anticipation. Alexandra kept telling herself to be calm, to be patient, to maintain an appropriate demeanor.

The alien ship's reaction drive flared into action. Semgee called out. "Captain! They're backing off."

Alexandra fought to hold her annoyance in check.

Proklyat'ye! I can see as well as you! "Prepare a warning shot. Let's see if we can persuade them that running may be costly."

No warning shot was ever fired. In the short time before Bright Victory's crew could even prepare the weapon, the projected image of the alien ship vanished, leaving behind the dark hulk of an outpost.

Alexandra spoke aloud what everyone else was thinking. "How can they jump from there?"

A moment passed while Bright Victory's first officer framed thoughts. "There's only one direction, Honorable Captain. Into featureless space where they have little chance of hitting anything." Without waiting for permission, he turned to the ship's navigator. "Analyze their wake ... and prepare an identical jump. Do not let that ship get free of us!"

CHAPTER 2
Escape

Hands splayed atop the instrument console, Eilen Macumbo waited for the next shudder. Feeling but a tiny bump, she released a long breath. The rumbling had dissipated. The drop maneuver had run its course.

Having shed the Raiju's great speed in a trail of space-time eddies, the ship's Riemann Drive now searched for elusive substance in the surrounding fabric of space. At less than half 'c', the ship hurled toward the red giant known as Holvar's Star. Eilen allowed herself to look up from the display console to see her captain standing within the outer fringe of the projection display volume.

Angus's ability to directly witness a drop still impressed her. She had once forced herself to do so. Never since had she repeated the experience. Doubled over with nausea was not the image of herself she most favored. Angus alone seemed immune to the debilitating effects of viewing a drop display. With the drop maneuver complete, he stood within the display, warping the field and distorting the view for those behind. Eilen began to wonder when he would step back and let everyone enjoy the view.

The field worked its wizardry, lending a metallic taste to each inhaled breath. Angus's distorted voice came from afar.

"Increase magnification." A whisper rose from the system officer's sleeve as he waved a finger across the controls.

The same part of her being that drew her to join Haven's Interstellar Service also allowed Eilen to understand Angus's reluctance. She'd stood in his place herself. With a little concentration, he could banish from his mind the muted sounds at his back and stand in his own private universe. The projection field's soft pressure and the deck beneath his feet would remain as the only reminders that he was not actually floating unencumbered in space, six billion kilometers from a strikingly beautiful red supergiant that never failed to produce the most spectacular display of any to be seen.

The star's sheer size inspired awe. As large as many complete planetary systems, it outshone every star within a thousand light-years, a brilliant flare among mere candles. Dropping into normal space around most stars would yield a projected image about the size of the nail on one finger of an outstretched hand. The Raiju dropped nearly three times farther from Holvar's, yet the huge star filled a large portion of the projected view. Swirls and eddies swarmed the star's surface, each one a tremendous maelstrom of unimaginable power, paradoxically exuding a hypnotic calm to hold viewers captive like the embers of a dying fire.

Raiju's destination lay hidden among the swirls, a minuscule black dot upon the seething sun's image. Plying a very close orbit around Holvar's, the small, dense hell-world called Sam Li's Cinder supported a cadre of skillful off-world engineers who exchanged a tiring and tedious life for great financial rewards in the recovery of refractory metals found there in great abundance.

Angus finally stepped back. The sigh in his voice reached Eilen's ears. "Disengage Riemann Drive."

While other members of the bridge crew admired the image of Holvar's, Eilen trained her attention on Angus. How old do you suppose he is? Thin grey lines streaked the black waves atop his head. Even he could not tell her from whence those waves had come. What little she knew told her he'd spent a parentless childhood, reared within the sterile arms of one of the League's outlying institutional nurseries. What scars did that experience leave behind?

Angus's unique status among the people of Haven showed on his smooth grey tunic. Upon any other Interstellar Service officer, the ribbon array integrated into the uniform's fabric would garner little attention. The identity of individual awards became lost in the mixture. On Angus's left breast, a single black-on-white striped ribbon stood alone above others. Worn by no other fleet officer, the award was given him by Haven's government in recognition of the singular act of delivering into the hands of Haven's guardians a League of Planets starship intact and undamaged. That he had singlehandedly crossed a 200,000 light-year void to do so only enhanced the story's allure. Only Angus knew the whole story. Would she ever hear it?

He seems worn, like the rest of us. The Raiju's four-month tour of six of Haven's inhabited star systems had levied a tax on everyone.

Sounding none too happy, Angus turned toward the bridge lift. "The ship is yours, Second. Inform the Cinder Station of our arrival. I need to rest a bit before we make our braking dive around Holvar's. Wake me before we reach the dive point."

Her captain's order seemed unusual but gave Eilen little pause. "Aye, Captain."

Angus generally reserved for himself the task of announcing Raiju's arrival. She suspected he liked the miners and found something enjoyable in their boisterous behavior. The miners would be waiting for mail, supplies, and for fresh prey to fleece in games of chance. More than a few would be looking forward to a ride home for recreational rotation. Raiju carried their replacements.

Hearing her shipboard title, 'Second', struck a chord. Would she miss it? Aboard the Raiju, the role of 'Second'— second in command, second only to the captain—had been pleasant duty. Now Angus's recommendation to Interstellar Command that she be given her own ship seemed likely to end her time aboard the Raiju. Glancing around the bridge she wondered if any of her crewmates knew of her potential departure. She would definitely miss each of them.

Under Commander John Singh turned her way, cocking his head as if to ask, "What?" Eilen answered with a cursory nod, thinking that she would be lucky to have as good a navigator on any ship that she might command.

The bridge crew's youngest member, Systems Officer Ivan Tanr, a new lieutenant enjoying the adventure of his first assignment, seemed engrossed in his work. Eilen smiled at the memory of his first day aboard Raiju. Angus had become quite annoyed, nearly rebuking the new crewmember, until discovering that the young man's rhythmic banter was as natural a part of his speech as was Angus's own precise Standard Galactic.

Eilen's smile softened as her eyes fell upon Deshi Henning, the ship's chief engineer, perhaps the oldest full lieutenant serving among the starships of Haven. Rising through the ranks, he'd become a seasoned veteran while the others were still in training. Eilen had to wonder if the man remembered with some regret the respect he once heard in his shipmates' use of the address 'Master Chief.' No one but Deshi could get away with the stern reproach that occasionally crept into his manner, especially when pointing out the evils of even a small breech in proper shipboard procedure.

Enough ... there's work to be done.

Holvar's presented a marvelous spectacle, but it also entailed one of the slowest approaches of any star, demanding a feat of precision starship piloting and adding another edge to the unique shape of this port-of-call. The Raiju would coast at half 'c' for a full watch before executing a close-in braking maneuver, whipping around the back of the giant star to slow into a rendezvous orbit. Their destination put them close to Holvar's full fury.

....

"Well done, Second ... a fine piece of helmsmanship. We've needed minimal course correction since pulling out of the dive." A sheepish grin came to Eilen's face. In spite of many years of service, her captain's acknowledgement and the nodding agreements of colleagues still managed to stir her pride.

The intense, high-gradient gravitational confines near the star enabled the ship's Riemann Drive to manage a good grip on nearby space-time but also required the Raiju to spend time within the massive star's tenuous outer atmosphere. Combined action of Riemann and reaction drives toiled to peel off speed, subjecting the ship to hours of buffeting. The maneuver taxed ship's systems and crew's nerves.

Raiju's approach brought a welcome picture of Cinder's orbiting station into view. The Cinder Station wore a gleaming shroud. Like a magnificent cape, the station's distinguishing trademark took form in a nearly hemispherical shield, 100 kilometers across, behind which the station found sanctuary from the incessant assault of Holvar's tortuous radiation.

Getting the Raiju safely within the shadow of that shield always occupied the captain's full attention. The station's static Riemann field adjusted the local curve of space-time to stabilize the orbiting dome, but it also presented the ship with a sharp gravitational gradient that demanded careful maneuvering. Under Holvar's intense glare, such protracted maneuvering only added to the tension aboard Raiju's bridge.

Although she saw Angus's attempts to hide his anxiety, Eilen could not help but register his inability to sit still, his hands frequently finding their way through his hair. There was nothing normal about the mining station's daylong silence and she could feel Angus's concern. Something was amiss.

In spite of her attention, she was still caught by surprise when Angus's loud orders suddenly rang in her ears. "All sensors active, Mister Tanr! Wide scan! Rapid sweep! Cease approach maneuvers! Second, prepare the ship for emergency departure!"

Raiju's second did not stop to ask why. Her reaction came without question or hesitation. The ship's captain had not issued a 'request.' Turning to the screen before her, she simultaneously activated several ship's systems.

A slight waver in Ivan Tanr's voice hinted at the effect of his captain's sudden order. "Nothing abnormal within our detection perimeter, sir. What might I look for?"

Replying slowly and quietly, Angus explained. "A starship, Mister Tanr ... an armed starship."

Ivan's blank stare asked for more.

"I call your attention to the profusion of small holes scattered about that heat shield. If you examine any one carefully, you'll see they were made with energy weapons. And, having deduced the cause of those holes, what would you further deduce about the vessel that made them?"

Every eye widened in recognition. The people of Haven had always known this day would come. Long ago, in fear of fortunes and futures, Haven's founders had fled in panic. For 600 years, the 200,000 light-year distance between the Lesser Magellanic Cloud and the Milky Way had protected the people of Haven from the unwanted attention of mankind's sole governing force. Yet the League of Planets had been there always, looming like a malevolent giant on the other side of the gulf. His own abrupt and perilous flight from the League had unwittingly taken Angus across that same gulf a mere 15 years ago. It was only a matter of time before a League starship did the same.

Eilen noted Angus's calm demeanor, knowing it belied internal turmoil, knowing he struggled within. The news must get back to Haven's seat of government on Russell Four. The safety of the Cinder crew, or even the ship's crew, would necessarily take a secondary seat.

"All right, Second. Stand off a distance and maintain emergency readiness. If Mister Tanr picks up any sign of the invader, do not wait for my order. Get this ship out of here as fast as you can.

"Mister Henning! Prepare a shuttlecraft. Instruct the mining crew to equip themselves with emergency survival gear. We'll remain nearby as long as we are able."

Henning's serious tone said much more than his simple words. "Aye, sir."

....

Angus Hirano glanced at the ship-time chronometer mounted above the projection field display, as he had done much too frequently all day. *It hasn't been that long. The shuttle left but an hour ago.*

His eyes fell to the small screen at his command station, feeling chagrin at the sight of fingers absently drumming on the armrest. The hand went quiet. He glanced around. Had anyone seen? Raiju continued to put distance between themselves and the space-warping influence of the satellite's static Riemann field. Angus's left hand brushed the Com control. A part of him wanted to talk to Henning, but he knew enough to leave the man alone. If possible, Angus would choose to be in two places just now. He wanted to be aboard that shuttle. He wanted to talk to the crew. Another glance at the screen showed him the same view seen by those aboard the shuttlecraft. He watched the mining station's image grow, itching to feel the craft's controls in his own hand. Darkness showed where operational lights would normally be. The radiation shield filled the landing craft's forward window, wrapping the tiny station in shadow. Angus knew what the shuttle crew would find aboard the dark station.

"Mister Singh, how're those NavCalcs coming?"

John Singh looked up from the console. "Nearly complete, Captain. The emergency jump course was completed some time ago. It may be approximate, but it wasn't really very complex ... The direct course for Russell Four is usefully complete and continues to be refined, with only minor adjustments remaining."

"Then both are ready to use?"

"Yes, sir."

"Plug in the emergency jump course. We may not have a great deal of time if we need to use that one."

"Done, sir."

Angus knew where he belonged. He may long to be aboard that shuttle, but in the very near future, one of only two things would happen. In either case, he'd be required here at the helm of his ship. Raiju would either initiate a hastened, but relatively normal acceleration dive into and around Holvar's wing and set itself on a course for home, or it would jump blindly into intergalactic space.

His earlier NavCalc request had raised quite a stir. No blind jump from so near a star mass had ever been documented. The immediate proximity of Holvar's Star rendered any NavCalc woefully imprecise. Kneading gravitational field and field gradient data into a calculated shape for local super-dimensional space, the Raiju's navigation computer produced a NavCalc that would likely work, but which, within the influence of Holvar's strong gravitational gradients, remained approximate. Any jump greater than a few light-years risked destruction. Only into intergalactic space, where no star mass existed, might Raiju find a long safe path.

I won't need it, but I'd be negligent not to prepare. The League ship seemed to have retired. No starship showed on Raiju's sensors. News of a ship from the Milky Way roaming freely within the boundaries of Haven must be delivered. If he could not deliver it in person, he'd at least ensure that Henning and his crew would stay alive to do so.

Angus knew what the shuttle crew would find aboard that mining station: no one and nothing. *That's what I'd leave.* The capture of any miner posed a risk to Haven's entire population. Nor would a single instruction set or bit of recorded data remain to be read, all wiped clean before the crew destroyed themselves in the briefest flash of the station's waste destruction chamber. He hoped the life support systems were still functioning.

....

The invader came out of the star itself. Almost before anyone knew what was happening the League ship's huge bulk filled the projection field, its near side covered with recessed weapons bays, looking every bit like the eyes of some enormous spider descending on helpless prey.

Only Ivan's astute attention and immediate action gave the Raiju any time at all, and only Angus's instincts and preparation gave them any chance to use it. He'd hoped for a return trip home, but he'd planned for the opposite. His precautions proved clairvoyant. The invader hadn't departed ... he'd lain in wait, hiding just over Holvar's horizon, listening. A quick dive through Holvar's wing now put the League starship within a few minutes of menacing Raiju with the same energy weapons that had destroyed the mining station. Angus's contingency plan immediately became the order of the moment.

"Emergency jump sequence. Now, Second, now!"

Anxiety disappeared. Angus became absorbed in the

performance of duty, acutely focused on what would surely be, the most dangerous contest in which he had ever pitted his skills.

That blind jump had just become necessary. Angus could only hope to lure the invaders into giving chase, leaving Henning and the miners free to warn the worlds of Haven. He could only hope to leave a trail good enough to follow ... but only just.

He no longer felt tired.

CHAPTER 3
High Grass

Conscious of his own heartbeat, Angus let his focus waver. In one long, slow breath he searched for calm. Edging deeper into the display volume, the projection field pressed like an invisible blanket across his body. Knowledge that the bridge bulkhead lay inches from his nose did nothing to dispel the impact of the infinite black void that filled his eyes. Speaking in a slow, quiet voice he forced the agitation from his order. "Aft view, Mr. Tanr ... wide field."

In the next few seconds, his pursuer would appear in real space. Then Angus's timing would begin. All dances depend on timing and Angus needed a well-choreographed dance.

A wave of nausea signaled the ship's transition through drop threshold. Moving not so much as a finger, Angus directed the next step in the dance. "Disengage Riemann Drive!"

The cue he gained from his ability to stare into the projected view of his ship's wake gave him only the slightest advantage. Would it be enough?

At near-light speed all radiation struck the Raiju from two directions only, bow-on and directly astern. Angus stood with his entire visual perception concentrated on the projection field, barely able to discern the dull glow of red-shifted radiation overtaking his vessel. His pursuer's reentry into normal space would broadcast a brief disturbance in the local fabric of space-time. Straining to catch a mere flicker, he drew another long breath.

Angus knew the League starship would give chase. They could do little else. They wanted his home base and to find it they must capture his ship or follow him home. A good decoy must dance well.

There you are!

Stepping from the projection field, Angus blinked in the bright light and focused on the chronometer above the aft control console. "Prepare to initiate jump sequence." In a detached pose, he watched the seconds tick by, one arm across his chest, the other propped upon it to support the hand on his chin. *All right. If they're any good, they'll need only thirty seconds to slow and train sensors, then another twenty to catch sight of us.* Angus held his breath. The seconds ticked by. *and ... right about now!*

"Initiate jump."

Angus ordered the Raiju's third jump of the long day.

....

Alone and as far from anywhere as anyone save Angus had ever been, the starship Raiju hurtled near light-speed through flat, featureless intergalactic space-time.

Nausea fading, Eilen felt relieved as she looked up from her instruments to see Angus standing in the projection field. The sight calmed her psyche. At that particular moment, seeing Angus stand as he so often did, immune from the ill effects of a drop display, lent a small dose of normality to the tension.

A moment earlier, she heard the order for a complete shutdown of the Riemann Drive, repeating a pattern set at the onset of Raiju's desperate flight. The tactic began to make sense. A disengaged drive allowed Raiju to maintain full speed. If that pursuing ship wanted to keep Raiju within sight, it would need to slow and activate sensors as it reentered normal space. Each time it did so Raiju pulled a bit farther away.

Stretching arms wide, Eilen arched her back, restoring life to stiff limbs. *How long can we keep this up?*

A glance at Angus, engulfed by the projection field, left hand pressed into the small of his back, told her fatigue grew there as well. The task of keeping watch on their pursuer extracted a toll.

I wonder just what he can see in that display. In principle, the projection field's aft view shortly after a drop should appear as a smooth, dull red glow. Angus saw something more. His escape plan depended on timing and the clock started at the exact instant of their pursuer's reentry. *This is no time to ask. Another time perhaps … if we live to see another time.*

The thought of instruction came laced with memory, a picture of the occasion of her first meeting with Angus. She remembered feeling grateful for the mere fact of standing next to him, relieving her of the common and uneasy distinction of being the tallest person in the room. A smile crept into her face as she tried to recall the subject of the instruction at the time, realizing that she could not. All she could remember was Angus.

At the time she had wondered as she had more recently, *how old is he?* Yet he seemed to wear his age easily, seeing the world through clear, confident eyes, sporting the awareness of a predatory bird. Thinking to compare notes with the ship's most experienced officer, she had once discussed Angus's background with Deshi Henning. Deshi had then offered the notion that their captain's customarily calm demeanor was not a true glimpse of the man, more shield than comfortable shawl. Deshi would go no further. When pressed, Deshi retreated, branding deeper analysis 'a breach of decorum.'

Returning to reality, Eilen wondered how many people Angus counted among those called 'friend.' *Not many. Would I be on that list?* As his 'second' for the last five years, she felt privileged to think she might be as close as anyone. Her home on Calivar, where a hardy few pulled a meager living from vast dry grasslands, had developed in her some regard for strong proud people who kept their own counsel. Angus trained by immersion and his example taught instinct as well as knowledge. *Lucky to have drawn him to train under.*

Now, three jumps into Raiju's decoy flight, things seemed to be progressing as expected. As far as Eilen could tell the League starship continued to play its part. Unable to see what Angus saw, Eilen could only observe and discern the events that seemed to guide his timing.

Angus's posture stiffened. *There's the first,* she noted. He held still a while before turning to stare at the chronometer. Eilen turned along with him, trying to judge the events guiding his timing. His next order came just about a minute later. "Ready to engage Riemann Drive. Lay in jump course ... maximum range. Initiate on my order."

His intensity and the close focus of the projection field added a hollow ring to his voice. Noting the elapsed time Eilen considered the possible sequence of events. *Nothing can happen until they reenter normal space. Then the only other thing Angus might detect is when they shut down their drive. So, Angus marks those events in the Aft Glow. Then he gives them just enough time to get their bearings, look around and ...*

"Engage Riemann Drive."

Then he gives them a chance to detect Raiju's space-time distortion, then...

"Commence Jump sequence."

Once more into the void.

....

Had any starship ever executed so many jumps in a single day? Eilen thought not. With the execution of the day's sixth jump, stark tension on the bridge had given way to a low-level unease, dulled by fatigue. When the League starship appeared again right on cue, Raiju's entire bridge crew took it as a reassuring sign. Angus's tactics were still working; events remained under control.

Exhausted, Eilen longed for rest. Playing the mouse in a tensely conducted cat-and-mouse game drained energy faster than anyone might suspect. Arms and legs responded slowly to her commands.

The Raiju's pursuers doubtless labored under the same strain. Eilen had to wonder what the League captain thought of the mad dash between galaxies. He had almost certainly never before taken 30,000 light-year jumps in such rapid fashion and likely found the bounding sprint quite unnerving. She could imagine that captain's outbound journey from the Milky Way as a composition of hundreds of jumps, taking great care to map each position and navigate precisely, ensuring a well-lit path home. The great leaps they now took were only possible in the featureless space-time between galaxies.

Three jumps and 90,000 light-years ago, Angus had established about a ten-minute lead. That those minutes would become important somewhere in this epic journey she had no doubt—but where?

Pushing back from her position before the instrument console Eilen stood and turned toward Angus, seated in his raised command station. Angus seemed lost in thought, wearing a vacant stare. His eyes came into focus as she took a step closer. "Captain, it's good to see your tactics working. You've managed to draw our pursuer nearly all the way back to the Milky Way. What I cannot see is how you intend to shake him in the end."

The question drew a smile. "You're right. You've seen most of the plan already. There's just one piece you haven't seen yet." Angus glanced at other members of the bridge crew. "Some of the others are probably wondering the same thing. The role of decoy doesn't always turn out well for the decoy, does it? Perhaps it's time to let everyone know exactly what we're doing."

As Angus reached to activate the ship-wide com-link Eilen saw a distinct change in his face. She'd seen the same change before. A starship captain wears many faces. Within the confines of the bridge, Angus might relax; content to work with the bridge crew as one among many. Eilen might casually approach that captain. The implacably stern face she now saw belonged to the captain of Raiju's entire crew. That captain had a duty to perform and there was nothing casual about the sobering notification he must make. How does one inform 150 people that they may never see their home again?

Drawing a single long breath, Angus let the alert signal fade before speaking. "Now hear this ... This is the Captain speaking. Some hours past I informed you of our encounter with the League starship at Cinder Station and of our decision to flee. We've come a long way since then. The Raiju is now nearing the Milky Way. We're all very far from home."

Angus paused, allowing the ship's company time to digest the reality of what they just heard. The stark message matched the grim set of his face and the emotionless tone in his voice. "The League ship remains on our tail and that's as it should be. We've succeeded in drawing it away from the Cinder Station and away from all our friends, families and neighbors. Our duty is clear. We cannot allow the Raiju to be captured. We must lose that ship. We'll either return home with Raiju intact or destroy her in the attempt ... That is all."

Eilen watched the stern expression drain from Angus's face as he mentally returned to the bridge. Turning his attention to the bridge crew, he spoke without the imperial tone of a moment before. "Our immediate mission has changed somewhat. While I'm busy keeping Raiju out of the League's reach, the three of you are going to begin searching for a particularly tight star cluster I remember from a long time ago."

Looking directly at John Singh, Angus began laying out his plan. "Commander, our next drop will bring us back into normal space very close to the Milky Way and, although the galaxy's presence should produce fairly gentle space-time gradients here, we'll need to take more care with the next few jumps. Run a systematic series of NavCalcs for courses running tangential to the galactic mass."

He then turned his attention to Ivan. "Lieutenant, set up a sensory autoscan for each normal-space period. The cluster I'm looking for has a beautiful shell of 'G' Types accented by a couple 'M' Types, all surrounding a single spectacular Type 'O' star. You can set your sensors to find that 'O' Type. Few stars shine like this one and I can give you approximate location coordinates."

By the time Angus turned to face her, Eilen had already considered what form her contributions might take. His instructions came as no real surprise. "Setting up to make use of those coordinates is your job, Second. The location coordinates I remember are based on triangulation between the reference position of Galactic center and a half dozen standard pulsar positions. Since Raiju's Nav Atlas contains no data for these reference points, you'll have to find them before my rough coordinates can do us any good."

Angus's instructions were understandable, but they stopped far short of explaining everything. Eilen had to ask. "Captain, if may I ask ... how is finding this cluster going to help us escape?"

One corner of Angus's mouth rose into a wry smile. "Of course, Second ... and your answer comes in the form of one last characteristic of that cluster. Among the stellar bodies surrounding that bright 'O' Type is a bound pair of neutron stars. The space-time tidal dynamics swirling within that cluster carry some interesting turbulence."

Absorbing this information, Eilen explored its implications. "So ... a turbulent space-time volume would prevent the League ship from following our wake if we jumped through that cluster, but wouldn't we have a devil of a time mapping a route through there in the first place?"

"Keep going."

"Unless, of course, you already know of a path through."

"Just so! And since I know there's a path, I can put Raiju in place to see that path and jump through with confidence. The League's captain will think more than twice before sending his ship through that cluster. He'll wait to map out the full space-time structure before trusting any kind of crude NavCalc."

As any hunter from the prairies of Calivar might say, Angus intended to 'lose them in the high grass.'

....

Eilen's smile nearly gave away the news before she spoke. "Captain, I think we've located your star cluster."

"Excellent! Let's take a look. Put a view into the projection field."

The vague curve of the Milky Way's underside filled the projection volume, spilling beyond the borders and leaving the graceful appearance of its more familiar spiral arms to an observer's imagination.

From the central instrument console, Eilen highlighted a small red dot within the nebulous fog of stars. "Here is where your memory puts that cluster relative to the reference points I found."

She then enhanced a second small bright yellow dot set

deeper within the fog of the galactic core. "And here is where we found a group of stars matching your description. I think maybe one of those nines you remembered might have been a six."

Angus could hardly contain himself. "Center the view on that cluster and expand."

The image spread outward until the fog resolved into individual spots, all moving rapidly. The viewer seemed to dash through the vast collection of stars at superluminal speed. When the view finally settled, a bright blue-white star shone at center while many smaller stars added weaker, cooler contributions to a dull glow engulfing the entire volume.

Angus rose from his command chair. "That's it! Now ... can you see how the entire cluster is bathed in weak luminescence?"

Joining the exercise, Ivan and John stared from their seats on either side of Eilen. John spoke first. "Yes. It's perceptible around the edges against the deeper black of space behind it."

"OK, Commander. I'll bet you can also tell me what's causing that glow."

John Singh thought for a moment before answering. "It would have to be caused by what remains of the original formation cloud combined with ejection mass from all those stars, illuminated from within by that bright one at center."

"All right. Now let me direct your attention to the right side of the image where you can see a somewhat brighter spot at the head of what looks a bit like a tail."

Angus paused while everyone examined the right-hand portion of the image. "That spot is formed by the two neutron stars. They're sweeping up material from the same cloud of stellar dust that permeates this cluster. Can you see how they've gathered the mass in their path and how their gravitational dance causes faint swirls in the nearby glow?"

Hands held wide, excitement in his face, Angus turned to face the members of his bridge crew. "That's the key to our escape!"

Perplexed, Eilen looked first at Ivan, then at John to see the same puzzled feeling written all over their faces. "Sorry, sir. I'm not sure what you mean. What is the key to our escape?"

Pulling his enthusiasm back to normal, Angus explained. "What I remember most distinctly about this cluster is the way it looks from a particular vantage. The havoc created by that pair of neutron stars gives the space-time topology there a peculiar character. If we put Raiju at just the right spot— somewhere just beyond the right-hand horizon there—then I can show you how the space-time topography takes on a toroidal shape and presents us a nearly clean hole to dive through."

"Won't the League ship be able to dive through it as well?"

"Yes, but they don't know that. Simply because I know where to look, we'll be able to find that low-turbulence path and develop a good NavCalc in much less time than they. Once we've jumped through that hole we merely need to quickly jump again. By the time the League ship makes the same jump we'll be long gone."

In spite of prolonged effort, Eilen and John failed to find a single-jump trajectory to put Raiju in place for the escape run—too much distance and too much star mass. They settled instead for a pair of jumps.

During the first jump period, Eilen became a model of focused action. If ever there was a time to summon every skill, to conjure every drop of cool professionalism, to recall every bit of confidence she had ever acquired, this was that time. She and John Singh pored over every bit of sensor data to produce a crude NavCalc, serving only to supply a frame for the more refined calculation they would eventually use. The next near-space period would provide enough data to get it close. All they would then need is a few refinements to safely make their escape.

....

Angus remained buried within the projection field. Eilen stood with John Singh, preparing to install a newly refined NavCalc. She had only just completed their setup, shut down the Riemann Drive, and was about to get a status from John. Angus's sudden order jolted her from the effort.

"Engage Riemann Drive! Initiate jump sequence!"

"Sir?"

"Now! Second, now!"

Perhaps the League ship had seen the pattern of Raiju's flight. Perhaps he took a gamble. It did not matter. Only a direct threat from the League warship would force Angus to jump again.

She felt the ship lurch into the jump. *I hope we don't pay too dearly for that ... lapse.*

....

The ship's distress rang in Eilen's ears and rumbled up through her legs. Angus's move into the projection field had come with more than a little trepidation. She knew they'd have no idea where they were when they were finally able to look around. On the one hand, the Raiju had certainly lost her tail, but at what price? Jumping through a dense and turbulent star cluster guided only by a crude NavCalc was a fool's mission.

They fell through the threshold. The Riemann Drive's groan became a deafening howl. The drive strained, screaming in protest. Angus turned from the projection field, shouting. "Abandon ship! Abandon ship! Emergency systems activation!"

The bridge of the Raiju sat near ship's center, an integral part of its inner core. Built like an onion, one concentric shell around another, 30 shells deep, Raiju held its Riemann Drive at the very center, a focal point from which the ship's symmetry aided instant adjustment of surrounding gravitational gradients. Emergency action called for dynamic refocus to protect as much of the ship's structure as possible. A severe hull breach gave the emergency response system a simple directive: preserve what you can, sacrifice the rest. In the worst circumstances, the Riemann Drive preserved itself and a close core, becoming an emergency escape module, containing only essential functions.

Standard emergency procedures directed ship's personnel inward. On this occasion, everyone aboard Raiju met their fate where they stood.

Most of the ship's compliment joined an expanding mass of debris that had once been the Raiju. Without the Riemann field to hold it together, the ship and everything in it exploded in a cloud of fragments. The ship's core survived the destructive gravitational tides only because the tightly refocused Riemann field wrapped itself around the smallest sustainable volume and sacrificed everything outside—cargo, fuel, hull … and crew.

Prepared for a harsh fate, Eilen was surprised to continue breathing and thinking. *Where are we? We'd have been better off to join the crew. I hope there's somewhere solid nearby, somewhere we might at least put down before we slowly die.*

CHAPTER 4
Lost Prey

The display volume settled into focus. Satisfaction chased the edge from Alexandra's voice. "and ... there ... you ... are."

That he felt pride in his captain's pleasure surprised Semgee. The alien's appearance, emerging on cue, confirmed their success. Astute observation and a rush of pattern analysis had placed Victory close enough to put the alien ship under its guns.

The advantage belonged to Victory. Alexandra wasted no time. "Weapons! Ready a warning shot!" The shot was never fired. Even as she issued the command, the alien ship blinked from the field. "Der'mo! How can they do that? They haven't had time to reposition." Her command came without thought. "Follow them!"

Knowing he could not respond as she wished, Semgee replied quietly, hoping to avoid fanning the flames. "Honorable Captain, this next jump will be difficult. We must take time to complete a more thorough navigation trajectory. The space-time topology here is quite uneven. There's just too much local star mass. We won't be able to follow the alien ship for minutes at least. I have no idea what technology allows that alien ship to jump so quickly, but I do know we have not the same capability."

Anger flashed onto Alexandra's face. She was not listening, nor was she prepared to wait. On this occasion, Semgee understood. Bright Victory had followed this alien ship through an intergalactic void larger than anything imaginable—the greatest hunt in the history of hunting. And they had cornered that ship! For such a chase to end in failure simply could not happen. Semgee felt his captain's frustration, but he would not let it rule his thought.

Alexandra's next order came in a slow, metered voice. "First Officer ... you will follow that ship. Now!"

There it was. The kind of impasse Semgee feared most. Dangerously wrong, his captain's order presented a harsh dilemma. *Would it be mutiny to defy her?* He could usually nudge her thinking in the direction of reason, but this time he was not sure he had the skill. She headed too rapidly down a destructive path. *An appeal to her vanity often works, or maybe to her ambition.* He'd need to phrase it properly. "Honorable Captain. Please consider. If we err here and the ship suffers damage, it may be difficult to explain in your eventual report. If, on the other hand, we perform all maneuvers in accordance with accepted procedures, we cannot later be criticized for failure."

The logic of the self-protective tactic was difficult to deny. Semgee watched his captain's face, carefully noting the hard lines recede as rational thought percolated through waning anger. When she finally replied, the words came weighed with resignation.

"All right Commander, do the best you can. I want a good jump trajectory, but get it done as quickly as you can. We're losing our quarry."

He could almost see the gears turning in her head, imagining how it would all sound in her mission report.

CHAPTER 5
Forest Rider

Turning his back to the outside vista, La'ann looked toward the interior shade of the forest. He loved Nahélé and drew strength from her verdant beauty. The great forest never turned away, never failed to soothe and renew his spirit. Perhaps she would do so now.

The strange event had left him shaken. *Tell Su'ban, I must.* The huge stone had streaked across the sky like some great howling creature, trailing thunder in the air, only to fall into the boundless marsh he knew as the Mokililana. It lay there now, still and dark, crowning one end of an ugly long gash in the green expanse spread well below and behind him.

A steady, deep hum rose from between La'ann's legs. Reaching down to touch Mœrai's soft fur, he gently stroked the side of his kùmu'lio's long neck. The simple act filled La'ann with a renewed sense of security. His head fell back onto the relaxed muscles of her powerful arm. He looked up along the arm's length to see it disappear into tangled vines overhead. Experience prompted a mental picture of the animal's curved claws firmly gripping dense ceiling foliage.

Hanging under the nexus of the colōfn tree's vine-covered branch, La'ann sat perched upon his mount near the western boundary of the great forest he called Nahélé. A fabric of leafy vines covered the massive tree's trunk and formed a living wall on his right side. Behind him the forest ended, falling abruptly away in a long, precipitous drop to meet a talus of forest rubble piled like boulders at the foot of a cliff. Only moments before he reveled in the expansive view spread before his high position in the living rampart that was Nahélé's western face. Outside of Nahélé's protective arms, Amon's fierce glare shone down from her place in the deep blue sky to sear the vast green Mokililana.

Visible from his vantage, the interior midfloor clearing stretched below and away from La'ann's position, offering quiet refuge in its serene beauty. Motion caught his eye. A serpent flyer swooped just below the ceiling greenery. Watching it fall toward the midfloor, he marveled at the superb collection of abilities ensuring the flyer a secure existence among the many creatures vying for life within Nahélé's arms. Thin wings held close, the flyer stretched its long body into a slim projectile, twitching small corrections into its plummeting course to fall hard onto some unsuspecting and unfortunate target.

In search of a better view, La'ann pushed the protective mask up onto his forehead before pulling the hood of his cloak over his head. Hidden again from Amon's brilliance, squinting eyes relaxed to gaze into the shaded clearing below. The forest's breath wafted over him, bringing with it the peaceful detachment he sought. Nahélé's arms embraced a rich tapestry of life, sublime dramas replete with equal parts peace and violence, a living tableau that always gave him reason to pause and savor his own existence.

The last remnant of afternoon rain fell from the forest ceiling. Brief, sharp flashes sprang from the soft shadows as a falling drop intersected an unimpeded shaft of sunlight from the upper forest. The soft impact of each drop on the cushion of decay covering the midforest floor bathed La'ann's ears with a barely audible patter. He enjoyed the elusive symphony as only an attentive and practiced listener could.

Through dim light hovering at the far end of the clearing, La'ann could barely discern an élobe cautiously making its way through waist-high greenery covering much of the midfloor clearing nearly a hundred arm lengths below. The élobe's broad footpads permitted erratic movement on the midfloor's spongy surface, a slow meander accented by brief dashes and petrified stillness. When frozen, La'ann could hardly see the animal, and only then because he knew where to look. Even as he followed it across the clearing he had to concentrate, losing it in a deep shadow, only to pick it out again with its next dash.

The familiar scene left him feeling calm. All was well. Nahélé's heart beat as always. When images of the strange flying stone again intruded into La'ann's mind they were considered with a clear head.

Tell Su'ban, I must.

Only the sight and sound of the strange rock's passing and the gash it left on the face of the Mokililana remained to bear witness to its existence. Seeking Su'ban's guidance would cost a day, maybe two. Within those two days the marsh would heal the scar and swallow the stone, leaving little trace of the insult it once bore.

Into the floating plain, go I must.

Within Nahélé's familiar embrace, La'ann feared little. The Mokililana gave him reason to pause. Common sense demanded fear of the floating marsh. A lightly considered journey to that forbidding place could only bring grief. Yet, even as he formed the thought, he knew what he must do.

A plan began to form. Water to drink he had. The high-forest cloak he wore would fend off Amon's angry stare. Footing meant everything in La'ann's world. Within the bags hanging along Mœrai's side, he kept a pair of midfloor boots. Whenever the need arose, this broad-soled footwear gave him the élobe's mastery of the soft midfloor surface. Would they not serve as well atop the sargasso surface of the Mokililana?

La'ann's ability to think through complex requirements was one of many reasons why he led hunting parties, why he sat now at the forest edge. On this occasion, he'd chosen a position near the western forest boundary perched just out of Amon's fierce midday glare, a good vantage from which to pick off ceiling runners. Sunlight assaulting the forest near the boundary's open edge would force runners emerging from the shadowy interior to slow and turn away, becoming good targets in the illuminating sunlight. He awaited the runners being driving towards him by fellow clansmen.

Tucked loosely within thick vines hanging from the root of one of the colōfn tree's large side branches, La'ann had an almost unobstructed view of the clearing before him. Observed from the eastern direction, where he could expect ceiling-runners to appear, he remained hidden. From its place along Mœrai's side, he extracted a dart-bow and rested it across her neck.

He chose to do so at an opportune time. As the bow came to rest on Mœrai's neck a ceiling-runner emerged, swinging fast from dense foliage above the far edge of the clearing. In a single, smooth fluid motion, La'ann lifted the bow and held its stock against his stomach as he pulled the taut line back, while, with his right hand, he reached toward the pouch across his waist. In the briefest moment, the dart was set, the bow cocked, and La'ann peered along the bow's length toward the swiftly tumbling ceiling-runner. As the runner came within range, La'ann held his breath and took aim; waiting for the moment it would slow and turn from the glare. The animal kept coming. As the distance between them disappeared, La'ann let his attention wander, fascinated by the head-on perspective at such close range. A vertical blur of swinging arms cut the image of the animal's thin body in half and a living lump of an eye jutted from each side, both blinking rapidly, regularly, and independently.

A glint of sunlight sent the runner into a sudden

correction. Long arms flew wildly outward, returning quickly into a smooth rotation and a wary new direction. La'ann squeezed the release. Remaining completely still, he watched the dart run true, its path etched in the air by a thin trail of thread, striking the runner just behind its near eye, almost at body center, and bringing an abrupt end to the smooth rhythmic motion of an instant before. Three arms faltered and fell away, numbed by the dart's venom. The body dropped, held momentarily by the fourth hand's long fingers. At the last claw's release, the carcass fell, held to a long arc by the tether thread. Climbing foliage grown thick below La'ann's perch softened its impact upon the pillar tree's trunk.

La'ann moved quickly, pulling the runner's body from the jungle growth and tying it to dangle away from the great tree. Before he had secured another dart to the bow, several more runners were already halfway across the clearing.

By the time La'ann was finally ready to quit, seven carcasses hung nearby. One task only remained, an unwelcome but necessary part of the hunt and one that no one would do for him. One at a time, he pulled the carcasses from their hanging storage. Making good use of his knife's keen edge, he cut every long arm from each carcass, tying them all to hang by one long finger. The poisoned blood from those arms took time to drain, but doing so preserved both the flavor and the value of the flesh. Blood flowed and La'ann turned the bright blade of his prized knife over in his hands. A treasured gift, it was all he had left to remind him of his father.

Into the loose net hanging on Mœrai's left side, La'ann threw the bodies. Carcasses were worth little, but their soft olive-brown fur had uses, and the skinned bodies would become fertilizer for the fields or bait for the swimming creatures of the underworld. Into the right-side net, he placed the arms. La'ann's secure place within the M'pepebato Clan had been largely earned, not for his eloquence at camp meetings, but for his keen eye and the valuable arms of ceiling runners that he supplied.

Waning daylight had begun to stretch and magnify forest shadows, telling La'ann it was time to rejoin his clan brothers in the night's bivouac. With the day's kill tied down and his weapons and supplies secured, La'ann urged Mœrai out of the position she had dutifully occupied for the last several hours. Mœrai returned a long low groan as she swung her forearm out, reaching upward for a fresh hold in the ceiling boughs. Quickly finding a secure placement for long claws, she moved out into the clearing, turning her pace into a steady swinging lope. La'ann pressed a knee into her neck, prodding her across the top of the clearing and into a well-used path through the hanging foliage.

He and Mœrai headed along the boundary zone, moving parallel to the forest edge. Longnight came tonight and Uko's huge looming dark side had already begun to cover Amon's face, even now dimming the glare beyond the boundary, permitting him to look with uncovered eyes across the Mokililana. Soon, the inner forest would be too dark for easy travel. They moved north toward the day's bivouac, where La'ann knew his clansmen, Ro'ann and Hol'imm, waited. For a while, La'ann enjoyed the feeling of Nahélé's breath washing over him. The forest released the day's tension in one long, slow exhale as marshland rose to enjoy Uko's company, flooding the underworld and pushing a river of air through the porous midfloor to flow out through the midforest volume. In concert with Mœrai's arms swinging rhythmically alongside, the gently flowing air helped La'ann to relax, pulling his thoughts away from the path ahead and back to the day's events, returning his mind again to ponder the meaning of the strange stone he'd seen cross the sky.

....

Deepening shadows became complete darkness as the

small group of forest riders prepared the evening camp. The only real danger could come from above. A few night-hunting serpents might climb from the forest floor, but they only posed a danger to smaller ceiling dwellers. Caution urged the riders toward the center of the clearing near the mid-span of linked arms from every pillar tree surrounding the clearing. Any approaching menace would be felt in the movements of ceiling boughs.

Each man set up a hammock, arranged so that the three hunters hung from the ceiling around a triangular space. Each one removed the supplies and saddle from their mounts, hanging essentials within reach at the end of a hammock. The hunters' three kùmu'lio hung quietly around the outside of the group, their keen senses providing better protection than any artificial device.

From components shared between them, the three hunters constructed in-place a fist-thick wooden platform to hang from separated points within the forest ceiling. The assembled structure filled the central space of their suspended encampment and supplied a charred depression within which to build a small fire. Burning too brightly in the darkness, La'ann placed an opaque screen around the fire until it settled into embers. A bright fire would always attract nuisances, so the hunters cooked the evening meal over the glow of low embers, just as they kept their conversation barely audible beyond the close boundaries of their small camp.

La'ann knew what he must do. *Small thing it is not, but ask I must.* He alone could expect to find the flying stone's resting place. Yet, if he hoped to return alive, he needed help to venture into that hostile landscape.

The Mokililana held real danger. Even as he contemplated the journey to where he'd marked the huge stone's resting spot, indistinct thoughts of the open marsh swelled into his consciousness. Pain came with them, not fear. La'ann tried to clear his head, but the memories would not leave.

He saw elation in his father's face. They had conquered. The marsh stalker lay before his standing father, hiding all but his father's head and shoulders.

The pain in his stomach became sharper.

His father's elation suddenly fell away. Horror flashed over the face in his mind. He saw the arm reach out. He felt himself pitch to one side. He heard the roar from behind. He saw the second stalker rise to full height. He watched his father raise his bow and reach for an empty quiver.

The pain tightened.

The scene blurred in La'aan's mind, just as the water in his eyes blurred the faces around him. No ... La'ann felt no love for the Mokililana, but he knew the dull pain in his heart would not prevent him from venturing out again.

Pulling himself back to the campfire, La'ann told Ro'ann and Hol'imm of the day's events, pausing frequently to answer questions from Ro'ann who found it difficult to imagine or to believe the tale he heard. "The sky, a stone cannot ride! From what place can such a stone come?"

La'ann had no answers. He had to agree. "Great mystery it is. Knowing, Su'ban will wish. To her, knowing, carry I must."

Hesitating but a heartbeat, Ro'ann rendered support. "With you go I must."

La'ann hoped his brother saw the gratitude he felt.

Skill with kùmu'lio made Hol'imm the better choice to stay. Mœrai especially disliked any separation from La'ann, and Ro'ann's mount was no different. Kùmu'lio cannot descend to the Molikilana. Their entire world was limited to the midforest ceiling.

The clansmen could afford to waste no time. Pulling down the bivouac, they set off toward La'ann's earlier hunting position. Darkness put the riders completely at the mercy of the senses and skills of their mounts. Able to hear, feel and smell her way along the route they had followed earlier,

Mœrai led, carrying La'ann as if he were one more satchel of cargo, putting him to sleep with her easy, quiet, swinging rhythm. In the morning he'd be thankful for all the sleep he might get.

Mœrai's snort awakened him. Eyes well-adjusted to darkness peered through the dim light filtering in from a clear night sky outside the boundary area. The bulky outline of the forest edge distinguished the clearing where he and Mœrai had hunted earlier in the day. He saw where the great colōfn trees ended and where the group must stop.

With not a word exchanged, La'ann and Ro'ann quietly assembled gear into back-born bundles, donned high-forest cloaks and boots, and lowered themselves down the outside of the exposed colōfn tree. There they swung themselves out onto the Kua'la, a gigantic talus slope made, not of rocks, but of fallen trees; a transition zone between the familiar forest world and the unforgiving swamp world of the Mokililana.

La'ann and Ro'ann stepped uneasily atop the dead hulk of what had once been the trunk of a living colōfn tree. With a single step onto the surface of the huge log, they changed from creatures at home in their forest into aliens wary of a hostile world. Turning anchors into the log, they secured both themselves and their gear and waited, waited for the outgoing tide, the dawn and the next stage of their trek. La'ann could already hear the low-pitched groans of logs grinding under their own great weight as the ebbing tide gained strength.

He sat knees drawn close, chin resting atop folded arms, gazing across the Mokililana's distant shadows. Rising above the flat, featureless form of the unlit Mokililana, the dark outline of a protruding isle stood against the twinkling forms of Amon's many kin arrayed above the western horizon. The isle gave La'ann a reference for his anticipated journey. At his back, Amon already awakened. He imagined her bright face pushing itself above the barrier-mountains guarding Nahélé's distant boundary in the east. He watched the edge of Nahélé's shadow form far out in the Mokililana and begin its slow march toward him. Until Amon fully awoke, he could watch without the protection of the high-forest mask lying within the hood of his cloak. He felt much less confined without it, able to see more clearly, breathe more deeply and smell air still laced with the scent of Nahélé. The sky brightened, chasing the sparkling eyes of Amon's kin from view. A bright crescent smile from one of Ūko's little sisters lingered in the deep blue sky above the horizon. Ūko slept, as she always did during Longnight.

Few of La'ann's clansmen ever came to look upon the unfettered beauty of the world beyond Nahélé. The people of Nahélé found constant comfort in the forest depths. The vast empty expanse of the western horizon gave solace to few, even less so in Ūko's absence. A glance to either side showed La'ann the colōfn trees rising above the Kua'la, their countless forms stretching into the distance and blending into a great impenetrable rampart, restraining and protecting Nahélé's bounty.

The slightest gentle airflow crossed his bare face, telling La'ann that Nahélé, too, was awakening to take in the first breath of the day, and warning him that the deep rumblings he'd already felt would soon grow stronger. The depths spoke in low groans, sending their message through his bones as much as his ears. He tightened his grip on the anchor beside him.

Staring up into the colōfn trees, he could barely make out Hol'imm and the kùmu'lio hanging just inside the edge of the forest ceiling. He waved toward Hol'imm. A weak light flickered and bobbed in response. Would he be able to see it later? Would the dense tangle of the Mokililana hide his view? They would need the reference. La'ann looked again toward the far isle. Their path lay between that point and here.

Another deep-throated rumble rose from the log. La'ann felt motion in his spine. The tidal retreat had begun. The forest shadow's edge crept closer. Amon's gaze would be upon them soon and the weight of her stare would press upon them all day. He'd soon need to retrieve his mask and retreat within the shadow of the hood of his cloak. First, however, he'd try to enjoy the slow ride, much less comfortable than Moerai's gentle swinging, but an exhilarating ride for a forester. Another glance up at Hol'imm told La'ann that they were moving faster. Hol'imm was now farther away, his outline barely discernable within the forest foliage background. Not a word passed between La'ann and Ro'ann as they rode out the ebbing tide, listening to strange noises completely unlike the muffled sounds of Nahélé.

Eventually, the receding tide began to slow, forcing La'ann to confront their climb down from the great tumble of logs. Their climbing skills were well exercised and they were at ease with the lightweight, strong m'pepalia-fiber ropes they carried. Yet a climb on this monstrous woodpile would test those skills more than La'ann would admit. Rising stiffly, he stood with somewhat less confidence than he wanted Ro'ann to see. He pulled an m'pepalia rope from his bag. To one end he joined a second, thin line and fastened the junction of the two onto the anchor he had already turned into the log. Feeling uncertain of footing, motion still evident beneath his feet, he set each step of the sure-footed high-forest boots firmly into the log and carried the two coils carefully out along the curved surface. Somewhere along the log's steepening curve he stopped and threw both coils out as far as he could, watching them arc over the log's remaining bulk.

The sound of La'ann tugging ropes from his bag pulled Ro'ann from his own contemplation and spurred him to action. By the time Ro'ann managed to secure his own lines, La'ann was already leaning backward against the pull of rope and stepping out over the log's curving bulk. The rope between La'ann's legs, wound out and around one side, across his body and over the opposite shoulder, to fall through his right hand reaching behind his back, a circuitous path harnessing the friction of his body to give him complete control over his descent.

Ro'ann managed to step up his pace, getting himself onto the steep curve of the log only a moment behind La'ann, who was looking down at their possible landing spots. Another log lower in the talus pile could be seen jutting at an angle from below the first and they were descending into a deep hole formed between it and a third log.

La'ann walked himself to his right and swung over to permit a step down onto a nearly flat area on the second log. Only as he pressed his feet into that log, was La'ann able to look up and see Ro'ann walking down behind. Satisfied with their first assault, La'ann reached out to grab the light companion line and gave it a sharp pull, releasing both itself and the thicker rope to fall from the log above. Ro'ann arrived as La'ann secured his ropes again, this time around the dried corpse of a thick vine that had once wrapped itself around the fallen giant. Testing and finding his anchor secure, La'ann moved off once again along the outside curve of the log before Ro'ann had time to retrieve his own ropes.

An impatient call from Ro'ann went unheeded. La'ann knew his brother chafed at their pace, but he also knew they had little time to spare. They would need every bit of a long day to find the flying stone and then find their way out again. They did not want to see nightfall upon the Mokililana.

A bit more than an hour's descent brought the pair to a point where the logs of the Kua'la plunged into the mass of tangled green forming the bulk of the Mokililana. The sure grip of high-forest boots no longer served a purpose and was quickly replaced with the larger print of midfloor footwear. The two men of the forest could afford little time to rest.

One task remained. La'ann turned back to stare up at the edge of the midforest ceiling, now high above, trying to find a mark, anything he could identify, something to tell him where

Hol'imm waited. Nothing called to him; the forest edge offered no feature to distinguish one point over any other. He stared in vain for many moments, hoping to find some pattern he might commit to memory. Hol'imm and the kùmu'lio had vanished. As he turned away, resigned to tackle the problem later, a flash of light brought him back. There was Hol'imm. With one long relieved breath and a smile, La'ann aimed a piece of burnished metal upward, delivering a return flash of Amon's rays.

Nothing more prevented their departure. The next few hours would see them winding their way through one vine tangle after another, slogging across the soggy Mokililana.

CHAPTER 6
One More Day

Lurid images fled in disarray. Searching for reality, Angus's eyes found only the faint glow of instruments upon the smooth domed ceiling of what had once been the Raiju's bridge. A soft whisper of air flowed somewhere within range of his hearing. The confines of his command chair forced a contorted twist as he sought to relieve an uncomfortable pain. Pulling himself upright, Angus glanced around the room. That he had awakened and still breathed gave him reason for hope. *At least, we should have time to think today.* Unbidden, the previous day's end came into focus. *The autopilot managed a decent landing. Amazing by itself.* The fact of that landing supplied Angus with two important pieces of information: nothing more than the Raiju's core module remained intact, and the planet outside would not kill them outright. Inability to meet either condition would have forced the autopilot to leave him and his crew in deep space with a crippled ship 200,000 light-years from home.

Angus scanned the area. In the absence of an expansive projection field display, the smooth forward bulkhead seemed oppressively near. Circumstance aside, little seemed amiss except dimmed cabin lighting and the slumped forms of three crewmembers asleep at their stations. *All that's left ... Time to see what lies without.*

Sliding silently from his command station, he stood on the deck, reaching suddenly to brace himself. With one hand on the station's structure, he straightened carefully. A second passed as he took note of the core Riemann field's absence, no longer giving definition to notions of 'flat' nor 'level.' Moving past a slumped John Singh, he acquainted himself with the bridge deck's gentle curve as he stepped toward Ivan's station at the instrument console's end. Gently shaking one arm, Angus whispered close to Ivan's ear. "Mister Tanr, time to get to work."

Arriving slowly, Ivan's return to consciousness began with the same blank stare with which Angus had met the dawn. Angus raised one hand in a bid for silence. "Softly, Mister Tanr. Let the others sleep. I need you to tell us what's out there. Can you quietly perform an assessment of our surroundings?"

Corners are difficult to find within a circular enclosure. If, however, by 'corner' one meant a low area, little-seen and little used, then a small, unoccupied portion of Raiju's bridge perimeter might be called 'corner.' After issuing his first order of the day, Angus quietly moved to the aft corner lined with emergency storage lockers.

Offering an energy ration to Ivan, Angus carried three others with him to stand beside his command station. There he filled the hollow in his stomach while pondering the day ahead. *Emergency stores will last a few days only.*

Ivan worked at his instruments. Eilen and John Singh remained asleep at their stations. Raiju's loss weighed heavy: one starship and 140 colleagues, friends, and crewmates. *We paid dearly. With luck, Henning and the replacement miners will live to tell the tale ... and justify the price paid.*

No amount of mental effort would bring his ship back, nor resurrect his shipmates. He should be thinking about survival. Perhaps fatigue had gotten the better of him, for Angus offered little resistance when his thoughts gravitated back to the chase's beginning, to his reaction upon finding one of the League's starships among the stars of Haven. For the second time in his life, he had found himself at the helm of a starship in blind flight, threatened by a League warship.

It was the only thing I could have done. There was enough information aboard to lead the League warship to every population center in Haven. I had no real choice. Either we ran or we destroyed the ship ourselves. Any other starship commander would do the same in my place.

It struck Angus as an ironic twist of fate that he should be present at the League's discovery of Cinder station. He understood better than most. The League of Planets' heavy-handed government had driven him out of the Milky Way galaxy just as it had once driven Haven's original settlers. Angus felt a kinship to those pioneers. He, like they, had fled to discover a new world, as yet unsullied by the League of Planets. Yesterday's incident seemed eerily similar to the events that brought Angus to Haven. And now he found himself again seeking survival on a new world.

A small tremor seized Angus's attention. Tension swept through him as his senses refocused onto the deck at his feet. Their escape craft might yet be in jeopardy. The deck shifted again. With one hand braced on the command chair, he put himself back to work. "Mister Tanr, can you tell me yet what's out there?"

Ivan could not hold his voice down. "Sir, it's remarkable, but this planet seems to support abundant life. I detect an atmosphere of oxygen and nitrogen, with minor amounts of carbon dioxide, ozone, inert gasses, and humidity. It's breathable, and there's water, but we may need to protect ourselves from that ozone. My first look at radiation levels also shows a high level of UV. The local star is throwing some mean light at us. I'll have more in a minute, sir."

"Very good, Lieutenant. Take a quick look at the attitude

sensors and accelerometers. I'm getting worried about the ground beneath us. How firm is our position here?"

Ivan returned to his instruments and Angus turned to wake the others, finding them sitting upright, shaking sleep from their heads. He picked the two energy rations off the main console, tossing one to each. In what he hoped was a light tone, he began regrouping his remaining crew. "Welcome to our new home. I hope you two are rested and ready to join us." Looking directly at his groggy navigator, Angus gave him a chore to get him going. "Commander, start assembling the emergency equipment."

Adept as she was at any task, a job assignment for his executive officer needed no real thought. "'Second', can you take some of the load off Mister Tanr and learn more about our new home? I think we need to know more about the landscape beyond the immediate."

Without a word, Eilen turned to her station console and began slowly activating instruments, interrupting motions to wipe sleep from her eyes. Angus watched her move hands over the controls, performing duties as familiar as breathing. The cabin had become nearly silent. The faint low hum of awakening instruments floated under mild scraping sounds escaping from the storage area. Angus could just hear Ivan humming to himself. Seeing his crew busy with routine tasks, Angus felt calm. He knew the feeling would not last long. Another faint rumble rippled through the deck. "Mister Tanr. What's happening?"

Composed by the performance of familiar duties, Ivan spoke evenly. "Sir, what I can see immediately around us looks fairly solid, but I don't have sensors to know exactly what's below this vehicle. I don't really know what's going on. I can tell you that we're completely surrounded by what appears to be dense plant life." Ivan then echoed what Angus had been thinking. "We may have to go outside to take a look."

"Not just yet, Mister Tanr."

Before Angus could finish the thought, Eilen spoke for the first time since waking. "Sir, a water haze is obscuring almost everything. I raised the antenna to get a look over the close brush, but I still can't see much. Only the long wavelength signals are able to penetrate far. I can just make out a high ridge off the port side about ten kilometers away. Otherwise, everything around us looks similarly flat."

Some time, and several tremors later, with their ability to probe the character of the outside world exhausted, Angus gave in to the inevitable need to venture outside. It took a little longer than strictly necessary for all four to get into protective gear; a precaution, since only Ivan and John were actually going outside.

Never before had the bridge of Raiju seemed so inadequate. The simple task of helping each other don protective suits designed for deep space transformed the bridge into a tiny cramped space and turned an otherwise simple procedure into a cumbersome ballet. While everyone else bemoaned the difficulty, Angus felt pleased that the clumsy activity kept everyone focused and pushed nagging fears aside.

He tried to keep a light tone over the intercom as he watched Ivan's back through the viewing port of the small airlock. "Mister Tanr, I trust you remember how to breathe in that suit. Are you ready?"

"Yeah, I'm ready. A little nervous, but ready."

Ivan held up a hand to emphasize the acknowledgment. The slight movement of his helmet might have been a nod. In their protective gear, both Ivan and John barely fit within the tiny space of the airlock. For either of them to turn and face the interior door was not worth the effort.

"And you, Mister Singh?"

"Likewise."

"All right, here we go."

Angus didn't bother to purge the atmosphere in the

airlock. Contamination of the atmosphere outside did not worry him; whatever they had brought with them into this alien world was certainly going to get out there eventually. The speed with which the world outside imposed itself on his crew did worry him. His hand moved slowly toward the airlock vent control. When the indicator signaled an equalized pressure, Ivan pushed open the hatch. A long exhale echoed in the intercom as both John and Ivan resumed breathing.

Through the viewport Angus watched Ivan unroll the escape ladder out the open doorway, kneeling to set it into fixtures. Compared to a proper descent vehicle, their vessel was poorly equipped. It struck Angus that this crude method of egress would be only the first of many compromises and improvised procedures they'd be forced to make.

Ivan's head disappeared below the bottom of the door opening and Angus moved to the instrument console. By the time he regained visual perspective, Ivan had already descended several steps. Reconnecting with Ivan, Angus's first words were bathed in caution. "Careful, Mister Tanr, I don't want to see your first step onto our new world start with a fall."

"A little late for warnings, I'm almost at the bottom. The ladder didn't even extend its full length. I can tell you already that the ship is well settled into very soft ground."

Through Ivan's helmet camera, Angus saw only the hands, ladder and hull. With growing impatience, he waited for Ivan to step away from the core's side.

The camera display shifted toward the ground as Ivan looked to take a first step onto the planet's surface. The ground shimmered in blue-green hues. Ivan's voice sounded doubtful as he extended his right foot. "I'm not so sure of this. I can see no place that looks firm." All seemed well until he shifted weight. "Whoa!"

Angus reacted before thinking. "Ivan!"

"I can hear you, Captain. I'm only a couple of intercom

centimeters away. Now, if I can just pull myself loose of this muck."

Eilen and Angus stood in silence watching Ivan's view as he extracted his wet foot from a clinging tangle of trailing green growth. At the sight of Ivan's foot firmly placed upon the ladder rung, Angus exhaled. "Mister Tanr. I think you'll need some additional equipment."

And with that statement Angus knew the planet was coming inside. Ivan could not hang outside on the ladder and Angus had no confidence the airlock sterilization procedure would handle the slime covering Ivan's leg. *Just a matter of time.*

One very long hour later, Eilen and Angus watched a close view of boots and hands as Ivan and John sat atop an inflatable platform, struggling with improvised soggy-ground footwear. Caution aside, Eilen worked without helmet or gloves, working and speaking naturally. "Having some trouble there, John?"

"Oh yeah. This is great fun. Trying to tie these cords while wearing these gloves is just what I was trained to do."

Ivan managed to secure the footwear well before John. Sitting with legs over the side and feet planted on wet, vine-covered ground, he tested his ability to stand.

"Hold on a second, Ivan. Let me get a line on you first," John said as he pulled his own legs over the side.

Through John's helmet camera, Angus watched Ivan take a few tentative steps. "This will work. It's a bit awkward. I have to move slowly and shift weight with care, but I think we can work with this." Ivan extended both arms. "What do you think?"

Like a kid with a new toy, Ivan seemed to be enjoying himself. Accidents, however, were something they could not afford, and Angus spoke for caution. "OK, Ivan. Take it easy. Need I say 'be careful' again? ... John, don't let go of that line... Ivan, can you pull back and give me a good look at the ship?"

In slow, measured steps, Ivan picked his way toward a tangled blue-green wall defining the edge of their present world. Ivan's camera swung with the motion of his head, alternating between the tangled wall and the ground one step ahead of his foot. Eilen switched the console display to John's cameras and she and Angus followed Ivan's progress from a distance. With every step, Angus's impatience rose. Angus wanted to see their vessel. Well before Ivan reached the foliage, he interrupted the march. "That's enough, Ivan. Take a break. Stop and turn around. I really want to see the ship's core."

As the round form of their vessel came into view, Angus pulled in a hissing breath. Ivan volunteered his own observations. "It's sitting pretty low, Angus ... and, the orientation doesn't look right, it may be turning." Slipping into analytical mode, Ivan thought out loud, "The spherical hull can't hold itself in preferred orientation. No footings seem to have deployed. Although, in this soggy ground, I'm also not sure what good they would do ... and, if it's not riding stably, we may have limited options."

Angus was already considering action. "Come on back, Ivan. I'd like you secure on the platform. We need to talk about what to do next."

Ivan's use of Angus's given name marked the new reality: the former starship crew was already becoming a survival group.

....

Momentarily spent, Angus stood upright. Excursion suits were not designed for ease of effort. The line onto which he'd just finished tying a bundle lay coiled at his feet. He looked down to the foot of the ladder to see if John was ready to receive the next one. Off to one side, Ivan caught his eye. Nodding to Ivan's waving arm, Angus wondered which test instrument Ivan had decided to set up first.

The plan was not without problems. Off-loading supplies had consumed a good deal of effort and they certainly were not going to come back inside. Deciding which articles to pull outside presented something of a dilemma. If they were concerned for their own safety outside, how then was it appropriate to risk their valuable emergency stores? At the same time, if they were unable to secure long-term shelter within the core vessel, then they'd need to bring everything outside eventually, and who knew how much time they would have.

Angus had one reason to be thankful. His fellow survivors filled him with pride. *As good a crew as I might wish for.* The prospect of exposing themselves caused no real concern. They simply got busy doing what they had to do.

He'd just reconnected with the work at his feet when his contemplation was assailed by a loud, high-pitched scream, piercing his ears with real pain. He looked up to see Ivan's flying body strike the far side of the bivouac platform and crumple in a heap. The impact sent a shudder through the raft, knocking Eilen off her feet. From his high perch, Angus turned eyes toward the spot where Ivan had been a moment earlier, stunned by the sight of a creature unlike any he'd ever seen.

The huge beast glistened. As though cloaked in a suit of polished tiles, its every movement sent waves of gleaming reflection running down its side. Twice the height of a man, the animal stood atop four hind legs and bellowed rage from the edge of the clearing. From a vantage above the surrounding foliage a long, narrow head turned to glare down at Eilen. Two huge, green eyes stared down recessed trenches running along each side of a long, shiny snout ending with a hooked beak. Eilen knelt on the bivouac platform trying desperately to pull a hand weapon from the emergency supplies. The angry beast flexed its two broad, spiked forearms, the same arms that had just hurled Ivan's body 20 meters across the camp.

Shaking off the shock, John hastily tossed aside supplies in search of a weapon. Finding one, he rose to see Eilen aiming a shot from one knee. The weapon flashed. A sharp crack echoed off the side of the core vehicle. A burst of smoke rose from the creature's torso, filling the air with the smell of ozone and singed tissue. The animal did not seem to notice.

John took careful aim and fired, raising wisps of smoke just behind one large green eye. The creature reared back, renewing its high-pitched bellow and swung a fearful glare toward John. As fast as he could aim, John fired one shot after another. The animal lowered itself into a crouch, holding massive forearms close and cocked all four hind legs, winding up to rid itself of John. At that moment, Eilen fired again, striking softer hindquarters, soliciting a visible shudder. Screaming anew, the animal reared a second time and turned toward her. Careful aim sent John's next shot directly into one eye, while Eilen caught the creature again near the opposite eye. The beast staggered and fell, hanging its head. Its bellow became a moan. Eilen and John kept up persistent fire as the creature slowed. Eilen took aim at a single point on the underside of its long neck, scoring repeated hits in that one place, until the creature's bellow became a gurgle and black fluid burst from its neck. With one last attempt to rise, the creature staggered and fell into the mush, sending forth a wave of stained water.

Arms outstretched, weapons aimed at the still body, the two defenders remained frozen, unable to decide if the ordeal had ended.

From his perch above the entire scene, Angus broke the silence. "I think you may have won."

Angus's voice rose over the hard breathing heard within every helmet. When he finally lowered his weapon, still breathing hard, John turned to look toward where Ivan had been thrown. "Ivan!"

Eilen crawled across the bivouac platform.

Angus could not restrain himself. Violating all his training he left the core vehicle unoccupied and climbed down to make his way toward Ivan. He struggled to pull himself onto the bivouac platform, feet sinking into soft ground. Eilen and John were bent over Ivan's body. John's low moan sent an ominous message. Nearing Ivan's still form, he saw blood flowing from four deep puncture marks.

Eilen turned a reflective visor toward Angus. "Can we get him back into the core?"

Without lifting his eyes from Ivan's body Angus replied in as emotionless a voice as he could muster. "I don't think it makes much difference. There are three of us now."

People have different mechanisms for dealing with grief. Most will withdraw. For the three survivors, their immediate escape from peril provided temporary refuge. John became detached, examining the holes in Ivan's suit, as if they were a mere curiosity on display. "These holes go deep. That scaly mantis made them with a single short swat."

While Angus struggled to don footwear, John sloshed around the platform to see more closely what had killed Ivan. The attacker's unmoving bulk lay on its side. A long narrow jaw gaped open, exposing three rows of sharp teeth, all appearing as lethal as a survival knife. Two forearms ended in long, hard scythes, lined with spikes as long as a man's hand and as thick as a thumb. A jumbled mix of hard scales covered the body, some colored dark blue-green and some shimmering with reflected light, marvelous camouflage for the surrounding jungle-world, and likely what diminished the effect of energy weapons.

John peered into one bulging, solid green eye, nearly the size of his own head. "Damnation! This is some kind of predator. You two should take a look at it."

Angus was not really listening. "I have to question our outdoor study plan. Animal life here may give us more trouble than we need. A strategic retreat back into the ship's core seems like the better choice."

Eilen agreed. "I'm not too keen on the idea of hanging around out here myself. The core seems much more inviting just now. I know we'll have to venture back out here, but perhaps we should give ourselves time to plan it."

John's face never turned from the scaly carcass. "And we'd better check all the hand weapons we have. It certainly looks like we'll need them."

Angus looked up at the sky. "We're all worn out and hungry, and I'm really not sure how much daylight we have. We should return to the core, eat and rest. We'll get accurate bearings on that high ground Eilen observed and make ready to move out tomorrow. I'm sure we'll need as much daylight as we can get."

Before that instant, events on the ground had kept Angus's attention away from the alien sky. He stared at a distant bright blue-white star riding an arc well below zenith in a dark blue sky. The opposite horizon now sported as large a moon as he'd ever before seen, filling a significant part of the low sky with a beautiful dull red-orange color.

He chided himself for the distraction. *I'll enjoy the sight later if we're lucky.* "Most of this stuff stays out here. We're certainly not going to take it all back into the core. Is there anything we should take back?"

Looking for a reply Angus caught his breath. The dense wet foliage behind John spread and a large sharp beak rose above John's head. Angus could barely shout. "John! Behind you!"

Eilen reached for her sidearm. John fumbled for the weapon on his waist clip. In the few seconds elapsing since Angus's warning, a second shimmering blue-green mantis pushed through the vines.

CHAPTER 7
Resignation

Victory's drop into real space came with a brightly filled projection display. The large, nearby blue-white star played host to a multitude of planetary companions and gave the bridge crew reason to be thankful for a carefully composed navigation trajectory. The star's image settled into everyone's mind and so did a disappointing certainty. The chase had ended. The prize had eluded capture.

"Honorable Captain, I'm afraid it is as I said it would be. We've dropped into this system as close to that blue star as reason would allow. Even here, the space-time gradient remains strong. To drop in any closer would have risked severe damage. It seems the alien ship fell through somewhere closer. Not far from that gas giant planet. Stresses there would have been catastrophic; almost certain to have torn the ship apart."

"Can we see any sign?"

"There's no sign of a starship anywhere. Another, less turbulent area might allow us to detect the space-time ripples of their wake, but here there's such a jumble of matter that it'd take days to decipher. Our last wake analysis would put them close to where we detect a broad arc of diffuse matter ... I'm not at all sure, but I suspect a close examination of that matter might reveal debris from the alien ship."

Not yet ready to accept failure, Alexandra considered options. How long might a return trip to the Lesser Cloud require? Finding that orbiting station again would take time. The flat structure of intergalactic space-time enabled very long jumps, but they couldn't simply retrace their steps. The frantic chase had not allowed for recorded bearings. Still ... it could be done without too much delay ... they had local bearings for that red giant star ... and it wasn't her problem to work out. She had a crew to do all of that. "How soon might we return to the Lesser Cloud?"

Semgee's face betrayed his opinion. "Do you mean directly from here?"

"Yes, that is exactly what I mean."

"Honorable Captain, please, if you will allow me, can I review with you some important elements of our present situation."

Here it comes. Alexandra knew the tone. Why did her First Officer always seem to throw cold water on her best plans?

Every shred of her being craved that alien homeworld, thirsted for the glory of its discovery, but still, she listened. With their original mission nearly completed, Victory had been ready to return home before the chase began. Perhaps a few weeks' worth of supplies remained in the hold. Was it not more important to report her findings as soon as possible? Her discovery and her otherwise successful mission might not win her an immediate seat on the First Council, but it would at least give her the right to return and find that alien homeworld ... and the council seat would wait. The alien world in the Lesser Cloud wasn't going anywhere. It would still be there when eventually they did return. And they would then have at their command the time, energy, and resources needed to find it.

He's right, of course. Maddening as it always is, he generally does give me good advice. Can't tell him that... but it does me no good to deny it either. No... it's a shame, but we'll have to set a helm toward home as soon as we complete our time here.

Their return voyage home would be tedious enough. In unfamiliar territory, Bright Victory would need to find catalogued pulsars and recalibrate their charts. A good navigator was well worth extra rank and she carried a full commander at that post. Finding their way home was merely an irksome task, requiring completion before she would be able to tell her story... and before she could graciously accept the glory that would be hers.

Alexandra began to wrap her thoughts around what she would actually report when Bright Victory arrived home.

CHAPTER 8
Encounter

The shriek froze La'ann in midstride. A moment passed before his breath returned and his heartbeat slowed. Kneeling, he placed a palm on the soft ground. It was near, very near. Rising warily, and with a nod toward Ro'ann, he renewed the pace, wondering why the beast should be out in the midday sun. *Under Amon's angry face, marsh-stalker walks. Normal it is not.*

Chance alone did not place the screaming 'stalker' nearby. Certainly, the object of their quest must lie nearby as well.

La'ann's wide, weight-distributing footwear imposed its own pace, coercing each step into ordained motion. Forced effort only strengthened the spongy surface's grip, draining strength that much faster. Wishing no surprise encounter with a marsh-stalker, the two natives paid heed to their every sense, brushing aside vegetation with one free arm, dart bows held ready in the other.

The last tangled vines gave way and La'ann peered cautiously into an open clearing. A loud, screeching bellow drew his eyes right. Some 40 or more paces away, he saw for only the second time in his life the daunting form of a marsh-stalker, standing upright, obscured in the halo of Amon's glare scattered from its scaly hide. The animal's forearms slashed the air ahead and La'ann realized he stared at its backside. Relieved to see the animal occupied elsewhere, he surveyed the scene. To one side of the enraged beast, a huge round stone protruded from the soggy marsh, its hard, smooth surface appearing completely unnatural among wet vines. The stalker rose well above the surrounding vegetation, standing more than twice La'ann's height, and yet the animal looked tiny beside the round stone, which showed only a portion of its great bulk. Yesterday, that stone screamed across the sky like some fell missile thrown by Uko herself. Today it slept in the mire.

The marsh stalker screamed anew. Knowing well how stalkers travelled in pairs, La'ann carefully scanned the area. Fighting the restricted vision left him by the mask around his eyes, he sought calm in long, deep breaths. Amon's gaze would quickly blind him without such protection, but it forced him to survey the scene in wide arcs, unable to move until he found that second stalker. *There!* Lying low, just beside the bellowing beast. Dead? Perhaps only one remained.

With one hand, La'ann signaled Ro'ann. Stepping out of the protection of thick vines the pair maneuvered carefully closer while the stalker's attention was focused elsewhere. Ro'ann moved toward the far side of the long clearing and La'ann to the near, each drawing on the experience of many hunts to know the other's intent. Approaching close enough to discern the texture of the stalker's hide, La'ann noted blackened spots where bright scales once glinted. This stalker was already hurt.

Ro'ann's dart struck first, met shortly by a second from La'ann, piercing the stalker in nearly the same spot. The beast bellowed louder, rearing high to turn and face a new foe. Falling onto all six appendages, the stalker's head swung slowly from side to side in search of its new assailant. Into its hind legs it gathered the force of another strike, sending ripples through the spongy ground. With arms waving above his head Ro'ann cried out. The beast turned toward the motion. In full knowledge of his brother's intent, La'ann waited. Not until the enraged stalker had its attention invested in Ro'ann did La'ann launch a third dart into its side. Immediately taking up the decoy's role, La'ann began screaming, swinging his bow in rhythm with his every wail. The stalker hesitated for a moment before twisting to aim a lunge toward La'ann. Hardly had the creature's legs collected beneath its bulk when yet another dart struck.

Head drooping, fury waning, the stalker turned again, slowly now. Sluggish movements evinced the power of four darts. Before the force of a strike found reality, the creature wavered. Its rear legs slipped and the stalker fell, striking the spongy surface and radiating waves of sufficient power to put La'ann onto a knee.

From that position, La'ann fired again while Ro'ann stepped wide around the prone beast to plant yet another into its side before it could regain itself. The stalker was down, at least for a while; darts prepared for a ceiling runner's small size would not last. Even six darts may not keep this one quiet for long.

Drawing a deep breath, La'ann glanced around the clearing. Silence now filled the space where a moment before the stalker's high-pitched screech had overpowered all other sound. Two marsh stalkers lay in the mire. The prone form of one loomed between him and Ro'ann, put down by their own hand. The other lay nearby, put there by what other force? La'ann stretched to see over the near stalker's form, protruding from the wet ground as high as his chin. The second downed stalker lay beyond, not far from the large, round stone. Behind the second stalker's bulk, he saw two small rounded shapes, of a size he might easily hold between two hands. Unnatural they were. Moving as if alive, each displayed a single shiny oval feature. The two round shapes sat atop larger figures covered white as the whitest blossom, something not from the marsh plain, not from Nahélé. *Ride the flying stone, they did?*

With a cautionary motion to Ro'ann, La'ann stepped around the near stalker and moved slowly toward one side of the huge round stone, seeking to put it partially between himself and these new threats. Ro'ann remained still, his bow at the ready.

These alien shapes worried La'ann. He held his eyes on them, noting how one turned with his movements. The second shape kept its shiny side steadily facing Ro'ann. *Intelligent, they are. Work together they do.* La'ann reassured himself with the feel of the loaded bow in his hand.

Reaching the side of the large flying rock, La'ann ran his free hand along its surface and confirmed the smooth hardness of it. *So large and of knife-blade made, fly it cannot.* A question to be pondered later. Just now his attention served better focused on the two intelligent stone-riders.

With the stone protecting one side, La'ann inched along, trying to maneuver behind the dead stalker, looking for a better view of these bobbing white beings. Before he quite reached a clear vantage, the closest being moved to the near side of the dead stalker and raised a white appendage. *An arm?* La'ann became yet more cautious watching that arm wave toward him in a manner to be respected. *A weapon perhaps there is.* Even as he formed the thought, a bright flash flew from the end of the raised arm to strike the nearby surface of the rock. *Command the hot breath of Amon these creatures can?*

La'ann touched his hand where the flash had struck. In a blink, he realized the truth. That flash might easily have struck him. He'd not have been able to avoid it. These were intelligent creatures; they had weapons; they felt threatened. Reconsidering his action, La'ann laid the dart bow at his feet and stepped back. He raised his arms. Surely, by such a move he would convey less threat. Ro'ann responded readily to a hand signal and did the same. The creature nearest La'ann lowered its arm and slowly moved from behind the dead stalker's bulk, awkwardly, seeming uncomfortable in the soft marsh ground. As its form emerged, La'ann exclaimed, "By Amon's curse!"

Their lack of faces and their white, shiny bodies may have hidden the resemblance, but now, he saw them walking upright on two legs, with two arms, hands and fingers, able to hold weapons. What else could they be? These creatures seemed very much like him.

....

Where had that second mantis-creature come from? Angus had not seen it until it rose from the ground and literally fell upon John, driving him with massive forearms into the muck. He had to reach John. Ivan was already gone. The thing's weight alone had probably hurt John as well. Four hand weapons possessed just enough power to bring down the first creature, now he and Eilen had but two weapons between them.

Soggy ground grabbed at Angus's feet. There was no retreat. The ship's core offered safe haven, but they'd never be able to haul John up that ladder. Cautious now, cognizant of the creature's resistance to their weapons, Angus fought to move close behind the downed animal, feet sinking with each step. He spoke into his helmet, "Eilen! Move up behind the other end of this thing."

Each step closer to the downed beast seemed to send the second creature into greater frenzy. Rising onto its rear legs, shrieking loudly, it brandished two large spiked arms, vainly attempting to chase them away. A ripple in the marshy ground sent Angus's first shot off its mark, striking the mantis in the side, with little effect. The shot succeeded only in pulling the creature's attention around, giving Eilen a clear shot at its left eye. She missed, striking low on its neck. Angus took care now with each shot, preparing to fire what might be his last remaining charge, aiming at what he thought was an eye. He never fired the shot, surprised by the animal's lurch. It suddenly turned away, showing its back, bellowing the louder.

What now? Angus strained for a glance at where he could only guess John Singh must lay in the thick mat. The animal's glimmering backside loomed immediately ahead, blocking any view. He turned to Eilen. "Can you see any sign of John?"

"Nothing."

The angry mantis dropped onto forearms, giving Angus a better view beyond. Angus pushed himself up to full height, stretching his neck to gain a look at John's body. Eilen's cry rang loud over the comlink. "There! What's that?"

In the direction of Eilen's outstretched arm, Angus noticed a shimmering shape moving near the edge of the cleared vegetation. He had difficulty discerning its true form, squinting to see it through a haze of color and glittering reflections. *Another threat? Whatever it is, that mantis doesn't seem to like it.*

Staring at this newcomer, trying to discern just what he saw, Angus noticed it change. *Was that an arm?* The mantis's scream rose to higher pitch, joined now by another wail, perhaps from the newcomer. Angus realized he was watching a second battle. The newcomer challenged the roaring creature. Then, even as he began to understand what was happening, a second wail drew his eyes to the opposite side of the clearing. He could just make out another bright, shimmering shape moving along the vegetation boundary. Everything came in pairs here. "Two of them," he said.

"I see it, too."

The angry mantis chose that moment to strike at the newcomers, shoving a wash of muck back toward Angus and Eilen, forcing them to seek protection behind the still carcass. By the time Angus rose to look again at the battle, the second mantis lay on the wet ground, all six appendages splayed out around it. The two newcomers approached closer and Angus saw how they moved upright on two appendages, while, in two others, carried a dark bow shape—intelligent bipedal creatures. That the bow shapes were weapons became clear as he watched them each release a projectile into the second downed mantis. He and Eilen could only stay hidden and watch the scene unfold. The newcomers didn't yet seem aware of their presence.

Angus watched the nearest newcomer look up and turn to survey the scene, completely passing over where he and Eilen crouched behind the first animal's corpse. Holding its weapon at the ready, the nearest biped moved toward the ship's core, reaching there as Angus wrestled his way around to one end of the downed animal's bulk.

Perhaps alerted by the motion, awareness seemed to arise in the approaching biped. It turned toward Angus. A dark, featureless hollow occupied the place where Angus might have expected to see some form of face. Angus rose slowly, feeling the adrenaline of the last many minutes, breath coming rapid and shallow; muscles tense. The second creature's demise gave testament to the power of the bipeds' weapons and this one now threatened to cut Eilen and him off from the safety of the ship's core. He took careful aim and fired a short burst, striking the core's surface just ahead of the biped's reach.

Watching the biped stop and examine the spot where the shot struck, Angus held his weapon ready, alert to the biped's weapon, ready to fire at a raised threat.

Another long moment passed. The biped stood still, facing Angus with the featureless hollow that should be a face. Angus waited, heart pounding, watching as the alien slowly placed its weapon on the ground at its feet, standing to hold arms free of its body. The gesture was easily understood: deliberate, intelligent, non-threatening, an intelligent attempt to defuse a tense situation.

Angus wasn't ready to grapple so soon with such a decision. Yet this alien being put one before him with a single peaceful gesture ... to disarm even slightly meant to place himself and his remaining crew in the care of these beings, about whom he knew only what he'd observed in the last few moments. At the same time, a cold assessment of their situation told him that, without some extraordinary intervention, he and Eilen were likely doomed. Solid ground seemed far away and the odds of them finding it very low.

Angus chose. Hooking his handgun to his belt, he slowly struggled away from the downed mantis, holding his arms in same open gesture as the alien ... *Now what?*

The alien slowly raised one arm to throw back a deep cover, replacing the dark hollow with the structure of a head. The face still stared back impassively, through a protruding oval. Raising its second arm, the alien pulled from his head a mask, revealing a dark-colored, very human-looking face, with eyes, nose and mouth, not greatly different from Angus's own. Angus's head reeled. The planet below his feet was many thousands of light-years from the nearest humankind. *"How can this be?"*

Angus felt helpless, caught like a floating leaf in the swirl of events beyond his understanding. The last few minutes painted a vivid picture. All around lay a wet, hostile world, where danger might spring at any moment from any direction. Yet here he stood, facing a native of this world, an intelligent being who'd sent a message. Baring himself of weapons and protection the native said he intended no harm. Now he asked for a sign from Angus. *And what do I intend?* The question really had but one answer. In truth, he had no real choice.

Raising two hands to grasp the hard sides of his helmet, Angus gave it a short twist and pulled it off. The new world fell upon him in a rush, attacking his every sense. Intense sunlight forced his watering eyes into tight squints, permitting only blurry sight. Every breath scratched at his throat, laced with an acrid taste and a musty odor. He fought down a cough.

The sight of Angus's bare head provoked a low sustained whistle from the native. For several long moments, the short expanse of ground between them fell still, until Angus tucked his helmet under his left arm, extended his upturned right palm, and said, "I am Angus."

Angus waited, feeling vulnerable and uncertain. Squinting under the cruel sunlight, he could barely see the marshland native. The wait didn't last long. Discomfort soon compelled an end, forcing him to return to the protection of his helmet, breathe easier and open his eyes. When the native quickly followed suit, retreating beneath mask and hood, Angus knew the native fared little better than he.

"Eilen, can you hear me?" Angus said into the comlink.

"Of course. Where would I have gone?"

Hearing Eilen's voice gave Angus some relief. At least his little unprotected excursion had not destroyed communications. "Did you see that bare-headed exchange between the alien and me?"

"I'm afraid I've had my full attention focused on this second alien. The one who has a projectile weapon pointed at me. What did you do?"

"The alien in front of me just came out from under his protective clothing and showed me a very human-looking face. I did the same for him and took off my helmet."

"And you want me to do the same? Not until this guy lowers that bow he's carrying."

Angus turned to see Eilen standing with her arms outstretched holding the second alien in the sights of her hand weapon. Before Angus could speak again, the second alien let his own weapon fall to one side. "You see," Angus said into the comlink, "the word has gotten around. We're disarming."

Eilen's weapon went onto her belt and she slowly raised both hands to her head, alert for any reaction. As she did so, the native, in one motion, flipped his hood back, then returned it forward again without removing his mask. Exposure seemed to be as pleasant for him as it was for Eilen and Angus. Followed his lead, Eilen removed her helmet and quickly replaced it, giving only a brief glimpse of her squinting face.

Both sides seemed to have reached a tacit understanding. Yet Angus vacillated. The import of the situation conflicted with something nagging at his conscience. He was forgetting something. *John!* The need for haste pulled him into sudden action. Angus moved as fast as he could manage, sloshing around the dead mantis, hoping all the while that his outburst would trigger no negative reaction from the native. The nearest alien did not move, nor did he try to hinder Angus's movement. Perhaps he understood what Angus meant to do.

A frustratingly slow slog led Angus to John's side. Kneeling to turn over John's limp form, he feared what he might find. Angus struggled to turn the limp body, unable to find traction in the soft ground. He was still adjusting his position when the near-native knelt beside him and helped pull John over.

The creature's blow had left a brutal mark. John's visor was crushed into his face. John never saw it coming, dead the instant that blow struck. And, in the moment it took for Angus to register the sight, the horror and the adrenaline of the last few minutes combined to sweep away all his carefully controlled detachment. In spite of everything, he let his head fall and wept.

....

Performed by a clansman of Nahélé, the stone-rider's clumsy efforts might have evoked laughter. The alien's strange form chased all such thoughts from La'ann's mind, leaving him wary. Without knowledge of the being's intent, La'ann could only remain alert, ready to defend himself. As the stone-rider made his way around the stalker's carcass, La'ann stood and watched, bow at his feet, until, at last, he saw the direction of the being's attention. The stone-rider's clan-mate lay on the marsh surface, unmoving and probably injured. There was no reason to interfere.

La'ann saw the alien kneel and struggle to turn his clan-mates body. There were many reasons for caution. La'ann disregarded them all. Instinctively, giving no thought to the many reasons why he should avoid interference, La'ann moved to help, kneeling beside the stone-rider and reaching to turn the limp form. The smashed facial front and the lifeless limbs left little doubt. One stone-rider no longer lived.

The realization hit La'ann at the same moment he heard the muffled sounds and felt the stone-rider next to him shake. Struck with the knowledge that this alien wept for his comrade, La'ann knew at once that these beings were as human as he.

Just as suddenly, he realized that these strange beings and the power that carried them across the sky were important discoveries, valuable to his clan. He must bring them to Su'ban. She would know what to do. He and Ro'ann simply had to get them off the Mokililana and back to the forest. Standing, he placed his hand lightly on the alien's back and said, "For you, wish I do, strength and joining from his spirit take. Go now, we must."

....

The sudden emotion took Angus quite by surprise. Perhaps he simply had no strength left to fight it. Surrendering to grief, he barely felt the hand on his back. When the planet native spoke, only a few word-sounds penetrated his helmet, "Ho 'opa' ... Oe ikai ... ho ... hapa o ... wé ... Ano ... ke ... ma ... pono." The unintelligible words meant little, yet the native's tone conveyed much. This native offered sympathy and Angus felt its sincerity.

Angus's wonder at the cloaked native's completely human action displaced his grief and filled his head with refocused awareness. *"What now?"* he thought for not the first time today. The planet native stood above him gesturing in wide-swept arm motions. Shimmering swirls of color washed over the native's scaled cloak. The native seemed to want him to stand. Rising, Angus spoke into his helmet receiver. "Eilen, you still with me?"

"Yes, Angus, I am."

"It's obvious. This native wants something. Can you understand his gestures?"

"I'm not sure yet, but I think he may want us to leave here and to go with them. He's pointing away toward the high ground."

"I was thinking the same thing ... and ... I think we should follow. We may be prisoners, but I'm not sure resistance would offer a better course. What do you think?"

"Do we really have much choice? We'd likely be dead without their help and we haven't tremendous future prospects on our own."

"OK. I agree. Grab a couple of emergency packs and additional hand weapons and let's see what's in store."

Neither of the two natives attempted to stop them as Eilen and Angus made their way to the platform that, less than an hour ago, was to have been their base camp. Now, pulling two packs from the pile of supplies and grabbing a couple more weapons, Angus could only wonder at the ease with which he placed Eilen and himself in the hands of these two completely unknown alien beings. Turning to rejoin his rescuers, protectors, or possible captors, Angus could see anxiety in their manner, the two of them now motioning in tandem. They wanted to leave in a hurry. The motions seemed directed at a hole in the surrounding foliage, where they obviously intended to go.

CHAPTER 9
Climb

Angus would remember little of the trek across the marshland. When later he might try to recall the ordeal nothing distinct would remain, blurred into one long, dull slog; a muddle of shimmering blue-green tangle, the passage of time marked by a somber dirge of wet, sucking footsteps. He would not remember when or where, but only that, somewhere along the way, something in his excursion suit failed, allowing the heavy, humid outside air to flood within and render every breath an effort.

Before the local sun buried itself below the horizon, he swam in his own sweat, the suit's fabric wrapped tight like a second skin, resisting his every motion. When the doleful procession eventually came to a halt, Angus's head hung. His arms drooped at his sides. His legs had become too heavy to lift. The boundless marsh lay behind and a rough, vine-covered slope rose before him. Finding support on a firm outcrop, he sat, too exhausted to do anything but breathe. For the first time in many monotonous hours, he was able to raise eyes from the ground at his feet.

A glance at Eilen presented a picture of how he must appear. She looked completely soaked, the fabric of her excursion suit clinging to her body as though she'd just stepped from a fully clothed swim. The sag of her shoulders and the hang of her head said she felt as he. As for himself, rejuvenation came slowly. All day, he'd focused on each step, concentrating on making careful strides, on placing each foot. The stop allowed him to ease the tight reins he'd wrapped around every fiber of will.

A glance at his two captors did nothing for his low spirits. They seemed immune to the ordeal, mocking his fatigue with their casual ease. The one Angus had begun to think of as 'Hump', swung the load from his back and set it down close to where Angus sat. The second captor, who had simply become 'The Other One,' similarly rid himself of his load. Freed of burdens, it was difficult to tell one captor from the other. With faces hidden in the shadow of hooded garments, no distinguishing feature set them apart. They blended alike with the marsh world, shimmering in the harsh sunlight like surrounding plant life.

Pulling a leather bladder from his gear, Hump shook it in Angus's face. Angus grabbed at the bladder, certain from the sound that it contained water, caring little if it did not. Pushing the visor of his helmet up off his face, he guided the bag's narrow neck through the opening. Thirst overwhelmed both caution and etiquette. His first taste of warm water turned quickly into one gulp after another until Hump pulled it from his lips, leaving another rivulet to join the sweat already trickling off his face. "Thank you," Angus gasped with all the breath he had left.

Reaching, Eilen pleaded. "If that's water, please, I could sure use some."

Angus gave himself a moment to catch his breath before answering. "If not, it does a pretty good imitation."

As Hump turned to offer the bag to Eilen, Angus saw the roots of another notion. Swinging his own pack from his back, he pulled it open and reached in to find a couple of ration bars. His efforts to unseal packages drew Hump's eyes, allowing

Eilen to grab a few more gulps.

Angus held out an unwrapped ration bar to Hump. "Perhaps you could use something to eat." Thinking that the purpose of his offering may not be obvious, Angus bit into the second bar while presenting the first. Hump's face froze before understanding dawned and his head bobbed as he accepted the food with the word, "Mélesi."

Following Angus's example, Eilen found ration bars within her own pack, unwrapped one and stretched an offering toward The Other One. The Other One looked to see his comrade chewing with abandon, and only then accepted the food from Eilen, acknowledging the gesture with the same native word, "Mélesi."

In that manner, a single native word carrying the apparent meaning of gratitude entered Angus and Eilen's vocabulary.

With rest also came Angus's first opportunity to observe his new world. The local sun's setting gave the sky's stage to the largest and brightest moon Angus had ever seen. Sometime during the long day, it had risen above the eastern horizon to follow behind the white sun. He had to marvel at the beauty of the sight, occupying so large a portion of the twilight sky that he needed to hold his flat hand close to block its image. It appeared near quarter-phase, only half-lit by the setting sun. Moonlight shone bright enough in its own right. Even the moon's unlit face threw down warm colors; red and orange hues fell from static eddies dancing across its surface.

Rising, Angus turned and faced the slope above, letting his eyes rise along its extent, stopping at the shadowed, flat barrier along its upper reaches. *A wall of some kind,* mused Angus, though its true identity momentarily escaped him. Revelation came with further inspection. A rampart indeed, a living barrier of trees the likes of which he had never seen nor heard. *They must be gigantic.* Their true size was difficult to gauge with their highest portions obscured in a layer of cloud and their distance unknown. As his eyes fell again to the near slope a more distinct picture emerged. Constituent shapes emerged from the jumbled surface to reveal their identity—innumerable splintered sections of immense hollow tree trunks, all lying like so many twigs in a heap extending along the forest edge as far on each side as one could see. All at once, Angus saw the war going on around him: a fierce boundary dispute between marshland and forest. The forest shedding the detritus of age to buffer the marshland's attack, while the marshland reached upward with gnarled webs of vines and creepers to tug at the fallen trees, striving to pull them into the mire.

Somehow Angus knew that the day's destination lay in those trees, and with that realization, he also knew that the long day was not yet finished. That they intended to climb into that forest seemed a daunting prospect. The path led upward through hundreds of feet of gigantic forest rubble. Angus was enjoying the wonder of it when Eilen brought him back to the immediate world.

"Angus, I'm stuck."

The diversion seemed at first welcome. "What seems to be the matter?"

"My foot is stuck to the ground."

Squatting to examine more closely, Angus saw a few thin fingers of marsh creeper curled around the edges of Eilen's crude soggy-ground footwear. He tried to pull it off, discovering it possessed a more tenacious grip than he would have expected. After several unsuccessful attempts, Angus thought to try another tactic. "Maybe we can simply take off those mush-walkers? I don't think we need them anymore. Our captors obviously intend to climb into this jumble of debris."

"You have my vote."

"I think I'll have to take off these gloves. They don't leave me enough dexterity to untie any knots."

Angus only turned away for a moment and was still

struggling with gloves when Eilen shouted again.

"Angus! It's pulling me down!"

When he looked again, Angus could no longer see Eilen's foot, but only her calf half-buried in water. Dark green tendrils wound upward to flay at her knee. He could see the leg descending. Grabbing at her outstretched arm, he tried to pull her free, finding no footing on the wet ground. With one hand held firm to Eilen's he reached for a second hold within the woven vines covering the surface on which he'd been sitting. Finding a grip, he strained with both arms, trying in vain to arrest Eilen's descent. Then, as if acting in concert with the disappearing ground, well-anchored vines in Angus's hand suddenly fell away, leaving him at the mercy of the pull. He fell, landing in a heap atop Eilen, who now found both legs sinking below the surface of a growing pool.

The looped rope falling onto Angus's chest required no explanation, but its use forced the release of a hand. With all the strength he could muster, he focused on the one hand holding Eilen's arm and slipped the other through the loop, lifting it as fast as he could manage over his head. As his free hand regained a grip on Eilen's arm, the rope tightened around his chest and joined the battle. Playing no more than a mere connection in the ensuing tug-of-war, Angus struggled to keep hold of Eilen's arm. Arms, hands, and shoulders strained together. Yet, as strain turned to pain, nothing moved. A raft of thin shoots rose from the water, waving in the air until they found a grip on Eilen's leg. She screamed anew. "Angus!" In seconds, she had sunk to her hips. Angus's arms began to fade; anxiety turned to panic. The strength of his grip began to fail. Angus struggled to maintain a grip. A black form fell into the water, sinking below the surface amid a whirl of thrashing arms. Angus had little time to wonder at what was happening. The stress in his arms eased, then the remainder released itself in steps until Eilen's body began to rise from the pool.

A few moments later, dripping wet, Angus stood atop firm ground together with Eilen and a very tall, near-naked, dark-skinned man, holding a gleaming knife blade in one hand and wearing a crescent of white teeth on an otherwise midnight-black face. The wide grin presented a most human expression, yet the broad face bespoke the man's distinct origin. Within eyes where Angus might search for expressive cues none showed. Whatever sparkle might be dancing there hid within a dark brown halo. No white setting surrounded the deep black pupils. Black-in-brown eyes gave little clue to what thoughts might lie behind. Only the grin told a story. Even the man's nose, flaring large and flat below those eyes, became lost in the glare of his smile. The grin disappeared when he spoke. "Hiki. Ée," he said, adding emphasis with repeated nods.

Feeling quite relieved and unable to discern which of his two captors might be speaking Angus anointed the man with a more appropriate name. "I'll just have to take your word for it, 'Grin,' old man."

In the aftermath of their brief duel with the swamp, Grin seemed to be having fun. Casually returning the knife to its place at his waist, Grin moved both hands to the sides of his head and raised them as if trying to lift the head from his body. On the second iteration of this little pantomime, Eilen looked at Angus, speaking aloud what he was thinking. "Should we?"

Angus slowly nodded. It had to happen sometime. Eilen placed both hands on the sides of her head and, with one quick twist, freed the hard helmet from its seat. Raising it off her head, she filled her lungs in one long, deep breath. "Tastes funny, but breathes well."

Seeing also how very wet and tired she appeared, Angus could only imagine how he must look. Removing his own helmet, he pulled in a slow breath. The air still seemed to come with a strong tang, but it felt good to freely draw in a deep lungful in the softer evening shadows and cooler temperatures. The huge moon's reflected light didn't fall with the same harsh edge as the sun's direct glare.

Grin watched with a renewed smile, obviously enjoying the show of relief. The soft tone in his voice suggested he understood. "Sikoyo kitóko. Ée?"

This time Angus couldn't help smiling, too. The cool air on his face felt every bit like the relief it was. "I'm sure you're right on that score, too, Grin." His own voice sounded strangely unfamiliar in the open air.

While Grin seemed to enjoy their moment of relief, The Other One stood aloof above the other three, silently recoiling the wet rope with which he had tried to fashion a rescue. When Angus turned a bared head upward, the man's face still lay in shadow within the hood of his cloak. Forgetting all normal proprieties, Angus stared at the man, curious to see the face under that hood. Perhaps The Other One understood, or perhaps it was merely his turn to act, for he dropped the coil at his feet and began to disrobe. The deep hood fell first from his head and a large pair of goggles came off to reveal the same broad, flat face as his partner's. Wearing no smile, the man's features gave no hint to his mood. With the shimmering cloak at his feet, he stood wearing only a sleeveless vest fashioned of a loosely woven fabric and leg coverings reaching only to midthigh. Having completed his transformation, The Other One laid a palm open and swept his arm in Angus's direction.

Angus needed little encouragement. He had spent entirely too much time in the excursion suit and shed it willingly. It might take a little longer than The Other One's loose garment, but it would come off all the same. Sitting on the moist log surface, he untied his improvised footwear and began to carefully open the seal, beginning at his collar and pulling down along the middle of his chest until he had exposed the shipboard uniform beneath. He was having a little difficulty pulling his arms from the sleeves when Eilen stepped close.

"If you'll just be a little patient, I'll be happy to help you with that suit." With her pulling the end of one sleeve, Angus managed to slip one arm out and pull it free of the suit. In like manner, he freed his right arm and both legs. Able to stand freely, he removed the helmet collar and carefully lifted it over his head.

He had just dropped the empty excursion suit at his feet and was enjoying the cool feeling of free-flowing air around his soaked shipboard uniform when he noticed Eilen staring at him with both hands propped on hips. Mock annoyance came along with her draw out words. "Any time you're ready."

"All right ... All right ... Your turn."

Less than a minute later, Eilen was free as well and the two shared in the pleasure of moving with some ease for the first time in a long while. Their enjoyment of such small fortune gave Grin yet more reason to display his teeth when The Other One came down to end their short rest with two short words to Grin. "Tokei sengeli."

The grin disappeared and, in the space of but a few moments, the two natives had secured their gear and turned upward. Grabbing his pack, Angus started up the slope, only to find The Other One pointing with obvious insistence at the small pile of discarded equipment. For some reason, it was not to be left behind. Angus hesitated, considering the awkward bulk of the package. Angus pled his case with raised eyebrow, spread arms and shrugged shoulders. A moment of blank stare preceded The Other One's pulled from his own pack a length of thin cord and quickly tied Angus's equipment into a small bundle, which he then hung at his own waist alongside a collection of already cumbersome equipment. Grin didn't wait to be asked, and in a few seconds had Eilen's equipment hanging similarly from his own waist. They began climbing from the swamp.

Freed of awkward footwear, Eilen and Angus found walking much easier in spite of the sloping path. Soft-soled shoes, made to grip a starship deck, were not the best choice for a moist, moss-covered log, but gave more secure footing than had the improvised marsh footwear. Steps came with some agility on solid surface.

Moving as fast as tired legs would allow, they scurried like so many insects both over and through the pile of hollow mega-logs, often finding themselves moving within dark, hollow spaces where moonlight found little power. As though alive, the pile seemed to protest their every step, complaining in a cacophony of groans, creaks, and moans. Chasms and cliffs there were, but none posed but the slightest obstruction. Gulfs wide enough to impede the strongest of climbers slowed them only long enough for Grin's bow to hurl an anchor into the far side, draw a rope through its eye, and swing across, there to secure a steady ropeway for the others to follow. Overhanging impasses presented hardly less challenge. Grin tackled each one with aplomb, able to pull himself upward hand-over-hand as effortlessly as any arboreal creature, all the while letting his white-toothed grin relay his feelings about the whole affair.

Both Eilen and Angus found inspiration in the display of skill. Grin especially seemed to have come alive within the mega-logs, while The Other One seemed possessed of renewed resolve. Grin's infectious mood even overcame Eilen and Angus's abject fatigue. Each new climbing challenge became a matter of pride, prompting Angus and Eilen to insist on surmounting each new obstacle independently, relying on their own efforts and asking little assistance from either native. In such manner the group soon found itself atop the last log just as fading twilight gave up its struggle with the night.

Angus looked in every direction, unwilling to believe that nothing more remained to climb. Yet as he saw that it was so and realized that the entire log-mountain lay below his feet, he knew that the grueling day had finally come to an end.

Sinking down upon the hard surface, he drew his knees close and lowered an exhausted head. When his eyes rose again, he took in the wide scene in the direction from which they had come. A display of stars in such numbers as Angus had never before seen confirmed in his mind that Raiju's flight from the League starship had led them to a particularly dense area of the Milky Way. Although engulfed in darkness, the low marshland still wrapped itself in a soft glow as starlight reflected from its countless mirrored leaves. A large bright crescent halfway up toward the zenith gave him reason to believe in a second moon for this planet. A gentle, warm, humid breeze wafted over him from out of the black forest at his back, and the pause allowed him to listen again to the litany of deep groans from the mountain of debris they had just climbed. He thought back to the start of their climb, remembering how The Other One had gestured upward saying, "Kua'la." It was just dawning on him that, as it continued to protest their intrusion, he sat now atop the place called 'Kua'la.' Had he not been so tired, the noise might have made sleeping difficult. But he was tired … and hungry.

Grabbing his pack, he rummaged for one of the energy rations, momentarily pushing aside another of his emergency items. It was becoming quite dark and, as he pulled out the ration, it occurred to him that he had just brushed aside something that might help in preparing the evening camp. When he again removed his hand, it held a personal hand-torch. Turning it over, he found the activator, a depression fitting nicely to his thumb. Without thinking, he pointed the device at the nearest of his two captors and pressed.

The bright beam caught The Other One standing with his head tilted up, coiling one of the ropes and staring at the dark forest wall. It startled him so completely he nearly fell over, dropping the rope and awkwardly regaining balance. Angus immediately extinguished the hand-torch and, momentarily blinded, muttered to himself, "Oh, Oh. That was probably a mistake ... and likely the last I'll see of that hand-torch."

As soon as both night vision and dignity returned, The Other One approached. Extending a hand, the man spoke. "Kosimba na koki ko?"

Angus had no trouble understanding what the man asked. Rising slowly, he put the hand-torch into The Other One's hand, watching him turn it over several times. At length, Angus held out a flat hand. The Other One hesitated but returned the device. Instead of taking it from him, Angus held the man's hand, turning the hand-torch into position for him to feel the activator. The device seemed small in the man's hand and his thumb completely engulfed the recess surrounding the activator. Pressing down upon The Other One's thumb, Angus exerted pressure until the torch beam suddenly threw a bright spot onto Angus's torso, eliciting a surprised exclamation from The Other One.

Armed with a marvelous new tool and the knowledge to use it, The Other One turned toward the dark forest and aimed a beam upward. For perhaps a full minute he waved that beam around the thick layer of foliage above their camp, then, after a little fumbling, extinguished it and continued staring at the area where he'd been playing the light. His purpose became clear when a feeble light shone from within the foliage and blinked several times. It seemed they had at least one more native compatriot nearby.

Expecting to have seen the last of it, Angus was both surprised and relieved when The Other One returned the hand-torch.

At that moment, Angus felt quite disposed toward The Other One, and easily acceded to the man's arm gestures, following him toward where Eilen and Grin sat. With similar gestures, the man asked them all to stand. Then, The Other One turned and looked directly at Angus. Saying slowly, "La'ann ... La'ann," he punctuated the words with two strikes of a fist to his chest. He then turned toward Grin and placed a hand on Grin's shoulder. "Ro'ann ... Ro'ann."

A few words, an obvious gesture, and a simple message, a message Angus had no trouble understanding, and a message that deserved a reply. Following the script given him, he stood to face the native who called himself La'ann and imitated the chest strike. "Angus ... Angus." He then turned toward Eilen and set his hand on her shoulder. "Eilen." Slow nods from both natives conveyed their understanding. With little else in common, the four trekkers fell into silence.

The one called La'ann lowered himself to the log surface, pulled both knees up close and wrapped his arms around them. "Sikoyo tōlala, Ahngoose." Barely had his arms secured their hold when his head fell to rest.

With only a glance toward Eilen, Angus followed the man's example, as he had done many times during the day, stretched out on the log and took in the dense field of stars before falling asleep.

CHAPTER 10
Arrival

A new day crept to life. The brightening sky loitered behind the forest wall while the western sky still entertained a host of stars. Deep shadow cloaked the marsh's far reaches. A layer of cloud hung above the night's bivouac glowing pink with the local sun's early efforts. Cool morning air and damp clothing invaded Angus's slumber. Sore muscles reluctantly yielded to slow stretching. Coaxing crusted eyes open, he saw the native called La'ann standing in dim light. Angus's cough rang harshly in the still air.

La'ann approached, carrying a sloshing leather bladder. Angus needed no encouragement. His parched throat awakened to the sound and he reached eagerly for the satchel, drinking in long gulps, expecting La'ann to pull it away at any moment. Surprised to drink his fill, he added the one native word he knew as he returned the bag. "Melesi."

The quiet setting, the cool air, the vista over the vast western marsh, or the mere fact that he was alive might have presented a tableau worth savoring. Instead, Angus's waking body chose the same moment to remind him of more mundane obligations. Fearful of offending, he wondered about local etiquette while glancing around in search of a private location. A soft noise drew his eyes left to see Ro'ann, back turned, standing beneath the curve of a cross-leaning log. At that moment, Eilen emerged from behind that same log. Neither she nor Ro'ann seemed concerned with the presence of the other.

Rising stiffly, Angus sought privacy behind the leaning log. His return met Ro'ann offering a sack of small bits. Perhaps hunger sharpened his senses, for the dried bits of food tasted as good as anything he could remember and he ate with the same relish he'd earlier given to the consumption of water. His eagerness elicited a wide grin from Ro'ann.

La'ann approached with a hand extended palm up. "Malili-móto nazali na koki ko?"

Angus heard the man's questioning tone, but could only manage a shaking head and shrugged shoulders, hoping the gestures might be understood as merely the ignorance they were.

Trying again, La'ann substituted arms and hands where words failed. Holding one hand upward, he waved the second hand just beyond the fingertips. Angus understood. Digging into his pack, he rose with hand-torch in hand. La'ann accepted with a slight bow, adding another tiny stitch to a growing fabric of trust between the two.

For the first time in what seemed a very long time, Angus found himself smiling, amused by the manner in which such a muscular man handled the hard, metallic device, turning it carefully as if it were a small fragile creature. Playing the torch beam onto an open palm, La'ann nodded at the wonder of it. Then, as playful as a child, he waved the beam into the thick foliage above.

That they intended to climb into that forest seemed clear. The local sun would soon rise above the forest wall and its glare would fall just as fiercely as it had the day before. The forest shadow had already begun a retreat from the marshland, its edge marching steadily nearer. The forest offered obvious protection. Yet, as Angus stared into deep forest shadows, their route upward seemed illusive. Between where he stood and the apparent protection lay naught but 30 or 40 meters of straight columns devoid of limb or branch.

As if in answer to his question a shout sent Angus's eyes searching, finally spotting a small missile flying from the high foliage, thin line in tow. The missile's appearance galvanized both natives into a well-coordinated team. Had he been counting Angus might have needed but one hand to mark the number of breaths that passed before Ro'ann had their combined equipment gathered into a single large bundle.

A second, bulkier package erupted from the thick leaves, falling heavily down toward the foot of the forest. La'ann gathered the thin line, drawing the heavier rope in from the shadows and across the rubble. While Ro'ann affixed the assembled gear to the heavy rope's end, La'ann sent a sharp jerk through the rope's long arc. No sooner had that message reached its mark than the far end receded into the foliage, pulling its opposite end through La'ann's hands. Every bit of equipment they'd lugged across the great marsh, weapons, food, clothing and water was soon swinging out toward the forest wall, restrained only by La'ann's loose grip as the light line passed through his hand.

In their simple efficiency, La'ann and Ro'ann won Eilen's admiration. "They do seem to know what they're doing, don't they?"

The comment elicited Angus's first full sentence of the day. "I was thinking that every bit of survival gear we have is now hanging at the end of that rope, including our hand weapons. Do you think we'll ever see them again?"

"That thought had not crossed my mind. I've been more concerned with the idea that in a matter of minutes it will be you or I dangling at the end of that rope."

Angus let his eyes fix onto the darkened roots of the forest. "Hanging over that black hole does seem a bit daunting."

Danger was not unknown to Angus. Years traveling

between stars had exposed him to hours floating in orbit above a planet surface, or in interstellar space, far from anything but the starship to which he was tied, separated from quick death by the mere thickness of an excursion suit. Those dangers seemed abstract and unreal. The prospect of dangling high above an uncertain black depth, trusting the integrity of a thin ribbon of unknown origin presented a much more tangible threat. And, with just about everything he owned rising into an unknown future, he felt naked.

The roped bundle dwindled to a dot before disappearing into the leafy shadows. Minutes passed before the bare rope fell a second time. Once collected, Ro'ann prepared another kind of package, tying off a couple of loop-holds near the rope's end. When ready, he slipped a hand into the one hold, a foot into the other and, with a nod to La'ann, swung out over the abyss wearing his characteristic wide grin. Minutes later, while La'ann gathered the rope a third time, Angus looked at Eilen wondering if she could see the trepidation he felt. She eagerly took the third turn. On the rope's next cycle, when no other choice remained, Angus put hand and foot somewhat uneasily into the loops and wrapped his other hand quite tightly around the rope section at his chest. The trip upward held no appeal. Declining every opportunity to gaze upon the beautiful, unfettered view of the marshland, or to look into the black abyss below, he focused his entire attention on his destination.

In a few long moments, Angus pushed his head through leafy branches to emerge between two large, furry bodies. A loud shout brought the rope to a halt and Eilen peeked from behind Ro'ann. "Angus! Slip your leg over that animal's neck."

Angus had once ridden a tamed beast, but he had come away from the experience with no comfort for the idea. He hesitated. Hanging from the overhead foliage by four large, furry arms, each longer than he by almost half, the beast sent an intimidating message of strength. A furry face swung itself around from the end of a very long neck to direct a bright yellow eye his way. Only Eilen's example and the equally unattractive alternative of remaining on the rope persuaded Angus to lift a leg and drop onto the furry neck. He sat still and wary.

Sometime later, La'ann's head appeared in their midst. Swinging himself in front of Angus in a single, smooth motion, he stretched forward and vigorously rubbed the animal's fur. "Mboté, Mœrai." The animal's response filled the air with a deep, resonant rumble, as much felt as heard.

The recovery of rope and line occupied the next few minutes. Ro'ann began pulling the heavier rope from its overhead hanger, gathering lengths into a coil about his shoulder. The bulk of that rope's length lay in a long, sagging arc extended far enough under the leafy ceiling to lose its far end in the shadowy forest interior. Ro'ann's coil had grown to many loops when a third rider emerged with the rope's end in tow to be greeted with great fanfare from La'ann and Ro'ann.

Following their newly inaugurated custom, La'ann immediately made introductions, saying as he pointed at the new rider, "Hol'imm." Then, shifting to point at Eilen, he said, "Ee'laan," eliciting a bout of head nodding from the man called Hol'imm. La'ann punctuated the last introduction with a reach backward to touch Angus's side, saying, "Ahngoose."

A few moments under the newcomer's intense stare made Angus squirm. Angus's discomfort seemed to strike a chord with the man, who bowed from the waist. "Mpasi nayoki." Pointing at Angus, La'ann offered an explanation in pantomime, passing an open hand around his own face. Another moment passed before Angus grasped the message. Hol'imm's bow came as apology for allowing the shock of Angus's white eyes and white skin to overcome decorum. Angus tipped his head to Hol'imm in acceptance of the man's gesture.

La'ann wasted no more time. Putting the group in motion,

he led them into the forest; one behind the other, riding inverted steeds along the underside of a living highway. The calm ride unfolded in soft filtered light, muffled sounds and rhythmic swinging motion, conspiring to pull Angus's head forward onto La'ann's back and usher him into much-needed slumber.

Sometime later he awoke, lying on his back, head groggy, stretched out between large furry swinging arms, staring straight upward at a tangle of thick vines. Pulling himself upright, he cleared his head, rubbed sleepy eyes and stretched sore muscles. A warm tone from La'ann welcomed his awakening. "Mai lalaki esika zonga o'zaki."

The world seemed to have brightened while Angus slept. *How long have I been asleep?* The forest floor had lost its former gloom. Where he had once seen mounds of molding detritus, scattered undergrowth, and deep shadows he now saw a bright clearing marked by regular, evenly spaced rows of vegetation. Cultivated fields! Movement caught his eye. Angus picked out many dark-skinned people moving among the rows.

Brilliant sunlight streamed through the ceiling above, bereft of the harsh edge of the open marsh. Angus tried but could not long stare upward, dazzled by the bright light. Sunlight seemed to originate equally from everywhere. In the absence of a distinct source, a shielding hand presented no relief. He turned back to look again at the surrounding scene noting how the formerly dense ceiling had thinned out completely, providing here only occasional clumps of shade. Somewhere between those fields and the forest top, where he had no doubt it continued to beat down a harsh wrath upon this world, the local sun's blue-white radiance had somehow softened.

Twisting completely around, Angus tried to find Eilen, seeing only Ro'ann's grin, until Eilen poked her face from behind the man's back, wearing a grin of her own. Excitement shone in her eyes. Why didn't that surprise him? She genuinely loved the great variety of the universe's creatures. He completely understood. She rode atop a creature new to her, one well adapted to life here in this alien forest. She loved it. It was her way.

Diverted by memories, it took Angus a moment to realize how the world around him had darkened. Ahead he saw only deepening shadow. Reflected light from the midfloor illuminated the near ceiling but faded to deeper shadow only a short distance ahead. Within a few swinging strides, before his eyes had adjusted to the low light, a weak illumination spread along the ceiling ahead, resolving itself into a regular array of glowing spots. Soon, the tail of an animal rose from the shadows surrounding each glowing spot. Animals like the one beneath him hung within suspended stalls, a stable. La'ann, Ro'ann and Hol'imm had certainly arrived at their home. The animal beneath Angus told him as much, snorting greetings to its fellows, returned in kind.

Did the entire place hang like these stables? An intriguing idea, but Angus doubted it. The stable area seemed much too dark and harbored nothing with the appearance of dwellings. He turned to see what Eilen might think of the place. Ro'ann's dark face was barely visible in the dim light. When a moment of staring failed to bring out Ro'ann's ever-present grin, Angus realized it wasn't Ro'ann at all. It was Hol'imm. Where had Ro'ann and Eilen gone? The question had no time to cause concern before La'ann turned into an empty stall.

The sight invoked memories. Angus had seen similar structures before. Somewhat smaller than his experience, the stall gave every impression of a common loading dock like many a planet-side trade station, where his cargo deliveries were loaded onto intercity transport. An opening just large enough to clear their mount's shoulders allowed their passage between two arms of a level, flat platform. Angus imagined La'ann or Ro'ann standing upon that platform tending the animal and its burdens.

A final swing of the big animal's arms brought the three of them deep into the stall, whereupon the animal announced her homecoming with a rumble that seemed to resonate with the walls. Her proclamation garnered attention. Before La'ann had dropped the reins, a man stepped into the limited glow of a single, teardrop-shaped vessel hanging from the ceiling. The man's clothing seemed similar to La'ann's, but simpler, without the many bits of adornment. Something in the man's eyes and bearing bespoke fewer years than La'ann. Although, why Angus thought so would be difficult to explain.

La'ann edged forward, waved an arm toward the platform. The gesture said all that was necessary. Angus pulled a leg from the far side and had just started to slip off the animal's neck when the attendant reached to help. As the young man caught a good look at Angus's face his eyes grew wide and he drew back staring, mouth open. Angus fell to the platform. A memory of Hol'imm's reaction flashed to mind. Thinking to allay fear, he spread arms low and backed slowly away from the startled attendant.

A pair of netted sacks fell onto the platform. La'ann spoke sharply. "Áwa! Yokamata!" Grabbing the bags, the attendant scampered toward the back of the stall.

Blood dripped from the sacks. The sight sent Angus's train of thought to La'ann's clothing. He now saw forest camouflage. The thought hit him abruptly. The fact of his continued existence owed itself to yet another random event, a hunting party's chance sighting of the Raiju core's emergency landing.

Glancing upward, Angus saw La'ann vigorously rubbing his hanging steed's neck. The two forest creatures conversed, La'ann in a language of words, the animal in low purring tones. The conversation ended when La'ann swung his far leg over, falling onto the platform as effortlessly as he seemed to do nearly everything. With a clear motion of his right arm,

La'ann bid Angus to follow. "Ahngoose! Yoya!"

A staircase set into the interior end of the stall led up to another, larger platform. There, Angus's eyes followed the length of a broad walk lined on both sides by stalls. The long arms of many animals hung from overhead. A long, flexible appendage extended from the snout of several animals. Angus watched those sinuous limbs disappear into hanging troughs, returning laden with water or vegetable matter. Turning to examine La'ann's mount, Angus saw the animal unfurl a tight coil and reach into the trough above.

Perhaps fascination showed in Angus's face, for La'ann chose that moment to identify the collection of animals with a sweep of arm and a single word. "Kùmu'lio."

The notion of domesticated animals reminded Angus of Eilen and her rural roots. Facing La'ann, he asked after her. "Eilen?"

Twisting half around, La'ann pointed over his shoulder toward one end of the stables. "Áwa."

Angus searched the dim light for a glimmer of La'ann's intent, finding a group standing at the stable's far end. Ro'ann's grin and Eilen's slim form stood together. The third member had to be Hol'imm. A surprising wave of relief washed through him. A few moments later, Angus stood before the only person who could possibly understand, the only being like himself on this entire world. She looked puzzled. "Angus. What's wrong? You're looking at me strangely."

"Nothing ... Nothing at all."

A grinning Ro'ann interrupted, directing a stream of native words at La'ann. The greeting came complete with a friendly slap to La'ann's arm. For the first time since their encounter yesterday, Angus saw La'ann smile, answering Ro'ann with a reciprocal slap and another unintelligible barrage of language. The friendly tone and the casual smiles reassured Angus. Shared ordeals had already built a tie between him and both natives. Their easy behavior helped deepen the bond.

The reassembled band followed La'ann through a nearby door and onto a small platform jutting into darkness. On his right, Angus saw a dimly lit stairway curving downward around the inner wall of a large, hollow shaft, its true extent fading into a black depth. The sound of his breathing reverberated off the curved wall. A smell of dank air and a faint echo of what might have been lapping water rose from below.

To his left spiraling steps continued upward toward another small platform, its underside cast in shadow from light spilling through a second doorway, perhaps five meters above and a quarter of the way around the shaft wall. The shaft's diameter was difficult to estimate but large enough to obscure detail at the opposite wall. Responding to Ro'ann's nudge Angus started cautiously upward, pressing his left hand to the wall.

The brightness at the upper doorway forced Angus to put a hand to his face as he walked outside. Seeing nothing but his feet, he recoiled sharply at the sudden noise, calmed only by La'ann's steady hand on his shoulder. When able to lift the hand from his eyes he was met with a wall of dark, staring faces crowding close on all sides. News of their arrival had spread.

La'ann stopped and stared at his small group. A moment later, arriving at either a solution or a decision, he uttered a stream of words at Hol'imm then abruptly walked away with Ro'ann on his heels.

Angus and Eilen moved closer to Hol'imm. Arms held high, Hol'imm spoke. In a spreading wave, the murmuring crowd fell quiet. Hol'imm waved his arms and the mass of bodies parted, opening a space between two walls of very curious and very tall, dark-skinned people. Like a bubble rising through viscous liquid, Hol'imm led Angus and Eilen through the crowd to a thicket-lined path where they left the sea of bodies behind. The path's other end opened into a secluded area. The murmur of gathered villagers could still be heard, dampened by distance and vegetation.

Hol'imm had taken them into a private area encircling the massive trunk of a single forest pillar. A long, deep, covered bench curved around much of the area's outer boundary, its expanse broken only by the rude interruption of a second entrance path. Living vegetation, woven into the contour of a roof, protected the bench's entire length, sloping toward the rear to form an interior space rising less than a man's height along the back wall. Inside, not a corner was visible; not alcove nor nook, nor interior wall, nor door. Spaces were defined by neat assemblies of belongings, clothing, weapons, tools and bedding, arranged regularly along the far wall and delineating the domains of individual occupants. Guarding two such near domains were two recognizable bundles, the total of Angus's and Eilen's possessions.

The sleeping bench stood awkwardly high for a casual step, but it gave Hol'imm a convenient seat. They all sat, enjoying the gentle, warm rain that had just begun, listening to the pleasant rhythmic patter on the flat wooden deck outside the covered shelter.

The quiet pause gave Angus a chance to take stock. His lightweight ship's uniform clung to sweat-soaked skin. He did not want to think about how he must smell after several days in the same clothing.

As if in concert with Angus's thoughts, Hol'imm rose and stripped off his light tunic to stand in the warm rain, raising his head to let it fall upon his face. The afternoon rain chose that moment to conclude its performance. Hol'imm looked up then waved for the two off-world beings to join him as he walked away. "Gyda ngai uta yo sengeli."

Angus stared for only a moment.

By the time Angus reached his feet, Hol'imm was already

moving toward the pillar tree. Eilen hustled to join him. Small rivulets of rainwater flowed across the smooth deck toward the pillar tree like so many spokes in a wheel. Walking around to the far side of the tree, Hol'imm stood before a conical container mounted above head-height.

Three light cords hung down, one from near the truncated cone's narrow bottom and two others from opposite sides behind it. Hol'imm grabbed one side cord in each hand and began to pull them alternately in opposition. The sound of sloshing water emanated from the tank above. A few moments of pumping brought forth an arc of white teeth on Hol'imm's face, which he continued to wear as he pulled the third cord to allow the shower of water to wash over him. He presented the cord to Eilen.

Possessing neither soap nor privacy, Eilen chose to remain clothed and merely let the clean water rinse salt and grime from her thin uniform. Angus removed his tunic and enjoyed the shower.

Upon return to quarters, they found added to their neatly arranged belongings a sleeveless tunic and a pair of short pants, loosely constructed and loosely fitted, more knotted than woven, covered with an array of small tassels.

Eilen looked at Angus, shipboard decorum still fresh in mind. He turned away. "Here, let me give you some room."

With the addition of a pair of calf-strapped sandals, the newcomers looked a bit more like their host. They were comparing notes when the runner arrived.

Their return to the common area felt quite different from the earlier crowd-filled experience. Empty now, it spread between dense hedge walls and the living pillars. Hol'imm walked steadily past the near tree and across the space, his footsteps making a soft slap against the flat wooden deck. Across the open area, Angus saw La'ann and Ro'ann waiting. He would later remember the short walk as his first fleeting glimpse of the quiet character of his new home.

From where he stood, his native friends appeared to stand near the lone open portion of the area perimeter, where no briar hedge rimmed the deck.

La'ann's hail cut short Angus's musings. "Ahngoose! Yoya osengeli!"

Native faces remained largely indecipherable, but the set of his friend's jaw, the sharp tone of voice, and stern posture told Angus all he needed to know. He hastened forward.

La'ann waited only long enough for Angus to reach the group then abruptly turned and stepped down off of the common deck. A nudge from Eilen in Angus's back put him in motion behind La'ann. Angus's first step into the amphitheater brought a hush to the assembled crowd. As he crossed the common area a moment before Angus had not been aware of the crowd's muffled voice, absently dismissing the background murmur as a natural sound of the forest and giving it no thought. With every voice suddenly mute the silence rang loud, adding exclamation to his awareness that all eyes now stared at his alien white face.

Imitating La'ann's manner, he stepped solemnly down the stairway, eyes fixed forward, unwilling to confront the host of probing faces filling the arced tiers to his left. Ahead and below, he saw two figures waiting at the lowest level, a flat circular section fanning from the pillar tree's trunk occupying the arena's focus. In stark contrast to the jumble of browns and greens pervading the entire crowd, the brightly colored headdress atop one man's head announced his importance. Yet it was the second figure that held Angus's attention. Standing next to 'Headdress,' a smaller person watched the descending group with steadfast intensity. The stout staff in her right hand stood taller than she. Why he perceived her as female he'd never know, but something in her bearing spoke of authority. A mat of short grey hair conveyed age and wisdom. Penetrating dark eyes, made intense by glowing light brown halos, seemed riveted on him alone. She watched his every move.

The ceremonial character of all he saw put Angus on alert. The occasion was ripe with possibilities, both favorable and perilous. He became conscious of his every action. A misstep might destroy every bond he and Eilen had thus far forged. With thoughts of many possible futures swirling through his head, Angus returned the old woman's gaze with the barest of nods. Her unwavering gaze filled him with unease.

Approaching Headdress, La'ann stopped. Headdress nodded and turned toward the standing crowd. Scepter in hand he raised his right arm. "Yokisa koki ko." Almost as one, the entire audience lowered itself onto the surface on which it stood. Imitating La'ann, Angus and Eilen sat on a bench carved into the bulging side of the living pillar behind. Only Headdress remained standing, waiting for the assembly to quiet. "Oyoka osengeli. Ka'ao ha'i, La'ann zala na." Angus heard only the name, 'La'ann.'

Headdress turned and sat, the metallic adornment about his neck jingling loudly. La'ann rose and stepped forward.

Beginning slowly, La'ann soon found a comfortable rhythm. Neither Eilen nor Angus understood even a word but La'ann's story was not difficult to follow. Sparing no theatrics, he related in grand gestures and recognizable postures the trek across the marsh plain. When La'ann demonstrated how he and Ro'ann finally brought down the second stalker, the entire gathering grimaced, filling the arena tiers with a unified hiss and arcs of bared white teeth. Stumbling across the platform, La'ann gave a fairly accurate portrayal of the alien visitors' inept trek. The crowd reacted with sympathetic groans.

Then La'ann turned to look directly at Angus. Angus knew a seminal moment had arrived. *The one thing I can do is show respect.* La'ann's gesture brought Angus to his feet and he found his cue with La'ann's hand on his shoulder and the words, "Ahngoose, nkómbó na," spoken to the crowd. Bowing deeply at the waist, Angus let his eyes fall toward the floor before straightening again to look into the crowd. The seated throng received him with two words. "Likamboté, Ahngoose." The response seemed to please La'ann. When the crowd responded similarly to Eilen's introduction, Angus relaxed. "Likamboté, Eelaan."

SANCTUARY

CHAPTER 11
The Midfloor

Jarred from sleep, Angus lay still. Moments passed as he mentally prepared himself for another day. When he finally propped himself onto both elbows, his gaze fell onto a pair of children running across the 'ann family area he now knew as the 'annliboko. Before being thrown among these people, Angus had not seen a child in years. The children's giggles rang like bells. In times past, their untethered glee might have brought a smile to his face. Now he merely stared.

Beyond the children, a group of women sat cross-legged in a circle, talking as they fashioned bowls and trays from the long flexible strips piled in their midst. Beyond them, perhaps 15 paces away he saw the huge pillar that was a living colōfn tree, one of many holding the entire village perched high within the surrounding forest world. He once travelled freely among the stars. Now his entire life was confined to this arboreal village.

Looking down the long sleeping bench, he saw no one. He alone seemed to have no reason to rise each morning. The thought swam through his consciousness. Past days as captain of an interstellar ship were filled with decisions, replete with activity. Now he wished for something to occupy his time. Learning the art of kùmu'lio care had improved Eilen's entire mood as well as her language skills. He should find something for himself.

At the moment, however, growing discomfort told him that mastering a useful skill would have to wait. He threw off the light cover, a blanket of loosely woven thick thread, into which small pieces of soft felt had been laced. Pushing himself into a vertical posture came with more than a few groans. He indulged in one good stretch before slipping arms into the lightweight vest that now comprised most of his wardrobe. Quickly pulling on a pair of baggy shorts, he stepped down off the sleeping platform, intent on making his way to what onboard the Raiju had been called the 'head.' Here it was known as the 'luba.'

Angus stepped onto the deck outside the sleeping bench, feeling its smooth, firm surface beneath his bare feet. Until recently he had never given the slightest thought to the floors he walked upon. The decks of the Raiju were designed with sophisticated alloys and structures, rendering them strong, stiff and lightweight; hardly a surprising achievement for a culture distributed across seven star-systems. The surface he now trod would have escaped his notice on any planet within Haven. Here, in what seemed a primitive forest culture, the deck's continuous, smooth, flat extent piqued his curiosity.

Leaving the privacy of the 'annliboko, he walked through the narrow connecting path, letting his hand pass along a head-high barrier of twisted briar on either side, feeling the thickly entwined foliage brush his palm, listening to the sibilant crackling of its leaves. Bringing his palm close to his nose, he inhaled the sharp odor; so different from the antiseptic passageways of the starships in which he had spent most of his adult life.

Angus emerged into the village commons. Industrious activity filled the area. The air smelled of wood smoke. Three small fires burned beneath round metal pots hanging from tripod supports. One hanging pot exuded fluid from an extended arm, filling a smaller pot upon the deck. A villager tended open pots hanging above unlit fire pits, while another pulled fiber from one pot and directed it onto a spindle.

One of the pot-tenders caught Angus's attention as he skirted the activity. "Mboté, Ahngoose." Not recognizing the speaker, Angus only nodded and returned the polite greeting. "Mboté." These people kept trying to pull him in, but for reasons he could not name, he felt unresponsive. Within the space of Raiju's bridge, it had not been so. There, he wrapped himself in competence, control, and composure. Here he walked exposed and useless.

Native attitudes remained reserved, always a nod or two; no disrespect, no impolite stares, but gazes lingered. Eilen consistently encountered smiles and waves, which Angus often wrote off to her darker skin color. Eilen was not quite as dark as they, but she stood out nothing like he did. The native reserve invoked memories of his orphaned adolescence and the coolness of his peers, dragging at his pride and dredging up feelings of doubt. If he were honest, he might admit to himself that his remote behavior fed the villagers' reserve.

How long had he been among them? The events of the last many days seem to have all blended into a single blurred tableau, devoid of distinguishing features. The first few days had been one long rest. Physically exhausted and mentally drained, both he and Eilen had slept almost entirely through their second day here in the village. Angus could recall arising very late in the day, awakening only to an urgency similar to that he now felt.

Which put him in mind of immediate needs and forced him to quicken the pace. He pushed past the place he called 'The Arena', which he had yet to understand, and then past the place he called 'The Theater', leading him to an isolated colōfn tree, situated on one far end of the village. Hastening his way through the open doorway in the tree's side, he stepped within and walked down one of the village's several sequestered spiral stairways. He fairly scurried through the dimly lit corridor below until he found one of several stalls where he knew he was welcome to relieve the growing pain in his abdomen. A few moments later, feeling much less anxious, he reached up to grab the rightmost of the two cords hanging above the commode. With several long, slow pulls he pumped water into the tank fixed above. A pull on the second line completed his morning's duty with a rush of released water. The apparatus no longer drew Angus's attention as it once had. It had now become one of many small technological oddities he catalogued amid what otherwise seemed a simple forest society.

Rubbing his chin, Angus stared at the retreating water. The discomfort of a growing beard reminded him of how completely his life had changed. Never before had he sported facial hair, but now, as he scratched at his nascent beard, he was becoming aware of just how much patience was required to grow one. He wished he had a razor... and a mirror, wondering what his hair must look like. What kind of society lived with pumped water and flushing toilets, but no mirrors?

Angus ran his tongue over the surface of his front teeth, feeling the film that seemed to have become a permanent part of his anatomy. His mouth felt irritatingly dirty. It dawned on him that someone, somewhere had long ago decided not to include a mouthwash solution in the emergency kit he'd managed to salvage. Not a sufficiently high priority. At the same time, he wondered, how long would it be before his teeth began to rot? *Not looking forward to that day.*

Emerging onto the commons deck, Angus stood with his back to the tree, staring at the village common and finding no particular direction to guide the day ahead. To his left was 'The Theater.' The villagers called it 'batomingi esika,' which Angus had learned meant 'many people place.' More often it was simply called the 'Mingi.'

Walking to stand above the Mingi, he looked down into its

descending ranks of wide, semi-circular benches, all inviting him to take a seat. He lowered himself onto the deck and let his feet dangle over the back of the Mingi's topmost bench. The central level, some distance below, looking smaller now than it had on the day he arrived. At that time the whole place had seemed a bit larger. Everything had been strange and fascinating and the Mingi had been filled with many curious, murmuring faces, all staring at him as he stood looking up from that low central level.

A few moments later Angus pushed himself upright, thinking he should do something useful... but what? Perhaps he should eat before deciding anything drastic. He made his way back to the 'annliboko.' The kids still chased each other, filling the area with joyful giggles.

Nearing his bunk, he saw a tray of food resting at the foot of his sleeping pad. The unattended tray was another small reminder of his drift away from the group. Everyone else, including Eilen, ate earlier and ate together; talking, joking and exchanging stories. He seemed to have fallen into an unsynchronized routine, gotten out of step, eating meals alone wrapped in his own thoughts. Solitary meals had been a part of starship command duty, but those former habits had also been forged in complete synchronization with ship's routine. Here it was different. Here an insidious ennui separated him from village life and fed upon itself.

Still pondering, Angus sat down on the edge of his sleeping space, next to the small tray of natural foods he had grown to enjoy as much as anything on his new world. Sweet-tasting fruits were a staple here. Fruit-bearing plants grew all around. He picked up a purplish-colored cut morsel, glistening with the juices he knew would flood his mouth as soon as he bit into it. It didn't disappoint.

His eyes wandered the 'annliboko. Rimmed by circular walls of either sheltered living space or impenetrable, tangled briar, it had only four narrow openings. One led to the common area, others to nearby family units. The colōfn trunk at its center dominated and defined the entire space, guiding the shape and position of everything else. From where Angus sat, if he trained his sight high along the straight vertical side of the tree looming over him, he could see a sliver of the side of what he knew was the tree standing in the center of the neighboring family unit, and yet another rising beyond that. The trees seemed to grow in a remarkably straight alignment. If he turned his gaze a bit to the left, along the other side of the same tree, he could see whole trunks regularly spaced along another direction, as though they had been planted by some great, uncommon cultivator. With his mind's eye he looked down from high above and saw the regularity of the trees with the village carved out among them; five family areas around the village rim, the luba on one end of an open common area, the Mingi, 'the Arena,' and the far-side egress route at the opposite end.

His lethargy certainly did not spring from his surroundings. Beauty came at him from every direction. Colorful blossoms graced the sides of magnificent colōfn trees. Blossoms in every size, shape, and hue he could imagine adorned trees as well as briar walls. Their spicy-sweet scents wafted through the entire village on every slight breeze, especially upon the daily flushing air currents that marked the pattern of Nahélé's life. Looking up as far along the colōfn tree as he could see, directly into the bright haze obscuring the topmost parts of the forest, he could see more blossoms hanging from the thick branches growing sparsely from tree trunks all around him. Some seemed to grow in midair.

Against the bright background, it was difficult to quite make out the structure of it, but Angus knew some sort of net hung above the entire village. What he could see was thicker supporting lines stretching between the colōfn trees, some distance below the first branches of foliage; the net itself wasn't visible, but he knew it must be there, anchoring flowering plants that seemed to grow suspended in the air above the village, fed by nothing but the afternoon rains.

An absent-minded bite of fruit sent streams of sticky liquid down the side of Angus's face, dropping through his open tunic and onto bare chest. Without thinking, he looked around for a cloth to wipe his face, an instinct born of former circumstances. In place of such former amenities he noted the small bowl fixed to the side of the central colōfn tree. A few steps to reach it and a few tugs on the plunger rising through the deck beside it, filled that bowl with water—one more incongruous bit of crude technology residing alongside the village's primitive beauty. As he removed the bowl from its resting place and stooped to empty the dirtied water slowly into a catch pocket fixed lower on the tree, he had to wonder again at the strange inconsistency of it all.

Angus walked back to his bunk-space, stepping up and into the rear, where laid everything he owned. The makeshift marsh boots he kept as a trophy to his adventure on the marsh plain were propped up against the wall. Everything he had taken from the landing craft was stuffed into the pack he could wear on his back. He now wore everything else he called his own; save only the hard-soled sandals he had been given that first day here. Their calf-length leather straps dangled from the metal frame of his marsh boots.

What was he now? Only a short while ago he called himself 'Captain' and roamed the stars. Those days were certainly gone. So ... what now? Not a captive, but what? Day after day, curiosity and excitement filled his former life. Now he had nothing to expect of the remainder of the day, nor of tomorrow for that matter. He longed to once again experience a drop into some unknown star system. *What am I doing to myself?*

Resolution began to take root. Might today begin his rehabilitation? He had already seen places on this world well worth exploring, just as he had once explored the cosmos. His first trip through the forest upon arrival now remained only as the foggiest of memories and he now had no idea of what lay beyond the dense hedges surrounding the village. It was time to see what may lie without. *And I know just where to begin.*

Angus knew how some of the village colōfn trees carried spiral staircases within their hollow interiors, like the ones that led to the kùmu'lio stalls or to the 'luba.' He also had seen many people come and go daily through another passage at the far end of the village common, opposite the 'luba.' *Let's see where those people go each day.*

Reaching into his pack, he found the hand-torch. Not knowing just where he was going, he had no way to judge what he might need. He didn't intend to be gone long and, since he'd seen people carrying only work tools in that direction, he felt certain that he wouldn't need his hand weapon. Shoes, however, seemed like a good idea.

Mind made up, Angus took a few moments to wrap sandal straps around his calves, and to dig into his pack for a cord he knew was there. In his former life, an item as common as the hand-torch would never have given him reason for a second thought. Remembering the reverence with which La'ann treated the simple instrument atop the Kua'la, he realized its new value. With no pockets it seemed rash not to protect it in some way. In his mind, he could see himself falter on those unnerving open steps within the colōfn tree, watching the torch beam fall from his grasp and disappear into blackness. Precautions might be prudent.

Ready now, with both shoes on tight and torch strapped to his wrist, Angus set off on the first independent action he had taken since his arrival. A little excited, he left the family area by way of the exit path on his immediate right, heading toward one far end of the village, where the path ended directly in front of an opening into the side of an isolated colōfn tree, completely enclosed by dense briar wall.

Arriving at that doorway, excitement ebbing, he stepped carefully through and onto a wide ledge inside the doorway. He looked down at the descending stairway wrapped around the inside of the hollow tree. A dim light shone through another door some distance below, barely illuminating a similar ledge at the opposite side of the dark well and the other end of the stairway. The poorly lit stairway spiraled more than twice around the side on its way down to that lower doorway, Gripping the hand-torch tightly, Angus drew comfort from the feel of it. With one hand on the tree's inner side, he stepped slowly down the well, playing the beam of the hand-torch on each near step. The firm, steady feel of each step fostered confidence and eventually brought him to the lower ledge without need of reassurance from the tree's inner wall. Through the lower opening, he saw a well-trod path outside, lined by low, loosely growing foliage. Extinguishing the hand-torch, he stepped into an area illuminated just well enough to see, engulfed as it was in the shadow of the village above. The ceiling opened up a short distance away and Angus's excitement grew as he marched down the path toward brighter light. Emerging from the shadows, the scattered heads and shoulders of a few people showed above an even field of nearly chest-high vegetation.

Farther down the path he was able to see down rows of tall, leafy plants, stretching away at an angle along both sides. Villagers moved between rows, stooping now and then to tend the plants. He watched field-tenders tossing pulled-up vegetation into elongated baskets propped upon a single plank with an upturned end. A short distance yet farther along the footpath, Angus saw similar activity being conducted nearer the path. He hurried along to get a better look.

Approaching the villager, he wanted to call out a name, but he could not recognize the face. Fearful of embarrassment, he was determined this time to press on. "Mboté," he said.

The field-tender looked up from his work, taking a

moment to recognize the interruption. "Mboté, Ahngoose. Malamu ozali?"

Aware that his light-skinned face could not go unrecognized, Angus heard a phrase he knew. The understanding gave Angus confidence. He returned the greeting. "Malamu nazali ... Ōzali?"

His efforts were rewarded with a wide grin and a nod of encouragement, "Malamu. Mélesi, Ahngoose."

Emboldened, Angus tried a bit more, asking, as he grabbed the end of a thick, fuzzy leaf, "Nini nkómbó?"

The grin widened considerably as its wearer readily supplied an answer. "Lipapú nkásá, Ahngoose. Nkómó oyo 'lipapú nkásá' bisó na."

With his small vocabulary exhausted, Angus ran out of conversation. as long a native discourse as he had yet conducted. Pleased with his efforts and with the new knowledge of this large-leafed plant, called 'Lipapú nkásá,' he nodded as politely as he knew how and turned toward the colōfn tree ahead. Additional walkway became evident as he drew close. A path encircled the girth of the tree, leading to other paths heading in two new directions.

Anointing the leftmost as most promising, he set off again. He would not have thought farm crops were something to foster emotion, but the sight of a different crop sparked his interest. Passing a few rows, he saw how the crop grew above his head, a kind of vine winding itself on hoops spanning rows to grow densely above an aisle three or four feet wide. Angus looked down each aisle in turn, searching for another field hand. After crossing the ends of too many rows to count, he found the path ahead again wrapped around both sides of another colōfn tree. Looking back along the path he had just walked he marked the colōfn tree behind and formed a picture of his return path. *One left turn,* he thought. *If I can keep track of the turns, the regular pattern of trees will give me a reference grid.*

On his left, a row of 'lipapú nkásá' plants ran parallel to the path. On his right stretched the many ends of hooped-vine rows he had just passed. He turned toward the tree ahead. On the other side, he recalibrated his mental map. *One left-turn and one straight-through, so far.* Ahead, the thick row of 'lipapú nkásá' continued its extent along the left side of the path, while the right-hand side now sported a third kind of crop, growing low to the ground. In brighter sunlight, Angus shaded his eyes. Across the field he spotted three people far off in the middle tending the crop with long-handled hand tools, faces hidden under brimmed headgear.

The low-planted rows offered little impedance, inviting him to venture beyond the confinement of the path. Thinking to make his way out toward the working group, Angus stepped off the path, picking footsteps warily. His open sandals offered scant protection and the soft ground seemed to give under his weight. He had meandered several rows before being stopped by a loud shout.

"Té, té, Ahngoose! ... Té!"

He looked up to see his hailer wildly waving both arms. Unsure of what transgression he may have committed, Angus turned to retreat and immediately discovered that traipsing into the field may have been a mistake. His planted foot fell into the ground, pulling him off balance and dropping him on his back, right leg buried to the knee. He lay staring up at the open midfloor ceiling looking into many thin fans of foliage receding into a bright glowing haze, thankful that the spongy ground had saved him from a good bump on the head.

Trying to right himself, Angus pushed back against the ground only to find it yielding enough to make rising more difficult than he might have guessed. He managed to get himself into a sitting position by relying on abdominal muscles alone. Then he tried to pull his leg out. He had extracted it no more than the width of a finger when the effort produced a sharp pain in his calf. Trying a second time, the pain came sharper. He tried rolling to one side to push himself up only to have his hand sink to the wrist. *OK, what now?*

Angus was about to call for aid when he saw clansmen making their way toward him. As they negotiated the last few rows, raising their feet carefully over each planted row, Angus saw the planks strapped to each foot and realized how they were able to walk while he sat immobilized in the soft ground. The first to reach him spoke with obvious concern, "Ahngoose! Malamu ozali?"

Thankful for the few native words he knew, Angus heard the meaning clearly. "Angus. Well, you are?" With a meager vocabulary, Angus hoped his answer would be understood. "No. Well I am not. Thank you, friend," he said in the native Batololému language. Unable to speak much more, he grabbed his leg and pantomimed pulling it out, indicating his predicament.

All three of his rescuers replied at once, "Té! ... Té!," holding their hands out to stop him from any more pulling. One continued speaking as he bent down to test Angus's leg. Angus understood only the first few words. "Well again soon you are, Ahngoose. Mpasi wænalawrpésa. Salisa bisotika."

The test-pull forced Angus to acknowledge difficulty with an "Ouch!" and forced his rescuers into another tactic. Angus sat passively and watched as they slipped long-handled, hooked field tools into the terrain beside his leg and pried at the tangle. It seemed to work. The hold on his leg had loosened when Angus felt something crawl across his ankle and up the back of his calf. "Hurry guys. I think I have company down there."

Lacking Batololému words to convey his concern, Angus tried to keep calm. While his friends worked on the tangled substance of the midfloor, he felt more and more tiny feet scurry around his leg. Then something bit. "YOW!"

The first bite came with more surprise than pain. Then bites came rapidly and Angus could not keep the pain from his voice. "Come on guys! This isn't a joke! I need that leg free, NOW!"

Pulling the terrain back with increased vigor, his rescuers finally enabled Angus to draw his leg from the thick, dense tangle of plant growth that formed the ground. As his calf emerged a plethora of toe-sized black creatures scampered back into the ground. Red scratches and bites covered the lower half of Angus's leg. A few trickles of blood running down the calf gave the only signs of anything amiss. Relieved, Angus reached to take a hand, rising gingerly to stand on the free plank dropped at his feet. "Thank you, friend," he said in Batololému, bowing for emphasis.

"Welcome you are, Ahngoose," said one of his rescuers.

Angus looked at each in turn, afraid he'd not be able to remember them when he saw them again. They knew him but he did not know them. He decided to rectify that situation. Striking his chest, he said, "Called Angus, I am."

The one still holding Angus up by one arm said, "Bisóyéba, Ahngoose." Then, with a glimmer of understanding, he followed Angus's lead. "Ri'nii," he said, dropping Angus's arm and striking his chest. Then, pointing to each, in turn, identified his two companions. "Li'nii pe Lo'nii."

The common 'nii' suffix told Angus they were siblings, but he couldn't quite say if they were all brothers. Li'nii's slighter build and more delicate features might indicate a sister. With her tunic fastened, it was difficult to be sure. Feeling a little embarrassed, Angus moved toward the firm path. "Farewell, friends." *Perhaps that's enough exploration for today.*

Ri'nii pulled on Angus's arm and pointed to the plank beneath him. "Zela, Ahngoose. Mibali osengeli." Then, taking one from his own foot, he reached to tie a second plank under Angus's feet. Standing on a single plank, Ri'nii motioned Angus to go ahead. Lo'nii and Angus, shuffled toward the path alongside each other, separated by a single planted row.

Stepping out of his borrowed field-shoes and onto the firm

path, Angus sighed with relief. *That's better.*

Lo'nii pointed toward the village. "Ahngoose. Su'ban na kipa o sengeli." Angus understood only the name 'Su'ban' and the oft-used word meaning 'must.' Shaking her pointed finger for emphasis Lo'nii spoke louder. "Sikoyo! Okei! Su'ban na kipa o sengeli!"

Angus turned and limped toward the village. *I really must learn the language.* Following his mental map, he moved along the solid path past the hooped-vine field, past the large-leafed 'Lipapú nkásá' crop and under the village's shady footprint.

Where's my hand-torch? Raising his arm, he knew immediately that something was not right. No weight. The strap dangled loose. *I should go back and find it.*

He turned. A sharp pain shot up his leg. Looking down, he drew breath through clenched teeth. In place of the leg with which he had awakened that morning stood a grotesque, swollen and inhuman appendage. His lower leg had grown as large as his thigh, flesh bulging purple through crossed sandal straps.

The hand-torch no longer seemed important. He stooped to retie sandal straps, inhaling with a wave of pain. Getting back to the village might have become a problem. By the time he reached the spiral stairway each step had become a test of will. Sweating profusely, Angus hissed each breath and pushed himself through the passageway. The dark stairway seemed hostile, the village level far away. The loss of his hand-torch seemed a great shame.

Right hand against the wall, holding his swollen leg high, Angus hopped up the first step, breaths coming shallow and quick. Ten steps later, sweat rolling down his face, unease turned to doubt. Will I ever see the top of the stairs? *One step at a time. Perhaps if I sat and negotiated each step backward.*

By the time he reached the upper doorway, each step had become a battle, requiring minutes to conquer. Sliding on his buttocks, he pulled himself through the doorway and propped himself against the tree. He bent to unwrap the straps. The throbbing leg protested every movement. Thoughts became muddled. He tried to focus. A dark cloud settled over his consciousness. He saw nothing more.

CHAPTER 12
Recovery

The image eluded capture. Eilen called. An old woman hovered. Awakening to bright light, Angus struggled to sit up, groggy, head pounding, trying to remember getting into bed the night before. The last thing he remembered was the many steps inside the colōfn tree.

Someone called. "Ahngoose! Yo batelemi!"

The 'ann family area came slowly into focus. Concentrating, Angus began to recognize a nearby face. He tried to speak. The face stood and ran off. She returned to speak with La'ann's voice. "Likamboté, Ahngoose! Batelemi ona. Mingi ntango lála ozali. Malamu oyoki?"

Understanding little but tone, Angus replied with one of the few native words he knew. "Mboté, La'ann. It's good to see you." Lightheaded, he settled back. "Whoa! ... My head spins."

La'ann knelt, placing a gentle hand on Angus's chest. "Olalisa, Ahngoose. Makasi té ozali."

An older person approached the sleeping bench, holding a cup with both hands as she negotiated the step. Reaching Angus's side, she lowered herself to one knee. Angus took the cup in both hands and sipped, letting the thin, warm, salty broth wash over his tongue. Hunger outran etiquette and he drank it down in gulps, handing back an empty cup.

The woman rose smiling. "Kitóko azali, Ahngoose. Ozonga na." She nearly bumped into Eilen as she stepped off the sleeping bench. "Ee'laan! Yo'uta. Malamu Ahngoose akoma."

Holding her gaze on Angus, Eilen nodded. "I can see that ... Mélesi, Tu'ann."

Hands on hips, Eilen stood at the foot of the sleeping bench, feigning annoyance. "So ... I just found out that you decided to rejoin the living?"

"Have I been away?"

"Yeah, you have! Four days now."

"Four days! Really?"

"You don't remember? You were delirious when they found you. If it weren't for Su'ban, I think you might have died."

"Died? ... of what? ... And who is Su'ban?"

The mock manner disappeared as Eilen stepped onto the sleeping bench to kneel where Tu'ann had been. "You really don't remember anything? Look at your leg." The lightweight blanket came away and a disturbing sight emerged. Wrapped from foot to hip with fibrous grey mat, cross-strapped by coarse twisted cord, the leg would neither lift, nor bend. "You'll have to wait for Su'ban to take all that off. She has charge of your leg at the moment."

"Who's Su'ban? And what's wrong with my leg?"

"You've seen her. She's the local 'medic'... and, as far as your leg is concerned, I can't really tell you. I wasn't there ... By the time I came back, your leg was wrapped and under cover and you were completely out-of-it ... Are you sure you can't remember anything?"

Angus searched his memory. "I can remember deciding to explore. I dug out my hand-torch and I walked down... wait... There was something about that torch?" Finding a mental thread, Angus began to piece things together. "Oh ... I lost it. After falling into a hole in the midfloor... then I was bitten by little black... creatures... Everything gets a little fuzzier after that."

"I don't doubt it. You were definitely in another world."

"Four days, you say?"

"Yes, four very anxious days for me. How are you feeling now?"

"A little weak I guess, and thirsty. Any water about?"

"Hang on. I'll get some."

Stepping down onto the village deck, Eilen walked toward the central colōfn tree, returning a few moments later with a shallow washbowl in hand. Water sloshed out as she stepped back onto the sleeping bench. Sitting up again, Angus gulped down what water remained, wiping drops from his chin with a forearm.

Eilen took the empty bowl. "Better?"

"Yes. Better. I should probably get out of bed. Help me up."

When Angus reached for Eilen's hand La'ann's restraining hand intervened. "Té, Ahngoose. Té. Su'ban zela na osengeli."

"La'ann's right. You should probably stay where you are until Su'ban can help you out of that poultice. Still hungry?"

Not ready to give in, Angus pressed. "Yes. I should get up and eat something."

"I don't think you have that choice. Not with your leg all trussed up like a newborn."

The thought of food sent Angus's tongue around the inside of his mouth. Something felt different. "Did someone scrub my teeth?"

"Probably. I heard Su'ban complain about your breath." Reaching into a waist sac, Eilen brought out a handful of short twigs. "Tu'ann gave me these. I'll bet one of your many nurses used some on you while you were out."

At the sight of something he understood La'ann brandished his teeth and waved a hand in front of his mouth. "Kosukola lino."

Eilen smiled. "Just as La'aan says, they clean your teeth. They don't taste bad and they seem to carry some kind of natural antiseptic."

Brightening, Angus took a few twigs from Eilen. "Tremendous! These little sticks will do a lot for my psyche."

"You think I can't imagine? You're not the only one who's feeling haggard."

Angus stared absently across the family area. "A shame to lose that torch."

"Who says you lost it? Isn't that it there, lying next to your pack?"

With effort, Angus twisted around to look toward the back wall. There lay the hand-torch, neatly placed among his belongings as though it had never been away.

Noting the object of their attention, La'ann explained. "Ri'nii ndako asimba."

As he mentally noted the obligation to young Ri'nii, Angus was struck by another facet of his new friends' character. These people placed faith in one another. Looking down the length of the sleeping area, he saw a number of bundled bedrolls lying against the wall at the foot of other possessions hanging from pegs, unprotected yet completely secure. What belonged to one did not exactly belong to all, but was protected by all.

Angus had resolved to repay Ri'nii's kindness when Eilen interrupted. "You wanted to know who Su'ban was? Well here she comes now. News of your recovery has made its way around the village."

A short woman approached the sleeping area, walking erect with the aid of a wooden staff. Lines etched her face, radiating from the corners of her eyes and defining the edges of her mouth. This face he had seen before, the same woman who stood next to 'Headdress' on the day they arrived, a face marked by wisdom and age.

Stopping at the foot of Angus's area, she nodded at La'ann. In La'ann's reply, Angus heard a respectful tone and realized he understood the native words. "Hello, Su'ban. Well you are?"

With a nod Su'ban acknowledged the greeting. "Well I am, La'ann. Good it is you asking." Her eyes then turned toward Angus. "Maladi makasi mabé ozwa. Malamu sikoyo ozali?"

Knowing only from her tone that she had asked a question, Angus said nothing.

Su'ban waved her staff at La'ann. "Sikoyo na bamona."

La'ann rose to offer a hand, helping the old woman onto the sleeping bench with somewhat more grace than she might have otherwise shown. Standing over Angus, Su'ban bent to examine the bandaged leg, sending a jingle through the many medallions hanging from her neck. As if by intent, the sound diverted Angus's attention long enough for Su'ban to tap her staff onto his bandaged leg.

Angus's exclamation came more from surprise than real pain. "Ouch."

Su'ban directed her next words to La'ann. "Ntango ekoki. Molangiti'eha sikoyo longola." When La'ann hesitated, she spoke more sharply. "Sikoyo!"

No third prod was needed. Drawing a knife from the sheath on his belt, La'ann carefully slipped the blade beneath the crossed bindings around Angus's leg. The fibrous dressing came away in layers, exposing first Angus's wrinkled thigh looking healthy and normal. Then the knee became visible, bruised and discolored.

The sight of his bare calf made Angus suck in breath. Whatever demons swam in the bites of tiny black midfloor creatures had left purple lines where sandal straps once crossed. Skin comfortably exposed on the day of his exploration now lay beneath a dark blanket of scabs and welts. He tried to bend his knee, quickly retreating as the effort pulled open scabs. "Aaiiee!"

Su'ban, on the other hand, nodded with approval. "Bisenga Nahélé na opésa. Ohini na owawéa malamuzuwaki."

Smiling, La'ann touched Angus's arm. "Kitoko ezali."

128

The common phrase meaning "Good it is" was becoming a part of Angus's growing vocabulary.

With a tap of her staff on the platform, Su'ban turned to leave. "Kitoko olálaki mingi, Ahngoose."

Angus answered simply. "Melesi, Su'ban."

La'ann rose to help her off the sleeping bench.

Rising, Eilen spoke while her eyes watched Su'ban's retreat. "A quick 'thank you' may not be enough. You don't know the half of what you owe her. She spent hours here while you were out-of-it, feeding you her concoctions and preparing that poultice around your leg." With a last word Eilen followed Su'ban. "Glad to have you back with us. Now I've got some work to do. I'll see you later."

As Eilen stepped off the platform she passed a young girl holding another cup. Angus understood the youngster's native words. "Many eat, Ahngoose."

....

A gift from Su'ban, the carved staff had become a part of Angus's wardrobe. Although running might present a challenge, with aid from the staff he could fashion the semblance of a walk. This morning he thought to join everyone at the morning meal.

Hobbling around the curve of the central colōfn tree, he found the 'ann family seated on the deck with all eyes trained in his direction, alerted by the clumping of his staff. For a moment, he hesitated. Several voices greeted his arrival. "Likamboté, Ahngoose." The kind welcome filled him with a surprisingly warm feeling.

The one called Ré'ann, whom Angus knew as family elder and a member of the clan council, rose to offer a seat. "Ahngoose, áwa ovánda." Once Angus had awkwardly lowered himself to the deck, partially filled trays came hand-to-hand to the space in front of him. At the sight of food, Angus realized that his desire to join the group might have quite ordinary roots. A healthy appetite had definitely returned.

Ré'ann swept an arm over the assembled food. "Olie, Ahngoose." A murmur ran through the circle as everyone shared Angus's obvious relish in the first mouthful. Placing a hand on Angus' shoulder, Ré'ann continued. "Ndako sikoyo okoma, Ahngoose. Kitóko ezali." Angus heard sincerity in the phrase 'Good it is.' When Ré'ann turned away, other conversations resumed and Angus had become a part of the circle.

Looking at the people around him, Angus felt chagrinned at how few he knew by name. Eilen smiled from across the circle. Seeing La'ann and Ro'ann to one side, he counted the two of them among those he knew. That he could recognize some others pleased him. At least he seemed to have finally learned to see these people in their varied subtle features.

Even as he began to enjoy his newfound membership the gathering started to dissolve. Eilen and Ro'ann stood first with a wave to Angus as they headed toward the common area. Like a call to duty, their departure triggered motion through the entire circle. People rose, turned and left, the day's activities taking priority over the conversations of a moment before. Angus remained with those few who stayed to clean the area. Last to leave, Ré'ann rose, departing with a friendly farewell. "Iniač, Ahngoose. Kobika malamu. Naino tokoloba."

Still ashamed of his poor native language skill, Angus mumbled what he hoped conveyed a similar meaning. "Goodbye, Ré'ann. Until another time you I see."

Setting his thoughts toward the day ahead, Angus looked at his still-discolored leg, remembering the last time he ventured out. *Perhaps a little more caution today.* He pulled the staff close and had barely succeeded in struggling upright when two children offered help. "Mboté, Ahngoose. Osalisa koki ko bisó?"

Although he did not understand what they said, their

smiles conveyed genial intent and Angus saw an opportunity to make friends and practice the native language. "Who you are?"

The question met smiles. With a flat hand on his chest, the taller of the two children introduced himself. "Lō'ann, I am." His brother repeated the gesture. "Né'ann I am."

Certain that no one in the village was unaware of his name Angus nonetheless felt an impulse to treat the two children with formality. With a nod, he flattened a hand on his own chest. "Angus I am." The gesture elicited broader grins from the two and probably solidified Angus's place in their esteem. As the children ran off, Angus hobbled toward the village common, trying to formulate a plan for the day.

Once through the connecting path, Angus stopped for breath. Staring at the deck, he muttered to himself. "Marvelous. I've become an old man. I can't even walk across the village." A picture came to mind. He saw himself on the bridge of a starship, leaning on a cane and almost laughed aloud.

From across the common someone called. Searching to find its source, Angus saw a raised staff in Su'ban's hand. Surrounded by a group near one of the fire pits, Angus surmised that she might be directing the preparation of one of her medicinal concoctions.

He summoned strength and shuffled ahead. As he drew near, the bustle of activity ceased. A tap of Su'ban's staff brought it quickly to life again. "Mboté, Ahngoose. Elengi otambola namoni ezali." Angus's beginner's ear heard only a portion of Su'ban's greeting. "Good morning, Ahngoose. Good ... you walk ... it is."

"Mboté, Su'ban."

Unable to recognize anyone else, Angus then sent a carefully pronounced Batololému greeting to Su'ban's entourage. "Mboté." A staccato barrage of voices and nodding heads rewarded his effort. "Mboté, Ahngoose."

Another tap of Su'ban's staff set everyone back to work and put Angus in mind of Su'ban's apparent role among the villagers.

Before the group, some sort of apparatus was coming to life. Two of Su'ban's assistants lifted a domed metal cover into place upon a heavy pot then fit a short cylinder into a receptacle atop the cover's center. Pipes and tubes lay on the deck waiting to be added. Su'ban said nothing. The tapping of her staff, which stood silent while everyone remained focused, seemed all the voice she needed to ensure accomplishment of the task.

In a moment of lucidity, Angus saw the woman's importance. He remembered La'ann's deference, the kind of respect La'ann gave to no one else, not even the clan leader called Ra'ahj, whom Angus had once anointed as 'Headdress.' When Su'ban spoke, La'ann deferred. It struck Angus that he stood beside the real power of the clan. Angus gripped the staff in his hand, thinking it showed Su'ban's real concern for his wellbeing, at least for now. He'd be wise to keep things that way.

Every movement Su'ban made came with a metallic jingle. Angus had seen the necklace before. *A badge of office.* This was the first time he'd had both the opportunity and the ability to look at the necklace closely. Bright gold medallions, individually etched in angular runes, hung in four loose strings from a rigid band around Su'ban's neck. Separated by similar strings of dull grey metal plates, the gold medallions spread across her breast in a broad ensemble. Her every movement matched the song of a wind chime with glittering light thrown in every direction. Angus made a mental note to one day ask about the meanings behind the runes.

Suddenly aware that he had been staring, Angus looked up to see Su'ban's eyes fixed upon him. Her steady gaze made him feel naked. Raising a hand to his chin, he dragged his fingernails, now a bit too long, through the whiskers on the lower half of his face. It occurred to him that he hadn't shaved for as long as he had been on this planet. The more-than-quarter-inch length of nascent beard gave him an idea of how long that had been; more than a month, at the least. He felt the back of his neck, finding yet more evidence in the shag at the nape of his neck. Almost two months. Looking at Su'ban's crew, he realized that none of her assistants showed even a hint of beard. Among these people, he'd seen none. What must they think of his appearance?

A drop of rain struck his arm and he noted scattered drops upon the surrounding deck. The afternoon shower had begun; somewhat earlier, it seemed, than yesterday. *Curious. Days here don't seem to march with a steady rhythm.*

Time to find shelter.

Expecting to see Su'ban's entourage scrambling for cover he instead observed their labors continue unabated by the rain. They had all removed their outer garments. Everyone enjoyed the refreshing cool rain, wearing only a light wrap about their hips. A little surprised, Angus noticed a young woman among them. He had not before then seen any of the adult women without clothing. Suddenly realizing that his attention might give offense, he searched for a place to avert his eyes, finding Su'ban's apparatus now completely assembled.

Angus gave the apparatus a long, careful look, thinking he'd seen similar contraptions before. A moment of inspection returned a memory from earlier days. He'd seen similar equipment used among Haven's rural populations in the preparation of alcoholic drinks. This particular apparatus, with its smooth, well-shaped metal components, seemed to belong elsewhere; alongside more sophisticated machinery.

The rain began to drum out a steady rhythm on the village deck. Angus looked up to notice Su'ban's scrutiny, her head cocked to one side. She beckoned him to follow and walked away from the cooking pot. Angus hadn't the strength to match her strides and only managed to catch up as she stopped and waited, rainwater dripping from her face.

"Many quick walk, Ahngoose. Rain now falls."

Pleased to understand words meaning 'rain' and 'hurry,' Angus saw in Su'ban's arm gestures a clear message, but he could draw no more speed from his hobble. The two of them became quite drenched before reaching her shelter opposite the Mingi. In a testament to her unique status, Su'ban kept solitary quarters, which she shared with a collection of tools and stores of varied containers that Angus could only surmise contained medicines and potions. Even the small step at the base of the bench floor, allowing her slight form to easily navigate her own threshold, had no peer within the village.

The raised sleeping bench provided a welcome seat for Angus, now worn out from a trip of only some meters. Su'ban had other ideas. Reaching to pull on his arm, she indicated her desire for him to enter. Getting himself up and into her shelter became an arduous task. Struck by the wounded pride of a weakened old man, Angus put little enthusiasm into a thank you for Su'ban's aid. "Mélesi, Su'ban."

As she turned toward the rear of her shelter, Angus could barely hear Su'ban's words. "Yo bökóeliko nazali na, Ahngoose."

That she had a definite purpose, Angus understood, so, while Su'ban retreated into the gloomy recess of her shelter, he stood bracing himself with one hand upon a heavy flat table occupying a prominent space. Watching her, he noted the several shelves along the back wall, filled with wooden boxes, earthen jars, and glass bottles. Su'ban stretched to grasp a small box, which she pulled down and placed next to several odd implements already laying on the table. Two more trips to the shelves completed her preparations. Fascinated, Angus watched Su'ban complete the steps of a well-practiced operation. Measuring with no more than her own hands, she stood above the table and carefully extracted a quantity of powder from several containers and added each to a stone bowl. Grinding and mixing with the aid of a hand-sized length of stone tool produced a uniformly colored powder, which she transferred into a heavy rectangular form containing a number of small wells. A matching lid fit atop the powder-filled form and, after several whacks with a mallet, Su'ban opened the form, upsetting it to discharge a number of dark-colored little pills onto the table.

One more visit to her stores produced a small leather pouch, into which Su'ban brushed the pills to present them to Angus.

Angus listened to Su'ban's instructions as he warily accepted the offering.

"Kisi na ozali, Ahngoose. Osalisa ikaika akopésa." Holding up one finger, she added, "Móko me, móko kisi." Walking to the open front of her shelter, she stepped off onto the deck into the afternoon rain and proceeded toward the fountain. Returning wet, she held a cup out to Angus and repeated, "Móko me, móko kisi."

The extended finger helped Angus understand. "One day, one pill."

"Mélesi, Su'ban." Without the slightest hesitation, he threw one of the pills to the back of his mouth and washed it down with a mouthful of water.

On his way back toward the 'ann family area, rainwater dripped from his nose but Angus felt much better than he had just a short while before. He found it difficult to believe that her medicine could actually work that well and that rapidly. *Probably only placebo psychology.* Yet, he walked steadier, shuffled less.

He was about to disappear into the briar-walled path when he heard his name called out. "Angus! Hold on." To all but Eilen he was 'Ahngoose.' He turned to see her trotting across the common wearing an exhilarated smile, a red flower in her hand. Hol'imm and Ro'ann trotted behind her, each hefting an animal carcass over one shoulder.

"What's the flower all about?"

"Nothing special. I just thought it was pretty. I pulled it off of a vine on the midforest ceiling. La'ann, Ro'ann, and Hol'imm took me on a hunt. Did you see what we caught?"

"I see the two carcasses."

"Yes. They belong to foraging animals La'ann called 'élobe.' We trapped them, and I helped do it."

Angus heard the excitement in her voice. "I'm a bit worn out. Can you tell me about it as we walk?"

"Oh... sure. We should get out of this rain anyway."

"Sounds like you did more than just watch."

A smile came through in Eilen's voice. "Yes. I did. I had a good time doing it, too."

"Go on. Tell me all about it."

"All right, if you're sure you'd like to hear; but let's first get ourselves under some cover." Eilen held out a hand, palm up. A light drizzle continued to fall.

"You have a point. We could get there a little faster if I concentrate on walking instead of talking."

Surprising himself, Angus managed to keep up with Eilen's steps. By the time they reached the sleeping bench, however, his fatigue had grown. He turned his back to the bench and let himself down with a thump.

Eilen set herself down beside him. "You all right?"

"Yeah, I'm all right. I've been hobbling around the village and I'm just a little tired out. Su'ban gave me something that seems to give me more energy, but I still need a little rest. Let me catch my breath." Angus leaned forward, let his elbows rest on his knees and took the load off his back. "Tell me about your day."

"Hol'imm gave me charge of a kùmu'lio. He calls her 'Chamoro.' I think she's warming up to me. She purrs when I pet her."

Angus again heard the grin and looked to see if it was

there. It was. "You've mastered the art of riding their swinging steeds?"

"Yes, I have, at least well enough to follow the others. Kùmu'lio are quite gentle and there's nothing to riding them. They seem to like it. The only thing I really had to learn was getting on and off."

"Where'd you go this morning?"

"We went some distance out toward what I've come to calling the 'north' direction. Hol'imm called it 'isáto mibali', which I don't understand since it literally means 'three men.' Maybe there's a place north of here called 'Three Men.' Riding along the midforest ceiling is quite fun."

"Quite the forest dweller you've become."

"Perhaps you're right. These people have taken me in. It feels like an honor."

"Feels a little different to me. I've become a bit more isolated."

"Are you sure that's not your own fault?"

"Perhaps. I seem to have been walking around in some kind of fog since we arrived. Then I go and take my first foray out-and-about and become incapacitated."

"Lucky for you Su'ban was here to fix you up."

"She seems to have taken some interest in me."

"You should be thankful. Su'ban is a leader here. You can see how she's given more respect than anyone else, including Ra'ajh. They call her 'Haku'iké', which I think means something like 'keeper of knowledge.'"

"I've noticed how respectful La'ann is with her ... and she seems to be a skillful healer. Look at this medicine she gave me." Angus pulled out the small sac of pills and emptied the contents into his palm.

"She made pills."

"Only one of many little out-of-place things here. This village isn't really as primitive as it seems. Have you noticed the little bits of technology that pop up here-and-there?"

"I guess I've noticed, but I haven't paid much attention. I've been having too much fun learning about everything."

"That's the truth, isn't it? You've been looking toward a future, while I've been mourning the past."

"You think too much about the Raiju. I try not to. If I did, I'd become as depressed as you ... and there's not much I can do about it anyway."

Thoughts of the Raiju and its crew sent Angus's mind wandering.

"Before we landed here, I was the captain of a starship, free to travel between stars. Here I need help to walk around the village."

"A little dramatic, don't you think?"

Angus had not heard. "The Raiju was really about the only home I'd ever known, and the people aboard her the only family I'd ever had."

"You still have me."

Angus studied her face, seeing it as he had not seen it before. "I do ... don't I." The words came out slowly. *More than a colleague ... there's no one here but her.*

Eilen averted her eyes. Angus realized he'd been staring. "I'm sorry. I got lost in thought."

"It's all right, but you should be thinking about what you have, not what you don't have. And you might realize that I've lost as much as you. When you were delirious and I didn't know if you were going to survive, I was as scared as I can remember being. The only thing that held me together was the reassurance from La'ann and Hol'imm that you would recover."

"We're no longer Captain-and-Crew, are we?"

"No, ... we're not. Shipboard etiquette is no longer in force." With that thought, Eilen rose. "You should rest. You're still recovering and I need to talk with Hol'imm."

Watching her walk toward the common area, Angus saw for perhaps the first time what a striking woman she was. An image of Su'ban's half-clothed assistant popped into his head. He quickly dispelled the thought.

CHAPTER 13
Another Mission

The chair's hard, uncomfortable seat was difficult to ignore. Sitting rigidly upright, Semgee pulled his eyes from the ancient, hand-painted image mounted on the wall behind Alexandra. The knowledge that he had not seen such artwork outside of a museum failed to inspire the reverence he knew his captain sought. The décor of her quarters was merely annoying and her self-satisfied expression seemed more irritating than usual. *Strange. She needs to raise herself behind that ancient wooden desk to feel important.* Still, he realized, few would be allowed to fill their quarters with such priceless antiquities. Her aristocratic lineage came with some elements of real power.

"Semgee, I'm sure you've heard. We've been given another mission."

On this occasion, Semgee had no need to feign enthusiasm. It would be difficult to match Alexandra's glee, but as soon as she broached the subject, thoughts of her annoying habits left his mind. "It is true, Honorable Captain, I have heard the news. May I ask how the Committee meeting went?"

In a rare display of good humor, Alexandra smiled. "Of course, you may ask... and I can only say, it was glorious! I may never forget how proud I was to bring such news to the

Committee."

Then the smile disappeared and, in the space of a breath, both her mood and the topic changed. "I had hoped to surprise them, but some hint of our news seems to have reached the Committee's ranks well before I arrived. I will trust you to take disciplinary action. It seems some of our crew are unclear in their understanding of the meaning of the word 'silence.'"

Diverting her ire, Semgee quickly returned to the subject at hand. "The meeting went well then, Honorable Captain?"

Alexandra visibly relaxed. Reliving the story gave her too much pleasure to resist. "Yes, it did. The entire First Council was present, even old General Chang, who, they say, never attends. All seats were filled. Conversation ended the moment I entered. When the First Secretary stood, I found myself suddenly alone in front of the entire Committee. He spoke directly to me, loud enough for everyone to hear, saying he had heard that I had some news for the Committee. I told him that I did indeed have news and, without even giving me a chance to take a seat at the table, or to consult my notes, he asked me to begin. It took me but a moment to gather my thoughts and then a few minutes to relay the story of our discovery at the red giant star and of our pursuit of the alien starship.

"When I finished, the First Secretary himself congratulated me on Bright Victory's tremendous discovery. It was a quite marvelous moment. Reliving it excites me still."

Semgee had to admit to himself that the experience would likely have been quite overwhelming for him. He prefaced his next question with a nod to her well-known ego. "I'm sure you were very gallant in your dress uniform, Honorable Captain. What then did you hear of the Committee's recommendations?"

He did not expect the frown he received.

"Nothing at that time, and that was a bit disappointing. As soon as the First Secretary offered his compliments and the applause subsided, they asked me to leave. I waited in a small side office until one of the Admiral's adjutants came to tell me that the Committee had ordered another mission and that I was to return to the ship to await official orders. I haven't yet even spoken to the Admiral."

"I'm sure, Honorable Captain, we will simply be asked to return and find the homeworld of whatever beings operated that orbiting station."

"I'm sure you're right, Semgee. But important issues will be buried in the details of the order, in the specifics of the Committee's direction for any engagement should we find the alien world."

"What direction would you have the Committee give us?"

"I'd be pleased to see them give us no direction at all, save that we use any means at our disposal to find that alien world."

"Is that likely, Honorable Captain?"

"I really don't know. I'm not sure what outcome the Committee would wish to accomplish. It would be foolish to plan too far ahead when we don't know with whom, or with what, we're dealing. The Committee will probably ask us to locate the alien world and return without making further contact, allowing time for further and more careful investigation."

"We should nonetheless be prepared to defend ourselves in any kind of confrontation in the event our presence is detected."

"Of course. That's just the kind of reasoning we'll use to arm ourselves to whatever degree we think necessary. I doubt that Fleet Command will argue too sternly."

"For how long a mission do you think we should plan?"

"What's the longest period we can remain out?"

Semgee couldn't help himself, becoming more engaged as the conversation shifted into a planning exercise. He leaned forward into the edge of the desk and began to vocally analyze the mission requirements. "Honorable Captain, I'm sure you realize that support supplies for the crew is the limiting factor. The length of our deployment will depend most heavily on the composition of our crew."

"Yes. Let's talk about that. I was thinking that we might put out with a skeleton crew and enable a longer voyage. Who among the crew can you say are indispensable?"

"Aside from you and I, Honorable Captain, we'll absolutely need to include skilled hands at navigation, weapons, systems, communications, and maintenance. Then, a skilled galley chief would also be wise."

Alexandra's face wrinkled. "Galley chief? Really, Semgee?"

"Yes, Honorable Captain, we'll be out several years and, while you might think it a nonessential duty, maintenance of the crew's morale will become an issue on such a long voyage and a skilled housekeeper will do us well in that regard."

"Can we get by with a single crew member covering each of those functions?"

"Yes, we can, at navigation, weapons, and at maintenance, but our primary mission will need full-time monitoring of systems and communications, and I would also recommend that we include a versatile, multi-role crewmember to back up wherever needed."

"I assumed you and I would perform that role."

Knowing that his captain would never actually step into any of the ship's more demanding duties, Semgee pressed the issue, "Of course, Honorable Captain, but we would be wise to protect ourselves against becoming too fragile. A versatile crewmember will make us more resilient."

"So ... where does that leave us? You and I, navigator, weapons officer, and a maintenance chief; two communications specialists, two systems specialists, a roamer, and a cook. That's eleven. Is that it?"

"It could be long and tiresome duty, Honorable Captain. Perhaps we can find two maintenance specialists, ... and ask them to also share cooking duties."

Alexandra heard but didn't skip a beat in her summary, "That still cuts our crew by several-fold. I like that. We could easily stay out more than two years."

Semgee was pleased. His captain seemed to have quickly embraced the character of the mission he'd been planning. One last requirement might actually be something she'd welcome. "Of course, it goes without saying, we'll definitely not be able to afford the luxury of a security force team."

Alexandra smiled.

Unable to entirely contain himself, Semgee thought to add one last point, in a futile effort to maintain a semblance of reality, "Yes, we could endure a long mission, ... but perhaps it will not be 'easy.'" Then, sidestepping the argument that his statement might provoke, he quickly pressed the conversation onto a related topic, with full knowledge that his captain and her focus on glory had not yet considered the tactical implications for a search mission into another galaxy. She concerned herself with glory... while he ran the ship.

"Honorable Captain, while I agree that it is not unreasonable for us to provision and plan for a two-year voyage, I would also respectfully ask you to consider the more important issue concerning the methods we might employ to guide our mission. I have been thinking about this matter and I have some recommendations I would like you to consider."

Her enjoyment spent, Alexandra hesitated a moment before finally relaxing to lean back into her padded seat, lace her hands together and press two extended index fingertips to her lips, "Of course, First Officer, I'm pleased that you've devoted some thought there. You have my attention."

Pleased with his captain's attitude, Semgee launched into explanation before her mood changed. "The issue with which I've been grappling concerns the search strategy we might employ to find our alien world. I'm sure, with only the slightest consideration, you'll agree that an exhaustive search method will be entirely impractical. The Lesser Magellanic Cloud is 'small' only by comparison to our own, Milky Way galaxy. It actually contains some two billion stars scattered throughout a volume of about two hundred billion cubic light-years. It's clear that we cannot visit them all."

Semgee suddenly feared he might sound too condescending. It was always a delicate balance. He knew his captain would take unkindly to any hint of patronizing, but he also knew she tended to miss important details.

Impatience laced Alexandra's voice. "Yes, of course. But we'd never try to do so, we'll listen for their electromagnetic signature."

Hoping to intercept any possible argument, Semgee adopted a more compliant tone. "Indeed, Honorable Captain, please let me continue."

With a dismissive backhanded wave, Alexandra's rising ire seemed to ebb. "Go on."

Semgee's relief softened his voice. "I ask you, is it likely that the civilization that created that close-orbiting station grew from life-originating seeds locally within the Lesser Magellanic Cloud? Or is it more likely that the civilization that we found migrated from an already-developed civilization present within the larger nearby Milky Way Galaxy?"

Enjoying his own story, Semgee didn't wait for an answer. "If we ask ourselves how long ago such a migrant Milky Way civilization might have made the journey across the intergalactic gulf, we might guess that, since the human race has only been traveling between the stars for about a thousand years, and since the League of Planets consolidated their realm nearly six hundred years ago, I might put forth a proposal and say that the alien civilization of the Lesser Cloud might, in fact, be of human origins and can thereby be only about two hundred to four hundred years old."

Semgee smiled with the realization that he'd captured his captain's attention.

She nodded as the thoughts formed in her head. "I'm beginning to see what you're thinking."

"I hope so, Honorable Captain. If my reasoning has merit, then we'll need to get as close as about two hundred light-years before we'll be able to hear any signals from their homeworld ... and my analysis tells me that, under that constraint, an exhaustive search will still require fifteen years or more of diligent effort."

Encouraged by Alexandra's softer tone, Semgee continued the tale, "I've been thinking ... since almost the moment we lost that ship on the far side of the galaxy... that their escape from our trap at the mining station revealed several things. First, it demonstrated their spaceflight capabilities, which, I'm sure you'll agree, match our own. Second, I don't think their choice of destination was a random accident.

"If I expand the first observation, it tells me that, since they can make jumps into intergalactic space in thirty thousand light-year leaps, then any point near the outer fringes of the entire dwarf galaxy is only about three or four jumps apart from any other point. Whereas, since only short jumps are possible toward the interior of the Cloud, a point deep in the interior is quite a number of jumps away from any point near the outer fringes. In a sense, then, the outer fringes are 'closer together' than are the interior points.

"Do you see what I mean, Honorable Captain?"

In one of her infrequent episodes of focus, Alexandra seemed to have been listening. Sitting upright, her voice carried excitement. "I do, indeed, Semgee! ... And I would add that there are likely numerous occupied worlds and remote stations under their control, which will increase even more our chances of finding a lead."

"Yes! And, since we discovered that remote orbiting station within about five hundred light-years of the galaxy's outermost fringe and in that portion nearest the Milky Way, I would propose that we confine our search to an area of the outer fringe centered around that station, limiting that area to about four thousand light-years in each circumferential direction, and add only about five hundred light year excursions along the radial direction. I think we can easily cover such a space in the two-year period we can devote to a single mission and I also think such a plan has a high chance of success."

In a smooth motion, Alexandra now rose from her chair and nearly marched around her desk. "Your analysis gives me even more reason to be anxious for our departure, Semgee. The sooner we get started, the sooner we can return to another glorious reception. How long do you think we yet require before we can set forth?"

"Honorable Captain, I have not been idle. We are, in fact, nearly stocked for a full voyage. I have now merely to appoint and enlist the necessary crew." Holding a steady gaze and looking directly at his captain as she stood at the corner of her desk, Semgee was pleased to find himself in excellent position to pose the request he had been leading up to. "A general order from Astrocorps Command would enable us to requisition the best-qualified crew members from their present assignments and to place our surplus crew members onto other ships. Can you obtain such an order?"

Alexandra hesitated but a heartbeat. "A good question, First Officer. The answer is certainly 'yes', but it will take a little time. I wonder if we can get what we need through informal channels. I think many of those whose skills we'll need would be prepared to request an immediate transfer, once they understood our mission. Perhaps I can more easily canvass appropriate Fleet officers to solicit some cooperation."

Well aware of his captain's love for the political, Semgee Marlowe rose smiling. "An excellent idea, Honorable Captain."

CHAPTER 14
Su'ban

So very different from everything he had known, so alien to the sterile environment of a starship, the rich, redolent air of the midforest awakened Angus's senses. Each breath captured a humid, aromatic stew, pulled from the stillness held between midforest floor and ceiling. Sweet and spicy smells from ceiling blossoms laced the sumptuous humor of the midfloor and the musty odor of his mount's soft fur. As if a veil had fallen away, Angus saw the forest world anew. With each swing of his mount's long arms, village boundaries fell farther behind and took with them the cloud of regrets and longings that had dogged his spirit. The stars may be forever lost, but a strange new and unexplored Nahélé stretched before him. Perhaps he might yet find comfort in this place.

A memory crept unbidden into Angus's consciousness. Ivan's rhythmic voice launched tales of thick, vibrant jungle air on his home of Granger Four. Quickly fleeing the emotional snare, he pushed the memory aside to seek again Nahélé's reality. Small creatures of many sparkling hues flitted from vine to vine. Hanging flowers entertained visits by creatures both winged and legged, each trying to out-shout the other in a dissonant symphony of whistles, clicks, buzzes, and chirps. Life thrived within the arms of the great forest.

Midday temperatures had just begun to make their presence felt. Tiny rills of sweat ran down the contours of Angus's face, finding their way into an eye. Absently pulling a hand across his brow, he watched La'ann pull up near a vine-covered colōfn trunk. As Angus neared the group, La'ann called to him. "Ahngoose! Where go, you do?"

La'ann's good-natured quip sounded clearly in Angus's mind. Finding courage in his understanding, Angus answered in heavily accented Batololému. "Nahélé, I am seeing, La'ann."

"Good hearing, your speaking is, Ahngoose ... Eat, you do?"

As he reached for the leaf-wrapped package, Angus glanced at Eilen. Forest food had become a favorite part of his new life. Taking only time to swallow the food in her mouth, Eilen offered her considered opinion. "Like it, you will, Angus."

Lunch and Eilen's easy manner fed Angus's relaxed mood. He leaned back to rest against his mount's strong arm and unwrapped the package, holding it to his nose and savoring the heavy aroma. The spicy flavors of forest food were becoming familiar. He quietly let himself eat while thinking of the morning's events.

They had not ventured far. Eilen had not exaggerated. Kùmu'lio made for easy riding. Hol'imm had offered one of the clan's youngest kùmu'lio. "Little trouble, give she will." This morning she readily carried Angus, happy to be stretching her arms with the older group, enjoying herself like any youngster. Could he find his way back? As if to check himself he turned to look in the direction they had come. Nahélé permitted an unobstructed view only so far in the midforest shade. Had they wandered much since leaving the village? He had not paid much attention. One short scan of their surroundings would unerringly tell La'ann and Hol'imm which direction they should follow. Might he someday learn to listen to Nahélé as well as did La'ann and Hol'imm?

Angus had barely finished his meal before a shout from Hol'imm jarred him upright. "Fulélé!" Spots of glare near the clearing center made it difficult to see along the line of Hol'imm's arm and, with no idea of what a fulélé was, Angus could only sit and await enlightenment. Eilen's shrug said she felt the same. Only La'ann's trained eye was able to spot the fulélé among the shadows of the ceiling foliage. "Fulélé!"

La'ann's explanation shed little light on the nature of the discovery. "For Su'ban," he said before urging Mœrai out over the clearing. Eilen started to follow but Hol'imm held up a hand to hold her steady. She and Angus watched the recovery of fulélé from their perch near the nexus of colōfn branches.

Hol'imm and La'ann reached only about a third of the distance from the clearing center when they pulled up. There, La'ann handed one end of his coiled rope to Hol'imm and let the rope play out as Hol'imm continued toward the clearing center. Standing upon the kumulio he called Moninga, Hol'imm anchored his end firmly within the ceiling vines and waited. La'ann stopped and pulled on the rope, stretching it taut between them. Satisfied, he wrapped it around a leg, calf and thigh, and turned the free end into several coils around his middle.

With a shout to Hol'imm, La'ann stood behind Mœrai's forearms and leaned against the pull of the rope. Then he leapt. Eilen stifled a gasp. Angus ceased breathing. La'ann fell. Everyone stood still watching the rope catch and pull La'ann's plunge into a great arc. Near the swing's nadir, directly under Hol'imm, La'ann kipped his lower body upward to propel his rising arc within reach of the ceiling vines. A quick grasp left him hanging by one arm buried in the ceiling foliage, one leg pulled straight by the rope and one leg dangling, looking completely unnatural so far from Mœrai's protection. After one quick wave to his friends La'ann reached toward the fulélé vine to secure his prize before letting his body fall from the ceiling into a graceful return arc.

Surrounded once again by Mœrai's strong arms, La'ann calmly retrieved his rope as Angus marveled. Consuming no more than a few minutes, the entire fúlélé recovery operation had left a profound impression. Angus felt sure that La'ann and Hol'imm saw their little swinging act as but one small piece of normal forest life. Yet the profusion of skills displayed in its execution left him realizing just how far from useful was the training of a starship commander. The ride back toward the village gave him ample time to ponder the nature of any place he might make for himself among Nahélé's people.

Angus had just stepped out onto the common deck. La'ann's footsteps echoed behind him in the stairway from the kúmulio stalls. Before Angus could limp more than two steps, La'ann brushed past him. "Again, where go you do, Ahngoose?" La'ann said with a quick backward glance. Ahead Angus saw Su'ban directing the preparation of another potion. La'ann seemed intent on that direction.

Limping near the working group, Angus heard the bustle of activity cease, to be immediately restored by a tap of Su'ban's staff upon the deck. Imperfect skills presented Angus a broken version of Su'ban's greeting. "Good morning to you wishing, Ahngoose. Good ... you walk ... it is."

Before Angus could frame an answer, La'ann held out his two cupped hands. "For you, Su'ban, gift we have." La'ann's uncommonly wide grin told everyone how much he welcomed the chance to please Su'ban. Although Angus had contributed nothing to the gathering of seedpods the row of gleaming teeth appearing across Su'ban's face made him feel almost as proud of the effort as, he was certain, did La'ann. Leaning on her staff, Su'ban freed both hands to accept the seedpods, tucking them into a waist sack before a free hand rose to touch La'ann's shoulder. "Well you do, La'ann. Pleased I am. Good it is."

With obvious pleasure, La'ann respectfully inclined his head and backed a step away before turning to leave. Angus took the cue and nodded as if to leave. Su'ban reached to restrain him. "With you, speaking I wish."

Standing silent, Angus waited for Su'ban's direction, only to see her turn and restore her work crew's effort with a rap of her staff. None of the three young faces staring up at him ignited any recognition. Angus inclined a polite nod in their direction and spoke in carefully pronounced Batololému. "Wishing good morning." The effort met with a collective return. "Good morning to you wishing, Ahngoose."

Another hard rap of Su'ban's staff grabbed Angus's attention with an accompanying burst of tinkling tones. Su'ban's serious face returned, then, just as quickly, her eyes refocused somewhere behind him. Turning, he saw Hol'imm and Eilen emerging from the stables, kúmu'lio care duties concluded. Su'ban followed their approach. Hol'imm had not quite closed the gap before she waved a hand in his direction. "Go, go! With Ahngoose and Ee'laan, I wish speaking."

Eilen's arrival seemed to galvanize Su'ban to action. Issuing a barrage of terse instructions to her crew, she turned to leave and at the same time, as though responding to her command, the afternoon rain began. The rain began to drum out a steady rhythm on the village deck. Beckoning for them to follow, Su'ban walked away leaving both Angus and Eilen hurrying to follow. Pushing incompletely healed legs as fast as they would permit, Angus gained the protection of her shelter as Su'ban deposited the valuable seedpods among her innumerable stocks of raw materials.

Perhaps if he had thought a bit about it, a tired Angus would not have presumed to sit himself down on the edge of Su'ban's raised bench. When she went stiff and stared down at him, Angus regretted the action, glancing at Eilen for support.

The insistent drumming of Su'ban's staff announced another intention. "Help me you will?"

Eilen helped Su'ban lower herself to sit next to Angus,

before hesitating at the choice of a seat for herself, finally choosing to put Su'ban between them.

Framed between the two outsiders Su'ban seemed small in contrast. Angus and Eilen rested their feet quietly on the deck. Su'ban's legs swung freely like a child's, belying the power she held over them.

Angus waited, trying to keep his apprehension in check. Silence seemed the best tactic. Except for the attention given his injured leg, Su'ban had heretofore left them largely to their own devices. He now saw Su'ban as the clan's soul and probably its conscience. Her scrutiny presented both risk and opportunity.

Su'ban first words seemed designed to put him at ease. "Well, your leg mends. Good it is."

Hearing a soft tone return to Su'ban's voice, Angus picked up the phrase, 'Good it is.' Added freely to almost any remark, much as people of Haven might say, 'so be it,' the phrase heralded her intent. Angus answered calmly. "Yes, Su'ban. For life in my leg, thank you, I do." Thinking to take a small positive step, he bowed in her direction. "Great, your life-force is."

Without realizing it, he had given Su'ban a good opening. "Also is yours, hear I do. A vessel of tool-stone made, La'ann speaks. Within such vessel, the air, you ride. True, this can be?"

Angus tried to compose an answer, watching the many wrinkles around Su'ban's eyes draw together as he struggled. Knowing she sought more than a simple 'yes,' he fought to form Batololému sentences that might convey more meaning. "Yes, Su'ban. Well, La'ann saw. Great life-force our vessel carried. In air, Ee'laan and me, it held. With great speed Ee'laan and me, it pushed. Gone now its life-force is. In the Mokililana, it rests. The air no more will it ride."

His answer was not much more than a 'yes', but the effort seemed to please her. Her next question came with a smile.

"This vessel ... by what clan made it was?"

The linguistic struggle again brought furrows onto Angus's face. Stammering, he stared at the deck as he tried to formulate an answer. "A large clan ... many people ... In the making of machines, skill they have ... 'Engineers' called they are."

"Of them, you are not?"

Angus paused again, unsure of just what she might want to know or of what he might say. In the end, he found little more to add. "No, Su'ban. From a clan called 'Pilots,' we are. In sky vessel fly, we can ... build sky vessel, we cannot."

Su'ban's eyes fixed on Angus, intently studying his face, eventually giving her thoughts a slow, quiet voice. "Like us, you are. And different, you are ... puzzled I am. Like us walk you do, but long your hair grows ... on your face hair grows. On Batonahélé heads, short hair grows... On Batonahélé faces, hair grows not."

Angus's hand rose slowly to his face. "Yes, Su'ban grow my hair does." Then, feeling a little self-conscious, he let his hand wander to the top of his head, noting how dirty it felt. "Batonahélé hair, it is not. Cut it I must."

Watching Su'ban's expression, Angus noted the many lines around her mouth and her eyes. *How old must she be?* No one else among the villagers was as sagely lined as Su'ban, giving her face an expressive character greater than most. Just now, Angus saw in her wrinkled brow how intently she strove to understand.

"What purpose to Nahélé's world, come you have? Here sent you were, yes?"

Speaking Batololému drew a mental toll from Angus. Su'ban's questions wore him down. He looked at Eilen, relieved to see his plea accepted. The silent exchange did not escape Su'ban, who turned to accept an answer from Eilen. "Fleeing we came, Su'ban. Escape harm we did. Seeking Nahélé's world we did not."

At these words, Su'ban paused, perhaps evaluating the truth of Eilen's answer. Eilen added what little she could. "From Nahélé's world we are not, Su'ban. A great distance, travel we did. From our world, Amon appears not. Too small for seeing, Amon is."

Su'ban slowly nodded. "To your world, return you will?"

"Return we cannot. Life-force, our vessel has not. Between Amon's sisters, travel no more we can."

Su'ban looked directly at Eilen. "With us stay you will."

Eilen composed a sincere face. "Yes, Su'ban. Stay, we must. To be with M'pepebato, thankful we are. And to be with Nahélé, thankful we are."

The interview seemed to be following a smooth course, prompting Angus to risk a question of his own. "Su'ban. Question, ask I can?"

"Yes. Together talking, we are."

"Su'ban, great knowledge you have. Where learn, you did?"

The question brought a smile to Su'ban's lips. "Haku'iké, I am. From old Haku'iké, learn I did. My 'kumuzala' it is."

Hidden among the many Batololému words, the one word nearly passed unnoticed. Angus looked at Eilen. "Kumuzala?" Eilen shrugged. "Something like 'reason to be', I think."

Eager to understand, Angus pressed on. "How long the learning you did?"

Su'ban seemed surprised by the question. She held up a single finger. "One day."

This unexpected answer gave Angus pause. Had he misunderstood? Eilen translated Angus's dilemma. "Su'ban, great your knowledge is. Learning one day only. Not possible it seems."

"So, it is. In the Dream World one day we lived. There learn I did."

Having no clarification to offer, Eilen shrugged. Angus returned to Su'ban. "The Dream World? Where it is?"

"Another day ... take you there, I will."

Unsure how he might pursue the question politely, Angus moved on. "Su'ban, from where ... village comes?" Lacking a Batololému word for house, or structure, Angus had used a word meaning everything from 'house' to 'family.' Had he captured the right meaning?

Su'ban's face tightened. "The village? Understand I do not."

"Village parts I mean; Sleeping places, Mingi, floor, Luba; into these things pieces came. With great skill village built. M'pepebato, build it, they did?"

Brightening, Su'ban seemed to realize Angus's intent. "Strength of arms give, M'pepebato do. Knowing give, the Haku'ike of the Bakeisiká do."

"The Bakeisiká Haku'ike. From what place begin does she? From what place begin her knowledge does? A place where knowledge of building they have ... is there?"

The wrinkles on Su'ban's face deepened. "Again, understand I do not. Carry within her knowledge, she does. Knowledge of M'boso, carry, she does ... Knowledge of M'boso, also carry, I do."

Poor skill thwarted Angus's efforts, but Su'ban's patience encouraged him. "Knowledge of M'boso, also you have? Build the village, you can?"

"No. I cannot. Such knowledge I have not. Her kumuzala it is. Mine it is not."

Su'ban's answer only confused Angus further. "Knowledge of M'boso, you have. Also, you do not? Understand I do not."

"Some knowledge within me, carry I do. Another knowledge carry, others do. Many Haku'iké, Nahélé holds. Within all Haku'iké, all knowledge remains ... Well, Nahélé's people keep." Placing a widespread hand on the necklace across her breast, Su'ban explained. "Here my kumuzala is."

Not much made sense. "Perhaps see, I do."

"No ... understand you do not. One day, with me, to the

'dream world' come you will. Understand there you will."

Su'ban paused and Angus pressed another direction. "Su'ban ... in Nahélé's world, a great village somewhere is?"

"'Great' village? 'Great' our village, is not?"

"Big, I mean ... much larger ... larger than many villages ... where people many are ... Counted, they cannot be."

"No ... such place, I know not. In Nahélé's arms, villages many are. Large some are; small some are. Like M'pepebato village all are."

Angus waved hands toward the deck. "Pieces of the village, from where come they do? The floor? Tools in the fields?"

"With Bakeisiká, trade we do."

"Bakeisiká?"

"Understand soon, you will. Come soon, they will."

For one long moment, Su'ban searched Angus's face. "Your kumuzala find we will." Then she turned toward Eilen. "Welcome here you are. Good living with M'pepebato you do." Her eyes fell toward the common deck. "Sent here perhaps you are."

Su'ban then lowered her staff to the deck and eased herself off the edge of the shelter floor. The interview was over.

CHAPTER 15
Underworld

Seldom did a restful night's sleep ignore La'ann's invitation. Yet he knew sleep obeys no master, visiting of its own accord or not at all. Anxious thought rendered this night's efforts futile. Sleep would not come. He told himself everything would go well. It always had done. He need only follow Ro'ann's lead and stay alert. He had done it before. Yet he could not sleep.

Nothing fearful stalked La'ann in the Midforest. The Highforest too held little dread. In these places, knowledge and ability kept him from harm. On the Mokililana, even Ro'ann would defer to his lead. Only in the Pō'ele did his abilities, skills and confidence flee. La'ann's respect for Ro'ann was never higher than when they descended into the Pō'ele.

Atop his sleeping roll, legs crossed, La'ann sought resolve. *No hold fear will take. Beside Ro'ann steady I will ride.* Uko's glow had begun to fill the upper forest. Soon it would be time. A second matter entered his thoughts. *Close watching, Ahngoose will need.* A first journey into the Pō'ele strikes fear into the bravest and the offworlder's abilities did not inspire confidence. *Ahngoose, keep near I will.*

Across the 'ann family home, beyond the colōfn tree, La'ann saw Ahngoose talking with Ee'laan. *Awake they are.*

Rising, he tucked his knife into the bands around his waist and stepped off the sleeping bench. *Strange they are. Of their being it is. Small thing it is.* Aside from events since their arrival, he knew only that they came from somewhere farther away than he could imagine, where they once controlled machines of great power. He wondered how Ahngoose made his way in that world. Ahngoose demonstrated no great skill at anything that La'ann understood. Ee'laan had skill with kùmu'lio and she had learned to speak the language of Nahélé. In the Pō'ele, where everyone must depend on each other, Ahngoose might pose a danger. Yet Su'ban asked that Ahngoose be taken into the Pō'ele, and Su'ban's wishes were not ignored. From a distance La'ann announced himself. "Mboté, Ahngoose. Mboté, Ee'laan."

As she looked up La'ann saw Ee'laan's face broaden in a smile. "Good morning, La'ann. Well you are?"

"Well I am, Ee'laan. Mélesi. Asking, kind you are."

La'ann looked directly at Angus. "Leave now we must. High the Pō'ele waters soon will be. Ready you are, Ahngoose?"

"Yes, La'ann. Ready I am."

The sound of clear Batololému words gave La'ann some hope for Ahngoose.

Su'ban had requested only Ahngoose's presence, but La'ann turned to Ee'laan nonetheless, wishing no insult. "Ee'laan, join us you will?"

"No, Mélesi, La'ann. With Hol'imm, go I will. The ways of young kùmu'lio, teach me, he will."

"Good it is. With kùmu'lio, good you are."

Anxious to get to the day's business, La'ann turned to Angus. "Ahngoose come, go we must. Malilibamoto, bring you will."

At Angus's blank stare, La'ann began to pantomime, but Eilen interrupted. "The 'cold flame.' He wants you to bring your hand-torch."

Leaving Angus to follow, Là'ann turned toward the common area. Paying little attention to the few small animals scurrying from the path, he strode rapidly past the briar-walls. Ro'ann would ask him to man the second boat. He did not like the boats. They were never still. The sound of Ro'ann's voice pushed La'ann faster, annoyed that he might be late.

....

Su'ban had asked for his participation. *Why?* Emerging from the 'ann family compound, Angus looked to find La'ann standing on the fringe of a small crowd gathered near the entrance to the stables. *Perhaps we'll ride kùmu'lio again.* The crowd began to break, filing toward the far exit tree. *The fields again. At least this time I'll be among experienced company.* Angus watched the group march past. *Curious. They all wear nothing but loin coverings.*

Walking at the end of the file, La'ann stopped to gather Angus. Angus offered the hand-torch. La'ann grunted an approval then reached to pull a leather strap from his waist. "Strong tied, it must be."

The work party became bunched in front of the colōfn tree exit. While they waited La'ann continued his inspection. He pointed to Angus's feet and chest. "Wet below, it is. No covering wear you must."

The instruction matched Angus's observation and left him wondering about their destination. Regular maintenance left the passageway adorned with woody stems on which to hang his things. Bare-chested, Angus grinned. Thinking that La'ann might share his amusement in their contrasting skin colors, he rubbed both hands over his body. La'ann's failure to share the joke surprised him. *Why the grim face?*

Stepping into the interior of the hollow tree, Angus heard muffled sounds blending into a low-pitched, drumming echo. The last time he'd descended these steps, he had nearly died.

Sparse illumination from a few algae lamps did nothing to bolster confidence.

The procession descended past the midfloor exit and Angus's pulse quickened. How far into that black nothing would they descend? What new danger would this planet throw at him from these depths? Moving ever lower, Angus stepped closer to the tree wall.

The darkness became thick, as if it had the power to absorb their feeble lantern light. Each footfall required more care. Were the dim algae lamps not present, a hand at the nose would not be seen. Even the view upward became lost in the gloom. Angus's apprehension grew when the stairway beneath his feet began to feel wet and slippery. Reaching for the security of the colōfn tree's inside surface, he found there a slimy film.

Ahead, Angus saw the work party disappear through an exit passage. Angus followed to find them all crowding onto a slick platform. His bare feet found uncertain footing. The world around lay concealed in darkness, yet he knew it was filled with water. Heavy, humid air smelling of damp decay carried to his ears the sound of isolated drops striking still water.

Several algae lamps, now clustered closely on the flat platform, provided barely enough light to allow movement. Seeing an opportunity, Angus pulled the hand-torch into his hand and shone it onto the platform. Among eyes accustomed only to dim algae lamps, the sudden glare brought instant confusion. Persuasion from both La'ann and Ro'ann restored a general calm and allowed Angus to illuminate the loading of two moored, blunt-ended skiffs.

The surrounding darkness devoured light as though nothing existed beyond the platform. Water lay all around yet Angus could see nothing. Without thinking he turned the torch beam outward, catching but a brief glint before a volley of verbal angst forced the beam's return. He would have to wait.

His hand-torch had become much too helpful.

Angus dutifully aided the loading until everyone was on board. La'ann moved to take his place near what might have been a prow of one boat. Both blunt ends looked very much alike. Waiting to take his turn, Angus watched La'ann step into the boat. La'ann's tall frame seemed unmatched to the boat's motion. Angus had never imagined La'ann as awkward at anything. When La'ann had finally seated himself, Angus stepped in easily to sit next to La'ann and quenched the torch.

La'ann pushed the boat away from the mooring to float freely on black water. Then he sat back with head bowed. "Now wait we must." A silence settled over the entire group; everyone huddled close, secure in a cocoon of soft algae-lamp light while the ominous blackness hovered just outside its reach. No one spoke.

Feeling naked in the cool air, Angus found it difficult to sit still. His curiosity nagged. *What's out there?* This time he acted more warily. "La'ann, Malilibamoto use I will."

At La'ann's grunted assent, he pointed a tight beam directly upward. Thick humidity gave the beam a canvas upon which to paint a visible path. Angus let his eyes follow the path upward, finding an illuminated end in a dense black tangle of vine ends, dripping with condensation. He knew instantly that he was looking at the underside of the midforest floor, now turned into ceiling.

The overhead tangle held itself just enough distant to render details difficult to discern. Angus strained both eyes and neck. Even as he did so, something squirmed. Aware now, Angus searched and found many-legged creatures creeping along vine highways, even as slimy, legless things slithered between them. The bottom of the midfloor was very much alive. Memories of his helpless entrapment in the midfloor's mesh came into Angus's mind and he imagined creatures much like those he now saw dining on his leg. As much as the sight fascinated Angus, so his torchlight presented the boats' occupants with a view they had never before seen. Everyone, including La'ann forgot claustrophobic fears and stared at the dark, squirming mass.

The Pō'ele ceiling stood only yards above. Its proximity gave Angus reason for wonder. *That tangled layer must be very thick! I should have counted steps below the midfloor exit ... There had to be more than fifty steps?*

Angus moved the illuminated spot away from vertical. Details fled as the beam touched vegetation at increasingly oblique angles and became absorbed in the distance. When he directed the beam to one side, another colōfn tree appeared out of the darkness at mid-distance and he ran the beam down the tree's side to intersect the water line.

Dousing the hand-torch, Angus let his eyes readjust to the diffuse light of algae-lamps and thought about what he'd seen. His mental picture of the great forest became more complete. Colōfn trees, standing like the pilings of a great ocean pier, supported the midfloor and the forest above and the midfloor's thickly woven tangle sealed off the dark world below. Every setting he'd seen on this planet seemed to exist above water: the forest above him now, the great pile of detritus in the Kua'la, the floating living mass of the Marsh Plain.

Excited and wanting to share it with his friend, Angus touched La'ann's arm. La'ann's somber response came in mixed words, some understood, some not.

"Quiet be. 'Koké máiho'i. Mbalanuivanda'... we will be."

Angus looked toward the dock. It had retreated to the fringe of algae lamp power. The boats had pulled away from the great colōfn trunk. A vague thought of losing contact with that tree rose in Angus's head. He followed the line running from bow toward tree. The far end looped around a thicker line running down the tree trunk. The boats will slip down with the tide yet also hold onto the tree. *How worn are those lines? How often are they replaced?*

Feeling the boat swing, Angus knew the water had begun to flow. Wave motion rocked the boat as current roiled around the colōfn tree. Loosening the line, La'ann let it out to full length, putting the boat in smoother current away from the colōfn tree. The tree's retreat left the boats marooned in a small cocoon of soft light from the algae lamps. Angus lamented the tree's disappearance.

Time passed slowly, giving to minutes the feel of hours in a litany of collective breathing and gently swirling water. Angus's stare caught the water's wavy surface in the diffuse glow of lamps. A tiny, bright glint moving with the current pulled his attention into the water. Looking deeper he noticed tiny lights in great number, a living school flashing randomly within a large volume. As he stared, a shadow spread across the group, a shadow moving against the current, something very large. Even as he processed the sight, he felt the boat rock in the large swimmer's wake. Angus tensed, waiting for another. None came. Perhaps the large swimmer had matters other than a small boat to deal with in the retreating tide.

One long, indefinite period later a sustained swoosh eventually heralded the bottom's arrival as the last few feet of depth drained from around the colōfn trunks within earshot. The boat hull found bottom with a gritty crunch and heeled slightly to one side.

Water still flowed around the grounded boat as everyone burst into action, knotting long tether lines onto rings arranged along the inside gunwales of each boat. Becoming lost in the darkness presented a danger to everyone. Nor was there much time to do what they had come to do. The tide would soon return.

Angus stepped out of the boat, feeling gritty sand between his toes, marking the coolness of it. Algae lamps held high fanned across the area. Standing on the wet sandy ground, La'ann looked across the boat at Angus. "Ahngoose ... malilibamoto."

Activating the hand-torch, Angus adjusted it to a wide beam and elicited an approving murmur from those who saw the Pō'ele bottom as they had never before seen it. Improved lighting aided the location of traps. Several framed structures, tightly wrapped in fine mesh netting were secured by line to a metal peg turned into hard, smooth surfaces bulging from the sand. Angus noted how the bulging surfaces wound through the sand nearby, protruding somewhat more in one direction while disappearing in the other. He would have followed the upside of one of the sinuous paths, but he knew he'd better keep the torchlight shining on the work at hand.

A shout from Ro'ann announced some success. "La'ann! Máioka!"

La'ann waved, then turned back to the trap in his hands. The tide would return. Peering into the nearest trap, La'ann donned a pair of gloves before reaching inside to pull out a wiggling creature. That catch went into a bucket held by a young person Angus did not know. Scenes of similar activity surrounded the area.

At some point, people began moving toward boats, and for a short time, Angus was able to divert the torch beam. Using a narrow beam, he found a single trap and followed the course of its anchor. From its beginning, he followed the hard protrusion to see it become an undulating wall growing larger as he followed. Soon he saw the full pattern of solid buttress roots, rising high to define the sides of canyons perhaps 20 meters deep before melding into the base of a mammoth colōfn tree.

Angus might have been content to stare at the spectacle of that colōfn tree somewhat longer had not La'ann reminded him of the peril outside the boat. "Ahngoose!... Now! You return!"

As Angus settled himself and turned off the hand-torch, La'ann finished his headcount, reporting the count to himself. "Nsambo. Awa nyé." In a hailing voice, hand cupped around his mouth, he reported the boat's status to Ro'ann. "Awa nyé!"

The boats' occupants sat close, leaning against each other in harmony with the boats' tilted posture. Within only a few minutes, the sound of small waves on sand and a slight cooling in the air announced the tide's return. The boat's stern gained buoyancy in the rising water, swinging slightly before the bow lifted free. The motion prompted several hands to search for gunwales and hold tight until the boat steadied and its occupants relaxed.

Everyone relaxed, except La'ann. For him duties remained. Pulling the paddle from under the seat, he dipped it into the water and began pushing the boat backward away from the colōfn tree and keeping the tether line taut. The effort puzzled Angus until the boat's keel bumped the first of the colōfn tree's buttress roots and he could see the wall of root rising from the water at the fuzzy edge of their light bubble. La'ann's effort to hold their small craft away from any possibility of becoming wedged then seemed quite prudent.

The boat swung sideways in the tidal current toward the opposite side of the colōfn trunk. Angus could see the glow of Ro'ann's boat caught in the same tide and swinging toward him. He stiffened and reached for the side, expecting a collision. When the approaching boat swung ahead of theirs, he saluted the experience of the two boat captains and the wisdom of unequal lines.

The current pulled both boats around to the opposite side of the colōfn tree and La'ann's paddling efforts became unnecessary. Replacing the paddle under the seat, he resigned himself to the quiet wait. The sound of the tide's edge on the sand was replaced by the sound of water flowing against the boat's blunt bow. In the isolation of their algae-light cocoons, with no visual reference in the blackness, there was little but their experience to disclose that they were now rising from the bottom. The boat's occupants retreated into private thoughts and allowed the deepening waters to carry them quietly back toward the midfloor.

Time passed and all remained quiet until a sudden wave sent many hands to the boat's gunwales. Angus looked into the water. Only black depth stared back. When the second wave struck more than one short gasp escaped the boat. Angus scanned the boundaries of faint algae light. Such a large wake belonged to a fairly large creature and it had come back for a second look.

The creature's third pass came within the illuminated radius and threw a strong wave against the side, exposing the tip of a dorsal or tailfin. The boat tipped hard. Flailing legs, a startling splash and a quickly doused scream jarred Angus's thoughts awake. He saw waves receding in rings. No one else moved. Hesitating only the time it took to pull the hand-torch from his belt, Angus rose, handed the torch to La'ann, and dove into the water.

Deep cold froze his breath as Angus fought a reflex gasp. Blind in the black water, he broke the surface to look for his target. Nothing but the boat lay above water. A couple of strokes propelled him to the taut tether line running into the water from the aft end of the boat. A deep intake of breath, a dive and a strong kick sent him down again, one hand loosely wrapped around the line. Pressure told him he sank deep; too deep, deeper than he liked. He felt his chest tighten. His lungs began pressing for air. The pressure behind his eyes became pain. He saw only darkness. Then he bumped into a body.

Wrapping one arm tightly around a small waist, ignoring aching lungs, he tightened his hand around the tether line and kicked toward the surface as hard as he could. The limp form weighed more than he would have thought possible. Like thick gel, the water resisted every effort. Alarms went off in his head, screaming at him to let his lungs fill. Each beat of his heart struck his chest, each pulse rang in his ears. Panic chased reason from his mind. His head swam and his vision filled with scintillation. The tether line fell from his hand. With a last vestige of consciousness, he set his legs kicking and his free arm pulling at the water.

Breaking into air with a rush, his free arm slapped the water. In one hoarse gasp, he opened his lungs to the air. Through water-filled ears, he heard a torrent of voices. La'ann's voice rose above the others. "Ahngoose! Ahngoose! Awa! Awa bisó na!"

Turning onto his back Angus held the young head above water and struggled to reach the boat with one free hand. An eternity later, La'ann reached out to grab a limp arm and pull both Angus and his charge close to the boat. A push from Angus and a pull from La'ann brought the slouched body over the side and nearly toppled La'ann. Angus bobbed in the water. For a moment he thought he might just rest there a while, until he remembered that he wasn't alone in the black water.

Angus reached to pull himself out, nearly sending another passenger into the water. Before trying a second time, he moved to the stern end and waved everyone forward. "Yokima!" he said, hoping he had the right word. One strong kick and a hefty pull sent him over the side, dripping water enough to add a couple of centimeters to the perimeter of the large puddle already formed in the bottom of the boat.

La'ann prodded the limp body. Angus realized that he knew the face—the young 'nii to whom he owed a debt. He urged everyone toward the bow. Draping Li'nii's limp form across the rear seat, arms dangling, Angus placed stiff arms onto her back. In slow motion he let his weight fall, feeling how far he might go. Water splattered from her mouth. Releasing his weight, he pulled her arms out and up as much as he dared. Upon repeating the same actions, Li'nii coughed, spit water and sucked in a wheezing breath of air. Many others breathed along with her.

Ro'ann's hails finally caught La'ann's attention. La'ann shouted to Ro'ann. Angus understood only the mention of his name.

Content to sit in the bottom of the boat, Angus sat feeling quite drained. The humid air helped but he was thankful for warm bodies around him. For the remainder of their ascent, he heard only the sound of Li'nii's breathing and of water lapping against the sides of the boat.

When La'ann finally shone Angus's hand-torch onto the loading dock, Ro'ann pulled his boat in close. The day's catch came out one bucket at a time. The boat's hull rose with each occupant's egress until Ro'ann climbed out and was able to pull the empty boat up onto a submerged mooring.

Many hands aided La'ann's turn at the small dock. Many hands reached to help Li'nii stand wobbly on the dock.

Helping others and unloading buckets of Pō'ele bounty, Angus stayed aboard until only he and La'ann remained. When he did finally rise, Angus found a host of hands eagerly reaching to help him. Atop the dock, he stood amid the entire work-party and endured a number of ardent pats upon his back.

Last from the boat, La'ann climbed out to stand smiling before Angus. "Brave you are, Ahngoose. Large my heart grows."

His own emotion surprised Angus. While he stood mute, La'ann pulled the hand-torch from his waist and turned its return into ceremony. With a sweeping gesture toward the exit door, he offered an honor. "Home, lead you will."

Angus trod the return steps with an energized gait and followed the beam of his hand-torch with some pleasure, climbing the many steps up to the village in the company of the low drumming echo of many footsteps.

Most of the workgroup dispersed. A few stayed to await the division of spoils. Bucket contents found their way onto the common area deck. Hard-shelled bottom-walking creatures wriggled legs in the air, flat fish flopped on the wet deck, long tentacles laid limp beside them. Ro'ann oversaw the division of spoils into five small family-bound piles and mediated a few small disputes over particular prizes. There were too few limp tentacles to go around. Ro'ann eventually knelt and cut them into smaller pieces, satisfying everyone. The disposition of a particular large-eyed creature was settled with barter. Ro'ann's ever-present grin aided his skills as a peacemaker.

Su'ban approached, staff in hand. As soon as he noticed her, Ro'ann grabbed the one sealed bucket and held it out for her to see. "Máioka, Su'ban."

"Pleased I am, Ro'ann. Good medicine make it will."

While Ro'ann enjoyed Su'ban's appreciation, La'ann could hardly contain himself, finally interrupting at Su'ban's first hesitation. Before Su'ban could register any displeasure, La'ann began speaking so rapidly that Angus understood little. A few gestures told him that La'ann presented Su'ban with a recount of Li'nii's rescue. La'ann eventually wound down and Su'ban turned to Angus and raised her staff. "A sign it is. For your future, looking, I do."

Carrying the prized máioka, Ro'ann left with Su'ban as La'ann and Angus walked back toward the 'ann family area. Reaching there, La'ann stopped and placed hands on Angus's shoulders. "Mélesi, Ahngoose ... Mélesi."

Angus accepted La'ann's simple 'thank you' with pride. At that moment, he could remember no other incident in his many years as a starship captain that felt quite as satisfying.

CHAPTER 16
High Forest

Angus followed La'ann and Ro'ann. Eilen hung back behind Angus. Both La'ann and Ro'ann wore the same glittering cloaks she had not seen since that first day on the marsh plain. The absence of Ro'ann's ready grin put Eilen on alert. Emerging from the briar-walled path the group met a filled common area. High-forest cloaks adorned each body. The entire assembly shimmered in morning light. *Well now! This is new.*

A barrage of greetings met Angus's appearance. "Mboté, Ahngoose." Hands reached to touch his arm.

So, that's it—Angus, the hero.

An open path ushered La'ann toward the entrance to the kùmulio stables. Before the tree stood a clansman looking very like Ra'ahj although sporting somewhat longer fuzzy grey hair. Although she had not met this man, Eilen knew of Ra'ahj's brother Ren'ahj. Her widening circle of friends had begun to pay dividends.

Nor had she ever met the man standing behind Ren'ahj. Yet she knew him as well. The long scar slashed across his face could only belong to one man. Ne'ban, she knew, oversaw the Hanging Gardens. She had heard the story of a long fall and of a young Su'ban's heroic efforts to save his sight. The exploit had set Su'ban firmly upon the path toward clan leader.

Highforest cloaks and many baskets in many hands told Eilen the assembly intended to spend their day somewhere among cultivated vines in the forest canopy. On any other day, Ne'ban and his troupe would be there already. Homage to Angus's exploit seemed to have delayed the day's work.

Ren'ahj raised a hand, sending a ripple of sparkling color across his body and a wave of quiet through the crowd.

With a respectful nod and a low sweep, La'ann theatrically presented the two senior clansmen. "Ahngoose … Ee'laan … Ren'ahj and Ne'ban, meeting to you I give." La'ann's formality seemed to require a response. Angus looked at Eilen. "Maybe you should say something."

"Not this time. You're the hero."

Angus drew breath, hesitating long enough to put together a few carefully pronounced Batololému words. "Ren'ahj … Ne'ban … from your greeting, honor, we have."

Placing a hand on each of Angus's shoulders Ren'ahj spoke in solemn tones. "Great fear, the black water brings … Much courage you have, Ahngoose … Proud brothers, we are." An assenting murmur ran through the crowd.

The declaration surprised Eilen. Did Angus understand how important the word 'brother' might be?

Ceremony complete, Ren'ahj announced its end. "Go now, we must." Privately, he added, "With us, come you must, Ahngoose … Su'ban say." Eilen could only assume the invitation included her.

Already in motion, Ne'ban made his way toward the kùmu'lio stalls. Behind him, nearly all those present, funneled through the entrance. Ren'ahj, La'ann, Ro'ann, Angus and Eilen then stood around a small collection of tools and clothing. Ren'ahj offered two lightweight cloaks. "In Wēkiu, wear."

The offer banished Eilen's doubts. She had never seen the Hanging Gardens. Her heart beat a little faster. Accepting the garment, she tested its weight. *A little bulky, but quite light.* A wide leather band around the middle and across the shoulders gave it substance. The remainder was a loose net of thick thread onto which were sewn an orderly array of small, thin translucent wafers, lending the garment a reptilian appearance. Turning a single wafer, she noted a tiny, shallow saddle, stiff enough to resist finger pressure, but thin enough to elicit careful handling. Oblique light threw off a changing array of colors. *Beautiful.*

Forest life had already begun to seep into Eilen's soul. Stripping off her tunic, she donned the lightweight cloak, giving no thought to the decorum of her former existence. As the cloak slipped over one arm, she noticed Angus blush and look away. She hastened to wrap the cloak around her shoulders.

A sack went to Angus. "Ahngoose, take this, you will."

Pulling one strap over his head, Angus let the bag hang at his side. Ren'ahj himself had more than one rope looped over his shoulder. A number of metal hooks, loops, and spikes dangled from the belt around his waist, jingling with every movement. La'ann and Ro'ann each carried a hooked pole and a bag slung around one shoulder. Eilen waited. Nothing more came her way. *What's my job?*

After one last look at his assembled group, Ren'ahj led them through the kùmu'lio stall entrance. This time, instead of descending, they climbed. Conversation stopped. The only sound became the regular beat of Ren'ahj's hooked staff resonating within the colōfn tree's hollow interior. Soft light spilled from regularly spaced holes in the tree's thick wall, gently brightening the spiral stairway. Eilen felt a steady, gentle upward flow of air. Monotony soon devoured an endless array of steps. Sometime later, a bit weary from the effort, Eilen walked out into harsh glare, quickly covering her eyes. Misty air glowed bright with sunlight. A narrow deck wrapped around the outside of the colōfn trunk, enclosed by a vine-threaded balustrade. Shimmering leaves covered nearly everything and Eilen saw the material from which her cloak was made.

Ren'ahj led his small band to a bench some ways around the great tree's bulk. Protective masks went on first. Narrow slits limited her vision, but Eilen could let her eyes relax. After checking the fit of her mask and tightening the loops of twine around her ears, Ren'ahj pulled the cloak hood over her head.

Next came another, thick-soled pair of sandals armed with a leather toecap. A hand along one shoe's sole revealed a profusion of tiny barbs. While Ren'ahj aided Angus, Eilen watched La'ann prepare working gear. Pulling from his pack a thin leather bladder, La'ann began filling it with loose fibrous material, packing until the bladder skin stretched tight to become very much like a large egg. After lacing up the opening, he wrapped it with a thick cloth and several long cords before slipping it back into his carry bag.

When all were ready Ren'ahj led them to a single opening in the balustrade. From there a walkway extended outward as if to float in the air. Suspended from a pair of graceful curves fixed higher in the colōfn tree, its opposite end lay somewhere obscured in glowing mist. Ren'ahj walked into the fog with Ro'ann close behind. La'ann waited as Angus hesitated at the threshold. "Ahngoose, go you must."

"Sorry, La'ann. Fear, I have."

"Brave you are. Behind you will I be. Go you must."

Angus tested the bridge with one foot before taking a few unsteady steps.

Wishing to cause no more motion in the structure than necessary, Eilen waited until Angus had opened a good distance before she stepped onto the bridge. As she moved away from the colōfn tree a moist breeze rose around her, swirling like a playful sprite. The long stairway climb testified to great height, but mist obscured the view downward and blunted the sensation. Yet the motion of both air and bridge gave her unease. Her right hand closed around the thick braided rope running waist-high between vertical supports and forming the top of a loosely netted railing along each side of the walkway. La'ann's presence behind her offered reassurance.

When the bridge's far end emerged from the fog, Eilen saw her three companions waiting against another colōfn tree. With faces obscured by hoods, she took the identity of each only from the gear they carried, the clinking tools on Ren'ahj's belt, Ro'ann's coiled ropes, and Angus's single sack. They were already in motion before she reached the platform. Around the curve of the second colōfn trunk, Eilen met another suspension bridge and a moment of bewilderment when her companions moved past it to step onto yet a third bridge farther around the trunk. *A network of aerial highways.* More confident now, she moved readily onto the next bridge. This one felt different. *Less vibration.* At mid-span Eilen greeted a young clansman. "Mboté." Grateful for the chance, she stepped around a basket of yellow fruit and peered over the webbed railing to see a hanging field of vines. *Ah! A vibration dampener.*

One arm-length at a time, the young clansman pulled sections of leafy vine over the bridge railing. A raucous, rasping wail greeted his efforts. Turning her goggled face toward the source, Eilen encountered a dark green creature rapidly fluttering just a couple of arm-lengths away, squawking in obvious displeasure. *This world is a marvel.* Rising airflow ushered a sweet, flowery scent past Eilen's face, filling her with joy for the breathing forest.

La'ann's voice intruded. "Come, Ee'laan. Wēkiu, go, we must."

The word 'Wēkiu' meant 'High Forest.' Eilen hesitated. "La'ann, Wekiu this is not?"

"No Ee'laan. Above Nahélé we go. To m'pepalia."

Eilen searched for translation. *Eater of wind? A new*

creature? A memory flashed to mind. Her little hand completely engulfed by her father's. They were going to see the animals. She tugged at father's hand. *C'mon, Papa. C'mon.* Her pulse quickened.

From the far end of the bridge, Ren'ahj shouted. "Large time, we have not."

When La'ann and Eilen caught up they found Ro'ann and Angus sitting on the lowest steps of another stairway, now wrapped around the outside of the tree, leading yet higher. Ren'ahj pushed past both Ro'ann and Angus.

The security of the colōfn tree interior was gone. Treads here wound upward haphazardly, often interrupted by the topside of a living branch. Branches grew thinner and more numerous. Arboreal vines intruded. Moist air left every surface slippery to the touch. In spite of the firm grip of new footwear, Eilen reached for the stability of the solid trunk. Venturing a quick glance at Angus, hidden behind both goggles and hood, she saw his hand also seeking the tree's steady bulk. Each upward step moved into younger, thinner branches, branches with less reach than those below, branches offering less protection from Amon's glare or from buffeting wind.

Restricted vision only added to her anxiety yet the protection of her mask could not be refused. Harsh, glaring light streamed from all directions, from below as well as above. In the profusion of leaves, throwing colors from every direction and illuminating every corner of the high forest, Eilen saw the moderator that turned Amon's punishing radiation into the comfortable daylight of the midforest.

Then the stairway stopped altogether. Stepping directly into the upper branches, Eilen felt them flex under her weight. The entire tree bent under the force of each gust of wind. Security required hands as well as feet. Her muscles tensed. Her heart beat in her chest.

The three M'pepebato clansmen seemed unperturbed.

Eilen could only envy the sure grace in their movements: quick, sharp, and precise. Ren'ahj stopped to pull a rope from his shoulder and tie it around his waist. Only after Ro'ann had the free end wrapped around his back did Ren'ahj resume climbing.

No one followed. The others waited, enjoying a short rest. A few moments passed before La'ann and Ro'ann silently settled the question of who would follow. A quick nod from La'ann released Ro'ann to scramble upward, trailing a second line for La'ann's hands.

Happy to catch a breath, Eilen looked out into thinning bright fog, becoming suddenly aware of the cold. The exertion of their climb and the engulfing foliage of the trees had, until now, masked the steadily falling temperature. Even in the bright light, the air seemed to hold little heat. Her cloak defended her skin from Amon's harsh glare but held little body heat.

They were no longer in the forest. The smells and sounds of the forest had fallen behind. Gone were the squawking and chirping cacophony of the flying and crawling forest world. In this high treetop, the wind swept away both odors and sounds. Here the air was crisp and clean, devoid of the forest's dense stew of sweet and spice. Here the sound of the wind reigned above all. They sat atop a cloud formed of the moist breath of the forest drawn upward and cooled in the treetops. Eilen could just see across the topmost cloud layer, looking solid in the distance. Only the very tops of the trees peeked above the cloud, many tiny islands in a vast white sea. In her mind's eye, Eilen saw here the birthplace of the afternoon rains that cooled the village below. The wind in her ear masked the call down from Ren'ahj.

She did hear La'ann's cry. With the ends of two ropes in one hand, he climbed down toward her. He seemed uneasy. The restricted space forced him to place each foot slowly and carefully. All at once, Eilen realized how much of a burden her untrustworthy skills posed to the three native clansmen. Finally securing himself next to her, La'ann wasted little time in tying her onto one rope's end. "Good it is," he said as he tested his handiwork.

Sending an alert upward with a yank on the line, La'ann then slid away and allowed Eilen to climb. A reassuring tug beckoned her upward. Taking each step with the same care she had seen in La'ann, she moved into thinning branches. The wind seemed to blow harder and set the treetop in motion, adding its own groans to the wind's howl, as if the great tree debated the merits of her intrusion. The taut rope felt reassuring in her hand.

The short climb left Eilen breathing rapidly, fighting the rarefied air. Unrelenting wind had coerced tree limbs permanently to one side like the bristles of a brush. The midforest dwellers huddled onto the leeward side, where Ren'ahj and Ro'ann had anchored themselves into the tree, one atop the other, perched as high as they dared. The tree swayed with every gust. At her arrival, Ren'ahj acted quickly, driving a kind of eyebolt into the tree trunk. Once he fed Eilen's line through, she too became attached. Scarcely had Angus poked his head through the lower boughs before La'ann appeared immediately behind. Five intruders lined the tree's top.

A shudder flowed through Eilen's body. She hadn't felt cold since arriving on this planet. Now she shivered as though naked. Ro'ann's shout drew her mind from the cold. "M'pepalia!"

Under a shading hand, Eilen tried to follow the direction of Ro'ann's outstretched arm. Distracted by the many-colored ripples of light from his cloak and hampered by her goggles, she found no object she might call m'pepalia. She did find the treetop filled with a dense web of gossamer filaments. The web gathered upward and rose from the colōfn tree's top as a single finger-thick rope.

Angus poked Eilen's leg. "Look! There. Can you see it?"

Letting her eyes follow the line upward, Eilen spotted the "wind-eater" nest riding high above the cloud layer. With no idea of distance, she could not judge the size of the elongated form at the end of the stretched line. *Can't be too small.* That it rode steady in the wind meant more than one mooring line. The distance and her restricted vision made it difficult, but she found a second line running between the nest and another treetop. Somewhere there was a third.

Ro'ann pointed into the distance. "M'pepalia."

Searching the deep blue sky, Eilen found a small speck. Further search yielded several more wind-riding m'pepalia and understanding awoke in Eilen mind. Here lay the forest clan's tended herd. The clan called themselves m'pepebato after the creatures they tended. To what purpose she could only guess.

Barely heard above rush of wind, the sound of Ren'ahj's voice drew Eilen's ears. eyes from the sky. Reaching with a hooked pole as high as he dared, she watched him snag the nest's mooring line. Ro'ann held the stuffed bladder in his lap and busied himself tying a thin line to its end. La'ann was occupied threading a thin wooden hoop into one side of the unfurled bladder cover.

The wind made conversation difficult and Eilen could do little but watch the work unfold, wondering all the while what her companions were doing and why she and Angus deserved the privilege of being there at all.

By the time Ren'ahj had hauled in a portion of nest line and managed to anchor it into the branches near his perch, he had only to wait a short time before both Ro'ann and La'ann completed their tasks. When La'ann finished, he handed to Ro'ann a long, open-ended sack, looking every bit like the sheath for some large phallic idol. Ro'ann joined the open sack to the bladder and carefully handed the assembled apparatus upward.

Loose coils of rope hung everywhere. What wasn't attached to one of the climbers or to the m'pepalia nest was attached to Ro'ann's assembled apparatus. Eilen watched Ren'ahj hold the end of the woven sheath open to the wind, allowing it to fill into a gently tapered shape. Releasing his hold, Ren'ahj let it rise, pulling line through his hand until it rode the wind like a toy kite. The purpose of the apparatus became clear as Eilen watched Ren'ahj fasten the kite onto a metal tool now loosely affixed to the m'peplia nest's anchor line. All the pieces of the puzzle fell into place as Ren'ahj freed the anchor line to once again pull taut and straight, presenting a smooth highway leading directly up to the m'pepalia nest.

Unwinding a thin restraining cord from a crude reel held between both hands, Ren'ahj dispatched his bladder-kite. It rose upon the anchor line, straining under Ren'ahj's control until it became a small dot and merged into the dark shape of the m'papalia nest. Ren'ahj passed the line reel down to Ro'ann and then began to pull a few arm lengths of the bladder-kite line back down only to release them a moment later. After repeating this odd process several times, Eilen caught on to the purpose behind the stuffed bladder—a simple lure. Ren'ahj fished for m'pepalia.

Do we intend to capture that creature? The idea thrilled her. Watching the high nest with anticipation, she knew that Ren'ahj had succeeded with his lure as he began hauling in his fishing line in earnest. For several minutes, loose folds of cord fell to Ro'ann, who furiously rewound it on the reel from which it had come.

Staring into the bright sky, Eilen tried to spot the ensnared creature, finding only disappointment at the sight of nothing more than the same small dot that had taken the upward trip.

The recovered fishing lure looked very much different now. A sticky wet coating covered the bladder. Avoiding its touch, Ren'ahj wrapped the bladder in dense felt cloth. Not until it was safely wrapped was Ro'ann able to satisfy Eilen's curiosity. Holding the cloth open, he showed her a deformed bladder, punctured by a pair of slime-covered holes, perhaps two finger-widths in diameter. Ro'ann beamed with satisfaction. "M'pepalia bite."

Ren'ahj had just milked his cow and captured venom for Su'ban's elixirs.

The wind-sack, looking fat and heavy, no longer billowed freely in the wind. Ren'ahj carefully pulled the stiffener from its opening to let the bag close, handing it down to Ro'ann with the opening bunched in his hand. Again, Ro'ann showed Eilen their spoils. An olio of small balloons and long, thin tentacles filled the bag. With one flat hand bobbing in the air Ro'ann explained. "Téa'éke. M'pepalia eat."

The words meant 'floating ball.' Eilen imagined the little balloons floating upon currents of air, dangling tentacles like a jellyfish in a temperate sea. She reached in to touch one.

Ro'ann yanked the sack away. "Te! Te! Ee'laan. Pain bad."

Yet another peril for the ignorant.

Watching Ro'ann and La'ann secure the day's spoils, a disappointed Eilen thought the adventure finished. Thinking they would soon leave the glorious treetop, she looked for direction. She was surprised to see Ren'ahj reach up and grab the m'pepalia's mooring line and begin hauling it in. With every tug, Ren'ahj fought the wind as it strained to draw him from his perch. Lengths of line fell to Ro'ann. Ro'ann bared his knife as Eilen watched in amazement. *Does he intend to set the wind-rider* adrift? His purpose did not become clear until she noticed how carefully he cut, only partially severing the line.

Returning the knife to its sheath, Ro'ann began unwrapping a single section from the twisted line, coiling a free length of cut line in one hand while the uncut portion fell toward La'ann.

Eilen's excitement grew with every meter of line accumulating at La'ann's feet. The wind-riding creature came ever nearer. She might see it after all.

The nest's growing image fed her imagination. Shaped like a tube, it seemed, as long as a man and nearly as wide around. A fairly large creature occupied that nest, and Eilen could almost feel its growing anger. Freed of the steady restraint from three taut mooring lines, the descending nest now fell prey to the wind's every whim, jostled by every gust and eddy. The creature within would surely arrive angry and dangerous.

The nest neared and Ren'ahj changed roles. Yielding the job of pulling to La'ann, he retrieved one of the long, hooked poles. With a wary eye, he held the pole at the ready. The creature showed itself in a single lunge. A strike from Ren'ahj's pole sent it in retreat. La'ann and Ro'ann tensed. Angus uttered in surprise. Eilen almost cooed. *Magnificent!*

Like some huge beetle, the m'pepalia's head filled the opening with a bright red shield, throwing off sparkling sunlight with every movement. Her love of all things living stirred in Eilen's breast. The shining face came in two, slightly concave halves, symmetrically arranged alongside a vertical central ridge. *That structure looks defensive. Does some more fearsome predator ride the air around here?* A row of hollow pits lined each side of the face-shield. *Olfactory openings? Why does it swing that big head? -Where are the eyes?* At both top and bottom, the facial ridge blended into a sinister tusk, bent forward in two long tapering curves, not quite meeting in front of the hard shield. *No oral cavity. How does this beast feed?* Even as she posed the question, the lower tusk erupted in a long, thin wriggling worm, emerging to taste the air. *Vertical jaws.* With rapid, repeated impacts, the two tusk-ends beat together. Straining to hear above the rush of wind, Eilen imagined she could hear a hard, clacking sound. *That creature is shouting 'threat' as loud as it can.* And Eilen knew exactly how that deep wound in the egg-bladder had been inflicted. *What a magnificent creature!*

Ren'ahj shouted to Ro'ann, not more than an arm's length away. "Cut! Ro'ann, cut!"

La'ann held the intact line steady and Ro'ann slashed through the loose line. Under La'ann's metered control, the wind drew the m'pepalia nest upward. Ro'ann added his hands to the process and, in much less time than it had taken to bring it down, they returned the nest to its place astride the wind. The m'pepalia would soon repair the damaged line, restoring strength to be harvested again another day.

They had what they sought: a section of m'pepalia fiber would become rope, a venom-filled bladder would supply raw material for Su'ban's medicines, and a sack full of téa'éke carcasses would become dinner.

Ren'ahj nodded to La'ann. "Down now."

Last to arrive, La'ann was first to leave. Angus quickly followed, perhaps too quickly. More than once Ro'ann was forced to brace the safety rope and contain a misstep. It seemed Angus had just begun his descent when Ro'ann set down Angus' rope to take into his hands the free rope tied around Eilen's waist. "Go now, Ee'laan. With care step."

Already wary, Eilen moved cautiously, as if the price of each foot placement may come too dear. *I will not slip. I will not slip.* On the way up, she had clearly seen every handhold. The downward journey now located each new foothold far from her scrutiny. On the way up her weight hung steadily below each shifting hold. Now her weight rode more precariously above changing footholds. Going down happened too fast. All at once, her weight descended upon an untested foot placement. The foot slipped atop a knot. Her ankle rolled. A jolt of pain rushed up her leg. Suddenly off balance, a handhold failed. The wind carried away her cry. "Nooooooo!"

A strong rope and Ro'ann's skill limited her fall to a mere few feet. She should have suffered nothing worse than a bruised side, but the sudden jerk threw her head against a bare branch. Dazed and disoriented, she hung upside-down. Blood pounding in her ears, she struggled to return upright. Nothing beyond hips prevented her from slipping completely from the rope's hold. Her head throbbed.

"AAAANGUS!"

The rope slipped. Eilen fell. The loop caught the crook of her knees. Hanging high above the midforest, upturned at the end of a thin line, she turned slowly like a spider's uneaten meal. Goggles dangled from one ear. Blood pounded in both ears. In the wind, Eilen heard the sound of La'ann's voice and struggled to make sense of the Batololému words. "Ee'laan! Slow go!"

Still groggy, she bent and reached for the rope, managing to get a hand on the loop. Straining every muscle, she pulled herself upright and wrapped a wrist and forearm around the taut line. Unable to see, she clung, breathing hard and fast, and waited for the pounding in her ears to subside. When wits returned, she lowered her body through the loop until it became wedged under her arms, letting her feet dangle free.

La'ann's voice carried over the wind. "Hold ... Ro'ann, hold!"

Eilen felt movement in the taut line.

"Ee'laan, swing you must"

Seeing only a blur, Eilen kicked both legs toward what might be the tree trunk. Upon her second try, she felt another hand pull the rope along with her effort.

"Again Ee'laan. Again."

The next kick met a firm hand around one foot and hard surface under the other. Then a reassuring arm wrapped around Eilen's waist. Angus's voice never sounded so comforting. "You gave me quite a start with that stunt. Please don't do it again."

Eilen would never remember the long descent. When she, Angus, Ren'ahj, Ro'ann and La'ann regained the security of the village common, La'ann helped her down to sit against the colōfn trunk and await Su'ban's attention.

Su'ban's examination hurt Eilen's body much less than it wounded her pride. A pair of probing hands and attention to

Eilen's protests gave Su'ban all the data she needed. "Mend, it will."

CHAPTER 17
Membership

Bright light filled Su'ban's shelter. The haunting shadows of previous visits receded now into the smallest niches, revealing the trappings of Su'ban's life, furnishings unseen elsewhere in the village: table, chairs, a raised sleeping platform, a stepstool. Several shelves hung from the back wall lined with tools and containers of many types. Larger items stood in stacks at the far end. Opening onto the common area, Su'ban's private quarters were large enough to house a good portion of an entire family unit. Her unique status shone from all sides.

The massive worktable had always been there, but now, as Angus and Eilen sat quietly awaiting Su'ban's wishes, its conspicuous presence added weight to Su'ban's importance. Laying a hand on its surface, Angus realized how very solid it appeared. The smooth, flatness of it spoke of capabilities yet unseen in the forest world. A mundane, unnoticed property in his previous life, here among Nahélé's people this simple quality seemed extraordinary.

A bowl of water rested alone atop the table. Afloat within the bowl, a small cup of oil held a flame flickering at the end of a thin stiff wick. A wisp of smoke rose to lace the air with spice. Rapping a knuckle on the tabletop, Angus sent ripples across the water's surface. A tiny boat traversed a miniature sea and he saw the flame's yellow-red colors reflect off minute dancing waves. Su'ban settled into the chair across the table; a tsunami rolled across the sea.

Is there excitement in that face? Hard to tell with these people. Angus had learned to read more obvious expressions. Smiles, grins, frowns and outright anger caught his attention, but subtle facial postures or glints of an eye remained elusive. A lifetime of reading colored irises framed in white left Angus ill-equipped to see emotion within black-upon-brown M'pepebato eyes. Now, the crinkles around Su'ban's eyes had Angus thinking he saw mirth there. The sudden summons had put him on alert. Su'ban did everything with purpose. They should be used to it, but it had been a while since her last call. Angus could only wonder about her intent.

Attentive to Su'ban's command, Angus and Eilen remained silent. She often approached her topic slowly, circling like a wary predator. On this occasion, she opened softly. "Upon you, dwell, my spirit does."

Su'ban looked directly at Eilen. "Learn you have, Ee'laan ... To our ways, you come. Pleased, I am ... Our speaking ... learn you do. Pleased, we are." With a glance down toward Eilen's bandaged ankle, she added, "For your pain, small fear, all M'pepebato have."

Then Su'ban stopped and looked into the small lamp flame. When her head rose again, her eyes settled on Angus. In a quiet, somber tone, she said, "For you, Ahngoose, uneasy my spirit grew ... Among M'pepebato, walk you do. See M'pepebato, you do not."

Letting her eyes drift again to the lamp flame, she spoke more slowly. "In another place, your spirit dwells ... For your spirit, much fear, feel I do." Then her tone changed. Wrinkles formed at the corners of her mouth and she looked into Angus's eyes. "In the Pō'ele, wake you do... For you now, Ahngoose, easy my spirit rests. Among us now, you are."

Placing a weathered hand upon the tabletop, she ended the thought. "Good it is."

Angus could think of nothing to say. Perhaps nothing was required. His gaze dropped to the hand on the table, tracing tendons radiating from Su'ban's wrist and the sinuous paths of veins, wondering how many years had etched the rugged landscape of that hand. He nodded in acknowledgement.

Su'ban's half-smile then hardened and a more serious tone returned to her voice. "M'pepebato, become, you must ... Good it is."

Angus had just enough presence to realize what a remarkable statement Su'ban had made. Did he hear correctly? He glanced at Eilen. Su'ban must expect a response. Conflicting thoughts swirled through his head. The honor of being considered a clansman should be acknowledged. At the same time, he wondered just what 'becoming' entailed.

While Angus sat formulating a response, Eilen's excitement took control, letting Su'ban know how pleasing the offer felt. "Great honor we have, Su'ban. Good it is."

Su'ban's soft smile echoed Eilen's feelings. "Good it is."

·····················

The filled Mingi hummed. Letting his eyes roam across the tiered assembly, Angus tried to count the many faces he knew, a number now grown large. The entire village might be present. Most of the 'ann family members sat atop the first tier and he realized that his presence and Eilen's standing among the group of neophytes on the Mingi stage had much to do with that fact. Eilen's apparent excitement seemed quite appropriate.

Unsure of just what he might expect, Angus tried to appear calm. Hands absently roamed over his head and face. The mat of lengthening hair and the long coarse whiskers felt strange. During his first days in the village, the pale color of his skin advertised foreignness. Lately, his alien stature was more loudly announced by the shaggy mane. Yet nothing concealed his blue eyes, still alien enough to startle any forest dweller unknown to him. The feel of his mane sent his mind back to another time when he had once stubbornly clung to the customs of his orphan origins, retaining natural body hair, choosing to conform through vigilant care, while Starfleet shipmates permanently shed theirs—another place, another time. Conscious of his hair, white skin and blue eyes, Angus looked into the sea of faces. *How must I look to them?*

Angus glanced at the three young people standing to his left. They stood soberly still. Perhaps they've seen it all before. Perhaps they felt little of the same anxiety as he.

Su'ban had said only that they would enter the Moésika and that it involved the ingestion of one of her potions. Eilen's explanation that 'Moésika' loosely meant 'Dreamworld' did nothing to ease Angus' apprehension. Su'ban's potions had proven quite powerful and effective as healing medicines. This one sounded more ominous.

Su'ban stood. A deep silence spread through the Mingi. Regaled in colorful cloak and headdress, Su'ban stepped forward and faced the crowd. She began with a steady cadence, reciting, in a somber, clear and full voice, what could only be a practiced litany. "Seekers today we have ... Seekers, to Nahélé, have come ... Seekers wishing people of Nahélé to be ... Allow them, must we?"

The entire clan answered, filling the Mingi with a loud resonance, "Yes, we must." In cadence, Su'ban continued, "To Nahélé, these children, who gives?"

Three couples rose from their seats on the first tier of the assembled clan and descended the side steps toward the center stage. Angus had just begun to wonder who sponsored him when he noticed La'ann and Ro'ann rising from their seats in the first row.

All three couples, as well as La'ann and Ro'ann, stepped

189

around the group of candidates, each finding a particular candidate to stand behind. Angus turned his head enough to see La'ann behind him and Ro'ann behind Eilen. The touch of La'ann's hand upon his shoulder awakened Angus's pride. The growing bond between him and La'ann gave Angus reason to stand straighter.

As sponsors assembled Su'ban turned and waited. She then spoke to the candidates. "Join us, you will?" Simultaneously from every candidate came the uneven response, "Join you, I will." Anyone unaware of the ritual litany might not have understood the jumbled aggregate.

Those few words seemed to comprise the oral ritual. Su'ban turned again to face the Mingi crowd. As she did so, a villager rose from the edge of the crowd and stepped down the side carrying a tray supporting six cups.

To the crowd, Su'ban spoke. "Leave you now, we do. To the Moésika we go. Return soon, we will." She then turned to face the five candidates and took a cup from the tray. The porter then passed in front of the five candidates, pausing long enough for each to remove a cup. Waiting until all five held a cup in one hand, Su'ban raised her cup. "With me, come," she said before tipping the contents into her mouth.

Only Angus hesitated. He held the cup close and looked into it. A couple of finger widths of dark-colored liquid stared back from the bottom. A sharp odor stung his nostrils. He looked up again, to see Su'ban's gaze fixed firmly upon him.

The warm liquid left a bitter taste in his mouth.

Searching his senses, Angus tried to capture the onset of the drug's effects. It came in a rush leaving virtually no chance to register the realization. A sudden warm tremor washed over every portion of his body. Muscles tensed. His whole body quivered. The moment passed and he felt no different than before.

He turned to look at Eilen standing beside him, erect and still, staring at the Mingi crowd. When she turned and returned a reassuring smile, he felt euphoric. His senses seemed enhanced. Strange new smells assaulted his nose. He looked down to see a small hard-shelled creature on the deck at his feet, absolutely sure he could hear the creature's footstep sounding loud and low like the resonance of a large drum. Then a deep silence fell and, for a moment he could hear only his own thoughts.

Su'ban waited, silently examining the group. "Follow me now." Angus flinched at the sound of perfect Standard Galactic speech.

Leading a parade of candidates up the side steps, Su'ban began talking. Angus's fascination at Su'ban's fluent command of Standard Galactic held him listening with rapt attention. How had she acquired such skill? Why had she chosen to plod along with his poor Batololému?

Upon reaching the commons deck atop the Mingi Angus looked back down toward the Mingi stage. La'ann stood frozen, his arm held out nearly parallel to the deck, a relaxed look on his face. Why was La'ann holding such an uncomfortable posture? Why did he wear that look on his face? Why was he not moving?

Su'ban walked toward her shelter where she climbed up to stand on the bench and looked down on the small group. She seemed more agile than Angus had ever before seen her. Angus looked upward to stare at a small creature silhouetted by the hazy glow of the upper forest. The creature floated still, frozen in flight, suspended above Su'ban's shelter.

Su'ban began speaking. Her voice sounded fresh and young but seemed to come from somewhere far off. She spoke of a time long past, when a people called M'boso roamed the worlds of the night sky doing Uko's bidding, eventually settling within the comfort of Nahélé's arm. She spoke of gifts, gifts brought from many scattered worlds met along the M'boso journey, gifts of knowledge; knowledge of many different kinds given to each village under Nahélé's protection;

knowledge allowing her to fashion medicines for the people of Nahélé. She told of the many different clans and of the many different kinds of knowledge they kept for Nahélé. Then she looked directly at Angus and seemed to speak to him alone.

In an instant, she stood before him, near enough to touch. Her eyes filled his vision. He became aware of nothing but the warm brown sclera of those eyes and the deep black pools they surrounded. When she spoke, her voice sounded loud and strong in his ears as if her lips moved not finger widths away.

In perfect Standard, she said, "Angus, heed my words. I have seen many years. Soon Nahélé will ask for my soul. The knowledge I carry must not be lost. The Clan will need another Keeper.

"You and Eilen came from the night sky like our ancient M'boso. In you I see new knowledge. You have been sent by Uko."

Su'ban then seemed to recite. She identified medicines. With each name, she spoke of preparation and uses. That much Angus understood, but much of what she said made no sense. The words seemed clear, but the meaning escaped his grasp. He knew as she uttered the words that she spoke in Standard, yet he could not hold the meaning, as though the ability to understand his own language had abandoned him.

Then, as suddenly as she had come to him, Su'ban stood apart, back upon the bench of her shelter. She stood quietly then turned to step down and lead the initiates back across the commons and down into the Mingi. As he descended, Angus stared ahead at La'ann and Ro'ann, still frozen in the same posture as he last saw them. In fact, no one seated in the Mingi had stirred in the slightest since he had entered Su'ban's Moésika. Understanding dawned. Time within Su'ban's Moésika flowed at a different pace than it did without.

Returning to the Mingi stage, the new M'pepebato clansmen filed behind their sponsors, closer to the colōfn tree, where a new set of cups rested on the backbench. Su'ban bid them all 'drink', as she lifted her cup, hesitating only to see them all follow.

Angus felt the cool, sweet liquid flow over his tongue. The cup had not been drained before the dull murmur of the Mingi crowd came flooding back into his ears. He watched La'ann's outstretched arm fall to his side as if he had only at that moment become aware of its weight.

In a voice loud enough for the entire Mingi to hear, Su'ban said simply, "Return we have."

The crowd responded with a collective, "Welcome, you are," and brought the ceremony to an end, prompting the gathered clan to begin rising and filing out of the Mingi.

Standing near the front of the Mingi stage, the sponsors remained. Su'ban's words came at their backs, forcing them all to turn to see their sponsored friends, now suddenly standing where they had not been but a short moment before.

La'ann turned, grinning, shocked not at all by the sudden vanishing act. Angus realized he now shared another profound experience with his friend, La'ann.

In spite of the stiffness and fatigue that seemed to have descended over his entire body, Angus felt uncommonly pleased. He stepped toward La'ann. Before he could speak Su'ban intervened. "Ahngoose ... Ee'laan ... with you speak, I will," she said as she turned and joined the crowd leaving the Mingi.

Su'ban walked surprisingly fast when she wanted to, briskly climbing the Mingi stairway and pausing for nothing as she made her way directly back to her shelter. Angus and Eilen followed to sit again at Su'ban's table and quietly await her pleasure.

For a moment Su'ban simply stood, leaning on her staff, looking at the two new M'Pepebato clansmen. At length, she said, "Hear all, you did not. Haku'iké be, you will not. Sad, I am."

Lowering herself onto a chair, she said, with resignation,

"Try again, another time, perhaps we will."

Angus tried to speak. His head swarmed with questions. Eilen interrupted before he could utter a word. "Su'ban ... Speak, may I?"

"Yes. Speak, you may."

In precise and respectful Batololému, Eilen ventured exactly where Angus had wanted to go. "The language of our home, you spoke. Know it how, you did?"

Su'ban hesitated. Her face changed, perplexed perhaps. When she finally spoke, her words came slowly, each word carefully spoken. "Your homeworld speaking, say, I did not ... The speaking of the M'boso, say, I did ... The speaking of your homeworld, hear, you did ... In the Moésika, so it is."

Considering Su'ban's message Eilen hesitated before posing another question. "Speak now the language of the M'boso, can you?"

"M'boso language, speak now, I cannot. In the Moésika, speak, I can."

CHAPTER 18
Nomads

La'ann had failed. Angus would become no hunter. Su'ban had failed. Angus would become no Haku'iké. A future within Nahélé's world seemed elusive. Years of travel between stars had left him with skills of little use in the great forest. The prospect weighed and blurred the distinction between one day and the next.

Midday cast a hazy glow over the village and a lethargic cloud over Angus's psyche. He stood silently watching as Su'ban attended a large pot hanging above one of the fire recesses near her shelter. Su'ban leaned on her staff while three young people dressed in minimum garments performed her bidding. Angus recognized only one young 'nii among them.

At Su'ban's request, the young 'nii offered a stick. Dipping it into the pot, Su'ban brought its end to her tongue, frowning at the taste. A quick gesture from Su'ban prompted the young 'nii to produce a long-necked earthen bottle, from which Su'ban poured a bit of content into the pot. She had almost replaced the bottle's plug when Angus held out a hand. "See, can I?"

Su'ban's questioning eye held Angus's arm still for a long moment before she extended the bottle.

Bringing the uncapped bottle near his nose, Angus wafted a hand across the top. A strong acrid scent arrived in a rush, sending the bottle in swift retreat. "Oohph!"

The bottle's return solicited a sympathetic wrinkled nose from Su'ban's assistant.

With her walking staff, Su'ban reached into the pot and pulled up a section of fat, swollen m'pepalia line. The bundle sagged and spread under its own weight, displaying the countless individual fibers from which it was made. Angus recalled how, as he carried the raw line down from the Wēkui, he had thought it suitable for fashioning a good rope. Now he saw the clan's ropes as more refined, fashioned of finer fiber. Yet, where were they woven? The village harbored no weaving or spinning apparatus.

A shout sent Angus's questions to rest among many such unexplained facets of his new world. Turning toward the sound, he saw a young villager running from the direction of the midforest exit-tree. "Bakeisiká! Bakeisiká!" It took him a moment to realize that she had come from the fields and that someone known as 'the Nomads' had arrived.

Furrows formed across Su'ban's brow. Without speaking, she turned abruptly to walk toward her shelter, leaving her assistants to complete without guidance whatever work remained.

....

Eilen immediately realized she must not linger. The 'ann family stirred. Situated next to Angus, her billet now lay only an extended foot away from giving him a waking nudge. He grunted and rolled away.

The morning meal came quickly, uncooked, and accompanied by little talk. The entire 'ann family seemed anxious to meet the new day. Even the little ones understood that dawdling would solicit disapproval. Cold breakfast fare allowed the deferral of cleanup chores. Trays and bowls remained on the deck as the 'ann family moved toward the commons. Eilen saw Tu'ann leave and rushed to catch up with her just outside the 'annliboko. A wall of backsides met them both. Tu'ann pressed forward and was given space. The 'ann family gathered around her. The 'imm family stood to the right, near the Arena, obscuring the Exit Tree path. Between the 'ann family and the 'nii group on their left, a cleared path led from the kùmu'lio stalls. Eilen could not see beyond the 'nii family but knew the 'ban and 'ahj families must stand there.

The first Bakeisiká clansman emerged, sending a murmur through the crowd. An ornate headdress and a jingling necklace gave him a leader's appearance. Where the headwear she had seen on Ra'ahj displayed colorful scales and feathers, the Bakeisiká leader's headgear was formed of dark, thin metal flakes, yet clearly served the same function.

Close behind the leader, a file of heavily laden porters followed. Looking toward the Mingi, Eilen saw its edge lined by neatly stacked piles. Even as she stared, the truth dawned. Trade goods, M'pepebato wares arranged for inspection. Distance obscured the identity of most piles. One grouping looked like large spools wrapped in white. *M'pepalia fiber?* Bulkier goods obscured other items spread lower and closer to the common deck.

Several pairs of Bakeisiká emerged carrying boards, planks, and thick beams. A large stack of building materials began to grow in front of the Arena. Seeing only men Eilen posed the question to Tu'ann, receiving an answer in carefully articulated Batololému. "Around us they are." Tu'ann's description of the nomadic Bakeisiká encampment left a vague picture in Eilen's mind of hanging structures, housing entire families. She still pondered the idea when someone touched her elbow.

Looking haggard, Angus still seemed somehow more alive and alert than she had seen him in some time. "What kept you? You've missed most of the action. In fact, you may have missed the best of it. They arrived in style, carrying goods up from below in quite a formal little procession."

"Yeah. I heard the commotion."

A murmur ran through the crowd, pulling all eyes back toward the Mingi. Craning her neck, Eilen observed Ra'ahj, headpiece and all, entering from the far end of the village. Exchanging curt bows with the Bakeisiká leader, Ra'ahj's arm swept toward the piles of trade goods. The Bakeisiká leader responded with a formal nod, turned and walked toward the assembled trade goods, joined in his inspection by several other Bakeisiká clan members.

The inspection of wares triggered the crowd. As the Bakeisiká group moved toward the M'pepebato wares, the entire village crowd flowed like water to spread between the piles of Bakeisiká goods. Finished ropes, metal tools, fabrics, bowls, and baskets were arranged near leather straps, bags, bladders, and foodstuffs. The village commons played host to a festive bazaar. Eilen noticed La'ann and Ro'ann threading their way toward coiled ropes as Angus strode toward the tools. The polished metal tools had not escaped Eilen's notice. She knew Angus had not given up the idea of a technological civilization somewhere on his new world. The tools fed his hope ... and kept alive thoughts of a possible return home.

Some part of Eilen wanted to move into the melee and examine the many displayed wares. Another part found the scene fascinating in its own right. The activity presented a new vision of forest life. An image formed of Bakeisiká nomads, flowing like blood through the forest organism, nourishing the living whole.

A sudden change in rhythm caught Eilen's attention. Su'ban stepped from her shelter, inserting an island of calm into the edge of the crowd. As Su'ban walked, the villagers parted around her. She moved through the assembly in a bubble of free space.

In a single pass, Su'ban inspected trade goods, stopping briefly at only two displays. When she eventually turned back toward her shelter, a small contingent of villagers followed, like pups behind their mother.

Eilen lost sight of Su'ban in the crowd until she climbed onto the raised shelter and turned to address a new assembly forming there. The scene seemed odd. Although Su'ban stood before the crowd she did not speak. Hands rose above the gathering, seeking recognition. Su'ban nodded and listened.

The entire scene piqued Eilen's curiosity. "Tu'ann. What there, M'pepebato do?"

"Trading, M'pepebato do."

"What speaking they do?"

"Their want, for Su'ban, they speak."

"For things trading, they ask?"

"Yes."

Su'ban leaned on her staff listening and nodded at each speaker in turn.

Ra'ahj escorted a pair of regaled Bakeisiká to join Su'ban on the raised bench of her shelter. In a loud, rhythmic, ritual statement, Ra'ahj thanked the Bakeisiká for their visit. Then he invited their leader to sit at Su'ban's table. Ra'ahj sat opposite. When Su'ban stood beside Ra'ahj, Eilen realized that the second Bakeisiká must be Su'ban's counterpart, the Bakeisiká Haku'iké. Trading began.

Nothing written, nothing calculated. When trading concluded, the two Haku'iké offered versions of the final accounting. An acceptance nod from each approved exchange of payment. Necklaces came off the two seated clan leaders and were spread on the table surface. On this occasion the M'pepebato clan became richer by the amount of three gold, one silver and two copper beads which the Bakeisiká leader removed from his necklace and laid upon the table. Ra'ahj picked up the metallic beads and incorporated them into the wealth of the M'pepebato village to be arrayed across his chest.

Thus, the commerce of Nahélé flowed.

Eilen wondered what the price of Su'ban's medicines had been. *Where is Angus? He should see this.*

....

A trading visit called for celebration. For the first time since their arrival, Angus and Eilen saw the Mingi play host to a midday feast. A roar of voices surrounded the Mingi stage, filled to capacity. Eilen wondered why she and Angus were seated there among dignitaries. *Su'ban's work for sure. What is she planning?* Beside her, La'ann spoke in her ear. "Ee'laan. Quiet, you are."

Su'ban was occupied with the Bakeisiká Haku'iké. Daughters of the same calling, they seemed to have much to talk about. Ra'ahj and his counterpart also appeared to have business to discuss. The Bakeisiká, it seemed, served another valuable function, as news couriers.

Discussion ceased as Ra'ahj rose. Standing with raised hands, he announced, "From you, hearing, I ask ... News, there is."

Ra'ahj returned to his seat, trading places with the Bakeisiká Haku'iké, who held herself silent for a moment. Assured of the crowd's attention, she began speaking in a metered, somber voice. "From Nahélé's clans, news, I bring ... In the north, crazy fire burned."

Using every bit of language skill at her command, Eilen barely made sense of the story. She tried to picture a burning colōfn tree, finding the idea difficult to imagine. The crowd reaction and the Haku'iké's somber tone told Eilen that uncontrolled fire fostered fear among the people of Nahélé.

The Haku'iké moved smoothly into a second story. "From Nahélé's clans, news, I bring ... the 'Ohebato, a sickness visited."

In this way, Eilen learned of recent events affecting several of the forest clans and saw how the Bakeisiká wove a unifying commercial web among the clans much as the Raiju and her sister ships had knit together the worlds of Haven.

The news report ended in a simple declaration. "Ending, my stories have."

But the Haku'iké was not completely finished. She also carried a more personal message. "From An'nii, greetings, I bring. For him speaking, I must ... Well, he is." The announcement brought her to one last topic. The Haku'iké then raised an arm toward the Mingi first tier. "Four others with us are."

At her bidding, four young men rose from the seated Bakeisiká group and made their way down the side aisle to the stage level. They arranged themselves to stand nervously in a row. The first stepped forward. "Lim'lii of the Máilobabato, I am. All day run I can."

In like manner, the M'pepebato clan became acquainted with Lor'aal of the Kùmubato, Kal'tie of the Libangabato, and Bor'ahm of the Uayémbabato. The Nomads were marriage brokers as well.

Then Su'ban rose to speak. "Story to tell, also we have. Speaking, La'ann will."

A nod from Su'ban brought La'ann to his feet. Spreading arms wide, he began. "Into the Mokililana a great flying stone fell. From a distant sister of Amon, visitors with it came."

And that's why we're here, thought Eilen.

With La'ann's animated telling, the origin of the M'pepebato clan's newest members took one more step toward becoming forest lore. Bakeisiká storytellers would spread the tale to all of Nahélé's villages.

Speeches ended and feasting began. Sometime later, Ra'ahj stood to announce that games would begin as soon as everyone could gather in the arena.

Sitting with Hol'imm and the 'ann family, Angus thought their seats high in the Arena venue provided a good vantage from which to view the event, better certainly than sitting close among the clan leaders at the bottom. On his left, Eilen sat wrapped in discussion with Tu'ann. La'ann's absence felt strange. From his second day on this world, La'ann was always somewhere near, protecting, explaining, and teaching. Angus's one solo journey nearly ended in disaster and La'ann had scarcely left his side since. Now he sat quietly listening to Hol'imm describe the likósisaka game while watching La'ann standing among M'pepebato teammates to one side of the Arena's lowest tier.

A mystery no longer, the Arena lay spread before him, arrayed with dangling ropes, perhaps half a hundred, hanging like a forest of stylized vines, each weighted by a gleaming metal cap at its free end. The technology embodied in the site's construction had long fascinated Angus and many times he'd guessed at its purpose. Now he finally saw the Arena for what it was: an actual arena, a three-dimensional field of play.

As Angus mused, Hol'imm talked. More words poured forth than Angus had ever before heard from Hol'imm, waxing broadly about how La'ann and Ro'ann were among the clan's most skilled rope handlers. Angus harbored no doubt of that assertion. Now he watched as La'ann, Ro'ann and four other M'pepebato contestants assumed the game's starting positions.

Differences between the two teams showed immediately. In unison, three Bakeisiká players grabbed ropes nearest the staging platform and readied swings. In a unified rhythm, they leapt up and onto the ropes in their hands, impressing the crowd with the beauty of synchronized motion. Metal epaulets threw off bits of sunlight with each kip of legs as each player's motion occurred at the same moment as the other, gathering each swing into a graceful arc parallel to its neighbor. These players played together often, a well-oiled machine, accustomed to the attention, accustomed to winning.

The M'pepebato team showed no such harmony, swinging into the field of play as individuals, no thought given to the coordination of their actions. Their swings seemed to take longer to build, longer to reach the second hanging rope, bland leather leggings and arm bands adding no flair to the effort.

In time, all players found starting positions, supported in apparent restful repose with legs enwrapped in rope, mounted high on the six ropes situated at each end of the playing field. The Bakeisiká team waited at one end, while the M'pepebato gathered on the other. A forest of empty ropes dangled between them.

The crowd quieted. The two teams sat and waited. Angus, too, felt anticipation, curious to see how this contest would conduct itself. Ra'ahj and the Bakeisiká leader rose from amid the lowest seats. As the pair ceremoniously approached the center of the low deck level, an arm reached up from below the deck to quietly deposit the ends of two thin lines at their feet. Ra'ahj looked at the assembled audience, letting his eyes wander all the way up toward those standing atop the village common level.

Angus heard none of Ra'ahj's welcoming words, focused instead on La'ann resting at ease with one leg wrapped around the rope hanging at one far end of the playing field. Why was he starting play from the position behind his teammates, farthest from center? If he was one of their best players, why would he assume such a defensive position? Surely, one of the village's best rope handlers would naturally sit at the forefront, ready to attack.

Talking stopped and Angus watched Ra'ahj bend down to pick the two lines from the deck. The game was finally ready to begin. Ra'ahj stood and pulled in both lines and by doing so also pulled out of its resting place the thick rope hanging at the center of the playing field. Gathering a bit more line, Ra'ahj soon had the field's center rope stretched taut in a line angled toward the seating area. Angus noted the fist-sized ball affixed to its end. A sharp yank from Ra'ahj to one of the two thin lines in his hand released the center rope free and set it swinging back into the playing field. The game was on.

Legs kicked and motion rippled through both ends of the arena. Excitement flowed through Angus, as much by the beginning of the game as by Eilen's exuberant hand on his knee. So much of what she did these days filled him with unfamiliar sensations.

The Bakeisiká team began as a unit, completely synchronized. Every player slid down to the same point at the same time, every player's legs kicked at once, every player's rope moved through the same arc at the same time, all aimed directly down the field, a beautiful display of teamwork.

So much so, that action at the M'pepebato end went nearly unobserved. In stark contrast to the Bakeisiká, the M'pepebato team began in uncoordinated fashion. Their motion built slowly, out of sync and in apparent disarray. While most of the audience watched the graceful Bakeisiká team, Angus watched La'ann.

Ro'ann and La'ann seemed to move in opposing directions. As La'ann's swing reached toward the center Ro'ann's swing reached toward La'ann. Before anyone on the playing field had yet attained a second rope, La'ann and Ro'ann had nearly brought themselves together. Nearing the top of their arcs, Ro'ann tossed his free rope end into La'ann's sure hands. La'ann immediately released his starting rope and became an additional weight upon Ro'ann's. With legs wrapped onto the rope's end, La'ann then extended his arms as he came within reach of the next rope closer to the center. As La'ann took hold of that next position, Ro'ann toppled down and latched onto La'ann's legs. The pair then swung together free of Ro'ann's starting rope, smoothly incorporating their additional momentum to propel themselves toward a new position.

The crowd grew quiet as they watched the new tactic take shape. Before any member of the Bakeisiká team had acquired a single new location, Ro'ann and La'ann had both made their way to a second rope and were in full swing toward a third. Everyone's eyes became focused on the two M'pepebato clansmen.

Two more ropes yet hung between the object ball and La'ann and Ro'ann's place on the field. Working together, the brothers needed but two swings to bring Ro'ann within reach of the next hanging rope and they had not yet exhausted their new tactics.

Reaching with his legs, Ro'ann hooked the next rope and as their backswing then drew him and La'ann away, he allowed the length of it to slip through his hold. While they swung back, both La'ann and Ro'ann climbed higher upon their supporting rope until they had the new rope completely extended and were able to secure themselves near its end. Ro'ann fixed his legs onto the newly acquired rope and then fixed his arms around La'anns legs. Bound tightly together, they dropped into another heart-stopping swing.

Angus held his breath watching Ro'ann swing upended clinging tightly to La'ann's legs. He was so enwrapped in their play that he nearly missed seeing the intent of their daring. The arc of their swing had just passed its nadir when Angus saw that it might bring the center rope within reach.

Bakeisiká players were just securing second positions when La'ann reached to grab the center rope. Ro'ann let go of La'ann and retreated as La'ann transferred himself to the center rope. In the memory of no living Bakeisiká had any village team so soundly controlled the opening of a likósisaka game. La'ann retrieved the object ball and remained low on the center rope, ball in hand.

Angus was not alone in wondering what the M'pepebato team would do next. Every spectator in the arena had watched La'ann and Ro'ann concentrate their efforts on the game ball.

Having secured it, the game moved into a second phase. Few observers had noticed how the remaining M'pepebato team members had swung into forward positions, around and behind the Bakeisiká team members. From that point on, Angus had difficulty tracking the many swinging bodies.

The entire Bakeisiká team seemed to converge on La'ann, who waited until their flank was exposed before timing a throw to Ro'ann, who had kept up his momentum and remained swinging in and out of proximity to La'ann. Ro'ann then wasted no time relaying that ball out and forward. A quick series of throws brought the game ball completely around the entire Bakeisiká team and gave the last M'pepebato player a chance to toss it into the funnel-shaped net mounted at the Bakeisiká end of the field—score and game; victory to the M'pepebato; one of the very few times the Bakeisiká had tasted defeat, and the quickest victory known to anyone.

Cheers rose from the entire M'pepebato clan, who greatly outnumbered the few Bakeisiká clansmen seated in the arena. Angus looked to La'ann and for the first time watched a grin as wide as Ro'ann's grow on La'ann's face.

With the game completed, players began to swing, one by one, out of the rope field to alight onto the arena deck; twelve bodies, glistening with sweat, chests heaving.

A cacophony of voices fell from the top ranks of the Arena as M'pepebato clan members congratulated the skill and success of their players. With a unified bow, the Bakeisiká team offered a congratulatory salute to their opponent's victory. Both teams then stepped to one side and filed back up the Arena tiers, dispersing into seats among the crowd.

La'ann alone remained standing on the lowest arena level, wearing a somber face, all signs of victory now forgotten. Seeing La'ann remain behind puzzled Angus and, as Ro'ann took a seat beside Eilen, his anxiety rose. "Happen, what is?"

Ro'ann's voice carried little life when he answered. "For M'pepebato, La'ann will fight."

Still bereft of a great Batololému vocabulary, Angus clumsily probed for explanation. "What meaning 'fight' you have? This happen, how?"

"Challenge, Ta'bor has given."

"What event cause makes?"

"Little knowledge I have. For challenge, small thing only Ta'bor needs."

A large, well-muscled man, not seen in the likósisaka game, descended the Mingi side steps, holding his head erect, staring straight ahead, obviously proud of his own strength. The outlines of every muscle were on display, advertising his power. His name rippled through the Arena crowd: Ta'bor, who made an art form of the gwar'a'saka challenge, who took every opportunity to confront others, who enjoyed the fear his reputation provoked. A large knife blade shone at his side.

Several M'pepebato clansmen climbed atop the Arena scaffolding. Pulling up most of the ropes, they reduced the hanging arena volume to a single small area—only seven hanging ropes, one central surrounded by an evenly spaced perimeter of six.

Ro'ann's explanation came in a low, monotone voice. Speaking to the air before him, he talked away his own fear. No object-ball would fly between ropes in the next match. Survival marked a victory in the gwar'a'saka. "With fall the gwar'a'saka ends ... or with blood."

Glancing down, Ro'ann noted another feature of the reduced playing field. "Net, remove they do not. Good it is. Always so, it is not. Today, midfloor, no one will see. With a cut only, perhaps this challenge ends." Then he looked toward the Bakeisiká man. "Knives, there will be."

....

La'ann stood on the side deck, awaiting the match's start, assessing his opponent. Familiar with the young man's reputation, he would be foolish not to believe that the man intended injury. Ta'bor held the entry rope in his left hand, staring fixedly into the rope arena, his right hand tightened into a fist, flexing forearm muscles. The muscular Bakeisiká clearly carried more weight than La'ann. La'ann stared at the man's solid bulk, recognizing it for what it was—a formidable weapon, one that might dislodge him with a simple blow.

Ra'ahj rose and stood between the two contestants, looking at each to accept their readiness. Acting as match judge, he dropped a hand and the match began. Both contestants swung into the field of battle using two near ropes hanging just outside each end of the restricted field. Their entry tactics gave the audience immediate indications of the character of each contestant's tactics.

The center rope offered strategic advantage: free movement in any direction. Upon the starting signal, both combatants swung to the nearest perimeter rope, reaching that rope at nearly the same instant. The Bakeisiká dropped his entry rope and executed strong kips, kicking out with his whole lower body, building momentum toward the center rope.

La'ann had never before been in a gwar'a'saka, yet faced a practiced foe. He was not without skill but felt unsteady, unsure of himself and of his tactics. He needed a plan, and he needed it fast.

The game began quickly. To those watching, La'ann seemed to lose the advantage from the very outset. While his adversary kipped toward the center, La'ann swung to acquire a perimeter rope without releasing his grip upon the entry rope. Allowing the perimeter rope's length to slip through his crossed legs he pulled himself higher on his entry rope. When he finally let go of the entry rope, his high position sent him arcing toward the midfloor. Near the nadir of his arc, he let his upper body fall off the rope, clinging with wrapped legs alone, to impart just the extra momentum needed to swing close enough to grab the center rope, just as he and Ro'ann had practiced.

The unorthodox maneuver gave La'ann immediate advantage. He had control of the center rope. It also placed him high without momentum. This game punished stasis; motion was key to survival. As he secured himself with an arm wrapped around the center rope, he turned to find Ta'bor swinging up at him, knife drawn and ready. La'ann saw the blade's arc and the strong arm behind it aimed directly at his chest. He had but one option. Releasing his grip, he plunged down the rope, grimacing in pain as friction seared his arm.

The tactic worked, allowing La'ann to avoid the slashing knife, but the effort still cost him a well-placed kick to the side of his head. Dazed, he fought to regain control. *Move! Move!* Swinging as much body as he could bring under control, he managed just enough perpendicular arc to escape by mere inches Ta'bor's return swing and a second blow.

As focus returned, La'ann set his eyes on his opponent, picking out adjustments the Nomad added to each swing. The man was good at this game. He had been here many times before. He wielded his knife ruthlessly ... and he obviously enjoyed it. With knives La'ann was no match. Body blows would likely gain less than they would cost against such strength and bulk. Leaving the center rope would get him out of harm's way for only as long as it took his opponent to establish the position for himself.

La'ann climbed high enough to speed his own swing and avoid another encounter with a Bakeisiká knife. Looking down, he took some comfort from the net. At least he would not fall to the midfloor. The rope dangled below. A stray glint rose from the rope's end. In that brief flash, La'ann saw what he might do. He possessed one skill his adversary had not yet seen.

La'ann stopped pumping. Both eyes followed the Nomad while La'ann gathered the rope's dangling end. A contemptuous smile spread across Ta'bor's hard-set face. La'ann saw his own movements being carefully assessed, another vicious slash or stunning blow being planned.

The attack took shape as La'ann moved higher yet, seeking to sap the force from his opponent's swing. Ta'bor arced forward, knife poised. La'ann tensed, every sense focused on the knife blade. A bit of rope slipped down from his hand. Ta'bor's arm thrust forward. The knife's edge arced toward exposed thigh. In a bright flash, the rope's metal-capped free end lashed out. The knife flew from the Nomad's grip and a howl of rage erupted from his lungs.

La'ann recovered loops into one hand, knowing by the angry sneer on his opponent's face that the contest was not yet finished. He moved down to invite a dislodging impact.

Ta'bor obliged, loading a hard kick into his swing. The swing gathered speed until, at the very moment of the kick's release, he saw the rope's end again streak toward him. Ta'bor had barely time to raise a limp defensive hand. As his attacker swept past La'ann let his upper body fall, jerking Ta'bor's entangled arm backward. What might have been a crushing forehead blow became instead a humiliating tumble. The Nomad's rope slipped through loosely wrapped legs as the big man fell to the net below, face warped in fury.

A simple rope had become in La'ann's hands a powerful weapon.

CHAPTER 19
Return

An appearance on the bridge had seemed appropriate. Bright Victory's return to the Lesser Cloud warranted the gesture. Now Alexandra was not so sure. The command chair seemed far away. Reaching to steady herself, she struggled to keep her head up. The queasiness seemed as strong as ever. *This is why I never command drop maneuvers.* She knew her crew felt the same nausea, but for them to see her similarly distressed might foster improper thinking, as though she were no different than they. *I should never let my excitement get the better of me.*

"How long before we can descend into near orbit, Commander?"

The lines on Semgee's brow told Alexandra that he saw the pallor on her face. *Proklyat'ye! I need none of your judgment.*

"Honorable Captain, we have begun already."

"So soon?"

"There is no reason to mask our approach and we chose a drop vector that already puts us into a proper trajectory. We have only to adjust our speed, which we are now doing. It will still require the remainder of the day to execute a braking dive and bring the ship into matching orbit with the inner planet." Pausing, he added, "I would commend the ship's navigator for his excellent and efficient guidance in our journey back to this star."

Chert yego poberi! Why must he always attempt to curry favor among the crew and undermine my authority? A brief flare of anger swept through her before Alexandra accepted the comment, perhaps softened by her pride in their prompt return to the Lesser Cloud. "Quite right, First Officer. Well done, Mr. Huang. Your performance does you credit, as it does those who recommended you for this assignment. Our return journey has been much less troublesome than I had imagined it would be."

With a respectful nod, Commander Joseph Huang, Victory's newly appointed Navigator, acknowledged the accolades. "Thank you, Captain. I'm grateful for your confidence, but I must mention that the spectral recordings taken of this red giant star on your first voyage made my job that much easier."

Considering her duties concluded, Alexandra gave a nod to the young man's point, before abruptly turning her back and walking off the bridge, relaying orders over one shoulder as she left. "The helm is yours, First Officer. Let me know when we near that orbiting station. I'll be in my cabin."

....

Victory's braking dive consumed most of the day before the ship fell into what seemed, for Alexandra at least, a maddeningly slow approach toward their quarry. Her nervous energy would not allow even the composition of one of her infamously self-serving ship's log entries to quell her impatience. Failing in her attempt to remain quietly in her cabin, she repeatedly stood only to sit again a moment later. When she finally abandoned the effort, she walked to the bridge to wait with everyone else.

Disinterest met her arrival. The eyes of every bridge

occupant were riveted on the expanded image hovering above the display area. In more normal circumstances, Alexandra would take note of the absence of a welcoming gesture. On this occasion, she completely ignored the omission, focusing immediately on the display image.

There she saw the same dead cinder of a planet, still seared by its huge near neighbor, as she had seen on Victory's first trip to this place. This time, however, no orbiting station appeared to lend the planet any unique importance.

"Where is it?" she asked as she came up beside Semgee.

"I'm afraid, Honorable Captain, that we haven't yet found it," Semgee replied absently, without diverting his gaze from the screen.

"Is it merely eclipsed by the planet?"

Answering slowly, Semgee's fingers pulled at his lower lip, his mind occupied elsewhere. "No, Honorable Captain. I suspect not. We've been watching long enough for it to have emerged if it were there." Then, returning to events begun well before his captain's arrival, he ordered, "Get in close and focus on that small blur just to the left edge of the planet image."

Expanding, the planetary image sank into the projector base, extinguishing its illuminated half and becoming only dark background for the apparent void that remained.

Semgee craned his neck, as though doing so would help him see the display image better, but the blur he had seen before seemed to have vanished in the expanded view. "What's that?" he asked. "There ... Is that blur real, or some kind of artifact?"

The entire bridge company, including Alexandra, craned to find what Semgee had seen. First to speak, she drew out her words, "Yes, First Officer ... I think you're right ... There is something there." Without thinking, she usurped Semgee's command. "Lieutenant ... center the image around that fuzzy spot and magnify the image further."

There it was, spread along a broad orbital arc, a sparsely filled volume of tiny glowing bits—the station's scattered remains.

....

Semgee Marlowe had never felt inspired by the décor of his captain's cabin—not at all how he would have done it, but, of course, nearly everything she did was not as he would have done it. Priceless though they were, the profusion of antiquities seemed oppressive and filled him with mixed emotions, reminding him on the one hand of his intention to apply for a transfer at the end of their last mission, and on the other hand, of the price he paid to join this historic mission. This time, he told himself, he would not allow her imperious manner to bother him. Now, as he tried to turn the conversation back to more useful purpose, he looked for a pause, lamenting her need to ramble on about the glory of it all.

"... I know you're right, Commander. It really hasn't been very long since we were here last—a matter of months only. And I was impressed with the speed of our refit ... almost unprecedented." A smile spread on Alexandra's face before she added, "That fact alone says a lot about how important this mission is to the First Council."

There's my opening. Semgee wasted no time. "Honorable Captain, the additional fact that we return to find a completely destroyed station also reveals much about the character of our quarry. If my hunch is correct, they certainly now know, not only that we're here, but also who we are and what we intend... and they do not want to be found!"

"Of course, but what can they do about it?"

"Not a thing, I'm sure. I would, however, propose that we waste no more time here and get on with our planned search."

"Can't we find a clue here? Anything to point us in the

right direction?"

"Perhaps, but let's just stop for a moment and ask what would be required to glean useful information from the debris here. We'll need to direct a focused Riemann field to gather it. That would slightly destabilize our orbit and require constant correction—small nuisance. In any event, there's only a slim likelihood that a clue of any real value exists among all that debris ... and sifting through it will take time ... a lot of time. Perhaps the Captain would agree that it might be preferable to get started on a systematic search since we both know it must be done."

Semgee watched the smile fade from Alexandra's face. *Perhaps I should have offered more support to her dreams of glory.*

Her acceptance came laced with irritation. "I suppose you're right, Commander. You usually are." Then she seemed to brighten and offered a new topic. "You know, since we discovered this star, we have a right to name it. What do you think of the idea of calling it 'Roshenkov's Star'?"

CHAPTER 20
Decision

Pulling the back of a hand across his brow, Angus tried to ignore the many rivulets of sweat. The day's cooling shower would be welcomed today. Warm afternoon sunlight filled the 'annliboko. A subdued hum of many voices filtered from the village common over the hedge-wall. Sitting cross-legged within the shade of his shelter, Angus examined the articles spread across his bedroll. Relics of another world, he had given little attention to these emergency supplies since his first day on the planet, when he took them from the core lander. Now, as if assembling an elite team of warriors, he questioned the value of each item. The likes of ration bars, hand-torch, radio/beacon/receiver, disinfectant, bandages, reflective blanket, a solar-powered distillation device, and a field knife seemed to offer easy choices. The hand-torch might buy passage from the Bakeisiká. Yet there were only two like it on the entire planet. Then his eyes fell upon the hand weapon. Reaching to touch it, his hand closed around the weapon's grip. The feel of its smooth contours sent his mind back to the last time he had discharged it. Memories of that first day on Nahélé's world flooded into his head: the sharp edge of light from the planet's white sun, the heavy odiferous air, his foot sinking into the Mokililana's soft, soggy surface. The long day returned in a complex mix of pain and struggle, joy and relief; the exhilaration of discovery scarred by the loss of shipmates.

The sound of Eilen's voice jarred Angus from his private world. "You seem to have calmed down a bit."

Without turning, Angus pulled himself back to the present. "Sorry, I was thinking about our first day here."

Eilen responded slowly. "I've let myself forget it."

Finally twisting to look at her, Angus saw Eilen's eyes returning from somewhere far off. *It really is a beautiful face. No other like it in Nahélé's world. We've seen so much together.* She seemed troubled. A cold unease swept over Angus. *What would I do without her?* Before finding an answer, he said, "Yes, I know what you mean. I was just thinking that Ivan and John would have enjoyed this world ... and these people."

"Which brings me back to what I think you're thinking. I'm not in such a hurry to leave here. Why are you?"

Angus had not yet articulated an answer to that question, not to himself or to anyone else. He took a moment before explaining. "It's obvious, isn't it? Somewhere on this planet, there's a technical center. Somewhere there's a city. You've seen the signs of it as well as I have. And then there's the nahélébato people themselves. They're so very human ... and where there's human life in the Milky Way the 'protection' of the League of Planets cannot be far away ... and where the League's forces exist, so does a starship or two. Don't you think we should find them?"

"Suppose we do find them? What then?"

"I don't know. I'll worry about that after I find a ship. I wasn't sure how we were going to explore, but these nomads now provide the means."

"You seem to have decided a great deal without sharing one word with me."

Another silent alarm sent a wave of tension through Angus's body. His nascent quest to find a city had barely taken form. That Eilen might not wish to join his quest had not occurred to him. Replying with as much sincerity as he could muster, he said, "I'm sorry. It all happened so fast I didn't have time to think."

"No. You didn't. Did you."

The rebuke struck hard. Angus struggled to frame an apology. He had not yet found words before Eilen softened the edge in her voice. "I've come to love our new community. I'm not in such a hurry to leave." Her eyes again drifted up into the trees. "At the same time, you and I are all there is, the only two of our kind. There are no others."

Forced to confront the ramifications of his decision, Angus stared across the 'annliboko. When he finally spoke, the labor of his thoughts laid a damper upon his words. "I must go. It's as simple as that. I can't just forget everything. The League will be hunting for Haven and, if there is any way at all ... I think we should try. If we don't, we'll always wonder."

Stiff from sitting, Angus stood to stretch, spotting La'ann emerging from the hedge-wall, already looking directly toward the shelter where he and Eilen stood. Standing silent, Angus waited for his friend to come near, certain that he'd momentarily be explaining all over again.

La'ann held his tongue only until he reached some ten steps distant. "Ahngoose! Ee'laan! Quickly you did leave. Troubled, I am."

In a moment's reflection, Angus saw his departure from the festivities. The thought of joining the Bakeisiká had seized him in a rush and his escape had become involuntary. Eilen offered explanation. "Join the Bakeisiká, we will." The fact that she included herself in the revelation was not lost on Angus.

In the time it took Eilen to say the words, Angus watched his friend's mood change from dimples to furrows. More surprising to him, was his own sudden regret at the sight of La'ann's fallen face. A long silence hung in the air. Concern laced La'ann's voice. "Leave us, you will, Ahngoose? M'pepebato now, you are. Leave, you cannot!"

"Leave, I must, La'ann," Angus said as he tried to formulate an explanation to this man who understood the forest so well and questioned little of what may lie beyond. "The 'village of countless people' find, I must." In a language having no word distinguishing 'city' from 'village', Angus had simply expressed his explanation in a fashioned batololému phrase, knowing as he said it that his words meant little to his friend and did little to explain why such a place might draw anyone from the clan.

A shout pulled all three heads to look across the 'annliboko, "Ahngoose! Ee'laan!" Young Ne'ann ran toward them, her little legs churning in a blur of motion. When she reached the four adults, her rapid breathing left little room for words. "With you, speaking, Su'ban wishes."

....

Su'ban leaned on her staff. From across her solid table, Angus stood awaiting her intent. Beside him on either side, Eilen and La'ann seemed unaffected by Su'ban's summons. Feeling tense, Angus could not keep his eyes from wandering. They fell first to the small drawstring purse laying alone on the table's flat surface. The table's straight rectilinear lines and sharp corners had never before seemed so foreign to him. Looking past Su'ban, he let himself roam the many crude containers lining the shelves in the dim recesses of her shelter. Across the table, uncomfortable silence lingered. The end of the day's festivities brought an uncommon quiet to the common area outside. Finally, Su'ban spoke. "To me my ears speak ... Leave M'pepebato, you will ... Uneasy I feel."

Digesting the Batololému words, Angus felt no real surprise, but, since only he, Eilen and La'ann knew of his decision to leave, Su'ban's statement still filled him with admiration. She always seemed to know what was happening even before it happened. He had intended to tell her personally, to explain his decision. Now, whatever explanation he might put forward would come at her insistence. Somehow the difference undermined his confidence. Would Su'ban object? Would she prevent their departure? Holding silent, he waited for her to circle her purpose. Her next words surprised him.

Su'ban looked down at the fingertips of one hand laid flat on the table. The simple act seemed to reflect the weight of her thoughts. Speaking slowly, articulating every word as though reluctant to part with them, she released her burden. "To you, close, become I have."

As she raised her eyes to look directly into his, Angus felt her sincerity before hearing it. "Many villages Nahélé holds. Counted between them, colōfn trees cannot be. Long away you will be."

For some time Su'ban held Angus's gaze. Angus searched the black-in-brown eyes peering from under the shadow of her brow, trying in vain to glimpse the soul behind them.

At length, Su'ban broke her hold and shifted weight, rising to stand erect. A wave of tension visibly drained from her body. She turned to La'ann. "From M'pepebato Ahngoose and Ee'laan will go. Within your spirit what thinking you find?"

Angus saw La'ann's head lift from the table to meet Su'ban's scrutiny. Su'ban looked for an answer even as La'ann sought the same in her. The question seemed to hang in the air. When La'ann spoke, his voice carried little of its normally firm assurance. "Within my head many feelings live. Days to come without Ee'laan and Ahngoose I do not wish."

The statement seemed to please Su'ban. Continuing to speak directly to La'ann, she unveiled another layer of thought. "Much wisdom in Nahélé's villages lives. For M'pepebato, such knowledge great worth carries." Dimples formed around the corners of Su'ban's mouth. Her face broadened. She smiled and said, "In days to come, Ee'laan and Ahngoose you will see. With them you will go. Your return I command."

The word 'stunned' would forever after bring to Angus's mind the look that swept over La'ann face.

Su'ban did not stop to give La'ann time to reply. Turning back to Angus, her voice softened and she said, "Perhaps your kumuzala find, you will ... Talk with you again, I wish ... Your return I ask." With those thoughts, Su'ban reached to pick the small sack from the table, holding it out to Angus. "With you, carry. Perhaps your return, help it will."

The idea that Su'ban might send La'ann to join his quest would never have crossed Angus's mind. Nor would any of the events that followed.

"With me, come," she said as she moved toward the single step that distinguished her shelter from all others in the village, the step that allowed her short legs to carry her down from the shelter's raised bench.

Living among the 'ann family during the past many months, Angus had never visited any of the other four private family compounds within the M'pepebato village. Walking now behind Su'ban, between dense brier walls leading into the 'ahj family area, he felt strangely tense. He knew the area within would look little different from what had become his home and he entered under Su'ban's authority. Still, with no invitation in hand, his steps required more effort than they should, as if his legs wanted no part of the intrusion.

Su'ban tapped her staff on the deck as she entered the compound. Looking up from their labors, several 'ahj family members acknowledged her arrival. Glancing neither left nor right, Su'ban marched past. From his place in line behind her, Angus forced a smile, nodding to each 'ahj, asking pardon for the transgression. Coming around the bulk of the central colōfn tree, the long, curved structure encircling the area came into view. Angus recognized Ra'ahj standing atop the shelter's raised floor, looking a bit naked without his official regalia and somehow much older.

Loud enough to carry the distance, Su'ban spoke as the group halted some little way from the edge of Ra'ahj's quarters. "From you help I need."

In the same moment that he asked himself why Su'ban stopped so far from Ra'ahj's shelter Angus also noted the way his neck bent to find Ra'ahj's face. Su'ban's keen intelligence never let her small stature interfere with her command of any situation. Ra'ahj understood. Stepping off the shelter bench, he brought himself closer to her level. "From me, wish what you do?"

As if it were her own, Su'ban took control of Angus's half-formed plan. "La'ann and four kùmu'lio I need."

Warily, Ra'ahj probed. "For La'ann speak I do not."

"For M'pepebato you speak. So it is?"

Obviously puzzled, Ra'ahj continued. "For what purpose these things you need?"

"Journey I wish."

Ra'ahj's eyes suddenly opened wide. "From M'pepebato go you will?"

"I go not. Ahngoose goes. Ee'laan goes. La'ann goes."

As the full picture took shape, Ra'ahj relaxed and began to act for the clan. "Long away they will be?"

"This answer, know I do not. Before they return, many Longnights you will see."

The exchange had reached the heart of the issue for Ra'ahj. Watching the internal struggle show on Ra'ahj's face Angus realized how poorly he had thought things through. Might Su'ban's plans derail his own?

"Leave La'ann must not. Also Ro'ann will go?"

Ra'ahj's concerns were now visible to all. The entire M'pepebato clan knew that Ro'ann and La'ann were rarely apart for long. Su'ban understood. "Your thinking I see. Good hunter Ro'ann is. One good hunter M'pepebato must keep. Ro'ann will stay."

Ra'ahj shifted direction. Su'ban's request included another

valuable clan asset. "Good with kùmu'lio, Ee'laan and Ahngoose are not."

Reluctant to step between two clan leaders, Angus held silent, unable to speak on his own behalf. In a silent plea for guidance, Angus looked at Eilen. As powerless as he, she could only send his way a slight shrug.

He need not have worried. Su'ban understood the clan and she understood Ra'ahj. "Hol'imm also will go. With Hol'imm, kùmu'lio will return."

....

Nahélé awakened from peaceful rest. Soft light filtered through thinning foliage near the center of every passing group of colōfn trees. Cool air flowed past Angus's face, bringing with it a flower-scented, verdant smell of the midforest and dispelling the musky animal odor of the young kùmulio on which he rode. Angus thought of La'ann's faith in a living, breathing forest and recalled the enormous tide at work below the midforest floor. Realizing how the gentle breeze would tell him in what direction they now traveled, he wondered if Nahélé inhaled or if she exhaled. *La'ann would know.*

Atop Mœrai, La'ann rode just ahead. Angus's mount had only to unfurl her long nose to touch Mœrai's curled tail. A train of riders stretched into the distance. Angus could see about 20 animals before others became obscured in the shadows hovering below the midforest ceiling. A new adventure had begun.

Between swings of Mœrai's long arms, Angus saw La'ann sitting straight, upright. Not once since they left the kùmu'lio stalls had La'ann leaned to pat Mœrai's neck as Angus had seen him do so many times before. Not once had he turned to look back.

Imagining himself in La'ann's place, Angus found

understanding. *Everything he's ever known lies behind, but he'll leave it there and steel himself to see only what lies ahead.* A backward glance might weaken his resolve. The thought of leaving Ro'ann standing alone on the dock might even now put tears in his eyes.

Angus turned to wave at Eilen riding next in line. *Could I leave without her?* She might feel as torn as La'ann. Or she might simply be following her Captain, as she has done for many years past.

Angus glanced at his side. With every sway of the kùmu'lio's arms, the hand-torch tied to his waist jostled against his thigh. The soft leather sac holding Su'ban's gift was tied there also. *And then there's Su'ban.* Would he have been able to leave at all without her intercession?

His mount's long arm brushed his shoulders. *Hol'imm will be annoyed at me for forgetting this young kùmu'lio's name.*

SAND AND SECRETS

CHAPTER 21
Caravan

In a pot above the small campfire, the evening meal simmered, filling the air with a savory aroma. Yellow flames licked the pot's sooty bottom. The fire's glow set an orange halo onto overhead foliage and illuminated the four kùmu'lio at rest around the private campsite. Had he thought to do so, Angus might peer between hanging kùmu'lio arms to see the flicker of a nearby fire burning amid another of the encampment's many family units. The suspended platform had space enough for sleeping rolls, gear, and a central fire. Not as large, nor as elaborate as other Bakeisiká camp units, but still more comfortable than the swinging hammocks of M'pepebato camps. Protected within a hexagonal wall of netting stretched between taut support lines, the four clansmen cloaked themselves in quiet conversation.

Each slow nod of Hol'imm's head lent weight to the weariness in his voice. "Far from our village we are. Worn, kùmu'lio are ... Worn, I am." Perhaps for Hol'imm the adventure had lost its shine. In sympathy with his kùmu'lio, he'd begun to miss home.

Angus felt a pang of guilt with each word Hol'imm spoke. His friends paid a high price to join his journey. The conversation needed new direction. "Quiet you are, La'ann.

Where your thinking goes?"

"Full, my head grows. 'Nahélé scar' much thinking makes."

'Nahélé scar' had become La'ann's name for the strange spectacle they had encountered the previous day. More than anyone else, he labored to understand the jumbled wall of broken colōfn trunks and boughs, a great inverted ridge of arboreal debris descending from a disjointed midforest ceiling to meet another ridge rising from the midfloor. Thick vines wove themselves throughout the broken scaffolding to bind forest wreckage into a formidable barrier. Kùmulio refused to approach, forcing the entire column to turn onto a parallel track. La'ann's knowledge of Nahélé and her ways furnished no explanation, leaving him bewildered.

"From Nahélé, strange speaking I hear. With two voices Nahélé did speak."

The light of the fire accented nodding assent. Angus's Batololému skills had improved and encouraged his participation. Evening conversation had become a welcome part of each day. "Truth you speak, La'ann. Fear the kùmu'lio had."

"Through kùmulio arms did 'Nahélé scar' speak."

As though objecting to the riders' very presence, the great debris barrier had filled the forest with deep rumbling dissent, punctuating the column's sidelong trek with a cacophony of menacing groans.

Talking to himself as much as to anyone, La'ann spoke slowly. "Close Nahélé lives, but apart. And to every friendly ear, her secrets she speaks. Loudly the scar did speak and Nahélé's pain make known. For me much thinking this makes. Understand I do not."

The gravity of La'ann's feelings held everyone silent until he chose to venture onto new ground. "And for Bakeisiká, also thinking I do."

The Bakeisiká presented another mystery. Of Nahélé they

were but in a manner different from any other clan.

Hol'imm agreed. "Many they are ... long, their line stretches ... Many kùmu'lio." Hol'imm's view of the world always involved kùmu'lio.

Snippets of high-pitched voices drifted through the ceiling foliage. Eilen peered into the distance. "Small ones we see not."

Drawing his eyes from the fire, La'ann perked up. "Truth you speak, Ee'lann. Hard faces only do we see. Of Nahélé they are. M'pepebato they are not. Batolému speaking they do. Another speaking also they do."

All four agreed. They had all observed Bakeisiká carry on private conversations through subtle gestures and tongue-clicks.

La'ann turned to Angus. "From you, no thinking we hear, Ahngoose. To where your thinking goes?"

Since the first day of their trek, the diversity of forest clans had fascinated Angus as much as any other part of the journey. "Many things, I see, La'ann. Of many clans, also full my head becomes."

"And many heads of Nahélé's children you and Ee'laan now fill."

Among the clans of the forest, Angus and Eilen had become celebrities. In pursuit of trading success, Bakeisiká leaders spread the story of Ahngoose and Ee'laan and their strange arrival into Nahélé's realm. The M'pepebato clansmen earned their keep merely by their presence and by the story's telling.

Silence enveloped the campfire. La'ann picked up one end of the rope coil beside him, inspecting it as though he'd never before seen its like. From where Angus sat, the rope end looked frayed, displaying short lengths of free cord. With aid from a small twig, L'ann poked and prodded the bulging rope's end.

Curiosity got the better of Angus. "La'ann, what you do?

Mend you make?"

Intent on his task, La'ann's answer came with no diversion of focus. "Yes, mending I am."

Angus persisted. "La'ann ... Your rope ... Hold, I may?"

La'ann raised his head to look at Angus; then picked up the coil and handed it to Hol'imm. Accepting the rope from Hol'imm, Angus set it atop his crossed legs. One end formed a tidy bundle, where strands from both the outside sheath and the inner bundle had been neatly woven into a single, intricate and tidy terminus. No visible loose strand hinted at any weak point. Only with great difficulty, and perhaps a broken nail, Angus surmised, might that end yield a stray thread.

The second end, the end on which La'ann had been diligently working, felt distinctly different. This end bulged perhaps three or four times the size of the first. A few loose threads remained to be incorporated into the unfinished knot. Held captive within the bulge rested something hard and round. With a short rap, Angus tested its weight against the platform floor, eliciting a dull clunk. A picture of Ta'bor tumbling from the arena scaffolding came to Angus's mind. "New rope, you make?"

"Yes, new using, I see."

The rope went back to La'ann and Angus thought about what that rope represented. He thought back to their visit with the 'Likosibato' clan, 'people of the rope.' In that rope, Angus could see the many revolving spools of the clan's kumu'lio-powered wooden apparatus and how they transformed raw m'pepalia fiber into the beautiful light ropes used throughout Nahèlè's many villages.

Their journey thus far had revealed many such Batonahélé clans, each contributing to Nahèlè's good health with the production of some essential material, tool, or commodity. Together they formed a distributed whole, nourished by a complex economic network into which the Bakeisiká nomads poured a life-blood of trade. The idea both captivated Angus and filled him with disappointment.

The forest's many simple industries seemed able to supply the people of Nahélé with every need. The existence of a technological center, some great 'City,' grew less probable with each new discovery. Nothing larger than a small village seemed to exist and each new day saw his hopes become that much thinner. Perhaps his energy would be better spent learning to live with what was. Yet one piece of the adventure still nagged. No origin had shown itself for the metal tools that sparked his imagination. Bakeisiká traders greeted all inquiries with silence.

....

As the next day's trek ventured forth, Angus sensed something different. La'ann and Hol'imm rode in tandem, something they had not done for quite some time. A preoccupation with local midforest vegetation engulfed the two clansmen as though they had never before seen its like. From his hind position Angus watched. The manner of his friends' conversation stoked his curiosity, finally spurring him forward. "La'ann, see what, you do?"

Waiting for Angus to approach, La'ann answered with a question in his tone. "New face Nahélé wears. Strange words today she speaks."

Angus had not yet formulated a second question when Eilen joined the conversation. "About what speak you do?"

Still peering into the midfloor, Hol'imm answered. "Small, colōfn trees are ... close, they grow,"

La'ann added, "Changed now, Nahélé seems. Strange she breathes."

The Midfloor did seem brighter, more fully illuminated than normal. Here and there, sharp streaks of bright sunlight broke through the midforest ceiling and, while each swing of kumu'lio arms carried a familiar scent of midforest musk, it came tinged with a taste of the Wēkiu, as if open sky was near.

From a hanging vine La'ann pulled a weighty seed. Holding his hand away from Mœrai's side, he let it fall. To Angus's mind the fall seemed all too short. A foraging élobe might let him judge the distance better, but none could be seen.

What meaning Angus drew from these observations came in the change he perceived in his two companions. The absolute confidence that Angus had come to expect as part of La'ann and Hol'imm's every word and action had vanished. He searched for reassurance. "La'ann, in what direction M'pepebato village is?"

Before answering La'ann twisted himself to look in every direction. His answer surprised Angus. "Know I do not."

Until that moment, La'ann and Hol'imm's wealth of knowledge had always filled Angus with admiration. Within the forest, no one would come to harm while in their company. La'ann's revelation startled Angus. "Why see you cannot?"

A long pause preceded La'ann's explanation. "Kamata vines. With water of the Pōele, Nahélé breathes. Longer upon one side of colōfn tree thirsty vines grow. Upon colōfn trees here all sides alike seem."

The explanation made sense but did little to extinguish Angus's concern. Had they lost their compass?

In their preoccupation, the four clansmen had allowed space to open between themselves and the column's rear. In the distance, the rearmost of the Bakeisiká column was barely visible. With a curt nod toward the receding riders, La'ann urged Mœrai forward, putting an end to the matter. "Come! Go we must."

Kùmulio are strong animals, agile and well suited to the forest. Swift, however, they are not. By the time the M'pepebato clansmen had closed the gap, the entire Bakeisiká column had come to a halt, which generally occurred only when they reached the day's objective. A halt so early in the day could only mean they had also reached their next trading venue.

La'ann seemed impatient. "Ahead ride I will. Village here see I wish." He pressed Mœrai past the nearest Bakeisiká riders before anyone could venture to join him.

By the time La'ann returned, his comrades were already setting up the evening bivouac near their customary position at the outskirts of the larger encampment. With no need for his help, his three companions allowed La'ann to sit silently atop Mœrai and await the platform's completion. Not until the others had settled onto the campsite did La'ann dismount and assume his place. The first flames of Hol'imm's fire flickered upward before anyone spoke a word. Then, in a calm and quiet voice, as though adding but a small observation to earlier discussions, La'ann made a surprising announcement. "No village there is."

All heads rose. Eilen spoke for everyone. "Trading we make not?"

"For trading Bakeisiká prepare, but upon the midfloor no village shadow sits."

At that declaration Hol'imm, Angus and Eilen stared while they grappled with its meaning. Every previous caravan stop had come with common features. Every stop came with a village and every village under Nahélé's care came with the same basic pieces: a central common area surrounded by family living areas, all built above an expanse of kùmu'lio stalls and a commercial loading dock. The village footprint always cast a large, dark shadow onto the midfloor below.

"With what clan do they trade?"

"Called N'gombabato, Bakeisiká say."

With a head now filled with the names of many of Nahélé's clans, Eilen looked for definition. "N'gombabato. Of what does this name speak?"

La'ann searched for words, brightening as they came. "People of the great sky wall."

Pressing the heels of her hands to her forehead, Eilen strained to translate each Batololému word. A moment later, she looked at Angus and erupted in Standard. "The Mountain Clan! Mountains! We're approaching a range of mountains."

Sound sleep evaded Angus that night, visiting only in fleeting fits. His high-forest cloak was no match for night air much cooler than Nahélé had ever before pressed upon him. A world outside of Nahélé loomed near, filling his head with possibilities. Sleep would bring the morning that much sooner, but that knowledge held little sway over his excitement. Sitting in silence, Angus met the slowly brightening morning with tired anticipation.

Eilen awoke before the others. "You seem rather quiet this morning."

"My restless night was no reason to disturb everyone."

"You couldn't sleep?"

"I couldn't get the notion of mountains out of my head, a new piece of this planet."

Before Eilen could offer more, La'ann awakened. "Batololému speak!"

"Sorry we are, La'ann. Sleeping you were."

"Sleeping no more I am. Amon awakes."

The sack of dried fruit in Hol'imm's outstretched hand supplied breakfast. The sleeping platform went quiet as the four clansmen gathered belongings. Then they sat to await the summons that customarily called them to the trading festivities. They would soon meet people from outside the forest for the first time.

Sometime later, Angus became the first to voice frustration. "No one comes."

The unusual delay also puzzled La'ann. "Truth you speak, Ahngoose. Why here messenger comes not?"

Standing, Hol'imm searched the surrounding campsites. "Gone many kùmu'lio are."

"To trading join asked we are not," Eilen said as she too

pushed herself up from the platform.

Angus's face turned hard. "Truth Eilen speaks. Asked we are not. Without asking I will go."

Last to stand, La'ann reached for Angus's arm. "Care take, Ahngoose. Strong anger Bakeisiká leader might feel."

"Go I must, La'ann."

Slinging a tied bundle of gear over his mount's neck, Angus reached to grab a bit of furry neck and pulled himself onto the young kùmu'lio he'd come to know as Tumtum. He had nearly made his way around the entire Bakeisiká bivouac before the others caught up with him.

Not far from the last vestiges of the bivouac area Angus found an isolated, narrow platform hanging from the midforest ceiling. To one side of its near end, a group of unburdened kùmu'lio hung tethered to ceiling foliage, bindings hanging loose. Angus pressed his mount close to the platform's near end. Looking along its length he could see the far end rise smoothly upward. Perhaps the sharp scent of the We'kui helped him understand, or perhaps Angus had become enough of a forest native to recognize the harsh edges of sunlight bathing the ramp's upper lengths, but he knew Amon shone down upon the sloping ramp's upper lengths. Dismounting, he set down his sacks upon the platform and retrieved his high-forest cloak.

Waiting only long enough for the others to dismount, Angus slung his gear over one shoulder and walked toward the light, unable to question why the weight of his gear helped to quell his anxiety.

That Hol'imm remained seated atop his kùmu'lio puzzled no one. Hol'imm was not one to leave kùmu'lio untended in unknown surroundings.

First to reach the top, Angus peered through narrowed eyes sheltered within the shadow of his cloak's hood. Another long platform lay atop the midforest foliage. Green branches of many trees surrounded the platform terminus just beyond the group of Bakeisiká standing near that end. Between the nomads and him, a neat arrangement of trade goods spread across the deck's one side. Beyond the traders, Angus saw no great colōfn trunks rising to hide the deep blue sky. Trees ceased their reach not far above where he stood. In the opposite direction, he noted a long stretch of flat wooden pathway disappearing into blue-white haze. Lost in a bright hazy sky, the appearance of what might be a mountainside loomed above distant treetops. His attention returned to the nomads.

Setting his feet, he became alert to their every movement. *Am I welcome or not?* For one long moment Angus watched the dark hollows of every Bakeisiká hood, imagining glaring eyes within each.

Brushing Angus's arm, La'ann stepped past and walked purposely toward the Bakeisiká. Angus tensed, then almost jumped at the touch of Eilen's hand on his arm.

Her voice came muffled by the hood she wore. "What's going on?"

"Not sure. La'ann seems to have taken the initiative."

Angus watched La'ann stop in front of two Bakeisiká figures identified by broad necklaces covering both chests—the clan's Trademaster and Haku'iké. Deference was evident in La'ann's posture and his every gesture. His words fell victim to distance and muffling hoods. Not until he turned and beckoned them to approach did Angus and Eilen realize La'ann's purpose.

As he walked slowly past the display of trade goods, Angus kept his eyes fixed upon the Trademaster, allowing himself only the slightest glance at the assembled wares. Stacks of ropes stood several coils high and he recognized Su'ban's medicines displayed in small clusters, looking like afterthoughts alongside batches of dried fruits.

The short walk occupied more time than the distance seemed to warrant, giving Angus time to see from within the hood's shadow the Trademaster's eyes fixed upon him. La'ann's right hand resting upon the hilt of his knife did little to quell Angus's concern.

Angus had nearly reached La'ann's side when the Trademaster's eyes suddenly lost their hold, his head and his attention turned away to refocus somewhere distant. In sharp repeated strokes, he waved the three newcomers toward the far end of the gathering. Responding to La'ann's firm grip on his arm, Angus complied without protest.

Slow, rhythmic reverberations announced the local clan's arrival through the platform beneath their feet. Pulling the hood of his cloak tight to shade his eyes, Angus strained to see into the bright haze. Many breaths passed before vague shapes slowly emerged from the distant end of the wooden pathway. Several more breaths passed before he could discern four-legged beasts plodding beside men. Each pair moved within a halo of diffuse color, a soft glow without sparkle. As distance diminished, indefinite images became heavily burdened creatures, evincing in the casual manner of their cloaked handlers, a line of docile beasts. Sturdy feet protruded below long white hair cascading down each flank. Beside the hairy animals walked men clothed in loose garments, belted and hooded and displaying the same white color as that covering the animals. Gripping long staffs, they marked each step with a coordinated strike to the platform. Only three others followed the lead pair. At the moment when wooden staffs simultaneously ceased their rhythmic beat, the mountain traders stood opposite their Bakeisiká counterparts.

The new arrivals immediately began untying bundles strapped atop their pack animals. Two handlers wrestled each heavy bundle onto the deck. The first bundle struck the deck with a metallic clank, putting Angus on full alert. Enduring the placement of all eight bundles, he waited much too long before seeing the traders unwind the first cover. When the cover finally fell back, rows of bright metal gleamed atop the heavy fabric. The sight made Angus's heart pump. There they were, his link to a more sophisticated world. Feeling Eilen's restraining hand on his arm he stifled a strong desire to pick up and hold one of the bright shapes in his hands.

Trading took a different form at this stop, all business and no social agenda. N'gombabato traders stepped forward to stand before the waiting Bakeisiká, exchanging slight bows before words were spoken. The Bakeisiká awaited the pleasure of their hosts. The first N'gombabato words came in heavily accented Batololému accompanied by broad arm gestures, inviting their guests to inspect the offerings.

Understanding only scattered words, Angus could not grasp what was being said. Frustrated to stand mute and idle, he struggled to hide his impatience. It seemed a long age before the Bakeisiká leader turned to invite his contingent to inspect the N'gombabato wares. Asking no permission, Angus joined the inspection. He picked up a hilted knife and ran his hand carefully over the bright, well-honed blade, feeling its weight, admiring the neatly wrapped leather hilt. Its mirrored surface spoke of skill and refinement, not a blade forged in any simple charcoal fire.

Barter began as soon as the two groups reconvened, facing each other cross-legged on the deck. Angus's impatience grew. *Perhaps the small numbers will promote a short barter session?*

On other stops, Angus enjoyed the haggling, but here the sound of it droned in his ears. Feeling his crossed legs beginning to cramp, he lamented the inability to stand and stretch. Although thankful for the protection of his high-forest cloak, the bright sunlight eventually began to extract a toll. Thirst became a priority. Perhaps physical stamina occupied a prominent position among the skills necessary for good bartering.

Angus began to think. A piecemeal realization took form. Another world exists outside the forest, a world where sophisticated tools are fabricated. The trail led outside. *Can we somehow attach ourselves to this mountain clan?*

Inspired, he searched for a plan. No flash of insight came forth. Initial excitement gave way to frustration. Among other forest clans, he and Eilen had always triggered curiosity. This new clan seemed different. There would be no evening entertainment. There would be no opportunity for La'ann to tell the tale. The mountain clansmen would see nothing new in their forest partners. Angus struggled. *What can I do? Any interruption might be seen as insult.*

Throwing back the hood of his cloak, Angus let his thick mane spill across his shoulders. Harsh sunlight fell hard upon him. The air seemed suddenly more difficult to draw in. Squinting against the glare, he shook his head and loosed long locks of hair. Keeping a sidelong eye on the N'gombabato spokesman, Angus ran nails through his beard. *I must look about as alien as anything they've ever seen.*

Talking stopped. The N'gombabato leader turned to stare. Traders on both sides looked for the source of disruption. Angus said nothing, attempting with a deep nod to return a respectful answer to the curious stares of mountain clansmen.

"Of what strange clan, this man is?" the leader asked.

The nomad Trademaster hesitated before offering introductions. "From far outside Nahélé, told we are ... Called Ahngoose, he is."

Hearing his name, Angus let his head fall.

A slight returned nod from the N'gombabato speaker allowed Angus to breathe easier. At least his breach of etiquette had not brought instant reproach. Then the N'gombabato clansman spoke directly to him, "Ninibato wapi, ozali?" Angus understood the accented Batololému words and knew the man again asked of his origin. Yet he hesitated, keenly aware that his answer would weigh in the granting of any future request.

Confronted again with the need to explain something he

knew would not be understood, he answered with no answer at all. In slow, carefully articulated Batololému he said, "Russell Four, called it is. Far beyond the Mokililana found it is." The heads of four N'gombabato clansmen bobbed inside loose hoods, apparently accepting his answer and his strange appearance as natural for anyone of such foreign origins.

Angus smiled, satisfied with his first step. Returning to the welcome protection of his hood, he sat quietly, allowing attention to return to the needs of the trade. Some time later the two leaders nodded, stood, and presented each other a formal bow from the waist. Thankful for the opportunity, Angus stood. A cool breeze flowed across the platform. It felt good.

The two trading teams quickly redistributed wares and collected their purchases. Angus watched, impressed with the apparent value of ropes and medicines. While two of the Bakeisiká clansmen rolled up every open display of metalwork, two others stepped to the assembled Bakeisiká wares and pulled away about a quarter of the ropes and nearly a third of the medicines before allowing N'gombabato clansmen to package the remainder. Su'ban's medicines seemed the perfect merchandise: small containers, sparing of weight and volume, yet high in value. What more could a trader ask for?

Seeing the end of the trade, Angus watched the Bakeisiká clansmen carry newly acquired property down the ramp. He quelled a slight panic. He had no intention of returning into Nahélé's depths. He needed to become part of the departing mountain clan's caravan. How he might accomplish this goal did not immediately present itself?

Could he buy his way in? What might he trade for passage? Time was short. He looked to find Eilen and La'ann standing beside one of the large beasts, stroking its white coat.

Walking toward them, he waited only until he came within hailing distance. "Eilen! La'ann! Speak with you, I must." Four steps later, he continued his thought. "Join the N'gombabato, I must."

The announcement did not seem to surprise Eilen. La'ann's eyes, however, became wide. Angus stood silent, watching the La'ann grapple with another difficult choice.

Momentarily incapable of thinking in Batololému, Angus mused in Standard. "Have we anything that we can afford to trade for passage?"

"You know what we're carrying as well as I do. I wouldn't want to part with the torch or the sidearm. The rest isn't worth too much."

"To us, but perhaps not to them. How about the reflective blanket?"

The wrinkles in La'ann's face matched the agitation in his voice. "Batololému speak!"

With a bow of her head, Eilen apologized. "Joining mountain clan, we wish. Blessing we seek."

As though all mental conflict had run its course, La'ann's expression went blank. "All trading with question begins. Wishes, known must be."

Angus stopped pacing. "Ask, you can?"

Only a moment's hesitation separated La'ann's stern face from the sight of his committed stride carrying him toward the nearest mountain clansman.

....

At the rear of a procession of woolly animals, the three forest clansmen listened to a deep rumble rising from beneath their feet. To both sides of the wooden pathway, treetops reached no higher than twice La'ann's height. Ahead, a rocky slope disappeared into bright haze. The weight of Amon's gaze fell heavily upon each hooded head. Everything they possessed rode on their backs. They were leaving the forest behind.

Upon stepping onto the first solid ground she had felt since arriving on this world-without-a-name Eilen voice erupted loud enough to turn the head of more than one mountain clansman. "Dry ground!"

For a moment the three foresters stopped to scuff their sandals in the dirt at their feet. Even from within the shadows of his hood, Angus could see how little La'ann's blank expression changed. "Where your thinking goes, La'ann?"

"With Bakeisiká alone Hol'imm will be. For Mœrai care Hol'imm will make."

That La'ann's thoughts might linger in the forest should not have been a revelation. Wanting to nudge his friend onto the new path, Angus offered reassurance. "Well Mœrai will be, La'ann." Then ventured a diversion. "For this hard world beyond Nahélé, what name is given?"

La'ann's answer came slowly and with a shrug of shoulders. "The Midfloor, the Mokililana, the Pō'ele, the Wēkiu. These places, my spirit holding is. Of this place no thinking I find." La'ann had become like Eilen and Angus, an adventurer, an explorer of unknown reaches.

CHAPTER 22
Patience

Yet again, Victory's most recent telemetry sweep had come up empty. Addressing no one in particular, Alexandra's voice carried an angry tone as she extinguished the projection field. "Why have we not seen anything?"

Able as his captain was in some ways, Semgee could never quite understand her inability to stay a course. She dealt poorly with uncertainty. Negative results never satisfied her impulsive nature. He could only think to explain, as he had done several times already, "Honorable Captain, I can only say again: it's too early, we'd be very lucky to have seen anything. You may recall that we were nearly a year into our last voyage before we stumbled upon the transmissions from that remote station. Our new mission will do much better, but we must be patient and let our plan take form. A few weeks of effort are simply insufficient to support high expectations."

Semgee watched his captain pace the bridge. Equipped with the temperament of a caged animal, she was often guided by instinct alone and completely out of sorts when restrained. Perhaps a bit more feeding would help matters. "Honorable Captain, perhaps I can show you the progress we've made. We have now explored a great deal of search volume within which we can definitely say a civilized planet does not exist."

Reactivating the projection field, Semgee displayed a three-dimensional map of the Lesser Magellanic Cloud. Instantly, the dwarf galaxy came to life floating above the projection field's defining collar, a dense swarm of tiny spots, some barely large enough to distinguish, a few large and bright enough to stand out from the rest.

He'd never admit it, but Semgee enjoyed using the projection field. The faint metallic odor stirred him, reminding him of the electrical storms he frequently enjoyed as a child.

Manipulating controls, Semgee shifted the viewing perspective until one very small, but very bright pulsating green spot stood out from the rest. "Victory is now here, Honorable Captain. The vertical axis in the image is oriented to Galactic standard; 'up' here is Galactic 'up'." The Milky Way is located in the direction of this vector." A solid, thin illuminated arrow immediately appeared within the image, its tail at the center of the fog, its point directed just above Semgee's right shoulder. With a second flick, it just as quickly vanished.

Semgee illuminated a second pulsating spot. "You can see how that vector and the location of the station we found defines the axis of our search volume."

Alexandra ceased pulling on her lower lip and Semgee allowed himself a little relief. Continuing in a more upbeat tone, he said, "Here is the search volume we plan to explore." A volume of tiny points on the image's outer layer turned violet, defining a wedge-shaped segment wrapped around the near end of the galactic vector.

"Now," Semgee punctuated his next statement. "Here's the volume we've already inspected." Another actuation eliminated all but a narrow, nearly tube-shaped volume of 'search wedge'. "You see how much remains before we can say we've given our plan an adequate trial?"

"It looks so small."

"Of course, Honorable Captain. But please remember, a

few months is not really a very long time."

"Yes, yes. You've said as much before."

Although he knew he had no choice, Semgee still had to ask himself if joining their new mission had been a mistake. Would the mission's importance ever make up for the unpleasant time spent with this person? When we succeed, she'll likely receive a seat on the First Council. *Will I ever command a ship of my own?* Perhaps.

CHAPTER 23
Nahélé's Edge

Renewal. Angus could feel it in his bones. The last few mornings had seen him awaken alert, ready, and eager. Pulling the bright new knife from the sheath on his belt, Angus examined the blade as he had done many times since he acquired it. The metal from which it was forged spoke to him. Not primitive, not simple, not low-grade black iron, it gleamed with noble immunity, completely free of the minutest worldly blemish, a truly civilized alloy.

He should be disappointed. Search efforts had thus far revealed no sign of industry, neither furnace nor forge, anywhere within the mountain clan's cavern. In an odd twist of logic, the failure reassured him. The discovery of advanced metalwork here among another primitive people would only disappoint. Yet somewhere a source did exist and the people of this cavern were one step closer to finding it.

Mornings in the cavern were something of a mystery, marked only by faint echoes of cooking pots and children's complaints. Angus had yet to understand how these mountain people recognized the beginning of each day. The natural concept of 'day' waited somewhere outside.

Cool and dank, the cavern bore a lived-in spirit, permeated by the musty odors of animal fleece, cooking fires, and seeping rock. Partway up one side a natural spring feeding a small pool overflowed into a stepped cascade and descended to the cavern floor. There it ran toward the opposite end to disappear under a low rock shelf. Open, flowing water kept the air humid and, together with a constant soft airflow, kept the cavern cool. The partnership worked overly well, rendering the cavern cooler than high-forest cloaks could resist. Stroking his new gomba-fleece garment, Angus admired the soft fur felt, thinking how well it served the mountain environment, keeping him comfortable within the cool cavern and able to repel Amon's glare outside.

On that morning, Angus enjoyed an easy mood. He felt cleaner than he had in a long time. Flowing water endowed the cavern with a public facility and Angus had just treated himself to the pleasure of a cleansing shower. Tingling skin lingered from the sand grit he had used to strip away the trail's deposit of dirt, sweat and oil. He could scarcely remember when he last stood beneath an afternoon rainfall. *Odd that Su'ban's alchemies don't seem to include any kind of soap.*

Local invention did, however, provide another delight. The soft garment came from the sheared fleece of the mountain clan's pack animals, 'gomba', as he now knew them. The shearing tool, a single strap of metal sporting two ground ends sharpened and bent upon each other, worked equally well on human hair as on gomba fur. Running a hand over a short, trimmed beard, Angus thanked Eilen's skill with the instrument. Light skin and blue eyes would continue to garner more attention than he might find comfortable, but his hair had lost its shaggy, unkempt wildness.

Feeling relaxed, he sat holding a cup of the hot mountain clan 'tea,' staring into the tiny ripples within the cup. Pictures of the Raiju wafted into his thoughts: John Singh scratching his chin before the navigator's consol; Ivan hunched over his Comboard; Henning standing with arms braced against the systems consol. The image morphed into the sound of

Henning's voice; a transmission from the mining station. Had Henning made it back to Russell Four? Had the Raiju's last action given Haven a chance to prepare? The knowledge that he would never know the answer to any of those questions weighed almost as much as the knowledge that his former friends no longer breathed.

Eilen's hail from across the cavern brought him out of the trance. "They're going out again ... trading ... and this time they're packing Su'ban's medicines and M'pepebato ropes."

In the excitement of her voice, Angus heard spirit. She no longer looked like the crewmate with whom he had once shared command decisions. Who was she now? *In one way at least, I'm quite lucky.* "We should join them."

....

The three M'pepebato clansmen walked at the rear of a short column of gomba. Cool flowing air whistled past La'ann's ear. Clothed in mountain garments and sturdy trail shoes, he suspected they were not going back to the forest. The mountain clan intended to do business with the 'Dryland Traders' and he knew of no such people among the forest clans.

Emerging into morning shadows, La'ann realized he had not seen sunlight since they entered the cavern some days before. Barely etched into the slope of the mountainside a single barren, pebble-strewn path led away from the cavern entrance.

Their journey had only begun when the lead handler nudged the first gomba through a sharp downhill turn, urging it off the trail and onto a flat, smooth rock outcropping, letting the beast find footing on the hard surface. Those behind waited to perform the same maneuver in turn.

La'ann searched his memory to find no trace of this path. It must lead to some destination other than the forest platform where they had left the nomads. The hard rock presented slight evidence of use. Proceeding slowly, N'gombabato handlers gave their burdened animals ample time to find secure footing. By the time a well-worn trail once again supported their footsteps, the path skirted the near end of the valley, along a shallow bench, tracking just above treetop level.

Loose ground was not La'ann's natural domain. He was both fascinated and unnerved by the sloping path. Placing each step with care, he eschewed the edge that fell away to his right. Yet, the sight of many small, densely packed treetops drew him there. Nahélé's voice rose in La'ann's mind, inviting him to look. A sudden insight stole into his thoughts. Below his feet he saw how each little tree held six neighbors close around, each trunk intimately joined to the others. Raising his eyes, he gazed out over the bright, white puffy surface of cloud hanging among the tops of the larger trees farther down the valley, taking note of the thousands of treetops poking their heads above the bright fluff. In his mind's eye, he saw the forest's birth here where he stood, its youth taking shape in a bound mass of little treetops, pushing its way down the valley to grow as it crept, becoming in the far distance the array of giant pillars that he knew so well, and finally forming the Kua'la in its death. He saw Nahélé not as many trees, but as one great forest—a never-ending, singular living organism, inexorably creeping down the valley.

The 'Nahélé Wound' now found a place in his store of knowledge. Where he had once seen mystery he now saw a boundary dispute between the forest organism of this valley and another crawling out of the next valley, a collision between two massive moving forests.

Buoyed by revelation, La'ann's face broke into a wide smile, pleased to add a new connection to his bond with Nahélé. Perhaps he alone understood. He wanted badly to share this new knowledge with Su'ban.

An upward gaze found sharp mountain peaks looming

over their path. Seen in earlier shadowed morning light, the sight might have revealed snowfields in shaded regions of the higher slopes. Now, Amon's bright light struck from high above the near side of the ridge, making it difficult to gaze toward those summits. Yet the air moved in cool swirls, giving La'ann reason to be thankful for the mountain robes he wore.

Some distance passed before his legs began to feel the strain of the trail. A life spent hanging from the midforest ceiling did not endow legs with great experience atop dry ground. Unsettled in unfamiliar surroundings, he stepped warily, unable to find guidance in well-developed reserves of knowledge. He missed the soft touch of Mœrai's arms. *Well be, Mœrai. Well be, Hol'imm.*

The gomba fleece robe served well. All morning it kept him warm. Now as the column made its way along the far side of the valley the garment shielded him from Amon's glare better than its bulk would suggest possible. He pulled the deep hood further over his head to better protect his eyes.

Monotony had just begun to dull La'ann's thoughts when the path plunged into the mountainside. Is this the entrance to another cave dwelling? Had they arrived at their destination? Air flowing through the passage perked up his senses and revived his morale. He threw back his hood. The air felt cool, if a bit musty smelling. Light in the passage became dim. No torch sconces lit the way. A lead clansman lit a torch, throwing just enough light off the walls to give those in the rear a beacon.

The deeper into the mountain they plunged, the more La'ann's comfort fled. The cave pressed upon him like a great weight. So completely unlike his verdant forest home, so foreign to his psyche, oppressive walls fanned fear. Like his feelings in the Pō'ele, close hard walls laid a clamp on his chest. Like the Pō'ele, he fought to gather courage, pulling deep breaths into his lungs. The touch of Ee'laan's hand on his back seemed to help. Reaching his own hand forward, he sought security in the feel of Ahngoose's back. Ahngoose's didn't seem to object. The connections settled his thoughts, giving him strength to resist the suffocation of darkness and close walls.

When the light ahead suddenly faded La'ann nearly called out. For a moment the darkness tightened its grip. What happened? Looking up he could just make out a faint glimmer. Some steps later he stepped out of the narrow passage and entered a wild underground room, large enough to swallow the dim torchlight and yet leave its far walls hidden in darkness.

What little light there was illuminated just enough ground to reveal a precarious trail. The column had not entered upon the cavern floor but stood exposed somewhere upon its flank. The path edge to La'ann's right dropped away into a featureless abyss. The sound of water drops falling into a pool echoed up from far below. A live, moist odor wafted upward, entrained in a gentle flow of cool air.

Fortifying his courage with the touch of a trailing hand upon the cave wall, La'ann wished for an end to the precarious path. Resurgent fears threatened to envelop him once again. He sought solace with thoughts of the gomba beasts ahead, calmly trudging forward, secure in their knowledge of the trail much as Mœrai trusted Nahélé's vine-covered paths. When the leading torchlight again reshaped itself, refocusing as the trail plunged into another close passage, La'ann's anxiety churned yet again. Relief at the precarious ledge's end became quickly dispelled by the oppressive weight of another confining space. Each step fell onto slightly higher ground and lifted him through a low twisting tunnel. Hard rock pressed from above leaving barely enough headroom for the animals. La'ann walked in a stoop, moving slowly through the restricted passage, ears assailed by the whine of flowing air and the close-focused echoes of hooves on stone. Breaths became more difficult to find.

Several times the passage gave way to multiple

alternatives, causing not the slightest hesitation or slowing of pace. Undeterred by black gloom, the column's leaders seemed to know every boulder, every turn along the dark trail as well as they knew the stones around their home fires. Darkness began to eat time as well as torchlight, dulling fears with monotonous, droning tedium. La'ann became thankful for small relief brought by the eventual weakening of the trail's upward march. When first he noted a change he was unsure of what he saw. Some moments later he allowed himself to take comfort from the sight.

"Ahngoose. Ee'laan. Light ahead, there is."

The truth soon became evident to all. A dim white glow seeped in from somewhere ahead, made visible by eyes sensitized by hours in darkness. The ceiling receded into the gloom above and the path began to wind through tumbled boulders, once a part of the ceiling. Eyes rose from the trail to peer ahead in anticipation of a glimpse of their destination. Even the gomba seemed to quicken the pace.

For a long while their surroundings continued to brighten until a uniform dim daylight reflected softly down from the rocky, rough ceiling of the widening passageway. La'ann knew that they neared an end. His nose told him well before his eyes.

"Camp there is," he announced, just before they rounded a final bend in the trail, just before it opened above the flat floor of a spacious cavern. The caravan took a turn to the right as they entered the open room, following a path circling down around the outside. Light streamed in from the left, where, some distance away the outside world vied for supremacy with the cave interior. Below, a wisp of smoke floated upward from a small campfire visibly burning on sandy, flat ground nested within a natural recess in a jumble of fallen boulders. A number of people sat around the fire.

....

In the language of the Omiswebantu, his name, Wezimunto, meaning 'starman,' became his when the night sky provided the only balm for his infant wailing. Within the tribe of desert traders, he was simply called 'Wezi.'

Just now, he watched the approaching file of Mountain People with mild interest, unwilling to let himself get excited over their arrival. He and his companions had enjoyed a quiet morning, resting in the cool shade of the trading cave in lazy conversation and he was in no hurry to disturb the calm. Bartering would begin soon, but there was no need to stir; he was already seated next to Mandingalo, who always spoke for the Omiswebantu traders during such sessions. He needn't even rise, suspecting that Mandingalo might remain seated, a tactic he's used before, displaying rude indifference in an effort to influence the bartering. Wezi sat in his customary place, prepared to translate between the language of the N'gombabato and his own Omiswebantu people's language. He would rise only when Mandingalo gave him a sign.

When Wezi finally took a good look at the approaching procession, he noted with some envy the very casual manner with which they led their pack animals down into the large open cavern, wondering if the animals might survive more than a day in the arid desert outside. A slight disturbance near the rear of the column caught his attention. Something seemed amiss. Three of the Mountain clansmen walked there alone, unaccompanied by pack animals, repeatedly turning their heads to gaze around the cavern, as if they had never seen such a place before.

'Out-of-character' might also describe Wezimunto, at least when compared to his brethren among the desert people. Not prone to the typically bombastic behavior in which his fellows took personal pride, he maintained more reserve. He was more of an observer, a thinker, and it was his observant self that now watched the last three members of the train of mountain traders. Their behavior seemed most interesting.

He imagined that an intriguing story might lie behind them and their slightly disheveled appearance. Their robes didn't seem to fall quite the same; didn't conform as well to the body forms beneath; weren't worn as comfortably as were others. Who might these three be?

....

The sight of another people from beyond Nahélé sent Angus's pulse up a notch. Glancing back at La'ann and Eilen, he found wonder in both faces.

As the small caravan made its way onto the flat cavern floor, he noted the 'dryland traders' sitting around a well-used camp area nestled into an alcove among boulders on the far right of the open floor. No one there stirred at the caravan's arrival, obviously quite accustomed to the sight. Rocks around the camp were blackened with soot. This camp had been in use for a long time. A broad rut, leading across the cavern floor, marked a well-used route from the direction of outside light.

By the time the caravan finally came to a halt, well removed from the area occupied by the small group of traders, Angus had already marked the carpeted display of wares laid out on the sandy cavern floor near the camp. He could only make out the rough size of the many items on display, but his pulse quickened with the sight. He was sure that a closer inspection would reveal an array of shiny blades in many forms. He had to remind himself not to run over and look. This new situation, with new tribes and commercial overtones, presented enough complexity to keep Angus alert to his own behavior. It would be prudent to wait for an appropriate moment.

The Mountain traders began slowly unloading pack animals, leisurely removing packages from their backs, moving slowly, as though bored with the whole affair. There was little for Angus to do but stand aside and avoid interfering. The slow pace of unpacking became difficult for him to watch, feeding a growing impatience and making him eager to lend a hand. His guides, however, moved in a slow cooperative dance, with a definite rhythm, serving some unapparent purpose and offering by way of invitation not even a glance in his direction. So, he stood, trying to look natural, knowing they all waited under the scrutiny of those seated not far away around the smoldering fire.

....

Wezi put on a stoic face, watching the charade with masked amusement. The lazy pace of the mountain tribesmen's unloading fooled no one around the fire's dying embers, obviously staged for the benefit of impending bartering. Not that it would have any real effect. Likely as much, Wezi mused, as would the feigned indifference of his own comrades, all part of a game the two groups played, and had been playing, since well before any of them now here had been born. In a short while, the real game would begin. He glanced at Mandingalo, noting the set of the man's jaw and how he mentally prepared himself for the verbal sparring to come.

In particular, Wezi watched the three 'odd ones,' as he had begun to think of them. Again, he saw how much apart from the others they stood and how they did not participate in the game. Again, he wondered who they might be. In his memory, only the mountain trader named 'Ubanimoboke' and a few animal handlers had ever participated in the business here.

....

The slow dance took its time, but eventually ended, leaving several piles of trade goods on the sandy cavern floor: rope coils, rolled bundles of gomba fleece, boxes of small glass containers—Su'ban's medicines—and a number of dried foodstuffs in various package sizes. Eilen was having a rather difficult time with the slow pace of things and wondered at the composure she saw in her two companions. The day had begun too long ago. Her small, hurried breakfast had long since ceased to satisfy, leaving in its wake growing hunger pangs, now becoming more difficult to ignore. Approaching the fire, she looked into the faces of her hosts. Hunger faded from mind.

Differences were evident in every facial line. If the features of Nahélé's people were sculpted from clay, a smooth landscape of hillocks and dales, the faces of 'dry land' traders were chiseled from stone, a sharp terrain of ridges and canyons. Numerous and distinct, the contrasts in appearance between the two peoples gave Eilen reason to wonder at the depth of separation between them. Such stark delineation would point to a deep, longstanding divide. Perhaps the trade connection before them has been as close as these two groups have ever come.

The man seated nearest the fire pit spoke. "Umbingelelo, Ubanimoboke! Sikahle?" he said evenly with both arms spread wide.

Eilen had only begun to wonder at the sound of a new language when she heard heavily accented Batololému words emerge from the man seated next to the first speaker. "Welcome, Ubanimoboke! Well, you are?"

The leader of the Mountain clansmen acknowledged the greeting with a slight bow. "Yes, Mandingalo! Well, I am. And you? Well you are, I wish."

Sending no eye toward the standing speaker, the translator repeated Ubanimoboke's words in the 'dry land' dialect, "Yebo, Mandingalo! Ngizwa kahle. ... Nakini kahle ngifisela."

All seemed well. Then, without the slightest signal, the

seated 'dry land' trader punched a long, accusing finger at the one she now knew as Ubanimoboke and, with a suddenly fierce facial expression, shouted loudly, "Nikukatha inhlonpho! Ngibona uthwala izibiphushile! Kungani kuenzafela mina!?"

Translating without change of gaze or expression, the man seated at the pointer's right hand then spoke again in quietly accented Batololému. "No respect, you hold! Worthless trash, I see. At me, why water from your mouth you do throw?"

For his part, Ubanimoboke offered his apparent attacker not the slightest reaction, but calmly folded his arms across his chest and returned an emphatic answer. "From mountain black heart, come, we have. Of great value, wares, we carry. Fool, you are, Mandingalo!"

Eilen cringed.

Again, without a glance toward either speaker, the translator merely shook his head enough to set in motion the silver ornaments hanging from his ears, and directed an even response in the opposite direction. "Sigaphuma intabakaba emnyama. Sithwala ngakuhulu inani. Wunina isiwula, Mandingalo!"

The desert spokesman rose in one motion. When the man raised an arm, Eilen expected blows. Instead, he extended the arm toward the display of trade goods and spoke. "Wenu impahlandini akwazi ukulingana nowethu."

Batololému words ushered from the still-seated translator, chasing the specter of impending violence from Eilen's mind. "The beauty of our goods, your poor trinkets, equal can not."

....

Unable to follow the exchange between the two leaders, Angus merely observed, catching only a word or two here and there. The banter of bartering had a familiar rhythm and Angus realized an opportunity would come to more closely examine the trade goods. He kept his eyes on the Mountain Clan leader, looking for any sign of an inspection round. It came in words. "Believe you, I do not. With my eyes, see I must."

Angus's pulse quickened. The translator rose to join the two traders. All three turned to walk toward the displays. Angus stepped in behind. The rebuff came intense and immediate. The Mountain Clan leader turned quickly pointing a finger directly at Angus's chest. "Move, do not!" Angus had little doubt of harsh consequence attending disobedience.

A wave of anger rushed through him before Angus reminded himself of how little he knew. Strict rules and rituals often accompany bartering everywhere. Suppressing his feelings, he let La'ann's gently restraining hand pull him back.

Out of earshot, those remaining behind could only understand the conversation by visual cues. A silent scene of broad gestures, of swept arms, shaken heads and menacing fingers presented a picture of continued bluster and bombast, as each trader in their turn either praised or denigrated the merits of individual trade items.

At one point, the two opposing representatives and their translator turned together to refocus attention toward the campsite and those standing around it. Angus stared back, convinced they were looking at him alone. The two traders' gestures drifted into a slower dance of head nodding. Their incessant dickering seemed to have entered a second phase, one that carried their eyes back toward the fireside. They returned to renew their positions sitting opposite each other across the cooling fire.

And haggling flowed from there. They had undoubtedly performed the same dance many times before, an exaggerated display of nodding, shaking heads, and slapped thighs; accompanied by fingers, both pointed and raised, singularly and in numbers, occasionally flashed in sets of ten spread wide. Both contestants employed enough physical posturing to render the exchange as exhausting as any athletic competition. Beads of sweat formed on the brows of both contestants. Their mutual bluster stood in stark contrast to the calm presence of the translator, whose face remained frozen in a stoic effigy.

And, for some time, it went on. Then, as if an alarm had sounded, the whole affair abruptly concluded. Things happened rapidly. The final tally seemed to be understood, implicitly. No reconciliation step, no exchange medium, pure barter all the way. No one wasted time in farewell pleasantries. Mountain clansmen in off-white robes soiled by the dust of the trail moved toward the displays of wares. Kneeling, they folded a ground cloth over the entire set of desert wares and wrapped them tightly for the return trip. A few rope coils were repackaged for shipment home. Perhaps, in spite of more forceful bluster, bargaining skills ran deeper in the mountains than in the desert.

A sudden moment of panic swept reasoned thought from Angus's mind. Metal knives and tools disappeared unexamined within fabric rolls. Re-laden pack animals were already being cinched for the trail. He had no intention of rejoining the return trip. Desert tribesmen, distinct in loose grey robes, also gathered wares. Angus's desires or even his presence concerned no one. What could he do? Quieting, Angus cleared his head and considered. He had to talk with the translator.

Which one was he? *Damnation! They all look alike.* Angus let his eyes roam from one to another, all scurrying around piles of newly acquired wares. There! The one with silver dangles in his ears, the one staring back, the one beckoning!

The translator's eyes met Angus's. He beckoned more forcefully.

Curiosity replaced the alarm in Angus's mind. *That's odd. Here I am, in a panic to talk to him, and there he stands waving me forward.*

Walking toward the man, Angus tried to appear calm, mentally composing a proper Batololému request for asylum. He needn't have concerned himself. The translator had other ideas. As Angus came near, the man bent down, picked up a coil of rope and tossed it toward him. Angus stumbled as he caught the rope's weight in both hands. Hardly had he recovered, when another coil came flying at him. Caught completely off guard, Angus was almost relieved when the translator spoke. "Quickly! Go, we must. Large distance, tonight, we travel."

The words were simple but the meaning escaped Angus's grasp. "Understand, I do not. With you, go, we do?"

"Yes. For you, Mandingalo trade makes ... To us, now, your strength belongs."

Angus's eyes grew wide. He stood frozen. Traded! Along with ropes and medicines. *Have we just become slaves?*

CHAPTER 24
High Desert

A bead of sweat leaked into Angus's eye. The path became indistinct. Pulling a sleeve across his brow, he blinked his eyes into focus. The load on his back grew heavier with each step. The translator's words echoed in his head. "... large distance tonight, travel we must." The bulky load forced his attention to the trail. Willfully placing each foot, he matched steps with the bearer ahead. The incline eased and turned to decline. A new set of muscles came into play. Angus strained to maintain balance.

With the downward slope came a view ahead. Soft light poured in through a wide opening looming some distance away. There lies the world of the 'dry-land traders.' As the ground grew level, Angus turned to search the train of bearers. *Where are they?* No recognition arrived before the man behind urged him forward.

Each time he cast eyes upward the opening grew larger, throwing more light onto the surrounding sand and filling the chamber with fresher air. As eyes adjusted to the light, so did his nose, becoming familiar with the scent of the air outside, tainted with the metallic taste of the Wēkiu. The outbound path rose to surmount a sandy berm filling the cavern mouth like a loose cork. Not until tired legs managed to push his eyes above the top of the berm, was Angus able to see what lay outside. The opening commanded a position high upon the brim of a wide shallow expanse, stretching into the distance. No end could be seen. Uko's broad face filled the landscape with soft light. Here surely was the 'dry land' of the 'dry land traders.'

And here, too, were wheels. The first he'd seen since leaving the Raiju. Wheels fit for solid ground. Several two-wheeled carts leaned against a large rock with wheels chocked and long wooden traces propped high. Animals to pull the carts there were also. Animals like none Angus had ever seen.

One animal in harness pawed at the ground. Tied into an array of nearby stakes, others restlessly pulled at their tethers, speaking in low resonating rumbles. Fearsome animals, every one seeming better suited to savage combat than to docile harness. Standing on two powerful legs, the beasts towered more than a meter above their handlers. Scaled hides glowed in Uko's radiance. Large heads swung in constant motion, stopping now and then to permit wary, yellow eyes to peer down each side of a long snout and focus a predator's vision upon anything within sight. Long tongues erupted in brief excursions, tasting the air. Short, menacing forearms ended in two sets of long, curved talons, evincing an ability to rip open any living thing unfortunate enough to come within reach. A long, muscular tail, stretching out flat above the ground, seemed to bestow upon each animal swifter movement than its bulk would suggest.

Angus held back. Other bearers walked around him to deposit loads nearer the tethered beasts. He'd seen claws before. Kùmu'lio had claws, thick powerful claws, claws adapted to gripping the midfloor ceiling foliage. Yet somehow, kùmu'lio claws appeared less intimidating than those worn by these animals. These claws inspired neither curiosity nor admiration. They inspired fear. The ease with which the many handlers managed the beasts filled him with respect. With eyes focused steadily on nearby animals, Angus deposited his load where others had already done, then turned to look for Eilen and La'ann. A hurried, anxious scan of his surroundings set teeth on edge until sighting them in the company of the translator. The casual manner of their approach dispelled his tension in one long slow breath.

In due course, Angus sat with legs dangling over the end of a two-wheeled cart filled otherwise with stacks of M'pepalia rope. As the cart lurched forward Angus shook his head in disbelief, finding it difficult to absorb how he and his three friends rode in silent captivity, like baggage, being drawn across a sandy desert by a creature born of a healthy imagination. Had his bullheaded quest cost them both freedom and fortune?

The look on La'ann's face spoke of other concern. La'ann stared wide-eyed at the vast, open space around him. How strange must it all seem? How different from Nahélé's protective arms? Noting Eilen's attention focused somewhere distant, Angus trained his eyes in the direction of her gaze. Two more carts followed theirs, the nearest far enough back to soften the presence of the unnerving animal pulling it. Behind the last cart a solitary rider sat atop one of the scaled animals.

....

Given half a chance, Eilen would always seize any opportunity to learn. Idly riding with a cart full of rope gave her just such a chance. As the cart jostled beneath her, she mused at her extraordinary circumstance. The fact was not lost on her that she sat upon an animal-drawn vehicle in the company of very human-like beings who occupied a planet far from anywhere such beings should exist. She let her attention focus on the solitary rider following the last wagon, watching how he controlled the bipedal creature he rode. Too far away to see his face, she noted the direction of his head, becoming certain that he watched her in return. The rider suddenly urged his mount forward.

The distance between them closed and Eilen forgot the flashing tongue of the rider's steed, concentrating on what little of his face she could see. One free end of a long scarf hung over his shoulder. The other end wrapped across the lower half of his face and around his head. Two deep blue irises shone like beacons from behind the scarf's protection, framed by light brown sclera within a darker facial frame. Reaching a place beside Eilen's wagon, the rider pulled up and allowed many seconds to pass, marked only by the creaking sounds of the caravan's wheels and the crunch of ground beneath them. That he intended to speak, Eilen understood. Why he hesitated she could not say. Eventually, the sound of accented Batololému revealed him to be the translator. "Wezimunto, called, I am."

Posed so calmly, the simple declaration offered a welcome invitation. Looking up, she held a hand to her brow and responded in kind. "Eilen, called I am."

The beast beneath the man called Wezimunto swung its head toward Eilen. A long, red tongue whipped the air above her head. A foul odor wafted into her nose. In reflex she turned away, drawing deeply on cool desert air to carry away the acrid smell. A distracting growl rose from her stomach, sending her mind to the pack upon her back. Food to sate her hunger had been there throughout the long day, but no opportunity allowed its retrieval. With legs dangling off the end of the cart, she thought of another use entirely. Eilen pulled the pack onto her lap and quickly found a sealed package. Tearing open the wrapping, she began eagerly chewing with a contented hum, purposely loud enough for Wezimunto to hear over the ambient sounds of the trail.

"Hunger, you have?" he asked.

Pleased by the success of her tactic, Eilen let a smile cross her face as she held up a second ration bar toward the rider.

The gesture seemed to amuse the man. He bent low and stretched to retrieve the offering. In the space of one cautious nibble, an experimental taste, and two healthy bites, the ration bar vanished. A nod conveyed the rider's appreciation. A foraging arm, a shoulder bag, and one moment later put reciprocal gifts into Wezimunto's hand. One stiff, dark, palm-sized chip fell to Eilen, who nearly dropped it as the cart hit a bump. A glance at Wezimunto's nibbling pantomime confirmed the chip's purpose. She bit down hard to tear off a piece. Firm, tough texture and an unknown but not completely unfamiliar taste told her she chewed upon dried and salted animal flesh. Looking up, she smiled and nodded, receiving two more pieces in acknowledgement.

An elbow into Angus's side made him aware of the offering. He stared at the unfamiliar items. She ripped off another piece from the morsel in her other hand, urging him to pass what she offered on to La'ann.

....

La'ann thought he knew the evening sky. He'd seen it many times from the edge of the midfloor, usually with company from Uko's broad arc on the horizon. In spite of all he had seen before, the desert sky enthralled him, so completely unbounded, as it was now, and harboring so many of Amon's sisters. Here was something to inspire awe, a completely unobstructed sky, becoming darker by each passing minute, and filling with so many of Amon's sisters to become as innumerable as the leaves on Nahélé's trees.

Until only a few days ago, Nahélé's arms had defined his world. Now he saw a new world stretching farther beyond Nahélé than anything he might have imagined. The trepidation of leaving Nahele's comforting arms had begun to fade, replaced by the exhilaration of discovery.

Accepting the dry animal flesh from Angus, he unhesitatingly drew it to his mouth and chewed without thought. Watching his own breath gather itself before his eyes in a visible cloud, he considered another new phenomenon. At times, in the cool air of the Wekui he had felt shivering discomfort, as he had in the water of the Poele, but here, wrapped in clothing thicker than he had ever worn, he felt a deeper kind of cold touch his hands and his nose. With a hand to his nose, he squeezed both nostrils to disturb the unfamiliar flow. Not all aspects of his new wide world were as fascinating as others.

....

Wezi had always wanted to talk with the mountain clansmen, to learn more of the world beyond the mountains. Trade protocol demanded he hold himself aloof, forbidding him from straying far from customary exchange. Fellow traders accepted his service with little or no appreciation and trading voyages had become dull routine. The novelty of outsiders added spice to the normally tedious return trip. Questions swirled in his mind, so many as to make them difficult to capture. It had been some while since he last found such pleasure in the exercise of his language skill.

And the 'odd ones' were indeed strange. He'd never before seen their like, especially the one with hair on his face, the one who sat sullenly silent. He leaned down, trying unconsciously to reduce the gap between his high perch and the one called 'Eyellen' riding the low cart beside him. The game they played had taken form without conscious effort from either side. It was his turn to ask. He directed his question at the notion of a forest. His first word jolted forth as his head bobbed with his mount's footfall. "Of ... a 'tree', tell me."

"Colōfn trees, called they are. In deep water, their feet stand ... The sky, their top touches ... Upon their branches,

Batonahélé live."

Wezi sat upright again, looking at the nearly featureless expanse of desert, finding it difficult to imagine the idea of 'deep' water, much less of a 'colōfn tree'.

Then the one called 'Eyellen', asked, "Of your beast, speak you can?"

Unsure where to begin, Wezi took a cue from 'Eyellen' and gave it a name. "Umgijimi Umqothu, called, they are. 'Jimi' we say." Pausing, he thought about where next to take his explanation, finally settling for nowhere at all. "As you see ... so they are," he said, spreading his hands wide.

"Run, your jimi can?"

The question inspired a soft hand to the animal's neck. A note of pride crept into his tone with his answer, "With great speed, run he can." Wezi was thinking of adding more when another idea struck. "With me, ride you will?"

....

That she might actually sit atop one of these scaly beasts had never occurred to Eilen. The notion prompted a moment's hesitation and forced her to give the animal a closer look. Ūko's diffuse evening light reflected from iridescent scales, surrounding the animal in a multicolored aura. Looking up toward its head, she watched the animal turn, as though aware of her scrutiny. A bright, wary, yellow eye peered intently at her. As if on cue, the jimi bellowed a deep rumbling groan, craning its neck and exposing a long row of sharp, cutting teeth. *"Obviously not an herbivore."* While the affection she heard in Wezimunto's voice was not shared, the animal did arouse her respect. Still, she didn't want to give offense to one among those she hoped might be called guardian, not master. Her answer came in a voice sounding much less firm than she intended. "Pleased will I be."

Urging the jimi forward, Wezimunto pulled even with the

driver, signaling with a vertical flat hand. Eilen hopped off as the cart came to a halt, then stood when the jimi squatted down onto the ground, stretching its long tail upon the ground. Pressed between the animal's thick thighs thrust high around him, Wezimunto beckoned.

Eilen looked at Wezimunto's outstretched hand, stilling her apprehension before taking hold. With one foot braced against the side of the jimi's tail, she swung a leg up to seat herself behind. Over his shoulder, Wezimunto said, "Hold, you must."

Even as he said it, the animal stretched the kink from its two strong hind legs, rising under her like a starship lift, pushing her to an unnerving height above the desert floor. Eilen's fingers wrapped themselves in Wezimunto's robe, feeling the taut muscles beneath.

Wezi yelled, "Hamba!" and struck heels into the animal's side. They lurched forward, one hind jimi leg swinging beneath them, sending the two of them leaning to one side. Eilen was not prepared, trying to hold steady with a handful of Wezi's robe, feeling the animal's tail muscles flex beneath her. On the second stride, she was ready and let herself move in sympathy. Two wide rocking strides later they had moved a short distance away from the desert caravan and Wezi felt better about letting the jimi show its power.

With a flourish, he raised his voice a little more, crying, "Hamba! Hamba!" as he kicked his heels firmly into the jimi's side, slapping at its flank with free reins. The jimi responded with another lurch. Two long strides later they were moving over the desert like a low flying bird, smoothly, as though the jimi's two feet no longer struck the hard ground. Cold air swept past Eilen's head. She could barely hear Wezi's commands.

One more 'Hamba!' brought yet another burst of speed from the animal, all the excess motion of a slower gait long since gone. The jimi rose high onto its toes, reaching out to swallow several meters of ground with each long stride, its tail straightened flat out behind, its neck stretched flat forward. Eilen felt the animal's muscles join in rhythmic waves, flowing from head to tail, sending all its strength down into smoothly swinging legs. It might have been an occasion for fear if the whole experience had not been so exhilarating.

It seemed to have barely begun when she felt the jimi's pace slow and the hum of cold air flowing past her ears begin to fade. Her body pressed forward against Wezimunto's back as the jimi's feet bit into the ground. With its last few strides, the animal absorbed forward momentum into upward flexing thighs and brought them to a halt. The jimi's exertion was visible with each exhaled breath in the cold night air. Wezimunto pulled the animal's head around to turn back toward the caravan, now barely discernible in the darkness.

Pointing up the shallow slope back toward where the dark base of the distant mountains met the level expanse of desert, Wezimunto said, "Look. Far, we run. Little time, we use."

Dim light made an accurate judgment of distance difficult, but Eilen could see that quite a bit of ground lay between themselves and the barely visible caravan.

Wezimunto prodded his jimi into a gentle trot, just enough above a walk to give him and Eilen a somewhat comfortable ride. He set them onto a slow, oblique course, aiming to intercept the caravan's path some distance ahead, unconcerned about any need to return quickly. Eilen pulled up the hood of her gomba-fleece robe. Warmth from the jimi's exertion felt good on her lower body but her ears burned with the cold night air.

Pointing into the darkening sky ahead Wezimunto said, "Ntombo awakens." A very bright star sat above the end of his finger, just beginning to clear the far horizon. The star seemed to captivate him. A moment later, he added, "Where Ntombo rises, we go."

The two riders fell silent. Wezimunto seemed lost in the

blackening sky and the myriad brightening stars. Eilen remembered the last NavCalc she had performed, reminding her how close to the Milky Way center the Raiju's last jump had taken them. Stars filled the sky, packed so densely that they shed enough light to pour faint illumination across the desert. For that moment, Eilen's life included nothing more than the star-filled sky above her, the jimi beneath her, and the desert trader whose back pressed against her.

....

An antsy Angus scanned the darkening desert expanse in search of the jimi and its riders. Twisting his body and craning his neck, he found them out of range of a normal speaking voice. Among surer friends and on surer cultural footing he might have shouted. As it was, he waited. All that could be heard were the sounds of conveyance: a wheel's squeak, an animal's snort, the crunch of sand and stone. The one called 'Wezimunto' seemed to be the lone chatty tribesman. Others rode within themselves. Unable to see Eilen clearly, Angus grew more nervous until they were nearly upon the caravan. "Eilen! Are you all right?"

"Of course, I am. Why wouldn't I be?"

Angus relaxed, dropped off the cart and walked toward the jimi. "Well, the way you and your trader friend took off, I wasn't sure you could hold on ... and ... I wasn't sure what sort of excursion your host had in mind."

Wezimunto urged his jimi to the ground. The rhythm and sound of Standard Galactic evoked a question. "Mountain tongue, speak, you do not?"

The task of dismounting required all of Eilen's attention. Wesimunto's question waited for a response until both her feet were back on solid ground. She took a moment to catch her breath, finally answering in Batololému. "No ... Wezimunto ... speaking of our homeland ... we use."

Instead of pursuing the matter further, Wezimunto surprised Angus by presenting himself. "'Wezi', to some, called I am."

Angus heard the personal invitation. Stepping closer to the jimi, he offered a hand. "Angus called I am."

....

The line of wagons rumbled across a flat broad valley, eating miles dimly lit by the densely starred night sky. Hours passed before the horizon ahead began to brighten and, upon reaching a hue that satisfied some criterion known only to their leader, the caravan stopped. Amon had awakened to chase them into hiding.

Leading the parade, Mandingalo's mount settled to the ground, and the other animals, both in harness and out, followed as one, taking their cue like a well-practiced dance. The three cart-riders nearly fell backward when their support suddenly rose high. Only Eilen refrained from letting out a sound, since she had been watching the lead animals and saw the settling dance take shape. Perched as they were, their dismount presented an awkward prospect. Wezi gave them a direction to follow. "Stay."

The removal of harnesses consumed little time and, with leverage from the long wooden traces, Wezi joined their driver to let the cart down slowly, allowing the three of them to step off the cart upright, dignity intact. Other drivers asked for help with their own carts. Anxious to help, Eilen welcomed the chance to study the draft animals more closely. Wezi bade her use caution, "Wary, jimi are. Smell you they do. Know you they do not. Near them, alert be."

One of the drivers waved, asking for help with his harness. Following his guidance, Eilen walked beside the unharnessed jimi and grabbed hold of a free trace. The driver had hold of the second trace. Together, with respect for the wagon's contents, they pushed the wagon back from the jimi and lowered the traces to the ground. The jimi sat alone, resting on the ground, reins dangling. Not until the driver had the wagon secured did he turn his attention back to the animal.

Eilen watched the driver's eye widen and heard him shout, "Amandla!" Seeing fear in his eyes she turned to see the jimi standing. She froze. A flare of nostrils, a sharp exhale visible in the cold air, huge feet scraping the ground all told her she faced an angry beast. She'd never know what small event might have, at that moment, tipped the animal's ire, for even as Eilen took in the nervous bearing, the beast reared, bellowed, and charged. In the small fraction of a second it took Eilen to see the sharp teeth, slashing claws, and crushing feet come at her, she reacted. In that instant she saw the certain death to be found in flight. Instead, she lunged, running directly at the beast, ducking below the snapping jaws and the arc of claws. Grabbing the thick tuft of long hair growing on the animal's chest, she held on with every fiber of strength she possessed. The excited jimi surged forward, dragging Eilen's useless legs across the ground.

With no target ahead in its field of view the animal slowed to a halt, panting, sending forth each breath with less and less force. The driver ran to take the reins. Able to stand again, Eilen released her grip and stumbled away. The same adrenaline, only a second before, propelling her to action, now washed over her, leaving her shaking. She looked around to see all eyes staring.

Rushing ahead of Wezi's long strides, Angus asked, "Are you all right?" The high tone in his voice relayed his concern.

Bent over to brace arms upon knees, trembling, Eilen failed to instill calm into her voice. "Yes ... I am," she said, feeling relief at the touch of Angus's flat hand upon her back.

Wezi's open mouth betrayed his amazement. "Proper act you make. This act only jimi boss knows. How know you did?"

Armed with absolutely no knowledge of jimi, Eilen had

apparently done the only thing possible to save herself from harm.

....

The three forest clansmen stood with Wezi to one side. Assigned no task, they watched the camp take shape. Two desert traders tended animals; others tended the shelter. A well-practiced routine quickly turned the contents of one wagon into an open tent rising above the sand. Air flowed freely under the shading cover and thick, woven carpets, held occupants off the sand. The end result provided a comfortable refuge from Amon's glare.

Still awed by the powerful animals, the forest clansmen never let their eyes stray far from the jimi, watching handlers tether each animal. With saddles and harnesses removed, reins staked to the ground, the jimi all settled onto the ground, hindquarters humped into the air, protected from the brightening sunlight by thick hide and reflective scales, heads tucked into curled tails.

As she rose higher, Amon's radiance became bright and white. The morning sky took a deep blue color, sparsely populated by soft wisps of high clouds; nothing like the thick layers above the colōfn forest. Jimi were grouped to one side. The soft aura they wore under Ūko's glow had become a myriad of scintillating reflections, glinting off iridescent scales like thousands of tiny mirrors. It became difficult to hold eyes upon them.

Sleep would come later, giving way first to a need for food, and discourse. Tribesmen gathered within the shaded tent, seating themselves cross-legged around a circle, with bits of dried food arranged in the center. Angus, Eilen, La'ann and Wezi sat on one side of the circle. Mandingalo sat opposite, flanked by unnamed tribesmen.

The desert language sounded warm between tribesmen,

sprinkled with a few chuckles amid chewing. Mandingalo did most of the talking. Everything seemed ordinary and calm—a simple rest stop. Mandingalo spoke in a low voice to Angus. Wezi translated. "Of your traveling here, Mandingalo wishes telling."

Angus looked to La'ann. La'ann nodded, a smile widening his face. He had developed the entertainer role and come to enjoy it.

With Wezi translating, La'ann described his first sight of the Raiju's lander streaking across the sky. When the story moved onto the Mokililana, La'ann rose to add emphasis. At his rise, Mandingalo slowly pulled a knife blade from the sheath tucked into his belt. Even in the shadows of the tent, the blade glinted while Mandingalo played with it. Then, without warning, and in a single swift motion, Mandingalo sent the blade into the woven floor at La'ann's feet. The knife sliced through the carpet, pinning itself in the ground not two inches from La'ann's toes.

La'ann froze, staring down at the knife still quivering in the ground.

In the time occupied by La'ann's disbelief, Mandingalo shouted. "Ukuma! ... Chanye amanga! .... L'umuntu fanelekhuluma!" He was not, however, looking at La'ann. Poised at the end of a straight arm, Mandingalo's index finger pointed like the sharp end of a spear, directly at Angus.

Wezi remained calm, directing muted words at the three foresters. "Please ... strong action, take not. Mandingalo's way, this is. 'Strong arm' meaning, his name has. To find his want, frighten, he does. To hear Ahngoose speak, he asks."

Angus closed his eyes to drain his reaction from his features, then slowly reached across his body to pull the upright blade from the ground. Rising with the blade in his hands, Angus held his gaze firmly on Mandingalo, meeting there a stern glare and stiffening posture. Around the circle, several other hands found knife hilts.

Angus let his eyes drop to the blade in his hands, taking in the four runes etched into the shining metal—Su'ban's M'boso runes. Bowing, Angus spoke Batololému as, with both hands, he presented the knife to Mandingalo. "Fine weapon, you have."

Wezi's translation came embellished with a respectful bow in Mandinglo's direction. "Niyadla isikahali esikhona." To Angus he added a smile. Angus's answer seemed to diffuse the tension. Angus lowered himself to the floor.

Reaching to accept his knife from Angus, Mandingalo acknowledged the respect. The brief drama had given Angus time to think. By the time he had again settled himself into a cross-legged position, he had also decided how to answer Mandingalo's request. He simply answered in Standard ... and looked to Wezi to pick up his tactic. "I'm sorry Mandingalo, but I don't speak any language of your world and, if I must tell the tale, this is the only way I can do it."

A blank stare came into Wezi's eyes. Returning the stare, Angus waited until Wezi's eyes widened. Wezi then turned toward Mandingalo. "Uyahlonga ulimi ukuhuluma. Umuntuhlwile fanelekhuluma." Angus could only hope he pled the case well.

The desert tribe's leader looked at Angus, finally nodding and waving the back of his hand toward La'ann, still standing as he had been during the entire exchange. Wezi spoke in quiet Batololému. "Forgiveness, Mandingalo asks. Story telling also, he asks."

In one long-drawn breath, La'ann found a second wind. Kneeling, he dug into his pack and pulled out his high-forest cloak to the murmured delight of his audience. Suitably garbed, he again launched into his story, which, on this occasion, took much longer than normal, since there were many questions. In the end, the desert tribesmen were completely fascinated, as much by the wonders of Nahélé as by the two outworlders.

CHAPTER 25
Far Mountains

Consciousness washed over Angus, chilling him like a gust of cold wind. He sat up. No one but he lay beneath the tent. Two tribesmen knelt opposite, busily rolling up the thick fabric atop the ground. He closed his eyes and filled his lungs with dry desert air, spitting it out again in a hoarse cough. His hand ventured to a nose caked full, forcing a sneeze and drawing chuckles from the nearest tribesmen.

Rising, Angus scanned the area, looking for friends. Hooded figures fitted jimi into harnesses. Faces hid within hoods. A jimi handler shouted instruction. Staring in the direction he thought of as West, Angus saw Amon's fading glare. The receding mountain range stood in silhouette, extending its shadow across the desert floor. The day's heat had already begun to drop.

I should stay alert tonight.

Angus picked up his belongings and stepped into the waning daylight. A tall hooded figure waved. *Wezi?* Two others hurried to secure a harness. Eilen pulled the cloth cover from her mouth and spoke Standard. "Here, Angus." Wezi extended a heavy, necked container. "Yomele." The Batololému word for 'drink' registered in Angus's mind. He managed only a few gulps before Wezi pulled the container away. In his other hand, Wezi held a long strip of cloth. Eilen demonstrated. "Let me show you."

Accepting the cloth, Angus followed Eilen's example, wrapping it around head and mouth. Breaths came softer. A tangy scent filled his head. Angus turned eastward to survey the surrounding desert. Scattered shadows of what might be small bushes dotted the vista. Patches of dark tone spread low here and there, perhaps some surface-hugging vine. Ūko's face peeked above the horizon illuminating the path they would follow, a nearly straight track delineated by the absence of all but hard-packed coarse sand.

In a very short time, the day's shelter was reduced to a small pile of bundles. While desert men occupied themselves with jimi, the three foresters were drafted into depositing the packed camp into the single unfilled wagon, where they also deposited themselves. The caravan resumed its march, leaving upon the desert little trace of its passing. The new day seemed to have lost the excitement of the day before, wrapping the foresters in a squeaky rumble of wagon wheels. Resuming his escort role, Wezi sought to break the somber mood. "Her face, Umuntukhulu builds."

In the cart, eyes rose from the ground and necks turned. Against a deep blue sky, the streaks of orange and yellow in Ūko's growing image seemed close enough to touch. A thin, dull red, crescent shadow partially consumed the lower portion. Angus wondered what kind of internal engine fueled the shadow's red glow, distinct from the portion still bathed in Amon's radiance. Eilen joined Wezi's effort. "Call her Uko, Batonahélé do."

The sparkle in Wezi's eyes evinced a smile hidden beneath the cloth on his face. "From the sky, before Umuntukhulu, Umuntubalele runs. Today, full face, Umuntukhulu wears."

Eilen pointed toward the glow behind the western mountains. "Called Amon, that one is."

The parade of carts rumbled eastward. While Eilen

engaged the translator, Angus looked to La'ann. "Far from here Nahélé lives." When La'ann failed to stir, Angus said no more. Perhaps his friend needed space to think. How much larger had his world become in the last few days?

Ūko's warm glow bathed the desert. Calmed by the sight, Angus filed it among the many alien landscapes he had seen. What would La'ann think of the unbounded reaches of interstellar space?

La'ann finally spoke. "Here nothing lives."

Angus raised an arm toward one of the desert's small shrubs. "Life there is."

"Colōfn trees they are not."

"Beauty there is."

"Yes, beauty there is, but without clothes I feel."

Afraid to awaken regrets, Angus joined La'ann in silence. The evening stretched into a well-lit night marked by the squeak of turning wheels and the muted rhythm of Eilen and Wezi's conversation. At one point Angus looked toward Wezi, admiring the man's impressive form sitting atop so formidable a beast. A thought struck and Angus pulled the cloth from his own face. "Wezimunto. Your knife hold, can I?"

Wezi stared at the desert ahead.

Have I stepped on some social custom? Angus wondered. Then Wezi took the reins in his left hand and reached with his right across his body to pull the knife from its sheath. An upward flip put it into his hand by the blade, whereupon he held it up to Ūko's light and stared into the blade's shine. A reflected glint came off the blade as Wezi leaned down to put the knife hilt within Eilen's grasp.

The man indulges me. Angus acknowledged the trust with a touch of the blade to his forehead. Holding the weapon flat in both hands, he admired the workmanship, noting how tightly the animal hide enwrapped the hilt. Lightly running his fingers over them, he studied the runes etched into the blade, the same four runes he'd seen on Mandingalo's knife.

More interesting yet was the blade's bright shine, completely free of blemish, smooth and ground to a keen edge. Angus gingerly dragged a light thumb across that edge. Looking for something on which to give the blade a more stringent test he glanced at his robe. Delicately, he dragged the flat of the blade along the robe stretched across his thigh, turning it until the edge just touched the fleece. A small mound of fine fuzz built along the knife's edge.

The bright blade in Angus's hand prompted La'ann to pull out his own knife. Holding it close to the one in Angus's hand, La'ann's face sagged. His most prized possession stood as a pale imitation of Wezi's magnificent blade.

As though he could hear La'ann's thoughts, Angus looked toward Wezi, noting how Wezi's eyes did not stray from the knife. "Wezi, your knife, how many years it has?"

Given an opportunity, Wezi seemed pleased to join in the knife's admiration. "Know I do not. To me, given, it was. Many years, kept it, I have."

The wary look in Wezi's eyes told Angus that perhaps the knife had already spent too much time in his hands. He passed it to Eilen. The eastern mountains seemed closer than they had been when the evening's journey began.

Under Ūko's soft radiance and in spite of the cool air, the wheels' drone began to pull a somnolent shroud over Angus's thoughts. When he awoke, he felt a harsh rasp in his throat. High-desert air had stiffened the skin of his lips. He rubbed them through the protective cloth. Wezi gave Angus a warning then tossed. "Here, look!" The small tin came at Angus directly out of the bright halo Ūko threw around Wezi. Wezi nodded approval at Angus's sure catch. "Your mouth, help, it will."

Twisting off the top Angus touched the soft waxy substance with the tip of a finger then set the finger to his lips. The balm tasted bitter. He was resealing the tin when he noticed the surrounding landscape. Low hills had replaced the flat desert. The caravan ambled through a narrow valley. Angus turned himself around to see a deepening valley and mountains rising in the path ahead. A brightening sky outlined peaks. Amon would rise soon. Another day would come into being before any real darkness had set itself between yesterday and today. It made Angus smile to recall how such celestial mechanics always amused John Singh.

Amon's imminent appearance set Angus's thoughts onto the need for shelter. Seeing no part of the narrow trail or the valley's sloping sides on which to spread a shading tent, he wondered if their destination might be near. He was still wondering as Eilen sat up and shook herself awake. "Where are we?"

"We seem to have left the flat desert behind. As far as I can tell, we're climbing."

Eilen strained to see ahead before returning to look upon the reddened crescent of a setting Uko. "Is that a sunrise ahead? What? ... No night?"

"The length of days seems to vary."

Foreign speech and questioning tones woke La'aan, who rubbed his eyes with the heels of his hands. "Leave dry land, we do."

Eilen offered a piece of Wezi's dried animal flesh. "Here eat."

The valley around them deepened as a brightening sky chased away the shadows. Shadows retreated up the mountain until Amon's glare began nipping the rear of the procession. The air warmed and the protection of a shady tent seemed more necessary than ever. Yet no one signaled a halt. Instead, without so much as a break in the rhythm of the wheels, riders donned protective gear. Angus watched Wezi pull a garment around himself to become a hump on the jimi's back, looking every bit like he was covered in jimi skin, throwing off glints of color to match the animal beneath him. Without cover for his eyes, Angus was forced to huddle within the hood of his fleece cloak. Wezi now peered from behind a pair of goggles.

Angus wanted to see the road ahead, but the sun's glare hurt his eyes. Yanking the hood of his cloak down low he peered forward. Only when he looked up did the sunlight become too strong. Experimenting, he closed the hood down to a narrow slit, imitating the restrictions of high forest goggles. For short periods Angus managed to keep the trail ahead in sight, but little comfort came with twisting to look forward or kneeling. He finally became resigned to seeing only where they had been.

The roadway hypnotized Angus as it emerged piecemeal beneath the cart. A few black stones passed nearly unnoticed before Eilen's sharply drawn breath awoke the observer within. As understanding crept into Angus's head he leaned forward as though to see better and only Eilen's strong grip on his sleeve kept him in the cart.

Half buried in the sandy ground, a corner showed itself, just enough to see the beginning of a straight edge. Then he saw two more stones, almost completely exposed, hexagonal sides around a flat face. Soon the cart stopped swaying and its wheels began speaking with a new sharp voice. The cart's wheels began turning atop a smooth, flat surface of interlaced black paving stones—a roadway, a decaying roadway losing form in ragged boundaries a cart-width away, but a roadway nonetheless.

All roads lead somewhere. With the arrival of purpose, the lure of a forward view gave Angus reason to strain his upper body. When Eilen joined him, La'ann inquired. "See, what do you?"

Unable to find a Batololému word for 'road,' Angus looked for help. Eilen pointed toward the ground behind. "Unchanging trail, La'ann. By people made. There, look."

For a moment La'ann marked the strangeness of the roadbed. As the wonder struck, he too, joined in the strained search forward, seeking first sight of their destination.

Wezi raised a finger toward the east. "Inyanga. Arrive soon, we do."

The name spurred Angus to work harder for a forward view. Balancing himself carefully, he knelt upon the cart bottom and laid his torso atop the cart's cargo. With care he would not slip off. Adding his hands to a tightly constricted hood, Angus shaded his eyes and peered into the distance. Inyanga remained hidden. Like the product of some colossal plow, the road cut a channel up the foot of a mountain, parting sparsely ornamented red-sand hills on either side.

The valley soon became a canyon and the gentle hillsides became rocky cliffs. Distance absorbed the black roadbed into a larger, indefinite haze. Yet, as the laden carts pushed their way further into the canyon distant lines began to resolve. Unable to fathom what he saw, Angus sought help from Eilen's eyes. "What do you see there?"

With a sharp edge in his voice, La'ann cut off her reply. "Batololému speak!"

Poor Batololému skills forced Angus into a short apology. "Bad feel, I do. What there see, you do?"

La'ann joined in the game. "Open mouth, I see."

Amon's glare fell from high in the sky. Crisp air seemed to glow with its own light. A new picture formed. The carts marched steadily toward an enormous gaping mouth framed by two large tusks striking upward as if from some menacing jaw.

As the distance shrank and the tusks grew taller Angus saw them for what they were: two round, straight, vertical towers standing like sentinels on each side of the roadway. An imposing set of four familiar runes graced the side of each. Wezi's voice reverberated off hard vertical canyon walls. "Inyanga."

Something unnatural lurked in those sentinels. Each turn

of the wheels foreshortened Angus's view and raised the runes higher. Looking past either column, Angus saw its vertical form defined by a sharp, distinct edge, but when he set his gaze upon them the runes appeared, not etched upon a distinct black surface, but floating somewhere beneath an indefinite clear boundary. In place of the reflected glint of polished stone, Angus saw only black depth, looking as though he could reach in and cause ripples. Passing close, Angus felt an urge to touch the near column, merely to prove that a hard surface would meet his hand. The jimi's steady pace soon left the columns behind to become engulfed in Amon's glare.

Eilen found her voice before Angus. "Angus! What do you make of those columns? I've never seen anything like them!"

Still grappling with what he'd seen, Angus tried to wrap some reality around his thoughts. "I don't know, but it's hard to believe they were constructed by these desert people ... I know you've been indulgent with my notions, but, perhaps you'll agree, there's something unusual here."

This time La'ann needed no translation. "Colōfn trees ... of stone, they are ... M'boso signs, I see."

Canyon walls became vertical ramparts clad in the same deep black stone of the roadway. The carts filed into a high, arched opening and Angus's fantasy came alive. The portal promised something extraordinary waiting just beyond the gaping dark hole. Previous doubts no longer really mattered. Purpose had always ruled Angus's life and, right now, he had a definite purpose: to see what lay beyond that doorway. 'Inyanga' might be the civilized center he sought. *What kind of 'city' can I expect to find underground?* A fantasy built from sparse observation, mortared with a bit of reason and a good deal of hopeful imagination had begun to feel real.

The cart passed under the arch and Angus threw back the hood of his cloak, straining to see past the shadows. Close walls covered in smooth stone amplified every wheel's creak. Amon's brilliance faded, but before any real darkness gained ground, ambient light penetrated from the corridor's opposite end. Were he a more profane man, Angus might have cursed the lead jimi, their bulk standing between him and an early view of whatever lay beyond. While his lagging cart remained a captive of the narrow corridor, the only evident aspect of the world beyond was how well-lit it appeared.

When the vaulted ceiling finally came to an end close walls maddeningly remaining. The one unrestricted direction for Angus's examination lay upward. The ceiling opened into a high dome, losing definition in dazzling light flooding down from innumerable bright circular spots festooned across its surface. *That can't be natural light, can it?*

Pondering the question, Angus failed to notice the sound in his ears. When the realization struck, he could barely contain himself, craning his neck like a child. As their cart cleared the last remnant of side walls, he put a hand on Eilen's shoulder for support and pushed himself up to stand on the cart bed. Able to finally see beyond the lead jimi, he gazed out into a large open square ... filled with people. The din of their many voices seemed like pleasant music.

Beyond the sea of heads, structures of only one or two stories rose around the plaza, nothing high enough to challenge the space above. No graceful high-rising structures pierced the void between floor and ceiling. Farther back, details hid in fading light, but nothing rose above what he could see in brighter light. A stone city, a primitive city, confronted Angus's gaze. The age-old technology of the pinned arch adorned curved doorways and domed roofs. Nearby, rough-hewn keystones reigned above a curious mixture of haunch stones, some crudely chiseled and some fashioned by a more refined hand.

Disappointment struck hard. Angus's excitement drained away and he sank down to the cart bed. Eilen noticed his slumped shoulders. "What's wrong?"

"This isn't what I hoped to see."

Eilen looked for herself. "You expected more, didn't you?"

"Yes. I did ... And then I find what? Another village ... larger, but nearly as primitive." Pointing upward, he added, "And, at the same time, look at those skylights, if I can call them that ... not exactly primitive work. They must be pulling in sunlight through a hundred yards of solid rock. Where are the people who put those things there? It just doesn't fit."

"Well, don't let it get you depressed. No matter what we find, we still need to deal with here and now."

"Of course. But please ... allow me a little disappointment."

"OK, but not more. We have a life to live where we are."

Once more put off, La'ann interrupted, "Batololému speak!"

Eilen attempted to apologize and explain in the same breath. "Forgive us, you must, La'ann. Wonder we see."

"Yes. Wonder also, I see. Many here there are. As Gombabato, within stone desert tribe lives."

The cart file found its way against the near wall toward a holding area. Jimi in stalls came alive. Jimi in harness answered greetings, sending ripples through the carts. Every rider urged his mount to ground. Yet none dismounted. People emerged like ants from a disturbed nest. Grooms with leather halters headed for jimi. Stewards pulling small barrows headed for the business end of carts. A well-practiced routine unfolded before them. A groom and two stewards approached. Two barrow-pushers waited for the groom to take charge of Wezi's jimi. Wezi tossed his reins to the groom, retrieved a saddlebag and slid off. The groom nudged the animal upright and led it toward the stalls. Wezi threw the bag over one shoulder and allowed the two waiting stewards to push barrows into position. The stewards stopped and stared at the three foreigners sitting between themselves and the cart's unloading.

Angus had seen the look on their faces many times before, on the faces of clansmen in every village within Nahélé's realm. Without waiting to be asked, he decided to simply let action show them who he was. Rising, gear still strapped onto his back, he stepped into the cart and began moving bundles to the fore where they could more easily be loaded onto the barrows.

With working room for only one, Eilen and La'ann hopped onto the ground. The barrow pushers hesitated but then proceeded to unload goods into barrows and take no further notice of Angus' appearance. Eilen and La'ann waited with Wezi.

The plaza outside roiled with activity, small standing groups offering a static background through which people flowed like water around stones in a stream. "As when the Bakeisika visit, it is," La'ann observed.

Eilen agreed. "Yes. A place for meeting and bargaining."

Strutting past the busy stewards, Mandingalo addressed Wezi in loud words and pointed at the foreigners. "Wezimunto! Woza! Bonaletha." Wezi translated in less belligerent tones. "Come, follow you must."

As Mandingalo led them around its fringes the Bazaar's business filled their ears. Passing a few structures, they soon turned left into a narrow alley. A warren of alleys later, the sound of the plaza had faded and all knowledge of direction had been erased from mind. The sound of their own footsteps on the tiled pavement echoed off close walls; walls made of set stones, some crudely shaped, others chiseled straight and uniform; some fashioned from natural rock, others from the unnatural black of the sentinel towers outside. Closed doors set into arched doorways occasionally broke the monotony of featureless walls. Light reached down with some difficulty through narrow spaces left between protruding second-level walls. They encountered people, people who paid them little mind, people who had business to attend, people wearing lighter, more colorful robes, people who perhaps did not often venture into the open desert.

The first stop came at the end of a short, vaulted tunnel opening into a well-kept courtyard, brightened by ambient light falling directly from the cavern dome. At center, a rough, black stone, standing as tall as Angus issued welcome with the soft sound of water descending a many-stepped slope.

Wezi followed Mandingalo around the fountain toward another arched doorway as he interpreted another command. "Here, wait, you will. To Imholi speak we do."

Lingering fatigue sent Angus to sit on a bench near the entrance. La'ann was first to notice the courtyard's hexagonal shape. "Like colōfn trees, around us walls are." A railed balcony graced all six sides of a second level. Within white urns in each of the lower level's six corners, small bushes grew with so many tiny yellow blossoms as to outnumber the dark green leaves.

Relaxing, Angus breathed air made fresh by both flowers and fountain. Eilen sat beside him. La'ann stood near, quietly listening to their foreign speech. Angus explored his frustration. "Something significant once occupied this place. Something much more than we can see now."

"I've noticed. Your instincts didn't lie. There was once a more sophisticated center here. It's just no longer here. Whatever once was seems to have fallen into disrepair."

"Those stone pillars outside are unlike anything I've ever seen. Whoever made them controlled more advanced technology than I see here."

"And what about the light in here? It seems natural, but how does it find its way through hundreds of meters of solid rock?"

"It's more pieces of the same puzzle we found in the forest. Bits of sophistication abound, but the people here don't seem to be aware of it, nor capable of fashioning any of it."

"Perhaps it wasn't so crazy ... This place may not be some lost Federation outpost, but where else could these inhabitants come from? They're much too human to be an evolutionary

287

coincidence."

Angus had no answer. She was playing with the same reasoning that had led him to the fantasy in the first place. The unanswered question hung in the air before Eilen shifted directions. "What do you think we should do now?"

"Wezi mentioned other sites further south. Perhaps we can make our way to one of those places? But ... I'm not feeling too confident that they'll be much different than this place."

"You're a little tired now. Let's not give up just yet. There's more yet to see around here."

"You're right. I am tired ... and don't worry. I'm not planning to jump from the top of a colōfn tree. It's just disappointing."

Standing patiently, La'ann used a pause in the conversation as a polite opportunity. "Far from Nahélé, we are. For Ro'ann, much to tell, I have ... and Su'ban."

The sound of those names stirred conflicted feelings in Angus. *Am I being foolish? What'll I do with myself if we go back?*

Wezi returned to escort the three forest clansmen back through the alley warren and bring them to a modest dwelling. Opening the entrance door, Wexi urged them through a narrow archway and into a small courtyard with but one other door. Graced by no fountain, the dimly lit courtyard sported a dead fire pit beneath a metal tripod, not unlike that above Su'ban's cooking fires. A set of side shelves looked to harbor foodstuffs.

Wezi opened the second door. The small dark room behind it contained a single low, flat platform and a chest in one corner from which Wezi pulled blankets, a bladder and an empty sack. Asking pardon, he left to return with a sloshing bladder and weighted sack. From among the food storage shelves, he took a few small sticks and several black lumps to start a fire.

CHAPTER 26
Footprint

The news seemed to have raised his captain's spirits. "I can feel it. They're nearly in our grasp."

If not for the massive antique desk and low, uncomfortable seat reminding him of where he sat, Semgee might ignore how she played with the gold buttons on her tunic and spoke to the wall. Does she really think the gaudy uniform impresses anyone?

"It is real progress, Honorable Captain. Not a chance encounter, as before. These signals were detected at a distance."

"How soon can we expect to fix a point of origin?"

"Not quite as soon as, I'm sure, you would like, Honorable Captain, but by late tomorrow we should be ready to maneuver into close-approach." Moving into more sensitive territory, Semgee summoned diplomatic skills. "There is a matter on which I need your guidance, Honorable Captain. May I elaborate?"

With a head-shaking glance toward the ceiling, Alexandra acceded. "Yes, yes, get on with it."

"Our approach should be conducted with some care. The signals we've intercepted are not rich, not the wide-band cacophony we might expect from a planet-wide civilization.

I'm afraid we've only found another outpost. Still, we must proceed on the assumption that whoever occupies the emission end of these transmissions knows of our previous encounter and, if we are to secure useful information, we'll need to minimize any warning time we give them."

"What you say all sounds prudent and natural ... It also sounds consistent with a need for speed as well. What's the problem?"

"I believe our mission will be well served by proceeding in several steps and obtaining more information along the way. Unless you object, we've already begun to initiate small jumps in the direction of that signal. I'm sure you will soon feel the first jump phase transition."

Drawing out the words, Alexandra acknowledged. "Thank you for the warning."

Semgee heard the piqued tone. It was often difficult to decide which would peeve her most: acting without expressed permission or adding unnecessary delay to an obvious action.

Noting evident signs of annoyance, Semgee moved quickly to explain the merits of his recommendation. "Once we can pinpoint the origin star we'll jump into a distant orbit and direct reconnaissance to establish the nature and exact location of the transmission source. We can then jump out again and set the ship onto a rapid approach trajectory, striking from a hidden position behind the star. Just as we did with the first outpost we found. A quick braking dive into a close approach orbit could then put us on top of them before they know we're there."

The idea's merits, at least, seemed to placate her.

CHAPTER 27
Intact

In long strides Wezi devoured the narrow alleys. The labyrinth gave Angus no reference to orient himself. Completely lost, he welcomed the respite when Wezi halted before the crowd-filled square. The cavernous ceiling and pervasive din told Angus he stood before the same bustling plaza that had greeted their arrival. He had hardly drawn a long breath when La'ann and Eilen joined and Wezi plowed directly into the throng. Angus was barely able to keep in sight the silver dangles hanging from Wezi's ears. Seething like a hive of insects, the crowd swirled around him. The follower's task became a harsh test of nerve and focus. Indifferent arms, hips and shoulders buffeted him from all sides. The scent of seldom-washed bodies assailed his senses. Not until Wezi stopped again did Angus catch up. Wezi stood waiting before a short, stone wall surrounding a small area of tables spread in front of a stone façade.

Stepping within, he bid his charges sit around a round table. At last able to view the milling crowd with some dispassion, Angus observed light, loose robes in varied muted colors. The square simmered with the flow of commerce, a market scene similar to those seen on many planets.

"Hunger, I have," Wezi said before leaving the three

foresters to themselves.

Speaking in Standard, Angus mused aloud. "Why do you think it was so important for Wezi to come here?"

Eilen's eyes stayed focused on the plaza. "I don't know, but I'm glad he did. This place is much more comfortable than his bare-bones room or that crowd out there."

Conscious of his lapse into Standard, Angus glanced at La'ann. Instead of the objection he expected, he saw La'ann staring at the crowd. Letting his eyes roam the sea of bodies, Angus felt some of La'ann's wonder. So many people living in the heart of a mountain must seem quite alien to a man nurtured within Nahélé's verdant arms. Angus's attention returned to the enclosure and he marked the tables within, simple stone pillars supporting a flattened round stone cap. Everything seemed made of stone. In his mind's eye Angus saw Su'ban's table and the M'pepebato village. The thread of commerce between this desert culture and the people of Nahélé seemed to have neglected to include any wood.

Wezi reappeared holding a tray, which he set upon the table. From the tray he then placed a half-filled cup before each of his guests, leaving one for himself at the empty seat. A wafer-filled platter remained.

Wezi sat and looked at his guests. "Eat! Eat! Eat!"

No one moved. Wezi reached to pick from the platter a browned, flat wafer.

The aroma told Angus that the browned rounds were baked, perhaps a kind of seed meal. Another, darker variety looked more like dried plant flesh. Angus decided to first investigate the drink. Thin and milky, it tasted bittersweet. He picked one of the darker wafers from the tray. Vaguely sweet, his jaws worked the chewy texture.

When all had eaten, Wezi spoke. "Speaking we must. From you learning I need."

Alerted, Angus sat up. *So ... breakfast comes with a price.* "Hear what, you wish?"

"Of your home village, tell me."

Angus glanced at his companions. La'ann's face remained unmoved. Eilen shrugged. Angus offered a simple beginning. "Within the arms of great trees we live."

"Of this thing called 'tree,' tell me.'"

The request stopped Angus cold. How can mere words conjure a tree's likeness for someone who has never seen a tree? Then, of course, a colōfn tree is something more than mere tree. For a very long moment, he stared at Wezi. When finally he spoke, his response came in the form of a question. "In the land between the mountains ... Things there grow?"

Wezi considered. "Yes. Low vines and bushes called ishihala there grow."

"Arms ishihala have?"

With thumb and forefinger spread a thumb's width apart, Wezi indicated a branch width. "Yes."

Placing two fists together, Angus twisted them upon each other. "Ishihala arms, bend not?"

Furrows appeared above Wezi's nose. Then his eyes widened and he nodded. "Yes. Ishihala arms bend not."

Eilen's nod kept Angus going. "In your thinking, very large ishihala see you can? Ishihala with arms larger through than one jimi on top of another standing?"

Effort again showed in Wezi's face as he tried to conjure an image of a tree so huge. "Difficult it is."

Angus reached for another wafer. Perhaps it was time to probe elsewhere. "Wezi, question, ask I can?"

"Yes. Good it is. Together speaking we are."

"To Mandingalo belong we do?"

Facial muscles again pulled at Wezi's. "Why ask you do?"

"For us Mandingalo traded, yes?"

The lines on Wezi face disappeared. "Yes. For you Mandingalo traded. To Umhwebi belong you do."

Before Angus could follow the thought, Eilen jumped in. "Wezi, Umhwebi you are?"

"Yes. Umhwebi I am."

Eilen smiled. "This food, Umhwebi make?"

As if unsure of the question Wezi responded slowly. "Umhwebi make not. Ubanondla make."

"Your robe, Umhwebi make?"

Wezi answered without reaction. "Umaluki make."

An arm gesture toward the busy plaza accented Eilen's next question. "Umaluki there are?"

Turning to look at the crowd, Wezi pointed at individuals wearing light green robes. "Three I see. There; there, and there."

As she asked the next question, Eilen looked directly at Angus. "Wezi. Your knife, Umhwebi make?"

Wezi's hand went to his waist. "Umenzimbi make."

Recognition must have shown on Angus's face. Eilen nodded and let her next question go unasked. With a gesture toward the crowd Angus took over. "Umenzimbi there are?"

Again Wezi turned and scanned the plaza, speaking as his posture returned to the table. "Umenzimbi I see not."

"Working place Umenzimbi have?"

"Next side plaza they are."

"Next side?"

Eilen spoke in Standard. "Perhaps he means across the plaza."

Minutes later the foursome pushed a trail through the plaza's bustling bodies. This time, at La'ann's insistence and in spite of Wezi's objections, La'ann tied them together like pearls on a string. Their second trip through the crowd brought them to a buffer clearing lining the far wall of the square. Wezi stopped some distance in front of an arched double doorway pinned at top by a rune-blazoned keystone. Wasting no time in ridding himself of the tether, Wezi threw La'ann's rope to the ground. Only then did he turn toward the doorway, leaving La'ann shaking his head as he recoiled the rope. Angus saw displeasure in La'ann's face. "Angry you are,

La'ann. Small thing it is."

"Wisdom you have, Ahngoose."

Wezi waved from the doorway. "Join us you will?"

Inside, a room spread left and right, enclosed by six sides and lit by several flamed lamps suspended from the ceiling. A score of strides might be consumed in crossing the room. Curtained windows on both sides of the doorway did little to dispel the gloom. Folds of dark red fabric softened the far sides, its color blending into shadows. Angus noticed none of those features. Instead, he saw how tables filled the room, leaving only enough space to walk between; round, flat tables draped in red fabric similar to that upon the walls. Upon each table were neatly arranged displays: tools, weapons, utensils of all kinds, some rough black matte, some dull grey, some bright, shiny, and looking smooth to the touch. "What place this is?"

The scope of the room fell under the sweep of Wezi's arm. "As you see, it is. Umenzimbi."

Stepping past Wezi, Angus walked to a round table, around which lay a number of short-handled tools neatly arranged in concentric rows. He picked up a small maul, noting the diameter of the wooden handle, made for a larger hand than his, a tool fashioned for driving a spike or crushing anything caught under a blow. He picked up a second. The weight felt strangely comforting. Pulling his arms apart, he let the two heavy tool heads fall together, striking and rebounding with a solid 'clack'. There was something satisfying in the sound of it.

The sharp sound drew a rebuke from Wezi. "Ahngoose! Touch not!"

As if in response to Wezi's command, curtains parted at the room's far end. A brightly dressed man entered; a man unlike any other Angus had seen in the city; wearing a short, bright yellow robe, reaching only to his knees. The man stood out sharply against the red room. A belt of shining discs drew his robe in at the waist. Tight white fabric covered his shins and, in place of strapped sandals, he wore what might be described as soft slippers, as yellow as his tunic. The crown of blue feathers drew Angus's attention to his head. This man certainly did not venture into the desert. Greeting Wezi warmly, the man let all know that he and Wezi were well acquainted. "Mukela, Wezimunto unhwebina. Isikhadedlula sobonana ngiyadla? Ngingakusiza?"

Wezi responded in equally comfortable tones, loudly enough to carry across the room, "Sawubona, Kwazimunto Umenzimbina. Abangane ngiyazisa." As he spoke, Wezi took a step forward, then stopped and looked steadily at Angus, raising a hand for emphasis. "Ahngoose, remain you must. To this man, speaking I will."

Attending Wezi's stern manner, Angus obeyed. Wezi then hesitated as if struggling for words. "Inhlonfo show you must ... As speaking to Mandingalo you did."

The yellow man seemed to diminish with Wezi's approach, although he was perhaps only slightly shorter than Angus. The stark contrast of his bright outfit and Wezi's somber, dark desert robes gave the smaller man quite a presence.

A couple of steps brought Eilen close enough to speak in the subdued voice she seemed to know was needed. "What's going on?"

"I'm not sure. Wezi told me to wait here and also demanded that respect be shown that man."

La'ann quietly inserted a simple observation. "Much wealth, here is."

In Batololému, Angus agreed. "Yes ... tools of metal we find."

Angus had no Batololému words to express the disappointment with which he struggled. The room before him harbored the very metallurgical wonders that he sought. Yet the culture outside held little promise for anything more advanced. "Place of making, Wezimunto seeks."

Too removed to hear the conversation, Angus observed the drama. Wezi and the yellow man moved as actors on a stage. Wezi assumed the air of a supplicant, his tale told with half bows and sweeping arms. Yellow Man responded with smiles and nods. When both heads turned to look toward the three observers Yellow Man gave them a nod. A short time later, with one last bowing plea Wezi pressed his case, only to be rebuffed by the little man's slowly shaking head and sternly pressed lips.

When the little man disappeared behind the curtain the room seemed to darken. Wezi trudged back across the room, shoulders slumped and frowning. "With me, come."

Outside Wezi stopped and regrouped in the relative calm of the quiet beach between the ramparts and the sea of people in the plaza.

"Ahngoose, sad, I feel. Your wishes make true, I cannot. Hold secrets, Umenzimbi do."

Angus tried to remain stoic, but he saw in Eilen's face that his disappointment must show. *What can I do now?* Kneeling, he set his pack on the ground, rummaged within to pull out the hand-torch. Eilen's surprise sounded in her voice. "You can't be thinking what I think you're thinking, can you? Angus, it might be time to reevaluate. You've found what you sought, or nearly so anyway. And we can all see there's no landing craft anywhere in sight, nor is there likely to be anywhere on this planet. For a short while it seemed real. It's not. Let go of it."

Angus looked at the hand-torch in his hand, turning it over as he listened to Eilen's plea, a part of him knowing she spoke truthfully, but another part unable to quickly abandon what had been fueling his days. In this place, the torch he held, an ordinary, everyday tool in his previous life, had value, and that value shouldn't be spent casually. While he struggled inside, he absently let his thumb brush over the power switch. The torch beam jumped to life and startled Wezi. "Ahngoose! What you do?"

Eilen moved to calm Wezi. "Wezimunto, no harm it does. Small tool it is."

Angus switched off the beam as he stood.

Wezi held out a hand. "Tool, it is? Hold it, I wish."

With only the briefest hesitation, Angus put the torch in Wezi's hand.

Turning the device slowly, Wezi examined each end. The wonder of it showed in his face.

With the hand-torch's return, Wezi jerked his head and put them moving again. "Another way perhaps there is."

Following Wezi through another of Inyanga's innumerable alleys, Angus noted only that their destination took them away from the comfort of natural light. The ambient light, coming as it did with greater intensity from the direction of the market plaza, became a compass, marking progress and perhaps marking a general beacon for their return.

Many twists later, doorways became scarce. Then stonewalls gave way to wreckage. Alleyways turned to serpentine paths separating piles of debris the size of buildings, scattered like raked fodder in a harvested field. Their path narrowed until, in the poor light, Angus began to tread carefully lest his ankles find a sharp edge hiding within the rubble. The meandering trail veered slowly to the right, eventually putting the feeble glow of the market Plaza over Angus's shoulder.

Air became still and thick, laden with odors in such variety as to defy identification, overlain by a distinctly human stench, of bodies well worked and unwashed. In all but absent light Angus threw fleeting glances over his shoulder, checking his companions. Eilen gave him no reason for concern, but for La'ann the oppressive place might prove too much of a burden.

A suspicion worked its way into Angus's psyche, not from heavy air, but from the evident ruin. The mounds of debris hinted at something once greater than what now occupied the mountain's heart. Peering at those mounds, he realized that all mounds were not the same; some were a collection of large stones, some of smaller stones, some of long metallic pieces, and some of black glassy stone. He had just begun to deduce what the sorted piles might mean when Wezi stopped, and almost at the same moment Angus heard the sound of activity. They had reached a clearing. No piles obstructed their view for a space of perhaps 30 paces. Torches burned in a number of points around the clearing and several people were at work.

With a word, Wezi named the people. "Izimumbi."

As if she knew the name, Eilen understood. "Of course, a scavenger guild."

The people at work did not appear as prosperous as Wezi. Clad in dark garments, looking worn, a few tatters hanging from a sleeve or hem, they pulled at the edges of a huge continuous slope of debris, a mother lode of rubble, stretching well to both sides and reaching up and back far enough to obscure its true extent. The kingdom of scattered mounds was the product of these people's energy and showed their place in the scheme of commerce. Raw materials to fuel all manner of construction and fabrication came from here, from the rubble left behind by some long-decayed former glory.

Angus stood and stared. A cold realization swept over him. Here was the 'city' he sought. The civilization into which he had invested such hope lay before him in ruin. Tangled wires and bent pipes wound around girders and beams protruding from a mass of shattered stone and glass. Equally shattered was any possibility of ever leaving the planet beneath his feet. His shoulders slumped.

Behind an open hand Wezi called a halt. "Here wait you will. With them speaking I go. With Umenzimbi, trade they do."

As Wezi walked away, Eilen saw his intent. "I think I see. If these scavengers trade raw materials to the metalworkers, then they form another path to the forges, a back door."

Surrounded by the detritus of a fallen civilization, Angus found his enthusiasm for the sight of those forges waning. "I'm not sure it matters much anymore."

"Fine time to admit that. Wezi thinks it's important. Let him play it out. What thinking, you have, La'ann?"

"Good feel, Nahélé's breath would give."

In his disappointment Angus still saw the wisdom in Eilen's remarks. She often had a feeling for the glue to hold people together. She would make a good starship captain.

With a raised arm Wezi signaled his comrades to join him. As they walked across the clearing, their path took them near a retreating, barrow-pushing scavenger, who kept one wary eye on them as he pushed past. A slight shift of cargo sent a metallic sound from the barrow. Angus turned to look. In the flickering torchlight a glint of bright metal shot from among the barrow's twisted tubes.

Angus almost reached out to grab the barrow before thinking better of it. "Wezi! Speak here, you can?"

Wezi advised caution. "Ahngoose. Care take. By this work, live, these men do."

When the scavenger set his load, Angus cautiously reached into the barrow to retrieve a small, bright metallic tile. Turning it in his hands Angus saw the bright gold wealth of the M'pepebato adorning Ra'ahj's chest. "Where find this, you did?"

Wezi intervened before the man could react to Angus's strange speech. "Lesi, la uyathola khona?"

The scavenger pointed back toward the debris mountain.

Peering at the rising slope, Angus could discern the earmarks of a trail, a path by which the scavengers might venture like prospectors into the mother lode.

"Wezimunto, find these bits this man can? Important it may be."

"To do this no reason he has."

"Trade with him we can?"

"With Izimumbi, trading never have I done."

Moments of unintelligible discussion later, Wezi's efforts did not seem to have progressed far. The scavenger seemed irritated. Wezi's hand upon the barrow prevented the man from pushing on. After some time, Wezi had achieved nothing. "Little time this man has. Trading, understand, he does not."

Eilen offered an idea. "New robe perhaps wearing, he wishes?"

With mock surprise, Angus spoke in Standard. "Oh ... So now you think barter might be a good idea?"

"Only for something we can replace."

A few moments of arm gestures and verbal banter brought Wezi another disappointing result. "Into the waste mountain, again today, go he will not."

Their efforts had reached a dead end and Eilen's patience seemed to have reached a limit. "Angus. I'm beginning to tire of the hunt. Why is it now important to you to find the source of those tiles?"

Although he knew that Wezi and La'ann had not understood, Angus could see in their faces that Eilen's feelings were shared. "I'm no longer quite so sure. The main reason for finding the forges was to find the source of the alloy from which those knives and those tiles were made." Angus stopped explaining. "Tell Wezi and La'ann that you wish to return. I don't want to drag you along on my foolish quest. But I do think I'm going to go up into the rubble and see if I can find the structure from which those tiles came. I want to get a sharper feeling for what the builders here could do, for who they were."

As if he had understood the exchange, Wezi threw out an opinion. "Now, all return, or none return."

"To this man speak. Trade, will he? For his knowledge and a flame, my robe, give I will."

....

From afar, a well-worn trail seemed to climb onto the rubble mountain. When seen close upon, the trail's form possessed slight definition. Nor did the surface underfoot possess a firm character. Reaching the gentle slope atop the broad plateau was a chore. Every step upward came with a slip backward, like trudging up a slope of small stones. Once the grade eased, walking still required care lest a careless step bring a sudden plunge and a nasty cut from broken glass or loose debris. Without his gomba fleece robe Angus felt naked. The thin fabric of his old ship's uniform was comfortable enough, but even worn under his forest village clothing, it was not meant to protect against anything more threatening than a well-controlled puff of air aboard the Raiju.

The bargain seemed poorly made. The directions Wezi had acquired did not guide as well. Guideposts carried meaning for the scavenger, but not for foreigners. Oddly shaped objects protruded from the general debris: a slim round bent pole here; a large twisted sheet of metal, there; and yet somewhere else, the intact corner of a much larger object. Feeling every bit the intruder, the eerie landscape laid dark colors upon Angus's psyche. What must La'ann think of this alien place?

Angus had only begun to tire when they ran out of landmarks. The flame's poor light in Wezi's upheld hand revealed nothing to lend the site any consequence greater than any other they had passed along the way. The presence of a 'small broad hill' matched the description of their goal, but, in the generally undulating context of the decayed landscape, such description left room for a good deal of doubt.

Although the rank, stagnant air had begun to erode his resolve and unease had grown with every fleeting glimpse of movement outside the illuminating fringe of Wezi's torch, Angus felt bound to explore. He had little doubt his companions would prefer to return, but they had invested so much to get here. Pulling the hand-torch from his bag he let the tight beam play slowly back and forth across the side of the broad mound, revealing little more than the ever-present, twisted amalgamation of refuse.

Yet, as the beam travelled up the mound, occasional glints hinted of something more; and, whether or not he'd found what he sought, Angus decided to get a closer look. A spot near the top displayed more glitter than anything yet seen. Abruptly, he left the path, such as it was, and stepped upward, quickly reminded of the care required.

Off the poorly delineated path the debris pile completely lost integrity. Each step became an adventure of its own. Surface appearances were deceiving. One spot might look solid yet fall open to the lightest touch, while another, looking quite perilous, might pass as steadier than most. Torn and twisted metal, replete with sharp edges, abounded. Treacherous in the poor lighting, an errant step could quickly become a gashed calf, or worse. Angus' resolve began to waver. Perhaps that deposit of glitter wasn't really worth the risk. After all, what did he really expect to find?

Intent on one last look around before turning back, Angus played the hand-torch beam around the pile one last time, finding a number of glittering reflections only a few steps from where he stood. The idea of departing again seemed hasty. He'd walked all the way from Su'ban and her fine polished necklace looking for a place where such things were fashioned. Standing now atop the disappointing ruins, he felt reluctant to turn his back before taking a good look.

Stretching as far out as he could reach without falling, he gingerly pressed a foot upon the top piece of debris. Feeling it hold, he shifted weight and felt the debris under his foot offer resistance—so far, so good. With all his weight now one step closer, he tried again, at first finding one more apparent stepping stone. Upon shifting weight a third time, the footing suddenly slipped. Flailing hands grasped nothing but air. He fell to a crouch. After one long moment of minor avalanche, the slide stopped as suddenly as it had started. Rising slowly, Angus played the hand-torch beam over nearby debris and almost immediately saw the new opening, marked now by a very bright reflection, just to one side of a deep hole. A closer look showed runes, etched deeply into a polished metallic surface, the same runes he'd seen floating in the obsidian pillars outside the city gates, the runes he knew as 'Inyanga'. It required some doing to temper his excitement. Drawing on every bit of newfound debris-pile knowledge, he climbed as rapidly as prudence would allow toward the hole, reaching it out of breath. When he was able to shine the hand-torch beam into the hole he saw the runes, larger now, large enough to be seen as the signpost they were, blazoned to one side of a support structure.

Directing the beam deeper, Angus saw a length of arched roof. Small glowing red spots moved quickly aside as the beam came upon them. A space like this would certainly attract occupants.

The flicker of Wezi's flame brought Angus's head back from the hole. The flame reminded Angus to preserve hand-torch power. He switched it off. The torch flames might hold at bay whatever creature scurried behind those beady red eyes. Perhaps he could hold that flame to one side and keep the fumes from his eyes. As long as flames worked, he'd use them.

With Wezi's torch in his hand, Angus dropped to his knees and shoved the flame into the narrow opening, hoping the little vermin could feel the heat. As he passed the flame from one side to the other, he saw dark shapes, scurrying to evade the light. Angus hoped the occupant carried a modest set of teeth, or claws, and, perhaps, a mild disposition.

Chest to the ground, he inched into the crack, shoving debris back as his feet sought traction. "Yuck!" An odor of dung and urine nearly brought his stomach into his mouth.

Sounds of falling debris echoed from somewhere ahead. Fighting the urge to breathe, he pressed ahead, pushing wildly until the rubble gave way. He fell forward onto a loose slope gasping for air. The torch fell from his hand.

Some breaths later Angus laid still. A low ceiling's gentle curve showed in the flicker of torchlight. Eilen's concerned voice called through the opening. "Angus! What happened? Are you all right?"

"Yes, I'm OK. Just kicked some debris down the side of this scrap pile. It opens up in here."

"Is it all right for us to come through?"

"Yes, that's just what you can do. I'll hold the torch here just to give you a target. You'll want to hold your breath. It stinks."

CHAPTER 28
Ground Station

The urge was too strong. Unable to contain himself, Angus turned away from the narrow opening and held the torch flame as high as he could, shielding his eyes with the other hand. The flame flickered near his head under a close ceiling. The flame struggled to penetrate the darkness, as if this hidden side of the crawlspace held more power over the feeble light. Dim torchlight illuminated the ceiling's curve descending above a cluttered slope of debris. He imagined a ramp or staircase lying beneath the rubble. He had hardly taken in the scene before Eilen's shout rose from inside the passage. "Hey! What happened to my light?"

Behind a clattering avalanche of rubble, Eilen emerged agitated and disheveled. Barely able to stand, she steadied herself in the torchlight. As her composure returned she turned back toward the crawlspace. "That narrow passage will be bad for Wezi and La'ann, especially La'ann."

Angus silently agreed. For all their proven courage and physical strength, he knew both natives would need something extra just to get themselves into that hole. The stench would put Wezi to gagging, and the dark, confined space would conjure fears enough to freeze La'ann's limbs. *Wezi first,* he thought as he called into the tunnel. "Wezi!

Come now you will."

At least the stench had confined itself to the crawlspace. The vermin living there likely foraged on the outside and only used the safe confines of that hole as home. Perhaps there was little of value for them on the inner side. When Wezi emerged, he moved farther downslope into the shadows to allow himself to stand and fill his lungs. One long breath followed another until he had cleansed himself of the disgusting encounter.

And that left La'ann alone at the other end. Angus imagined himself in La'ann's place. The thought of squeezing into that dark, stench-filled confined space weakened La'ann's knees. And at the same time, the thought of shrinking before this barrier already surmounted by his friends stiffened his spine. Angus had no doubt where the balance would fall.

Angus shouted through the crawlspace, "La'ann come. Space here there is. Far it is not." Then he handed the torch to Eilen and he let himself slip downslope. Sharp-edged sounds rang off the hard ceiling, each footfall setting loose sliding waves of detritus left behind by an 'Inyanga' lost to time.

Near the bottom, a hard floor appeared beneath the debris. In the weak torchlight a faint reflection caught his eye. Angus picked it up. He held a small bright tile, not half a finger-length on each side. It looked like the pieces of Ra'ahj's necklace, like the currency of the forest, similar, but not quite so. This tile was more colorful, not metallic, a small piece of hard mosaic.

The clatter of debris echoed from the ceiling behind as Angus's three companions joined him at the bottom. Regaining the flame, he held it high to keep its light from his eyes and picked his way carefully down the smooth ramp, kicking aside scattered bits with his toes. He had stepped only a short distance when his raised arm began to protest. The torch fell and in nearly the same instance anxious calls rose from behind. Angus was not the only one feeling uncomfortable in this strange space. Changing torch arms, he kept walking. The air seemed drier and less mobile the deeper they moved. The corridor came to an end at the edge of a black volume large enough to swallow the torchlight. Air hung motionless. Angus pushed the torch out past the edge of the void, seeking assurance for another step. One cautious step later a hint of reflecting torchlight returned from the far side. Angus moved forward and a round, domed room emerged from the dark. He looked down at the floor. The fine dust there had not seen the slightest disturbance in some time. He had to wonder how long it had been since a sound was last heard here.

As the torch moved two other doorways became visible. The closest appeared on Angus' left and he ventured toward it, finding in the illuminating torchlight another vaulted passage. He hesitated only as long as it took to assure himself of his companions' continued presence, then, without a word, he led them into the second passageway, listening to the sound of his footsteps echoing louder as hard walls pressed in again.

An end came into view not many steps later. The room beyond sent back reflections well before they had reached the corridor's end. As Angus drew closer, he saw something other than walls in the opening. By swinging the torch wide from side to side, he could see movement in the reflections. The prospect of finding something more revealing, pushed him quickly into another room, this one extending far toward his right.

The builders of this buried complex seemed to approve of arches. A familiar vaulted ceiling covered the long room. The floor ended sharply at a straight edge four or five steps in front of where he stood. With his eyes he followed the length of the floor's edge; first left, where it ended at the base of a flat wall, then right some distance to end at another wall. The place felt familiar. Many times before, Angus had stood in similar places. He knew he stood on the platform of a transport station. In some distant past this place once welcomed visitors from somewhere else, or perhaps, sent them away. Holding the flame as high as he could, he advanced toward the edge, watching how the flickering light reflected from an area above the platform, watching the reflection move as he approached. Even before his fingers reached its surface, he knew what they would feel when they touched the transparent barrier. He watched the light dance within the curved barrier, sliding his hand upward and arching his back to follow the curve up toward the top of the room where it disappeared into the ceiling. Looking through it, he could see the same curve continue in the form of an opaque dull surface, descending to form the wall opposite, forming a smooth, circular tube. Glancing left, Angus saw the tube end abruptly at the same flat wall forming the left end of the platform on which he stood. To his right, a second flat wall defined the platform's length. This wall, however, stopped at the barrier, leaving the interior side pierced by a gaping hole boring deep into the mountain. About halfway between where he stood and the far right-hand wall, a section of the clear curve stood high from the remainder, while next to it, a matching opening gave Angus all the proof he needed to see how that curved section once filled the opening beside it.

The conclusion that he stood on the loading quay of a station had just settled into Angus's mind as Eilen's voice broke into his thoughts, "Angus! You've been searching for a transportation hub. It looks like you've found one."

With barely an acknowledgement Angus extended the flame torch to Eilen. "Here. Hold this," he said. "I know it's just a waste of power t, but I want to have a look down that tunnel." One hand braced on the outside surface, he leaned into the barrier opening and let the narrow beam of his hand-torch drill into the tunnel. It revealed little more than the flame had done, except perhaps that the tunnel ran deeper than he could see. *"How far does it go,"* he wondered. *"A few kilometers? A few thousand? and what's at the other end? Another Inyanga? Something more."*

As he pulled the beam back into the station, Angus let it trace the path of a short wall rising from the tunnel floor and aligned along its spine. *A mono-track? A power feed? Magnetic lift?* In his imagination, Angus saw a tubular vehicle riding that spine, filling the cavity, speeding through the tunnel, perhaps piercing only rarefied air ahead. Or perhaps even aided by the thrust of air pressure from behind, like a pellet in a toy air rifle. He pulled his head out to look more closely at the manner of that door's closure. The door's edges seemed to be formed into a channel. A glance at the edge of the opening showed the same channel inverted. The two were meant to fit together tightly. Did they form a seal? Probably.

Caught up in the discovery, Angus wanted more, yet knew he would not get it. Unless they were prepared to walk into the depths of that long, dark tunnel, the ancient station seemed to have shown them all it had to offer. Angus looked at his companions, quietly standing together, awaiting direction. He was yet ready to declare an end.

Extinguishing the hand-torch, he reached again for the flame and started back toward the station entrance. "There was a second door back there. What do you say we see where it leads?"

In but a few minutes Angus and his friends were carefully stepping down the curve of another dust-covered sloping ramp, descending into another dark room, a not very large room. The air temperature fell distinctly as they entered, adding to the feeling that they had discovered a new feature of the City-that-Once-Was. Light from the flame torch flickered off circular walls, blending into a broad curve of ceiling. Small, scattered pieces of loose debris sent an occasional crunch from underfoot. The sound reflected from the hard wall, returned to their ears from all directions, amplified enough to make Angus feel like he intruded in a sacred place.

The room's unknown purpose seemed to involve the single structure standing alone like a focal point in the center.

Nothing else was present. Not high, nor large; the size of a small booth. All four explorers stepped around it. There seemed to be no entrance. Like the room, a single surface encircled the cylindrical structure. Angus mused that it didn't seem much larger than the small express lift he'd seen on many starships, lifts rarely used and generally reserved for emergencies, the kind that could whisk one, or possibly two, crewmembers from one deck to any other in mere seconds. Those vehicles possessed obvious doors and weren't freestanding. *Still*, thought Angus, *perhaps it stands here at one end of its travel, at the top of a conveyance shaft extending below this level. There should be a door here somewhere.*

Holding the flame close to the booth surface nearest the entrance ramp, Angus noted a somewhat different sheen. A patch of differing texture stood out. He reached out to explore. It felt slightly rougher than the surrounding surface. Nothing happened. *Irrational to expect anything operational.* Absently, he wiggled his spread hand, alternately touching the panel with fingers and thumb.

A collective jolt hit both Angus and his companions when, with barely a whisper, a portion of the curved side suddenly slid open, bathing them all in bright light. La'ann and Wezi bolted backward. La'ann fumbled for his rope, momentarily unable to see. When eyes came open again the four stood before a small circular chamber defined by a smooth metallic wall. In contrast to the exterior room, the interior floor was clean, free of dirt and debris.

La'ann and Wezi backed slowly away. In one hand La'ann carried his rope at the ready, ready to use against whatever strange force was at work here. A moment of caution before Angus stepped toward the opening, eliciting a sharp warning from La'ann. "Ahngoose! No!"

"Safe, it is, La'ann," Angus reassured, when, in truth, he wasn't quite so sure. He wondered at the chance of taking some irrevocable step. Although, having seen chambers very like this one, he had reason to believe he knew what might be expected. Still, he couldn't be sure. What did he really know about the purpose of this small chamber, or of its builders? Not a thing. Stepping inside, he stood still for a moment feeling a small bit of relief when nothing happened. The action of lights and doors had already spiked his blood with adrenalin. "Inside, come you can," he said with a short wave.

Two quick steps brought Eilen inside, forcing Angus to one side. La'ann and Wezi approached more cautiously, taking their steps slowly, warily. La'ann stared up at the domed ceiling pouring soft light down into the small area. Wezi was tall enough to reach a finger up to the lit surface, reacting with some surprise when it did not feel warm. With some degree of wonder, he said, "Hot it is not. Like the handflame it is, Ahngoose."

Even Angus and Eilen were startled when the door slid shut behind them. Although they had seen many similar events in their lives, this one came as a surprise. No assurances of any kind sprang from Wezi or La'ann's experiences. They were suddenly trapped in a small cage. Before anyone could speak, the chamber began to resonate with a deep hum. Low-frequency vibrations rose through the soles of their feet. Angus put a hand to the wall, steadying himself, feeling slightly dizzy and lightheaded. A light nausea welled in his stomach and he was struck with the thought that he'd felt like this before—during jumps. Bewildered faces around him told Angus he wasn't the only one wrestling with a strange sensation. He had hardly begun to confront the implications of what he felt when the humming, the vibration, the odd sensations ceased, and the crowded chamber went still and quiet.

Angus's eyes turned to the barely visible lines of the chamber door, silent and firmly closed. He stared intently at the wall on both sides, searching for another control panel. He reached out to touch an area near the interior position opposite of where he had touched before, allowing his hand to spread and wiggle in much the same way as he had before. The door slid open. With the first crack, the air in their chamber rushed out with a hiss.

STARS AND STATIONS

CHAPTER 29
Another Outpost

The pretense seemed tiresome, but Semgee always knew where his duty lay. Watching Alexandra's expression, he saw the imagined triumph already forming in her mind. *What might it be like,* he wondered, to serve with a more dispassionate, logical captain, someone with whom he might compare notes, someone with whom he might jointly plan ship's operations, someone from whom he might learn.

"Honorable Captain, if you would permit, I do have some news."

Semgee watched Alexandra's face assume its familiar, firm 'I'm-the-Captain' set. "Go ahead, First Officer. I'm listening. How's our approach coming?"

"I'm afraid, Honorable Captain, not quite as we might have hoped."

Not the kind of statement Alexandra wanted to hear. Furrows formed on her brow. "What do you mean? How so?"

Why, he could not explain, but Semgee decided that no mincing of words would help on this occasion. "Since we dropped into real space near this rather unremarkable, G-Type star, we've been unable to reacquire the signal we've been chasing." He let that statement sink in before touching on its consequences, which he knew she'd find more difficult to hear. "We can only conclude that the transmissions ceased some time ago."

This time she surprised him with what seemed like calm acceptance. Propping an elbow upon the desktop she allowed her cheek to settle upon her closed hand. "Can we say nothing more?"

"I'm pleased you asked, Honorable Captain. And, yes, we can say two things more: Our distant standoff position tells us the cessation likely occurred more than a month ago and we do have a probable site which may yet yield additional clues."

Brightening, Alexandra looked up again. "How so?"

"Our survey reveals several planets surrounding the star, a large gas giant herding several significant moons, a couple of frozen worlds farther out, and a single rocky planet in moderately close orbit. It is not unreasonable to expect the signals to have originated from that rocky world.

"That sounds promising. Why didn't you say so sooner?"

"Honorable Captain, I thought you should know of the signal loss. Its absence carries another likely implication."

"And just what might that be?"

"Our quarry is now alerted."

"And you think so, why?"

"The signals we intercepted were almost certainly from another outpost. The pattern of transmissions and their sparse content told us as much. The fact that they stopped transmitting some time ago tells us these aliens probably abandoned this outpost. It's not worth the effort, but, if we jumped back out to a distance nearer our last encounter, I'll bet we'd be able to reacquire that signal."

"I don't suppose there's anything we can do about that now ... and, besides ... it's of no real consequence. We're well-armed."

"First, we still need to find them. I'll prepare a dive into a near orbit with that rocky planet and we'll at least see what we can glean from what we might find here."

"On your way out, send in that weapons officer ... What's his name?"

"You mean, Commander El-Hashem?"

"Yes ... We'll use that rocky planet as the target. I need another weapons test. I'd like to get a better idea of exactly how many square kilometers we can obliterate with what we have at our disposal."

CHAPTER 30
Orbit

Bitter cold washed across Angus's feet and caught the breath in his throat. Leaning forward, he peered into a dimly lit world, disappointed by the sight of what seemed to be the same smooth-walled round room that had been there before the door closed. Yet the cold air said something had changed and his ears registered new sounds. This room sounded different, sharper, in concert with the cold stiffness of the air; even the opening door's faint hiss carried a metallic edge. As Angus and his companions stood inside the small chamber, a soft light rose within the room outside, radiating uniformly from every point in the ceiling bulge.

One cautious, toe-first step took Angus into the room. Air cold enough to freeze flesh bit at nose and fingers. He mourned the loss of his gomba robe and, even as he did so, he could feel on his face the heat radiating from the wall. Holding his companions still with an upright hand, he gave himself a silent moment to glean the heartbeat of the place, feeling, more than hearing, another low hum. The place was alive.

By her wide-eyed expression Eilen told Angus that she felt it too.

One after the other, Wezi and La'ann stepped into the room, alert and edgy, a pair of caged animals suddenly freed.

In one quick glance Angus saw how alien this place might seem. No experience in his two friends' lives matched anything here. The very air they inhaled, sterile and free of floral scent, was unlike anything they had ever before breathed. Yet Angus felt alive and filled with anticipation. Everything here felt strangely comfortable, not unlike other places he had seen.

Chiseled into the structure of the facing wall, a smooth ramp curved upward to disappear into the ceiling somewhere around the room's rear circumference. Driven by thoughts he could hardly allow to form Angus walked directly toward the ramp and began to ascend. So rapt was he in his quest for the ramp's upper end that he had not noticed his three companions lingering in front of the small entry chamber. He'd already walked halfway up the wall before his thoughts turned their way.

Using what he hoped was a calm manner, he asked, "See more, wish you do not?" His voice rang loudly off the hard wall.

A silent moment filled the cold air before La'ann asked the most pertinent question. "This place, what is?"

"I know not. Places like this one, seen before, I have." Reluctant to lend any reality to the vague impressions he'd been entertaining, Angus spoke without thinking. "Far from Nahélé, perhaps, we are." Then absently lapsed into Standard. "Eilen, are you seeing what I'm seeing?"

"It does seem to have a familiar feeling." Waving a hand at Wezi and La'ann, she let herself continue in Standard. "C'mon gentlemen, our guide awaits."

Neither La'ann nor Wezi missed her intent and followed dutifully, if hesitantly, up the ramp.

Angus resumed his upward march until he saw through the ceiling a clear, star-filled night sky. They were no longer in the heart of the mountain. Enrapt with the sight, he had nearly stepped into the room above before he noticed the absence of a floor. With half his body still below the level of what should have been floor, his eyes took in a view from many miles above a sunlit planet surface. Surprised, he looked back down the ramp, seeing his friends staring upward. Stepping back down the ramp, he ran his hands across the solid, opaque sides of the passage, reaffirming its solid definition.

Eilen asked, "What's wrong? What do you see?"

"I'm not sure. We seem to be emerging into midair."

Wezi may not have understood what was said, but he understood the furrows on both faces in the exchange. "Nini okotála?" he asked quietly.

Remembering to whom he spoke, Angus offered what little explanation he could. "Strange again, it is. High, we are. No floor, there is."

He looked up through the opening and again stared into a star-strewn night sky. Alerted now, he stared at the edge of the ramp as his upper body rose above the floor level, seeing the sharp boundary. Beyond the end of the ramp, where there should have been floor, there was simply clear space, and far below, thousands of kilometers of planet surface as it might be seen from higher than any bird could fly.

Unable yet to believe what he saw Angus took in more of the room, noting a solid, opaque annular boundary holding its bottom edge high above the planet below and separated from deep space atop by a clear, hemispherical dome. Returning his eyes to the planet, he picked out mountains, deserts, and oceans of both green and blue. His eyes told him one thing, but his reason sowed distrust. The enclosed room at his feet and the still air around him told him he could not possibly be standing before an open window, freely exposed to the miles-high perspective before him. He carefully extended a hand toward the planet, almost losing his balance when the hand suddenly met solid resistance. When a second, more controlled probe met similar results, he ventured to step up and onto firm, hard, flat surface, invisible to his eyes, but definitely present underfoot. Standing now, visually unsupported, miles above the beautiful day-lit planet surface, he marveled. Another carefully extended toe succeeded in finding yet more solid support. Rising confidence helped him believe that one more step would not send him tumbling toward his death.

"Oh! Stars of Heaven!" Still standing on the entrance ramp Eilen reached out with her hand to feel the hard, invisible barrier.

Angus turned back to see her standing near the top of the ramp. His eyes followed the surface of the ramp down into a solid well, yet he saw no visible existence outside the perimeter of the opening, no sides, no structure; the opening's depth apparent only within the confines of its outline, a two-dimensional, infinitesimally thick window in the three-dimensional volume of high planetary atmosphere.

"Quite something, isn't it," he said with no little awe.

Vague suspicions coalesced in a single burst of realization as Angus walked without fear to the edge of the room. A single, very bright, blue-white star dominated the deep space scene outside. He knew it as well as if he were standing on the Raiju's bridge. If he looked carefully, he was sure he might be able to find among the bright points before him the far away tiny image of a crescent Uko, reflecting Amon's brilliant fire. He was back in deep space, back where he belonged.

A gasp from La'ann drew Angus's attention from the deep space scene. La'ann and Wezi were kneeling close to each other at the top of the ramp, unable to even stand above the edge of the abyss. Eilen stood suspended above what Angus now knew as a dynamic view from somewhere in the high atmosphere of Nahélé's world. As Angus watched La'ann's hand reach to touch the invisible floor, another striking feature of the display became visible. Glowing red runes appeared suspended below the entrance. The runes gave the gate a label; a label to match the red spot visibly pulsating on the planetary illusion beneath their feet.

A marvelous illusion it was. The NavSystem aboard Raiju could project a three-dimensional image of an entire galaxy; one which Angus could manipulate like a toy. Yet the image before him was infinitely more sophisticated and powerful. Only with reluctance did he pull his eyes away.

Armed with perspective, Angus on other aspects of the circular room, being drawn immediately to the dark outlines of other exits arrayed around the floor's outside circumference. He counted five others, and a sixth near the center of the chamber, before which Eilen now stood.

"Angus ... come here," she said without taking her eyes from the hole in the air above Nahélé's world.

Walking directly, but slowly over to where Eilen stood, Angus stared into another spiral ramp, leading downward, becoming steeper as it fell away.

"Now where do you think that goes?" he thought aloud.

"I don't know, but I suspect I'll be amazed when we find out."

At Wezi's hail the two of them pulled their eyes out of the hole to see their two companions, standing at the top of the entrance ramp. "Forget us, you have."

Eilen took sympathy. Stomping her feet on the invisible floor she said, "Out come. Safe it is. Lies, your eyes speak."

With a show of trust, La'ann looked directly at her, steeled himself, and stepped out onto the floor; then, retaining his unwavering focus on Eilen, he took three more steps before stopping to stare down at the tremendous drop below his feet. Pounding the invisible barrier with his foot, he assured himself of its reality, then quickly closed the space between them.

"Brave, you are," Angus said with a hand on La'ann's shoulder.

The three of them watched Wezi walk nervously, but

steadily across the room.

Angus waited only until Wezi stood beside him. Then he looked down the spiral ramp, thinking aloud, "Shall we see where this goes?" and stepped into the hole-in-the-air.

It felt more level than it looked. Visually, he should be falling forward, but he felt no incline. His sense of balance said he walked upright. Knowing his eyes could not be trusted he closed them and allowed his mind to override his eyes. When he opened them again the ramp had flattened and became the floor of a short corridor, a corridor of smoothly curved walls and no corners. Angus's firm sense of 'up' and 'down' seemed to dissolve. Peering at the far end, he saw the pathway wrap itself 'upward' and around the sides. He continued forward waiting to feel tipped by the path's curved journey up the wall. The feeling never came. His eyes continued lying, but nothing seemed amiss underfoot.

Prepared now, Angus saw nothing surprising as he emerged into another domed room. This end of the passageway opened to a floor filled with stars, surrounded above by a transparent dome through which he saw another view of deep space. No longer awed by the sight, Angus rose out of the floor into the center of the room alert to the possibility of additional exit portals. He found them, visible in the floor as black patches where no stars could be seen. They showed themselves as he moved. Changing perspective imparted a corresponding change in nearby stars. Stars winked in or out of view at the edges of black portals.

Eilen, Wezi and La'ann followed and stood close with Angus in front of the central entrance. The stars in the floor here did not seem to instill the same fear as the planetary view. Perhaps a night sky seen below one's feet was much too far from experience to inspire fear. Nor did the view through the clear dome carry great fascination. Stars overhead they had all seen before.

As his companions spread themselves around the room,

either staring down at the image in the floor or gazing out through the clear dome, Angus focused on the portals, marking a route to an exit portal directly ahead, visible from where he stood as only a black void in the field of stars captured in the floor. Shifting his perspective, up or down, or side-to-side, he guided his steps by the portal's occlusion of individual stars, watching them wink in or out of view as he walked. He had nearly reached his goal when Eilen's call turned him around.

"Angus! Come here. I've found something you'll want to see."

He found her nearly behind him, perhaps a third the way around the room standing near another exit portal. Eilen's beckoning gesture was enough to also pull Wezi and La'ann from their explorations. By the time Angus approached, Wezi and La'ann were already waiting close to where Eilen stood several steps away from the shadowy print of one exit portal. As he drew near, Eilen said, "Watch there," and simultaneously pointed toward the floor. Angus, Wezi, and La'ann all looked and, as they did so, Eilen stepped closer to the portal. A star in the floor image became noticeably brighter, then shone brighter yet as she took a second step. When Angus turned back to say something, he caught sight of the nearby portal, now softly illuminated from inside and clearly sporting a descending ramp. Eilen drew back again and they all watched the bright star and the illuminated portal fade in unison.

"Angus! Do you know what we've stumbled upon?"

"Yes. I think I do. I'll bet the other end of this ramp will put us before a small chamber very like the one that brought us here, except this time it will be linked to some other satellite orbiting some other star."

Eilen nodded slowly, her eyes never leaving the darkened portal. In a low voice, sounding almost afraid to hear her own words, she said, "It sounds too fantastic to say aloud ... but I'd

call it a transport system ... an interstellar transport system."
Angus felt but did not see Eilen's eyes turn to look at him. He
stared down the darkened ramp. Then, before Eilen could
speak again, he stepped toward the portal and stood above the
ramp, mesmerized, watching the illumination rise,
anticipating his next steps.

"Angus, stop. You know what you'll find down there.
Before you go any farther, let's think a bit."

Angus looked up from the ramp. "Don't you want to see
where it leads?"

"Yes, I do ... but perhaps we could slow down a little. I'm
afraid we're becoming too enthralled by the whole thing ...
moving too rapidly. We have no idea what we might find at
the other end of the next portal. We don't even know whether
the planet portal will work in the other direction."

The worthy thought touched a logical nerve. Angus looked
again down the ramp then back to her.

Eilen continued, "Besides, it's been a long day. I'm tired
and I'm hungry. Perhaps, before we rush off into unknown
territory, we could at least test the return trip."

"Perhaps you're right. I was getting ahead of things. Shall
we go see if there's a return trip in that lift chamber?"

Wezi and La'ann stood by, politely ignoring the exchange
in Standard that they could not share.

....

It was difficult to judge how long Wezi had been away. He
returned with both sack and the bladder full. Without a word,
he hung the bladder on a peg, set the sack down near the fire
pit, and set himself to preparing the evening meal. In the space
of a minute or two, he pulled the tripod off the previous day's
ashes and arranged a fresh charge to fuel a new fire.

Wezi's procedure evoked both amusement and
amazement. Such primitive fire-starting methods were new to

Eilen. Even as she admired the skill she saw in his efforts she also saw how she might use the occasion. Seizing the opportunity, she decided to reinforce the growing relationship, saying, "Wezi, fire make, can I?"

If Eilen intended no hidden agenda, Wezi's puzzled expression might have drawn a smile from her. "Happy be, I am," he said, offering his two fire-starting implements. When she declined to take them, Wezi watched intently as Eilen rose and moved to her survival bag, picking out an item small enough to hide in one hand. Settling herself again, she unfolded the small item, transforming it into a thin wand before inserting its one end into the kindling. A few seconds elapsed before the tinder bundle burst into flame. Wezi's appreciative reaction was just what she had hoped for. Carefully returning the marvelous little instrument into a compact package, Eilen extended an open palm. "To you, give I do."

The small fire warmed the little courtyard of Wezi's home, giving it a comfortable feeling and, after unrolling three small carpets near the fire for his guests to sit upon, Wezi turned it into a pleasant setting and a good place to talk. Perhaps Wezi understood the duties of a host as much as he understood the need to chase the day's turmoil from everyone's head.

Taking note of the calming effect the fire seemed to have on La'ann, who sat completely wrapped in thought. Eilen wondered if he might not be reminded of many a quiet hunting camp shared with Ro'ann.

Angus stared without seeing. Eilen watched him squirm beside the fire, knowing his thoughts still lay somewhere else.

Relaxing, Eilen momentarily forgot the unforgettable day and simply enjoyed the fire's friendly feel, listening to a faint flutter from the yellow flames. Drops of fat ran off the small carcasses Wezi pushed around the mesh grill, sending occasional pops into the room. An appetizing aroma rose from the cooking, tempting Eilen to ask about the animals being prepared. A vision of the not-quite-visible creatures scampering around the wasteland plateau pushed the thought from her head.

Her eyes returned to Angus. She saw him still in deep space, captivated by the day's events. He should be thinking like his former self, like a starship captain. Perhaps she could nudge him back into the role. Wezi was starting to pull their meal from the fire. As Wezi passed to each person a stone bowl in which lay the not-quite-charred remains of some small creature, Eilen decided it was time to prod Angus from his solitude. "Angus, what's going through your mind?"

At the sound of Eilen's voice, Angus directed a blank expression her way. At length he said, "I've been wondering about the power behind this fantastic system we've found. The feeling I get in the transport chamber seems quite like what I feel during a jump. It strikes me that the power behind it may be similar to the Reimann drives of our ships, as though the system builders were able to couple and focus two Reimann drives to control a narrow corridor of space over interstellar distances."

Eilen had to smile to herself. Angus's analytical skill was still intact. She need only nudge it into motion. "I've been thinking, too," she said.

The day's events had at least left Angus in good humor. A smile spread across his face and he threw a little taunt her way. "Well ... That IS a good sign."

Ignoring the bait, Eilen acknowledged the mild rib with only the slightest grin, "Yes, it is. You need to try it, too. If we were back on the Raiju and preparing to send out an excursion team onto some newly discovered planet, what sort of plan would you demand?"

Angus looked hard at her. Sitting back, thinking, he rubbed his chin. She saw the wheels turning—a good sign. Perhaps she had done the right thing. Picking up a piece of dinner, Angus started to gnaw on what might have once been some creature's forelegs. When he finally spoke, his answer came from a somewhat different direction than Eilen expected. "Translate for me, will you? I'm afraid my Batololému skills aren't up to it. Wezimunto! Can you measure time?"

The sound of his name drew Wezi's attention. Eilen's translation elicited a short nod as Wezi rose and stepped to one of the cabinets, extracting from it a shaped stone. Reseated, he placed the stone on the floor before him. All could see how its top had been worn into a smooth, deep, conical depression. The purpose became clear as Wezi removed and separated a top half from a lower; then, while holding the top half firmly in his left hand he raised the lower half to pour from it a flow of sand into the depression of the top. Having emptied the lower section, he repositioned the upper portion back atop the lower, releasing, with the removal of a restraining finger, the sand to flow through a small hole in the bottom of the conical hollow. They all watched the sand slowly disappear and return to its original place within the lower section.

Angus anointed the demonstration. "And thus, elapses one 'sand period'."

Eilen's translation went elsewhere. "Wezi, La'ann ... About the room-that-moves, more tell, I must."

CHAPTER 31
Without a Starship

Wrapped in private anticipation, no one noticed the blank walls of Inyanga's back alleys, nor did they see the mounds of sifted debris or the mountain of wreckage as they retraced yesterday's journey. No one said a word as they crawled through the reeking low tunnel and stood again before the 'room that moves.' When they eventually found themselves atop the unseen floor of the orbiting station's planetary reception room, the four explorers, bound now by an experience shared by no other living being, quickly crossed the room, showing only passing interest in the beauty beneath their feet or the bright stars shining through a clear dome. La'ann and Wezi's world had grown well beyond the bounds they knew only yesterday.

Wezi's face betrayed no emotion. He stood before one of the orbiting station's two active outbound portals, knowing what to expect. The 'room that moved' looked distinctly like those he had seen before. It no longer held any power over his psyche. He stooped and opened the sack he'd carried, withdrawing another, smaller bag and from that the stone components of his sand-timer. From a lidded container, he poured a measured portion of sand into the receptor-half and looked up to acknowledge his readiness.

One had to admire the simple ingenuity of the primitive device, crude and clumsy, but portable and functional. Deficiencies in accuracy and precision didn't really interfere with utility.

Waiting only for Wezi, Angus met everyone's eyes in turn. "Ready, we are?" Eilen's nod freed any doubt. "In five sand-turns, return I will. If return, I do not. Follow you will not."

Wezi's silent nod and a last glance in Eilen's direction seemed to remove the only impediments to departure. Turning about, Angus stepped toward the door. With a final look back, he smiled and reached to activate the panel.

A barely audible whoosh sent Eilen's hand to her chin, stilling there the quiver she knew might form. Fear is often born of ignorance, but in this instance Eilen's knowledge and experience fed her imagination and stoked her fears. Her companions knew of danger from their fellows, or from casual misadventure, or perhaps from Nahélé's wild creatures, but none of these were evident in the strange sliding door. They waited calmly for Angus to return. Eilen alone knew how the closing door would send Angus across distances so vast as to defy explanation, and to what? All evidence told her the door would open for him on another satellite not greatly different from the one on which they stood. Yet she could not be sure and doubt gave birth to fear. Although she would never admit it, the idea that she might be left alone on Nahélé's world filled her with dread. It was the second time Angus had put such fear into her head, the second as unwelcome as the first.

She looked down at Wezi's timer, wondering why the sand flowed so much more slowly than it had the night before. A dimple had scarcely formed upon the sand surface, yet Angus' departure already seemed hours distant. Five sand-turns was an unreasonable wait. La'ann's hand upon her shoulder gave her a start. "Good man Ahngoose is. Return he will."

The gesture brought all of Eilen's concerns to the surface. By the time Wezi set the next turn in motion, she was pacing.

By the end of the fourth turn, she knew she would not allow the very protocol she had approved to restrain her. If Angus failed to appear by the end of that fifth turn, she would find out why.

With the fifth sand-turn nearly within the receptor, Eilen confronted her intent directly, turning to stand directly in front of the closed chamber door, acutely aware of how foolish it seemed, of how she might very well send herself to whatever demise prevented Angus' return. Stilling her breath, she reached to touch the activation panel, conscious of La'ann's close presence. She looked at La'ann, who only nodded. He understood. Still squatting near his timer on the floor, Wezi took note, finally rising to stand behind his two friends. Their silent votes tipped the balance. Eilen's hand touched the panel with a degree of certainty that had not been there a second before. When that touch failed to bring forth action, frustration became anger and she hit the panel again with force. Was Angus's fate to be resolved so emptily? Was he to simply disappear without explanation? No! She'd struck the panel several times, showing no sign of ceasing, when La'ann drew her arm away. Her head fell and rocked slowly side to side. "No. No. No."

Neither she, nor La'ann, nor Wezi could find anything more to say. A heavy silence befell the three companions, amplifying the chamber door's whoosh as it opened. Eilen looked up to see Angus standing within, his expression tightening as he took in the scene without. "Happen what?"

Before Angus had even finished, Eilen lapsed into Standard, nearly shouting, "Angus! Where have you been?"

Angus's mouth opened as though he intended to speak, then closed again. Then, in a quiet manner he said, "Truthfully, I really don't know. I can only say it wasn't much different than this place."

At the sound of his voice, the anger seemed to drain from Eilen's face. Furrows reformed themselves into a mock scowl.

"That's not what I mean! What took you so long?"

"I arrived on another orbiter and I went over to look at the planetary side. I didn't think it would take long."

Eilen could hardly contain herself, staring at the growing beard covering his unkempt face. Her reply carried enough volume to ring in the hard-sided room. "You disregarded the instructions you drafted yourself!"

Reaching to put a hand on Eilen's shoulder, Angus's voice softened. "I'm sorry. It won't happen again."

The apology allowed Eilen to relax as Angus's arms engulfed her.

As if he had actually understood the exchange in Standard La'ann took the opportunity to convey his own feelings. "Returned you are. Good it is."

Angus freed one arm from Eilen's shoulder to wave them all into the open chamber. "Come. All go, we can."

The transport chamber was not designed for four people, but the short trip gave no one time to become uncomfortable. Emerging into the star-bound side of another orbiter, they all stood and momentarily admired the view through the clear dome, another field of countless bright stars, as beautiful as the one they left behind, but distinctly more rarified. They stood most certainly in another small corner of the galaxy, somewhere far from Amon's neighborhood.

"Tell Wezi and La'ann that I found active portals here for two other destinations, but nothing active on the planetary side. In fact, the floor on that side is dead and dark."

"... and you're itching to try one of them aren't you."

"Of course, I am."

Eilen paused, firm lines settling in her expression. Her posture conveyed a clear message. "No ... I don't think so. This time it's my turn." She waited for an argument that never came.

Occasional exchanges of Standard between Angus and Eilen no longer seemed to vex Wezi or La'ann. On this occasion the two native speakers merely followed their off-world companions across the room to stand looking down into the nearest active portal. As they approached, a star glowed bright red and a vertical line of runes pulsed to life just off the right side of where they stood.

"Have I seen those runes before?" Angus asked in Standard.

"No," Eilen replied. "These are different. It reminds you of the Inyanga station only because the first rune is the same. This ramp is definitely going somewhere else."

Angus stepped down the ramp.

The room below surprised no one. They were met by the familiar sight of a smooth-walled, round room, its center occupied by a single upright small cylindrical chamber. Gathering before the chamber door, Angus ceded the lead to Eilen, stepping to the side. Eilen looked at Wezi and La'ann. "Go I will. Stay, Angus will. My job it is."

Eilen laid her hand on the activation panel. The door remained inert. After a second failed attempt, Angus reached out to show her his perfected technique, wiggling his spread hand to let thumb and little finger alternately touch the panel in two places in a rapid four-touch sequence. The door slid open. Eilen gave Angus a slow nod, as if in deference to his dubious skill, then stepped into the chamber and turned. The closing door separated her from her companions.

Although she did not feel fear, the mere fact of standing alone for the first time in quite a while disturbed Eilen more than she would have thought possible. This transport chamber was no different than the other two she'd ridden that morning and she had every reason to believe it would function as had those others; but somehow this time, filled with no one but herself, the small space felt oppressive.

Her mind had barely wrapped itself around her feelings when the door slid open and she stared out at a cold, empty room. Taking a single step outside, she felt a sharp cold wash over her body. She nearly retreated before sensing the heat flowing off the wall. *This is what Angus felt that first time.* She hadn't yet reached the bottom of the exit ramp before she remembered the 'immediate return' protocol. As she stepped back into the chamber she thought, *Perhaps, Angus's recklessness is understandable.*

Arriving to find the others as she had left them, Eilen directed a mild jab at Angus. "You see, Angus, it's really not a difficult protocol to follow." An elaborate half-bow from Angus acknowledged the rebuke. Wezi's unchanging face showed no emotion. Only La'ann smiled.

Solo mission accomplished, Eilen waved everyone into the chamber. "C'mon." The crowded transport chamber felt more comfortable.

Although he stood nearest, at the door's reopening Angus stepped aside. Pleased, Eilen walked directly toward the upward ramp, thinking Angus's leadership skills were returning. The top of the ramp on this occasion offered no surprise and no impediment. Eilen stepped into another reception room, adorned, like the others she'd now seen, with a field of innumerable bright stars shining through a clear domed ceiling and the image of a different star field shining up through the invisible floor. She stopped and stood motionless for a moment, taking in the metallic edge to her own footsteps and the odorless, antiseptic quality of the air. Behind her the others spilled out onto the floor and fanned out across the room, no longer awed by the sight, either above or below. Each of them examined the room under direction of their own priorities. Angus stepped directly toward the nearest of the remaining five exit ports; Wezi and La'ann both had their eyes focused down into the floor's image. The deep-space scene through the dome brought Eilen back to life. "Angus!"

Reacting to the loud ring of her own voice, she quickly reduced her voice to a more subdued tone, almost a whisper.

"We seem to be in the company of a rather nice-looking red giant." Pulled from the disappointing discovery of a lifeless second exit port, Angus looked in the direction she indicated. A brilliant and distinctly red-colored star stood out, shining with greatly more intensity than all others within view. Angus held up his hand to gauge its size, then turned and walked toward the central ramp leading to the planetary side. As Eilen drew near Angus pointed into the floor. "You see? There!"

A distinctly bright red star stood in the floor image just to the right of the planet-side walkway entrance. No mere coincidence, Eilen felt confident that it was the image of the red giant. She let Angus take some satisfaction from his discovery, "The perspective is different and the distance is greater, but I think you're right. That's the same star."

Angus's excitement still sounded in his voice. "Let's go see the planetary side?"

An unlit planetary side greeted their entrance. Stars shone through the dome, but no image adorned the opaque black floor. No one moved away from the entrance portal. Angus's voice carried disappointment. "The same as I found on the station before this one."

Returning to the star-side terminal, an ebullient Angus stepped out and started to march toward the exit portal directly across the room, announcing his plans. "Shall we find out how many other active stations there are?" A couple of steps later, he stopped. "Wait a minute. I forgot which one brought us here."

"I'm turned around myself," Eilen had to admit. "Wezi, La'ann. Return trail, know you do?"

Wezi extended his right arm toward the nearest port on his right. "Here."

"Yes ... and I found this one dead," Angus said, indicating the port directly in front of the internal passage. With his back to everyone, talking to no one in particular, he walked toward the next portal on his left. "Which means I haven't yet tested this one."

Angus only slowed as he neared the next portal, reporting his findings aloud. "OK. That's one more working." Without stopping he continued around the room. The other three watched Angus circumnavigate the room. He hadn't quite made it back to where they all stood when he reported the tally. "Three dead, three alive," he said in Standard. A step later, he stood holding fingers in the air, repeating himself for Wezi and La'ann's benefit. "Misátokúfaka, misátovánadaka," he said in his best Batololému, rewarded with smiles and nods. At least he spoke well enough to be understood.

Reverting to Standard, Angus looked at Eilen. "We know where one goes, that leaves us two more unknown destinations to explore."

Eilen allowed her face to broaden in a smile before turning to walk toward the next exit port along the same path Angus had followed. Reaching there, she didn't even hesitate but continued down the ramp as if she had done so all her life.

It surprised no one that the next star-side terminal could hardly be distinguished from the last. Their similarity seemed their most characteristic feature, as though whoever had created the transport stations had done so in large numbers, like so many factory-made personal vehicles.

The next terminal floor floated above a star map seen on yet another scale, smaller stars were visible in much larger numbers. Cloudy nebulae obscured vast regions, imparting a galactic scale to the scene.

A kind of implicit process had begun to form. A quick visual examination of the room and of the star-filled space outside the dome preceded by only moments a silent walking survey of the exit-ports, this time conducted by the entire group. Wezi was the first to speak, pointing as they slowed in front of the first active port, halfway around the perimeter. "Umuntubalele ... Inyanga."

Remembering her long conversation with Wezi during the

desert crossing, Eilen recalled the name he had given to Amon. "Amon? Wezi speaks."

Looking where Wezi indicated she could see a set of runes marking the port. The pulsing star image carried a distinct blue-white tint, but the image was too small to conclusively tag as Amon. "Wezi. Mean what, you do? That star, Amon is?"

"As first sky-door, writing is."

"Know it you do?"

"Yes. In my spirit, see it I do."

Angus caught the thread of their conversation. "It's easily verified. Shall we test Wezi's memory?"

"Of course. And let me do one thing more," Eilen said, walking back toward the port from which they had shortly before emerged. "As I thought, the signature star here is quite bright and tinged red," she said, allowing her navigator skills to take the thought further "With distinctive markers like these and enough time, we might map out where we actually are, at least in relative terms."

Still standing with the others at the threshold of the port ramp, Angus wanted to hurry her. "All right, let's see if this port takes us back to Amon's station?"

The new station's star-bound terminal room gave them nothing to identify. Amon would be visible only from the planetary side. So not until they walked out high above the surface of Nahélé's world did Wezi's prediction become reality by the singularly bright nearby star shining through the clear dome. Angus acknowledged the obvious, setting a raised finger in circular motion. "Circle, made we have."

The language effort didn't go unnoticed, nor was it unappreciated, eliciting vigorous nods from both La'ann and Wezi. Angus's elementary characterization of the morning's astronomical journey poured a cooling dose of normality over the entire activity.

The moment seemed appropriate for a rest. While her companions looked on, Eilen walked toward the Inyanga planetary port and sat. "Hunger now, I have." From a distance, she appeared to sit in midair high above Inyanga. When the others joined her, Wezi pulled dried foodstuffs from his bag and she passed around a canteen of water. The water quenched thirst and reminded each of them how dry was the air they'd been breathing.

After quietly eating, La'ann spoke. "Within Nahélé, trail, I know. In this place, lost to me, trail becomes."

Realizing how uncharacteristically quiet La'ann had been all day, Eilen used the opening. "One danger only, losing trail is. More dangers there are ..."

....

Angus cavorted like a child with a new toy, enthralled to find the floor adorned with a bright planetary image. The discovery was worthy of celebration. La'ann and Wezi's world no longer held him captive. How many other worlds might he yet find? Wearing the replacement robe Wezi had given him, he presented a comic figure. Much too long, his legs found unhindered movement only when he gathered fabric under the belt line, letting folds fall out around his waist. Wezi's gift gave him a distinctly un-Angus-like appearance.

The floor's image displayed a large part of a whole planet, as might be seen from a vantage higher even than what they'd seen above Nahélé's world. A single feature dominated all else, a white polar cap covering perhaps a third of the visible hemisphere. The white cap stood in stark contrast to the black void of space behind it and put a sharp edge to the curve of the planet. A terminus shadow's edge arced across one side. No expanse of green gave any hint of forest; no Nahele here; no long mountain ridges broke the flat monotony; no expanse of blue-green ocean shaped any kind of shoreline. The polar cap's white color stood in contrast to the uncapped planet surface, appearing soft yellow-brown adorned by broad streaks of pastel umbers, ochers and tans, as if put there by the strokes of some tremendous brush. Stray wisps of clouds followed long arcs across the image, evincing atmosphere, water and possibly weather.

A bright red spot shone here similar to the one indicating Inyanga's location on Nahélé's world, placing the location of a planetary terminal well within the confines of the white polar cap.

Wezi and La'ann's puzzled faces prompted Eilen to explain. Pointing to the brightest star visible through the clear dome, she made an attempt. "Wezi, La'ann, understand you do? Under Amon's gaze, Nahélé's world sits. Under the eyes of that star this world sits. Another world it is; Nahélé's world it is not, the world of the 'Isihlabthikhulu' it is not. Down on it we look; from a place higher than a téa'éke floats." Searching the two faces, looking for signs of recognition, her eyes met only even, impassive expressions, conveying little.

Looking directly at the two natives, Angus tried to stir up action. "Good it is! With me down, who will go?"

Neither one moved immediately. La'ann stirred first. "With Ahngoose, I go."

Angus was pleased to see his friend take up the challenge, the friend who saved him from death-by-Marsh-Stalker, the friend who led him across the Mokililana. It was time to renew the bond.

Eilen seemed surprised. "Wait a second. Are you saying you already want to change our new procedure?"

"Yes. I think we should. I've been thinking that we made a mistake with the stipulation of allowing one person to go it alone. I would propose that we send two, appointing one to stay with the chamber ready to return if anything goes amiss."

....

The door opened to an absurdly cold, dark room. Breaths

came rapidly as if atop a high mountain. No radiating heat blunted the icy edge. Yet no obnoxious odor assailed Angus's nose and, as he peered out into the black it seemed he could see a dull glow on the opposite wall. If the terminal rooms' commonality held true, an exit ramp should be just there. He stepped cautiously out, trying to quiet his rapid breathing, testing the air, ready to jump quickly back into the safety of the transport chamber at any hint of malevolent scent. La'ann watched and waited; waited until he could wait no longer before releasing a single long exhale. The chamber filled with his condensed breath.

Stiffening cold lent a clumsy edge to Angus's movements. Perhaps he'd parted with his old gomba robe too easily. Wezi's replacement gift offered scant protection ... and the anteroom here showed no signs of warming. Angus tested the local gravity, bouncing his own weight against the strength in his legs. Perhaps this planet was larger than Nahélé's world, but not by much. La'ann chose that instant to step out. The chamber door slid shut, plunging the room in darkness.

In the darkness Angus froze, waiting for eyes to adjust. A second or two passed before he realized that a feeble glimmer of light flowed into the room. He could barely see the outline of the nearby transport chamber. He could just make out a faint blue glow emanating from a point high behind the transport chamber, about where he knew the exit ramp would lead.

Where the exit ramp should have been the hand-torch beam threw back glistening reflections. He followed tracks running down to find them spread from the foot of the ramp into a frozen pool on the floor. Retracing the route upward he found the exit path blocked, entirely encased in a solid wall of blue ice.

Angus stood and stared at the frustrating barrier, refusing to be so quickly barred from exploration. At low power setting his sidearm might melt a pathway through. How much power remained? Then those frozen tracks pointed to another problem: where would melt water flow? The room floor seemed flat and level. The chamber threshold looked flush with the floor. What might happen if melt water were to flow all the way there? Not worth the risk.

Angus doused the hand-torch.

Their first extra-system foray left Angus exhilarated. Not much to show for the effort, but no one hurt and now he knew there are other worlds to explore.

CHAPTER 32
Excursion

"Honorable Captain, I find no indication of habitation." The young lieutenant spoke slowly, hoping to keep any nervous edge from his voice. The bulky excursion suit made him feel uncomfortable, constricted, which only added to the twinge of fear he felt as he approached alone an alien habitation on an alien world. Ships' systems he understood, but he was never trained as a frontline soldier, and the thought that he was the most expendable among Bright Victory's skeleton crew did little for his confidence.

He now stood near the one structure among the several around him that he knew would likely house living quarters and sensing equipment, evident not in its size but in its substantial construction and in the sensory antennae bristling from its roof.

His captain's voice sounded clearly in the confines of his helmet. "I don't think we need to concern ourselves with proper etiquette. Blow a hole in it and get in there!"

Li Jie Chan spoke again, carefully, trying to sound confident, keeping his voice even, having never before spoken directly to his captain. That she had chosen to insert herself into ship-to-ground communications laid a dramatic emphasis on the importance of his mission. "It shall be done,

Honorable Captain."

The hatch itself told the lieutenant something about its builders. They were no bigger than he. He stared at it, looking for a strategic point to direct fire, aware of the hatch's function as a pressure cap. It certainly opened with a swing about the obvious hinges on the right, so he took aim at its center, where he expected to find the latching mechanism. A moment before firing, he hesitated, lowered his arm, imagining debris ejected by a sudden release of pressure exploding toward him. Taking a cautious couple of steps to one side, he raised his arm a second time and fired a focused beam into the center of the door.

Muted by the rarefied atmosphere, Li Jei heard only a dull thud from the short blast. His discharge produced a rapidly thinning cloud of hot gas erupting only from the door's vaporized metal substance. That the weapon's blast was joined by no burst of escaping pressure gave Li Jei all the evidence he needed to understand the status of the station's interior.

Entering carefully, he found the station deserted. No surprise there, but the familiar look of it came as a shock. The appearance of obvious facilities stopped him cold. Crew quarters, storage areas, work areas, all appeared strangely similar to those he might expect to find on one of the League's more remote working installations.

A shrill and testy voice sounded in his ear. "We need every bit of information we can pull from the place. Can you see any data storage equipment?"

"Yes, Honorable Captain, but access may take me some time. I'm pleased to report that I'm fairly certain I've identified data access ports and, if I can also trace a power feed, I should be able to gain access to the data storage equipment. If I can fit a transceiver to one of these access ports, I may be able to capture stored data."

Knowing that he would need to explain, Li Jei took a breath, hesitating before he ventured into more dangerous territory. "However, Honorable Captain, if I may ask a small concession."

"Yes, Yes, ... Of course. What is it?"

His captain's obvious irritation prompted Li Jei to speak slowly, trying hard to hold his own annoyance in check. "Honorable Captain, I need to ask for some indulgence. I'll be hampered by one important problem. Our equipment was obviously fashioned differently from what I've found, and, since I'm not very efficient working in this excursion suit it may take me a while to accomplish functioning connections."

....

Semgee had been able to find no advantage in all the data so far analyzed. There was no particular scent to follow. That somber fact left him quite disappointed and armed with no better recommendation than to resume the systematic search plan that they had been executing, something he knew his captain would not wish to hear.

"I afraid I must agree with you, Honorable Captain. The information so far retrieved has been very disappointing." It was another of the many times when he really wished his captain were more accommodating. He needed to think more clearly, more freely; to lean back and let his thoughts roam; but the stiff, upright chair his captain provided for guests would permit no such freedom. He really should leave to think elsewhere.

Alexandra seemed surprisingly calm. "They do seem to have performed a rather thorough purge of their data banks. They knew we were coming, did they not."

"Yes, they did. I would be negligent not to acknowledge what is now an obvious fact: the inhabitants of this dwarf galaxy know we're looking for them. And I can only guess why this outpost needed to be abandoned. Perhaps it was a little too near our initial contact and wasn't all that important. It does seem like a mere exploratory outpost."

Semgee brightened. "At least we now know for sure who our adversaries are. That outpost's general appearance tells me its inhabitants were as human as you and I ... and also confirms my theory ... We've almost certainly discovered the fate of those ancient rebels. Their flight took them here, all the way into another galaxy. We now hunt their descendants."

Although he felt certain that Alexandra must have entertained the thought, Semgee also knew that she would avoid confronting it. Now his statement put it immediately before her.

A reluctant acceptance sounded in her voice. "I suppose you're right, but it's a shame. It reduces the impact of our discovery ... and now I have to wonder if that knowledge helps our search in any way at all."

Almost as if her words had triggered the action, their conversation was interrupted by the intercom alert.

....

Reaching to open the channel, Alexandra spoke more harshly than she intended. "Yes. What is it?"

"Lieutenant Chan here, Honorable Captain. I believe I have some encouraging news and I respectfully request permission to enter."

She briefly considered denying the request. That thought triggered another. She should soon inform her new skeleton crew of the realities of her world. Interruptions were seldom welcome. On this occasion, however, she and Semgee had reached an unpleasant impasse. The diversion might help. "You have it," she said in the direction of the door.

The young lieutenant entered wearing an obnoxious grin, so obviously full of himself that Alexandra made a mental note: he would certainly need a bit of personal attention aimed at achieving a proper adjustment of attitude. Then again, he wasn't bad-looking, and he was young enough. Perhaps he could be useful to alleviate her tension in ways the others couldn't, another of her privileges as captain.

Li Jei drew himself into an erect posture and offered a proper stiff salute to the ship's ranking officers, the prideful grin still full on his face. "Honorable Captain, First Officer, I didn't mention it before, since I had not then been able to gain access to its contents, but I did find something significant inside the outpost." Raising his hand, he revealed a small object, held between thumb and forefinger. "This is a personal data storage device." The grin on his face became wider.

Damn his adolescent pride! thought Alexandra. She stared at her grinning crewman, becoming angry at his obvious enjoyment in the face of keeping his captain waiting. She had quite decided to berate the young man before he continued.

"I found it in the outpost crew's quarters, in the back corner of a small compartment. It contains images."

"Of what, may I ask?"

Leaving the answer to Alexandra's question hanging unanswered in the air, Li Jei diverted the moment to ensure his superiors knew of the credit he deserved. "It took me quite a while to rig a working connection and read it, but I got there eventually."

Which of course was not what Alexandra wanted to hear. "Yes! ... Yes! ... and WHAT did you find?"

Too wrapped in excitement, Li Jei didn't even register her displeasure. "Personal images, primarily what would appear to be of one crew member's family and friends. I examined them carefully, since they confirmed our suspicions surrounding the nature of the outpost's inhabitants, but then I found something more interesting."

Once again Li Jei paused and Alexandra let loose her growing ire. Her tone left no doubts of what she thought of his minor theatrics. "WELL??"

Li Jei went quickly to the heart of the matter, though

perhaps with less confidence than he had but a moment earlier. "I think I can help us find their home world ... I found what may be a very helpful clue."

"And ... just what might that be?"

"If I may, Honorable Captain, it would help if I can take control of your comscreen. I wish to project the images."

Not yet convinced, Alexandra marked her assent with an exasperated arm gesture. "Please! By all means ... Go ahead."

Stepping toward the far wall, Li Jei touched the panel. The ancient artwork displayed there momentarily dissolved into deep black. His audience's eyes lost focus in the vague blackness, only to be pulled back with the appearance of a new image: a man wearing tight-fitting clothes stretched around a muscular body, stood atop a small hill in the foreground with an arm raised in greeting as he smiled at the camera. The man's clothing seemed out-of-place, more in tune with an indoor café than the starkly beautiful scene around him. The hill on which he stood fell off into a broad vista of sand drifted into dunes, defined by hues of tan, taupe, beige and copper, sculpted by wind into smooth mounds and wavy ridges, punctuated here and there by sharp, rocky outcroppings and darker shadows. A blue sky met the horizon, darkening in its higher reaches and surrounding a small sun, hanging just above the horizon, its pale white color brightening the far, left corner of the picture.

Watching for acknowledgement, Li Jei began walking them through his reasoning. "You see the small setting sun on the horizon? ... Well now look at the shadows."

Shadows extended forward in a direction toward and to the right of the camera. Something about them didn't seem quite right, however. They seemed a little broader than they should be and each darker on one side than the other. Once Alexandra and Semgee had become intrigued by the scene, Li Jei continued, "There's a second sun off the image and higher in the sky than the one we see. The planet here is in orbit around a binary star ... and that's not all.

"Although the resolution recorded in this image is much too low for me to actually determine a spectral type for that setting sun, it seems to be a somewhat unusual hue, given the atmospheric conditions evident in the image.

"So ... although I probably can't prove it, I suspect this image was taken on the surface of a planet in a circumbinary orbit around a double star ... one in which the smaller of the binary pair is a helium white dwarf."

As he spoke those words, Alexandra noted the young man's excitement, looking directly at her, waiting for the import of his statement to register.

Semgee caught on before she did and usurped her chance to catch up, blurting out the conclusion that Li Jei had come to tell. "... and ... that's a rare occurrence among the stars of any galaxy."

"Exactly, sir! It's a marker, and certainly visible for millions of light-years in all directions. We can stop jumping around and begin to search this galaxy for a helium-white-dwarf-binary-companion star."

CHAPTER 33
Alien planet

Nothing seemed different, yet everything had changed. Angus stepped up into a familiar terminal station. Today's wonder came not from the station's existence but from the promise of where it might lead. A destination Angus wanted badly to discover. "The large M-type, I remember. It's the only way I could tell you which port we came through yesterday. Most of these ports all look the same ... We should somehow mark them so that we don't become rats in a maze."

Had he paid any attention Angus would have seen the smirk on Eilen's face. "You know, of course, they are marked."

"Yeah. And if I could read these runes the name tags would mean something to me."

Eilen turned toward Wezi. "Wezi, these symbols, to you speak, they do?"

"Speak they do not. See them I do."

"Understand, I do not. What meaning you have?"

"Within my spirit, see them I do."

"Ahh. For us, 'remember', word is."

From his pack Wezi extracted a flat, rectangular object. "Scratch them, I have."

This revelation drew everyone close. Pulling back a protective cloth, Wezi uncovered a rectangular matte black object. Lines of exposed bright metal shone through the black finish on one flat side. Runes identified each node in a web of lines. Angus's eyes widened. Wezi had made a diagram of the transport network. Turning to look at the scene projected on the floor, Angus compared the rune-set identifying Amon, then stepped away to examine the runes floating in the floor image next to the M-type star.

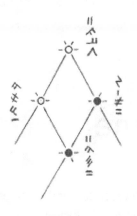

"Wezi! Well done!" Angus's Standard speech required no translation. The corners of Wezi's mouth turned upward. "That's one problem solved. Now, is anyone interested in seeing where this last active port leads?"

Minutes later, standing atop another station's planet-side terminal floor, they were met with a very different sight than any they had thus far seen. No planet-surface image greeted their arrival; nor did dead blackness herald the demise of whatever outpost had once existed there. Instead, the station's planet-side floor displayed an image similar to the outside view. Within the floor image, a single star outshone every other star within view. A small crescent reflection evinced the presence of at least one large planet.

Puzzled, Angus stepped toward the nearest portal. Somewhere past halfway a hint of motion caught his eye. With one more step he was certain. The image in the floor shifted, expanding with each step closer to the portal. Four steps later a small inner planet filled the floor. Standing at the portal lip he looked into the image at his feet. A bright red spot shone out from a location within a deep, rugged chasm that seemed to girdle the entire world. Retracing his steps, he watched the planet recede back into the system image. Without speaking he walked past his friends and continued toward the port opposite, feeling oddly satisfied when the image expanded again and pulled a second small planet from obscurity. His close approach activated another bright red indicator poised on the edge of an expanse of frozen black swirls in what was probably the remains of a once flowing expanse of molten rock spewed from some angry spout.

Angus stood straight, looking across the room toward the first port. The view below his feet looked no more appealing than the first.

....

Interior light spilled from the transport chamber as the door slid open, penetrating only far enough to illuminate the near floor. The reception room's far reaches still hid in gloom. Breaking the darkness with the beam of his hand-torch, Angus probed the room's extent, finding familiar smooth round walls, a shallow domed ceiling, and a ramp curving up the opposite wall. Tiny glints of light returned from many points in a profusion of shiny black floor debris. They seemed to be somewhere within the lava flow.

A pungent sulfurous odor struck Angus's nose and brought water to his eyes. The torch in his hand was now the only one left to them and it remained to be seen just how far it might guide them. His eyes began to burn and fill. Entertaining fleeting thoughts of stepping from the chamber, Angus instead stretched to close the chamber door. The isolation suits of his former life had always felt like a nuisance. They seemed now more valuable than he ever thought possible.

Their first steps back into the clean air of the orbiter came with a rush of gasping breaths. La'ann's face instantly told everyone what he thought of the clinging sulfur smell. Through halting breaths, bent over with arms braced on both knees, Angus reached into his limited Batololému to let La'ann know he agreed. "Good air, here is. Good it is."

"Perhaps we might take a look at the other one?" Eilen offered.

No more than halfway across the terminal room, Wezi announced, "With Ahngoose, I go." Their last foray had reminded Angus more keenly of the dangers inherent in first steps upon alien planets. Were they crossing a desert Wezi's skill would not be questioned but his complete inexperience with alien environments might be a liability. Certainly, Wezi and La'ann could not go alone to a planet surface. Could he let even one of them go? It seemed like introducing a novice rider onto the back of a spirited mount with the rudiments of riding yet to be mastered. Looking directly into Wezi's eyes, Angus said to him, "Wezimunto, danger there is." Wezi seemed to pay no mind. Perhaps his pride was tweaked, perhaps he was growing bored waiting, or perhaps his curiosity was growing; in any case, Angus could see the determination in Wezi's face. He waved an arm in the direction of the portal, thinking, *All right, Wezi, you're a grown man and a solid member of our little band. Let's go.*

....

Forewarned, Angus balked at exposing themselves too fast. Prodding himself and Wezi to fill their lungs he inhaled deeply several times, holding the last one before tripping the door. At the thinnest crack, the small chamber's air rushed out with an audible hiss, raising dust from the floor outside. Angus felt his lungs expand and pressure build behind his eyes. Atmosphere there was, but thin, very thin. The smooth, edgeless room looked eerie in weak, reddish light falling through the opening at the top of the ramp opposite. A thick layer of red-orange dust covered the floor.

Scant atmosphere spelled real danger. Memories welled to remind Angus of what an excursion suit rupture felt like. He was well aware. Still, he could not resist. He stepped out, playing the hand-torch beam at his feet. Wisps of dust rose only to fall rapidly back to ground in the thin air. Impressions of his sandals showed on the dust-covered floor. *The first steps seen there in a very, very long time.* Dim reddish light fell through the opening atop the ramp like the glow from a bedroom nightlight.

Holding Wezi still with a raised flat hand, Angus walked to the base of the ramp. His first upward step sent a warning, slipping in the dust upon the smooth slope. Another careful step later, well before he'd gained any sight of what might lie above, his lungs began to scream. With one last look at the top of the ramp, he listened to better sense and turned. At that moment, his heel came down too hard onto the lower slope and slipped, throwing him off balance. Normally, such a fall onto his rear portions might evoke laughter, but not here. A cloud of dust rose as Angus hit the floor, and his lungs erupted into the thin air. Fighting to regain breath, Angus felt the panic rise. His head spun with each failed attempt to draw in rarified, dust-filled air. Wide-eyed, he looked toward Wezi, still standing in the transport chamber doorway. Fear filled Wezi's face. It was the last thing he saw before losing consciousness.

CHAPTER 34
Exploration

Ooph! What was that? Where am I? Eilen! Where are you?
"Angus! Open your eyes!"

Her face hovered above him like a hazy moon, floating before an indistinct backdrop. *What happened? Where am I?* A picture formed in his head; a picture of Wezi standing in the transport chamber door. "Where's Wezi?"

"He's here. Look." She pointed to the prone figure nearby. Angus saw La'ann kneeling beside Wezi lying immobile on his back, face obscured in shadow, robe covered in red dust. Beyond Eilen, a sliver of star-filled dome shone through the exit above the transport chamber room and Angus knew he was back on the orbiting station. He started to sit up. His head swam and fell back onto the floor, sending a jolt through his skull.

Eilen placed a hand on his chest. "Stay still for a while. Let yourself come around."

"What happened?"

"You tell me. When the chamber door opened, we found you and Wezi lying on the floor, unconscious. The sight threw a scare into me. We tried to revive you there in the chamber, but neither of you responded. Hearing your heartbeat gave me some hope and we moved you out here. I didn't breathe easy until you started to revive."

"There was no air, but light showed from above the chamber room down there and I tried to get a glimpse. I slipped, fell, and knocked the breath out of me. Last thing I remember is seeing Wezi standing in the chamber."

"He must have gone out and dragged you back."

Angus looked again at Wezi. "I should be thankful he's such a strong man."

The sound of Angus's voice sent a fleeting smile across La'ann's grim face.

Trying again to sit up, Angus found more success. In dim light, he could discern only the distinctive outline of Wezi's prominent nose. His dark-in-dark eyes remained hidden behind closed lids. Only after La'ann's expression lost its concern and the corners of his mouth turned upward did Angus realize that Wezi had returned.

Awakening with no more decorum than had Angus, Wezi's questions followed a similar pattern. "What place, I am?"

La'ann said what everyone surely felt. "Good, your voice to hear is."

Reaching to grasp Wezi's hand, Angus welcomed him. "Strong you are. Happy I am."

For the first time Angus could remember, a white arc of exposed teeth spread across Wezi's face.

Distilling a bit of insight from the near-disaster, Eilen spoke slowly. "Warning, see you do? New world, danger brings. Frightened I am." Then, as her eyes focused again on Angus, she added, "Worn we are. To Inyanga, return we must."

Even in his weakened condition, that idea did not sit well with Angus. Slipping into Standard, he let himself go. "Hold on. We still have most of the day ahead of us. Don't you want to see more? There's no telling what we might find. The people who built this transport system must've left something else significant behind somewhere. They may be out there somewhere; alive and well."

Eilen did not want to hear it. "You two almost died! At least, you'll agree that, without proper equipment, planetary exploration carries high risk."

"I'll grant you that, but it's something of a waste to drag ourselves up here and then leave before the day is half spent ... and, to repeat myself, can you think of any more worthwhile way to spend our time than to explore this stupendous thing we've found?"

"How do you feel about limiting ourselves today to a survey of what stations we can find and leaving planetary explorations for another day? Perhaps when we've devised better ways to protect ourselves."

"All right," Angus agreed. Then, noting the very perplexed looks adorning his two other friends, he ventured a grin, "But, you'd better let these two in on the plan. They seem a bit put off by our disagreement."

Slowly pushing himself to a knee, Angus let Eilen convey the essence of her issues to La'ann and Wezi, ending her explanation with a query to Wezi, "Well now, you are?"

Wezi started to speak but stopped as Angus rose beside him. With help from Angus's outstretched hand, Wezi managed to get one foot up under his rear and then allowed Angus to pull him all the way upright. Steadying himself atop both feet, Wezi looked at Eilen. "Well, I am."

Angus put a hand on the back of Wezi's shoulder. "Friend, you are," he said, then paused to add, "Another world, find we can." Turning abruptly, Angus walked toward the exit ramp, leaving the others to follow as Wezi managed to clear the last fog from his head.

By the time the other three caught up, they found Angus in the star-side terminal standing in front of the second working portal.

"See anything interesting?" Eilen asked.

"Nothing significant. This next destination seems to be

just another small yellow main-sequence star ... shall we see what's there?" He stepped down the portal ramp.

The next station did prove more interesting. An active planet-side image completely erased any lingering doubts Angus might have had. He immediately began meandering around the room with his eyes focused deep in the floor.

In spite of her doubts, Eilen rejoined the effort. "What do you see?"

It was at first difficult for Angus to discern exactly what the planet's image was telling him. He saw a bright white surface marred here and there by faint streaks of slightly darker color. Before he had found interest in any particular feature, La'ann stood beside him. "Move, it does," La'ann observed, pointing toward one of the darker streaks. Following La'ann's lead, Angus moved from foot to foot, changing perspective. The motion accentuated the colored streaks and showed them to be wisps of grey clouds drifting high above the background surface. The realization catalyzed Angus's thinking. High clouds demonstrated the existence of atmosphere and possibly of water. Perhaps a planet surface excursion would not be so rash here. The surface temperature didn't look encouraging. What looked like an immense expanse of frozen wasteland didn't speak well for an extended stay. Angus stared at the small illuminated red location indicator, looking for any sign that might convince him of the potential there for an extraordinary find, something to make the risk worthwhile. He saw none.

Returning to the transport chamber, they next found another inactive planet-side station with no wondrous scene to enliven the black of space outside its clear domes and only one additional active starport, a completely uninteresting station, as if its entire purpose was merely to ferry travelers between two, more relevant star-ports. Perhaps there were limits to the distance any single station-jump might be able to project its travelers.

The disappointment of the third station quickly disappeared upon entering the fourth. Stepping onto the star-side terminal room the travelers found themselves in the midst of a beautiful cluster of several tens of bright stars. Space outside the clear dome danced like a swarm of bright, glowing stellar insects, all vying for mating rights on a black summer evening.

Eilen was reminded of her old duties. "Damn! I wish I had my old instruments. I could have fun examining this cluster."

La'ann's voice conveyed the awe he felt. "With their beauty, honor us, Amon's sisters do."

For a short period, the compelling sight pushed other interests into forgotten corners. Then Angus drew himself away and returned to the mission. Leaving the others to their admirations, he delighted to discover six active star portals, leading him to suspect that at least some ports led to destinations within view through the dome. For a while he tried to match the floor image to outside reality, but, the floor's very different perspective left his efforts inconclusive. In the end, it wasn't all that important and the station's planet-side still beckoned. He walked into the internal passage.

The view through the planet-side dome lost a bit of its luster in competition with the gleam from a very bright image in the floor. The planet in the floor was alive. Huge clumps of thick white clouds boiled up from the lower atmosphere, in spots reaching great heights. Darker regions flashed with internal discharge. Small patches of the planet's surface managed to poke a head through breaks in the cloud cover, showing solid green—a dense jungle, or perhaps another tangled Mokililana. The surface of this planet harbored life in great abundance. A trek to that surface would certainly see dangers taking the form of living things.

Well before he saw her, Angus felt Eilen's presence. Strange how well he knew the sound of her footsteps, and how well he heard them. *Sound seems amplified in here.* Kneeling, he felt the floor's hard surface with all five fingertips, giving it a gentle rap with his knuckles—hard as polished stone, an impervious barrier to all but light; a surface to be felt, but not seen.

"This one looks quite lively," Eilen said.

Angus picked up the conversation without lifting his gaze from the floor. "Yeah, but with what? ... I'd very much like to see a bit more of that world down there. This cloud cover makes it difficult to learn the extent of things. I'd feel a little better about a trip down if I could learn more from up here ... parts remind me of the Mokililana. I'm inclined to take a look."

Eilen began slowly, matching the tempo of her words to Angus's rise from the floor, ensuring she had his attention. "You may recall ... we would almost certainly not have survived the Mokililana without the help of our native friends."

In Angus's mind the death of friends blended with a tortuous slog. "Of course. A prudent reminder ... but, at least, I think we should put this one on the top of our candidates for a return date."

The sound of Wezi's voice carried a warm tone. Perhaps the recent misadventure had drawn him more deeply into their small band. He was now as much one of them as anyone. "Something find, you did?"

Pointing toward the world below, Eilen showed Wezi a glimpse of a very lush world. "World alive is. Where clouds are not, there look. Green it is."

Before Wezi could react, Angus had already set out toward the exit ramp. He met La'ann as he stepped into the passage. "La'ann, with me come. Try again we will. More to find there is."

Already forgetting the ripe planet, Angus wondered what new planet awaited discovery. Was there any chance of encountering the architects? *Planet-side terminals seem wrapped in decay. Still ...*

Stepping again into the star-side terminal, Angus glanced around, moved by the impressive display of stars, momentarily undecided. He enlisted La'ann's aid, "Think what, do you, La'ann? Which door, take must we?"

La'ann turned his head, first one way, then the other, slowly surveying the room, then settled his whole body into a new position, facing left across Angus's field of view and, with a jab of his chin, said, "There. Like Isato Mibali, it is."

Following the line of La'ann's gaze, Angus immediately saw why La'ann favored that particular portal. Like the formation of stars above Nahélé that marked the northern direction, three bright stars aligned to point a celestial finger down toward the portal.

Angus stood still admiring the view and realizing how contented he felt. Events had taken quite a turn. From an arrival punctuated by harsh survival, his life on Nahélé's world seemed to have settled into a lethargic existence leading nowhere. Until Nahélé's nomads set him in motion to find the civilized center he had begun to suspect. Now he stood here, amid the most fantastic machine he might ever have imagined. Yes, he felt good.

Standing next to La'ann, Angus had to appreciate the part that his native friend played in his new adventure; La'ann, the brother he never had. The thought struck him just as Wezi and Eilen emerged from the internal passage. Wezi, whose strength had just saved his life; and Eilen, who now occupied a place in his life no other could ever match. Suddenly, the allure of his former life aboard the Raiju seemed to fade into a pale and forgotten shadow. That Wezi should speak seemed to fall in line with the spirit of the moment. "Chosen you have?"

"This one to La'ann belongs. Choose, he did."

Nearing the exit portal, Angus stepped aside and, with a sweeping gesture, bid La'ann lead Wezi and Eilen down the ramp toward the next station.

Wrapped in private expectations, the four star-travelers

362

arrived onto the floor of the day's newest revelation. Where the last station bathed in the grandeur of a tightly woven tapestry of bright stars, this station's terminal dome spun a view of stars in a fine, loose, delicate lace.

A tour around the circumference of the star-side terminal room met nothing but dark, dead portals—the end of the line. Disappointing, but the planet-side terminal remained to be examined. A quiet, contemplative mood had grown among them. No one spoke as they all stepped out atop the image in the planet-side terminal floor. The world below their feet rekindled the awe in all.

Angus was struck silent by the sheer beauty of it. Wezi and La'ann drew audible breaths. Eilen reacted. "Oh! Look at this one!"

A water world, covered in deep blue—a real ocean, one of the miracles of the universe. Surely, creatures swam beneath that blue surface. Without another word, they all fanned out across the floor, every eye fervently searching for the locator beacon, asking where a journey down to that world might take them. A few moments passed before anyone found it. "Here!" La'ann said finally, his normal speaking voice ringing loudly in the silent room.

Standing alone near the room's single active portal, La'ann stared down into the floor, unmoved by Angus's approach. Drawing near, Angus quickly saw the object of La'ann's gaze. A meandering shoreline running across their view from away on their left to near on their right hand, marking a sharp transition from the deep blue ocean color to a light brown landmass. Angus let his eyes follow the shoreline, telling himself that it ran along a northwest to southeast direction. By such convention, he saw their small view of the planet surface separated into a northeastern half covered by landmass and a southwestern half, covered in blue water. Not far northeast of the shoreline, a change in color marked what had to be a range of hills, or perhaps mountains, shadowing the shoreline along nearly the entire length. Angus traced the line of hills down, turning to his right to see them flanked by featureless dry land around a southern edge.

Mottled foothills separated the dry tans of the lowlands from the dark green of higher valleys slopes. Near the lower edge of those hills, the bright red locator beacon appeared, blinking like an insistent alarm. Curiously, as though the one gave birth to the other, a dark green, serpentine line rose from the terminal beacon's location and meandered down toward the ocean, finding the water in a small fan of darker color. Little imagination was required to see that line followed a flow of water ending in a delta at the edge of the sea. The dark green color would easily result from an abundance of plant life, slaking its thirst along the water's course.

The entire picture felt warm and welcoming. Even their high-altitude view of Nahélé's world had not presented a picture quite so comforting. Angus reminded himself that Nahélé's reality was much more benign than the satellite view had shown. The picture before him seemed more welcoming than had Nahélé's world.

A long silence passed before Angus broke the mood. "This one looks like one we might visit."

"It does look inviting, doesn't it," Eilen agreed, pulling a hand to her chin. "Perhaps we can, at least, take a preliminary look."

"Here. What, it is?" Wezi said, moving to squat directly over where he had been looking, a point immediately above the small delta where that course of water met the sea. Wezi's simple curiosity drew everyone to his side and enjoined all eyes to the discovery. "Look. There. See it you do?"

Bending low, as though by moving one single meter closer the kilometers-high view might be improved, Angus peered intently at the patch of green forming the river's mouth. Eilen saw it first. "Yes. I think you're right, Wezi. There is something odd there. See ... near where it begins to widen ... the color changes and there's a pattern."

Now everyone focused on the apex of the delta fan. Was it unusual in some way? La'ann gave his realization a description. "Like the midfloor fields it is."

Nature does not generally play in straight lines. Straight lines are created, a product of intelligence, yet here were straight lines, decorating the edge of the delta. That small piece of the surface of the planet below was inhabited; by whom, or by what, one could not answer by staring down from kilometers above.

"Where's my hand-torch?" Angus asked no one.

SHIPS AND SHELTER

CHAPTER 35
Junglegrass

A faint swoosh accompanied the door's opening. Chamber light spilled forth. Something large and solid waited outside the light's edge. Before moving a limb, Angus cautiously drew in a small breath. Finding no issues, he ventured forward, hearing in his first, hesitant steps an unfamiliar dull echo. The usual metallic edge was absent. The room felt smaller.

Eilen's hand-torch came to life, illuminating a far wall covered in a swarm of snakes. The smooth-walled room they had come to expect lay hidden behind a knot of thick, sinuous ropes, some as broad as a well-muscled thigh, entwined with thinner arms and fingers. The naturalist in Eilen spoke first. "These look like roots. Some large plant has sent roots down into the transport terminal in search of whatever it needs. You can see how the lines tend to converge there where the top of the ramp would normally penetrate the ceiling."

Angus stared at the wall of roots. "I suspect our hand weapons will have little trouble blasting through it ... and I'd very much like to see what things look like outside. I'm in favor of blowing a hole through that root wall and climbing out. Does anyone object?"

"I don't, but Wezi and La'ann should have a say."

Rummaging within his pack, Angus found his hand

weapon. "Fine. Let's show them instead of explaining."

While Eilen searched for her own weapon, Angus swept an arm aside, telling Wezi and La'ann to stand at his back. Aiming at the center of the root-mass, he fired. The root-mass exploded. Wiping moist plant tissue from his face, Angus turned to see Wezi and La'ann doing the same, looking quite put-off by the task. By way of apology Angus said, "Too much strong."

Caught in a crouch, Eilen received the spray on her backside. Weapon in hand, she rose and passed her hand-torch to Wezi. "Perhaps two less energetic beams can accomplish the task a bit less messily."

A second later, the edge of the ramp showed through a two-meter round hole in the root mass. Behind a steady barrage of moderate bursts, the two energy weapons cleaned the ramp up to the room's exit. A short time later their efforts had produced a tunnel to the level above, where a flat, level floor remained from whatever structure had once housed the transport terminal. There they were forced to stop, leaving Wezi with no reason to continue holding the beam of Eilen's torch. He played it at their feet and stood with Angus. La'ann and Eilen were surrounded on all sides by a woven wall of vines.

Forgetting himself in his confusion, Angus said in Standard, "I have absolutely no idea in which direction we should move. Which way is 'out'?"

Although he could not have understood, La'ann offered a suggestion, "Libókobamoto ... kill it, you must."

As Wezi played the torch beam around it seemed that the tangle of roots had woven themselves less densely on this upper level. Spaces existed among the tangle of larger roots. Wezi extinguished the torch before anyone asked, leaving them all in complete blackness, seeing only the random fleeting scintillations of saturated retinas. Angus turned himself to stand sequentially in each of four evenly spaced positions. No direction seemed to distinguish itself over the others.

In the darkness, Wezi, said, "Here, look," but, no one could see in which direction Wezi looked. Angus convinced himself of the merits of one particular direction. "Wezi. Cold Flame, life again give." The sudden glare shuttered every eye, to cautiously reawaken seconds later. When he could once again see clearly, Angus found his three friends all facing the same direction as he.

Wasting no time in analysis, Angus fired in that direction. He and Eilen pushed ahead, encouraged in short order by thinning vines and the eventual appearance of the withered remnants of old leaves. The tangle of twisted sinews soon became thin enough to offer a convoluted path through which any one of them might climb without the need for blasting. Dim natural light filtered down through dense foliage. Stowing both weapons and torch, they crawled and climbed, moving over and around but always upward through a snarl of vines. The temperature rose.

Climbing through tangled vines became strenuous, sweaty work. The suffocating jungle exhaled a moisture-laden breath, drenching the interlopers in their own perspiration. Sweat-laden cloaks became weighty burdens and dragged upon every protrusion. Minutes began to feel like hours. In the lead, Angus soon began to fade. When would it end? Desperate to get a glimpse of what lay around them, Angus turned from the slowly rising path and began climbing directly upward. Perhaps he could find a place to see above the tangle.

Nothing came easily. Everywhere he looked sinuous plant stems as massive as small trees wound around each other as if each sought the other's demise. Angus found footing on one sturdy stem after another, struggling over barriers whenever their many pathways crossed. A steadily rising path seemed elusive. When at last only smaller, leafy vines filled the space above, he stopped.

"Help I need," he said as the others caught up. He held out his pack for Eilen to hold, while he pulled his arms from the sweat-soaked, clinging cloak.

Before Angus could free himself, La'ann put out a hand, held Angus's arm and said, "No Ahngoose ... Climbing, I do." Allowing no argument, La'ann proceeded to strip himself down to the forest clothes he'd been wearing beneath one cloak or another since saying farewell to Mœrai.

While La'ann climbed higher no one spoke. Straining to keep the barest glimpse of him in his sight, Angus watched La'ann pick his way upward until he disappeared into leafy growth. Not many minutes later, La'ann returned. Everyone else waited as La'ann sat and let his breathing slow. Eventually he stood and extended an arm. "Far, forest goes. No end," he said. Twice, he turned and extended his arm and said, "No end." Upon turning himself toward the fourth direction, he broke into a broad smile and said, "One way only, end, it does."

The vine-choked jungle stole all sense of direction from Angus. La'ann's ability to find bearings in the thick growth put him in the lead. Tenacious vines were a determined opponent, steadfastly resisting the travelers' every effort. With cloak wrapped now around his pack, Angus still sweated from every pore. The effort to keep pace with La'ann put into his mind the day La'ann's skill took them across the Molikilana, sweating weight from their bodies much as they did now.

Stepping over a small vine stem, Angus paid it no mind, oblivious to the twitch his misstep produced in its frozen demeanor. A moment later, Angus heard Wezi yell, "Ahngoose!" On unsure footing, Angus required a moment to secure himself. As soon as he turned, he saw Wezi on his rear with a leg wrapped in a small vine. Angus had only begun to wonder how Wezi might have accomplished the strange pose when a second loop dropped over Wezi's head. Wezi eyes grew wide. Behind Wezi, Eilen stood with her hand weapon at the ready, searching for a point of aim. La'ann eased himself close to Angus with knife in hand. A narrow beam from Eilen's weapon struck a serpentine section above Wezi's head bringing forth a flow of black fluid. Wezi's eyes closed, his mouth opened wide, struggling for breath. Angus raised his hand weapon, looking for aim at the very moment a sinister form rose from below brandishing a dark cavity larger than Wezi's head. A series of muscular rings arrayed behind the gaping hole pulsed in regular waves. Around the mouth, a ring of fat cilia waved anxiously as though each writhing tendril competed with its neighbors for the first taste.

Eilen's second shot cleaved the ghastly head and send it plunging into tangled depths. A tremor washed through the worm's long body. Wezi gasped for air. Standing opposite, Angus watched helplessly as the worm's dead weight pulled Wezi from the wide vine-trunk. Wezi's flailing arms sought a hold. "Ahngoose!" Falling to the vine surface, Angus stretched a hand and grasped only air.

The loop of rope flew with purpose, finding Wezi's flailing arm and wrapping itself even as Wezi closed his grasp. The dead worm dragged Wezi over the edge. "Hold!" La'ann yelled as he let his own body fall off the vine. Eilen screamed, "Nooooo!!" A wave of horror swept through Angus. Not quite able to process what had happened, he lay prone on the vine, arm stretched to no purpose. Eilen stood frozen with weapon raised. No one moved.

Then La'ann's voice rose from below. "Ahngoose! Ee'laan!"

Pulling his head over the highway vine's edge Angus peered into shadow, afraid to confront what he hoped not to see. Relief replaced horror.

Wezi dangled there, legs kicking empty air, one arm wrapped in La'ann's rope. La'ann hung a bit higher, providing a well-placed counterweight to Wezi's weight. The swirl of emotion now made room for admiration of La'ann's extraordinary and very quick thinking.

That worm's attack left senses awakened. Danger lurked amid the giant vines. When a freshening scent and cooling airflow signaled the possibility of an end, anticipation hastened their efforts.

The vines did finally thin, but any elation over the victory was dampened by another sight. A sheer cliff rose above their perch at the jungle's edge, separated from the last reaches of twisted vines by a moat of vacant space. A downward glance revealed a tale of jungle vines struggling to climb the wall. Some distance below, the jungle met the wall head-on, sending upward from the meeting place countless grasping runners. Several weathered, lifeless vines hung from the edge of the precipice, withered skeletons marking the results of failed climbs.

Staring at the gulf, La'ann pondered any attack on the obstacle.

Angus had other thoughts. "La'ann. Worry not. Here we stop."

"Cross it I can, Ahngoose."

"Believe you I do. But worn we are. And water we need. Return we must."

Speaking Standard, Eilen sounded relieved. "I think you're right. Now that we have some idea of what we'll need we can return better equipped."

Wezi's news changed the picture. "Light we have not. Cold flame, lost it is."

The unwelcome announcement threw the discussion into silence. Angus tried to imagine climbing through the maze of tangled vines in darkness. "Flame torch make we can."

La'ann's disagreement came in two steps. "Here, nothing burns. Above, hard land there is." Then, breathing deeply he added, "Breathe, I must. Down again, go I wish not."

The gulf looked daunting but spanned only a couple of meters. La'ann's decision was made. He stood and pulled the rope from his waist, dropping several loops at his feet. Tying a loose loop into the rope's weighted end, he laid a length out straight behind him and stretched an arm to find a grip. His arm whipped forward to send the weighted end flying toward the wall. The first attempt dropped away.

La'ann aimed his second try a little more toward a protruding length of dead vine. The second throw snagged itself. La'ann stretched the rope taut, testing the strength of his anchor, straining until the end loop slipped off and fell again. Somewhat encouraged, his third attempt went in the same direction. Again, he tested and met firm resistance, absorbing every bit of muscle La'ann could exert.

"First up, I go," La'ann said as he grasped the slim bridge he had fashioned.

Angus's voice held concern. "La'ann careful be. Strong it is not, I think."

The better part of an hour later Wezi, La'ann, Eilen and Angus sat atop the plateau. A dense carpet of green foliage filled the ravine from which they had just climbed, stretching to the distant side and appearing so nearly flat and solid that one might imagine walking across it. Around them in every other direction stood dry grass as tall as Angus. Securing a footing had also formed a trampled clearing large enough to allow them all to sit and take stock.

The effort to reach the plateau had left them all panting and drained. A gentle breeze wafted across the jungle-filled canyon, drawing the sweat from tired bodies and setting it free into the air. Exhausted but happy to be done with the humid jungle, everyone sat gathering breath. Saturated robes came out to lay atop grassy pallets and dry in the sun and breeze. In the back of every mind, the same thought: How will they ever return to the transport station?

La'ann tied bundles of grass to mark the spot on the canyon rim. Then Wezi stood and announced, "High my head is. Leading now I do." No one objected. Wezi looked along the canyon's course. He had but two directions to choose.

Somewhere beneath the canyon's green canopy water flowed toward the possibility of cultivated fields. Which direction? Putting the canyon on his right, Wezi set forth.

Thick and tall, the grass hid from all but Wezi what lay ahead. Bound only by the canyon, it seemed to go on forever in every direction but one. The wafting breeze set a grass-filled horizon in motion. The waves fascinated Wezi. Dry, flowing air pulled moisture from his cloak, cooling him.

Settling into rhythm, letting each step follow the swing of his arms, Wezi swept the grass aside. The blue expanse of clear sky riding above the golden hue of an unbounded ocean of grass reminded him of clean, open desert. He felt calm, content to push on as long as there was light to guide him.

In this manner, some distance passed below everyone's feet while sunlight faded into a deepening red as it crept toward the horizon ahead.

Wezi stopped. "There away, light I see," he said, pointing in the direction they had been traveling. A bit of sunlight reflected in the distance.

....

The grass ended abruptly, cutting across their path in a straight front. Four faces peered through carefully parted grass stems, staring at a small group of domes. Angus had seen such a scene before—prefabricated structures, a small farm. Scanning the area, he tried to identify the purpose of each dome. The farthest seemed to be a dwelling, distinctive in the number of windows piercing its shell in two levels. The structure closest on his left made itself known less from its appearance than from the sound of motors operating within—a pump house, drawing water through the thigh-thick pipe running away behind it toward the river that flowed from the shallow remnant of the upstream canyon. The other two significant structures, one low and wide and one much taller than the others, would be needed to house equipment and animal feed or such. But for the unknown character of their location, the pastoral scene might otherwise be reassuring.

Angus's head swam with questions needing answers. *Where might we be?* A few more steps would leave all cover behind. Are we prepared for an encounter with whomever or whatever lives here? What else can we do? There's water here. Less risky if we fill up after dark. The local sun is already low. Not long before evening settles. Perhaps we can also get a look at the shape of these farmers. We'll have to regroup anyway.

"Sound what was?" Wezi said in a low voice.

"Hear something you do?"

"Yes. As before I hear."

"Still be. Also hear, I do."

The animals came at them at once. In the space of a single breath all four humans stood exposed with their backs to the farm staring at six snarling heads protruding from the grass. They looked like long, thin dogs but low to the ground; owning a long snout and a prehensile nose. Beady eyes set wide aside told of poor eyesight. Perhaps they didn't need to, or couldn't, see much in their world of tall grass. One dog rose off front paws waving his long nose around. Perhaps they relied on scent rather than sight. These dogs evolved, not to see above the height of the grass, but to hide within it and gain advantage with other senses. Four unwashed humans made for easy detection.

From all but one dog came a low steady growl. The odd one loosed a succession of yips and snorts, marking him the pack leader. A fleshy scar across his snout and a single protruding spear-of-a-tooth left no doubt of his role as hungry carnivore. One yip-howl from Scarface spread the dogs apart trying to outflank their prey. At the second yip they all moved forward with bared-teeth. End dogs pressed closer on each side. Two energy weapons gave the four humans one advantage. Occupying the left side, Angus fired at the closest dog, already threatening to get behind him. His first shot elicited a loud howl and left that dog without a paw, limping but not retreating. Scarface barked out another order and his troops settled into constant motion. Accurate shots became more difficult. Blending into a continuous blur of motion, in and out and back and forth, the dogs relentlessly continued closing the trap. Angus felt for the spread control on his weapon, not daring to take his eyes off the animals. At this short range, he should be able to blow that snarling head completely off. The moment the nearest animal saw the weapon turn away, it lunged. Angus had barely enough time to retrain the weapon and fire, hitting the animal's hindquarter and forcing a retreat. The odor of singed fur filled his nose. A second dog lunged even as the first retreated. He had little time to wonder why the shot had not done more damage. Unable to re-aim, Angus brought the butt of his weapon down upon the second animal's head, forcing another quick retreat.

Eilen's first shot missed, raising a cloud of dirt behind the near dog. The dog seemed to gain courage. Her second shot struck hindquarter, raising both yelp and limp.

Energy weapons weren't their only defense. The weighted end of La'ann's rope lashed out at the dog holding the far right, winning a satisfying yelp. Slinging whip snaps about wildly, he held back the entire snarling right side of the formation.

Wezi stood tense, knife in hand, waiting for a chance to slash at a pair of snapping jaws.

Angus fired madly. A hasty third shot missed. Never before had efforts on the training range seemed so worthwhile. His next shot struck home again and, to Angus's horror, barely singed a spot of fur. He'd finally run out of power. Another completely ineffective shot confirmed his fear. "I've run out!" he shouted above the sound of snarling dogs.

With every dog firmly in view, Eilen edged closer to Angus, reaching to pull Wezi's cloak as she moved. Scarface sensed the growing advantage and, with a sharp bark, sent the left-side dogs pressing to within a short thrust away from sinking tooth into flesh. Eilen succeeded in forcing them back one more time, firing several quick shots in rapid succession.

La'ann continued snapping off whip shots, holding the right flank at bay, but the dogs watched, learning the rhythm of his rope until a snap of jaw finally pinned it long enough for two more to get it between their teeth. La'ann and his rope were out of action.

The four humans bunched close. Frail as they felt, the four still moved toward the last remaining gap. Angus readied himself for a vicious hand-to-claw fight. He focused on the nearest dog, listening to its snarl, seeing the intent in its eyes and the tension in its legs and trying to anticipate the moment it would spring. The flash of decision came and Angus set his legs to receive the lunge. At the same instant, a loud crack rang out as the dog's right hindquarter exploded, sending it howling to the ground. Startled, Angus stared at the writhing dog. A second later he turned to look for the source of the sound. A man standing upright took aim along the barrel of a shoulder weapon. Another sharp crack split the air. No yelp followed. The shot separated its target from life with an explosive loss of the animal's head, leaving it slumped on the ground in a heap.

Much more quickly than it had begun, the confrontation ceased. Scarface and his troops disappeared into the high grass, leaving two corpses to mark the spot.

Angus, La'ann, Wezi, and Eilen held a steady gaze on the still-quivering reeds even as the last dog slipped between them. Only when he was sure of the dogs' departure did Angus turn to confront their rescuer. Angus's hand weapon rested empty on the ground. The native had not yet lowered his weapon, still holding it at the ready, pressed into his shoulder, aimed, as far as Angus could see, directly at him.

"Who are you?" the man said in clear Standard Galactic

speech.

CHAPTER 36
Captive

The door clanged shut, adding cold exclamation to Angus's return. Easing himself onto the narrow bedframe, he looked around, noting the psychology on display: the much-too-heavy door; the small, stiff bunk; the high, tiny window; the hard, grey walls. The cell was not built for comfort, neither physical nor mental, it was designed to wear its occupant down ... and, until not more than a few minutes ago, Angus would have said it was working.

How long had it been since he lost the Raiju? He was no longer sure. The passage of time had become an abstract notion. Struck by the irony of the situation, he allowed himself a lopsided smile. The League had caught him after all.

Grey metal stared at him from walls, floor and ceiling. A bit of outside light fell from a single opening opposite the door, perched too high to allow a view of anything but a small patch of sky. Two narrow, covered slots adorned the heavy metal door, both opening from the outside. His captors kept an eye on him through the high one. Trays with food and water slipped through the low one. A seat in the far corner covered a commode. The cell was well suited for the slow torture of solitary confinement.

Earlier that day, he had been certain of the garrison

prison's success, instilling the despair for which it was intended. The dismal cell was beating him. The mental strain of only a few days of interrogation had drained him. Keeping his secret was a struggle. The secret of Haven must be preserved. No representative of the League could discover even a hint of his origin. Awakening that morning with a head full of fog he had felt his resolve weakening. He knew he'd not be able to hold out forever. Then the day's interrogation brought a break in the dark clouds, a patch of sunlight to lift his spirit. Today he learned more than had his interrogator. Today he knew there was a way out. He need only hold out a little while longer.

His cot felt more comfortable than it ever had. He began to think, reviewing what he knew. Recalling his capture, he remembered the shock of hearing Standard spoken.

The four explorers could offer little resistance when security personnel came to take them. Uniforms, mannerisms and speech told Eilen and Angus that they had stumbled onto an outlying League settlement, an early-stage colony, just beyond exploratory, a small permanent settlement with emerging agriculture. Such a colony would be frequently supplied with essentials—regular visits by League starships. When Angus noticed the schedule posted on the wall of the reception room of this very building, it had not seemed like much. Too small to read, it might have only been a duty schedule, but important enough to post.

Now it all fit together. Angus's interrogator's anxiety had given rise to one little slip. Wanting desperately to demonstrate achievement, he had mentioned how his chance would come in two days. The remark added color to the broader picture: a somewhat overweight and sloppily uniformed garrison commander, who carried the rank of Major, too high for this backwater post. The man anxiously wished to redeem himself from whatever misstep had sent him into exile and four mysterious, alien-looking prisoners were just the kind of spice that might get him the attention he needed.

This backwater colony possessed little, yet among its first permanent structures had come a detention center. What did that say about League priorities? Still, the League had not supplied it with more than rudimentary interrogation methods. Angus and his companions need only keep up the pretense. *Eilen will speak only Batololému. La'ann and Wezi can do nothing else.*

More sophisticated methods would wait until the prisoners were transported to a larger, more established security facility, a facility that would also be able to identify Angus Hirano. The League of Planets had a long memory, especially when pertaining to the theft of one of their cruisers. Neither Angus nor his companions could be allowed to reach that place, not if the people of Haven were to escape the ignominy of existence under League rule. *We either escape or die trying.*

Angus began thinking in earnest. A glance at the hem of his sleeve bolstered his confidence. *A bit of luck there.* The lapse spoke again to the garrison commander's lack of Security Force experience. Standard protocol would dictate confiscation of a prisoner's own clothing. Yet his Inyanga robe remained. They'd left it as his only covering. Perhaps they thought the growing stench would help the tongue loosening process. A good strategy in theory; the sterile smell he'd noticed upon arrival had long since fled, outmatched by the odor of his own body. Angus rubbed his hand over the fabric, remembering his last meeting with Su'ban and comforting himself with the knowledge of what remained hidden in the hem of its sleeve.

Mind wandering, he thought about how amusing it was to watch his captors grapple with the sudden appearance of four strange humans. A smile grew. The contents of their carryalls didn't help matters, especially the hand weapons. Fashioned strangely, they appeared different from anything the garrison commander had ever seen, closer in some ways to weapons he'd only heard of from long ago.

Angus was having difficulty maintaining a consistent story. The garrison commander did not quite see how a faulty NavCalc and a much-too-stressful drop might cripple a starship. The story was not succeeding—too many details for Angus to explain. His very scruffy appearance did not help.

The major clearly wasn't satisfied, nor was he concerned. His failure to wrest a true story from his prisoners may have vexed him, but he remained confident in the power of methods at the disposal of a more capable unit. The League's security forces had many and better located elsewhere. The truth would come out and there would be glory in the story. The major was counting on it.

And Angus was just as certain that he'd be the first to receive the bulk of more capable attention. No. There was no question about it. Angus could not let himself fall into the hands of more capable interrogators. He'd simply have to escape.

....

No one had visited for quite some time. Angus had to wonder why. Had it been more than two days? Three? He couldn't be completely sure. Fatigue was starting to play tricks, and he had no idea of normal daylight patterns here. He was no longer sure of the pace of days or of much else. How many meals had he been fed? How long had it been since he last spoke to any of his companions? He was beginning to lose patience. Plans, however, were taking shape.

....

Another trip to interrogation. The drab corridor was

becoming quite familiar. How many times now had he made the journey? Angus tried to get a peek into another of the holding cells, desperately wanting to see one of his friends. It wasn't a large colony. There were only four doors. He and his companions likely filled them all. Before he could even get an eye to the high opening on the door, the guard behind him shoved the butt of his weapon into Angus's back. They continued toward the far door on the opposite side of the corridor. Angus knew it well—the only other room he'd seen since taking up residence in the small cell he'd just left.

Reaching the far door, Angus glanced through the clear top-half panel, surprised to see a new face. A uniformed officer sat at the opposite end of the table within. Angus recognized the uniform—a ship's captain, wearing a Service Dress uniform. *A supply ship! Why would the ship's ranking officer come here? And why would he wear a formal uniform? Gotta admit, the man looks good.* Angus strode into the room, walking a little more upright than he had been a moment before.

....

Happy to be outside for the first time in many days, Angus smiled as he walked out of the Security Building. Sunlight on his face, a gentle breeze flowing across his body, and a tang in the air combined to make him feel alive. Sometimes it doesn't take much.

The four prisoners walked in line, manacled to each other hand-to-waist with forearms bound together wrist-to-wrist, elbow-to-elbow. Angus realized how difficult it would be to run or strike any kind of blow. The League's security forces had been doing this sort of thing for a long time. No prisoner of the League would ever surprise a guard with any well-directed elbow.

Today's events signal something unusual. The last time

Angus had been able to speak to anyone outside of interrogation had been upon arrival. Now he was anxious to speak to Eilen. He needed to convey some inkling of his plans. There might not be another chance. He was last in line. She walked ahead in front of them all.

Angus looked up to realize that Wezi might not understand what he was about to say. At least he could draw some comfort in the fact that the guard beside him would certainly not understand.

In as clear a Batololému as he could muster, he said to Wezi's back, "'Dream World medicine', I have. When give I do, you eat. La'ann and Ee'laan tell."

"Understand, I do not," was all that Angus got out of Wezi before feeling the sharp jab from the business end of a shoulder weapon. The guard behind him barked. "Shut up and keep walking! Let's get this done. You really stink! You know that?"

A small bus waited out on a road running between several buildings. At the bus door, guards separated the prisoners and, one by one led them aboard to be re-bound into separate split-bench seats, next to a window on alternate sides, leaving an empty bench between them on each side, as good a job of isolation as the small space allowed. There was no chance to speak. With all four prisoners secured, the two guards sat themselves down on the single long bench in the rear. The garrison commander boarded last, walking down the center aisle to sit in the rear. Angus had to wonder if things were going according to his hopes.

As soon as the bus cleared the last building in the small settlement, Angus saw a planetary cargo shuttle parked alone on a flat, clearance. His heartbeat rose. Won't be long now! Angus was happy he had spoken when he did. *If Wezi can only pass along the message ... and if I can only get a finger into that hem.*

....

The orbital flight encountered little more than typical atmospheric buffeting. Exterior views are an unaffordable luxury on a simple cargo shuttle, but it didn't matter. Each change in the vehicle's motion added a small brushstroke to Angus's mental picture of the ascent and evoked scores of welcome memories.

Snug seats for perhaps 25 filled the forward compartment, leaving room for a larger, open cargo area in the rear. From his position in the front row, bound as he was, Angus could see no faces. Thinking that Wezi and La'ann likely did not share his pleasant assessment of the trip, he imagined what expression they might be wearing.

Close approach to the orbiting starship came with its own litany of maneuvers and conveyed a clear picture to Angus of the shuttle's position at each step. Angus couldn't keep himself from judging the pilot's clumsy docking maneuvers.

Restrained by lines binding his forearms to the seat beneath him, Angus could only sit and wait. Would the opportunity show itself? Will he be able to use it if it does? How many of the ship's crew descended for R&R and how many remained aboard? The primitive outpost offered little as an R&R station, but bored starship crews will take what they can get.

Excitement pushed even these worries from Angus's mind. He felt like a little kid, excited, as he had when he first saw the vast bulk of any starship. Since then he had seldom sat in any but the pilot's seat, and he had never sat anywhere quite so restrained.

The starship's Transfer Bay did not seem as large as many Angus had seen. He found himself again at the rear as the four prisoners walked off the shuttle. He observed things arranged in a manner fitting his picture of the situation. Cargo was assembled on mobile pallets to one side, a group of crew members were standing in formation, arrayed five by five, awaiting their turn for planetary R&R. Angus reflected on the fact that supply ships would not be expected to sport a large crew.

It felt good to be free of restraint. Angus looked down at the small pill in his hand. Things were about to change.

CHAPTER 37
Celebration

Alexandra's stateroom seldom played host to merriment. Only a grand occasion would prompt her to pour libations from her private liquor supply, the kind of liquor for which only someone of her station might develop a taste.

"It's a great moment ... a great moment for us all," she said, turning the bottle up to let the last drop fall into her own glass. Setting the bottle down on the desk behind her, she turned and lifted her glass to salute her bridge crew. "I congratulate you all for a job well done."

With a second nod, Alexandra tipped her head back and threw the sharp liquid into her mouth, swallowing in one quick gulp. Ceremony concluded, Semgee noted the change in her expression. He took the initiative. "Duty calls, gentlemen," he said to the small gathering. "Semgee, would you hold for a moment?"

"Certainly, Honorable Captain."

Before the door to her cabin closed behind the last crewmember, Alexandra had already stepped behind her desk. She spoke with her back to Semgee. "We need to plan an endgame here."

"I have given the matter some thought, as I know you would expect, Honorable Captain."

"Of course, you have, Semgee. Can I hear your recommendations?"

Semgee hesitated, knowing his analysis would provoke reaction, trying to frame a positive, or at least well-composed, answer. "First, I'd like to remind us both of some obvious weaknesses in our position."

Seeing no change in her posture, he continued. "We are but a single ship and we carry a mere skeleton crew. Yet we must be prepared for a hostile reception. We don't understand the strength of our opponent; nor do we even know what sort of weapons we may face. We don't even know with what kind of alien beings we're dealing."

Uncharacteristically, Alexandra sat still, pulling at her lower lip, staring at the stateroom door, giving every indication of listening.

Semgee pushed ahead. "Honorable Captain, I think we would be wise to mark the location of the alien world we've discovered and return home to escort a full fleet back here."

Then, realizing he'd erred in the omission of one crucial argument, he added, "The First Council would undoubtedly place you at the head of such a fleet. It would be a big feather in your cap."

Alexandra sat up, turned to face Semgee, settling folded hands on the desk in front of her. "Yes ... It would be ... but an even bigger feather would be mine if we returned with a signed treaty and an emissary to give our accomplishment some teeth. They would almost certainly vote me onto the First Council before any fleet returned. Our deeds will be recorded for posterity. It'll be historic."

She did, at least, give her First Officer's argument credit, acknowledging his appraisal of Victory's readiness for action, "I agree. We are light, but we have a very capable ship, with extraordinary firepower ... and we did include a skilled weapons officer among our crew. I suspect we'll get no resistance at all, but should we encounter any, I think a suitable demonstration of the power of our weapons, perhaps against a sizable population center, will secure a rapid capitulation. We haven't, after all, seen anything in the two outposts that we've thus far examined, to lead us to believe these aliens possess any kind of technology to overshadow our own."

Glancing away, Alexandra refocused somewhere behind Semgee. "You do have a point about the limits of our small crew. I would propose some caution. Our small numbers will render unwise any thought of allowing a departure of any crewmember from the ship ... and, I think we'll have to be careful. We should allow no more than a handful of aliens on board. Communications will be critical. Perhaps we can transfer personnel using a shuttlecraft in orbit. I'd like you to devote a little more thought to those matters."

Alexandra paused before returning her eyes to look directly at Semgee. "Tell Commander El-Hashem to prepare another test program for his weapons system. I want to see how rapidly and how utterly we can destroy an entire city. I'm sure he'll agree. We should be prepared. I expect the sudden loss of a few hundred thousand, or perhaps a few million of its citizens will ensure better cooperation from our foe."

CHAPTER 38
Intergalactic

Angus felt at ease. For the first time in a very long time he was completely at home. His earlier dirty, disheveled appearance had felt so alien alongside the sterile surfaces of the ship. With a glance at La'ann, he noted how loose gomba fleece robes appeared unseemly among the crisp lines of the bridge space. His friend's neutral expression revealed little of how the forest native might view the freshly commandeered shipboard clothing Angus now wore. Appraising the bridge deck of the League starship, Ganymede, he had to appreciate its neat, orderly appearance. The projection field's central location told him he was not aboard the old Raiju, but in many other respects, he was in familiar territory.

The projection field held a beautiful image of the Milky Way filling the entire display. Pointing to a dense bright spot not too far from the nexus of one of the Milky Way's arms, Angus tried to give his friends some perspective. "La'ann, Wezi ... bright spot ... there. You see? To Amon's home, close it is. By great distance, tiny Amon becomes. See her you cannot. Small she is." Angus paused to see if his ideas were gaining traction. "... but there Amon and her sisters be. Count them you cannot. Like all the leaves on all the colōfn trees within Nahélé's arms, or as the grains of sand in the 'desert between the mountains' they are."

Futile... neither La'ann nor Wezi had even the slightest grasp of what they saw or of how far from their world they now stood. Nor did that fact seem to give either of them reason for concern. Angus could see how comfortable they both were. So strong a trust had grown from the past days' adventures that little more than the sight of Angus and Eilen's own easy comfort was required to put the two natives of another world at ease.

Admitting failure with a shrug, he caught Eilen's crooked smile.

"Valiant effort ... but I don't think you're getting through." Then Eilen took her thoughts in another direction. "I'm not sure I believe what happened. It all happened so fast I think I may be as numb as they are. One minute I'm walking off the surface shuttle, trying to make sense out of the words Wezi whispered in my ear. The next thing I know I'm tying members of the ship's crew into the shuttle seats." The amusing memory brought on a smile. "At first, I didn't understand it at all. Not until the restraints suddenly fell from my wrists and one of Su'ban's 'dream world' pills appeared in my hand. Then it all made sense."

Angus nodded. "I'll have to give Wezi a medal. If that message doesn't get delivered, things might have gone badly awry. I really needed everyone ... especially him. I'd never have been able to do it alone. The 'dream world' gave me freedom, but it didn't give me either the strength or the stamina to manhandle the ship's crew by myself." One thought led to another, pulling his mouth into a wry grin. "I wonder what that ship's captain and his crew thought when they found themselves seated in the shuttle hold with nowhere to go. Gotta be frustrating to realize that, without weapons or excursion suits, they're stuck there until we restore pressure in that Lander Bay."

The thought gave Angus reason to muse. He continued

thinking aloud. "It strikes me that I've now stolen two of the League's starships. It could become a habit."

Then he settled back to the business at hand. "How many more jumps do you think we need? I'm a little anxious to show Wezi and La'ann something of our home?"

CHAPTER 39
Fate

Alexandra stood erect, preening, straightening her uniform for the fourth time—her full-dress uniform, a gaudy garment that came from some long-ago period, adorned with gold buttons and colorful medals. She always held her head a little higher when wearing it.

"Think of it, Semgee! We'll be the first to extend the League's borders to another galaxy. Could there be any greater glory?" Unrestrained, she rambled. "I'm a little disappointed we never had the opportunity to show them the real power of this ship. Too bad. They should have seen it. They'd never then question our authority."

Semgee wasn't at all disappointed. The rapid turn of events surprised him as well. For once he agreed with her. It was a historic moment.

Observing the entire expanse of the Lander Bay, Alexandra and Semgee stood within the comfort of the ships' environment, thick transparent doors standing between them and the hard vacuum of the other side. Bathed in the bright lights of the Lander Bay, the angular shuttlecraft settled onto the deck, a wash of engine exhaust flaring silently beneath its bulk. Heavy outer bay doors were already narrowing the gaping hole, sealing the bay from the vacuum outside.

Almost disappointed to watch those doors close, Semgee's mind had not yet settled. Immediate events vied with the beauty of the view through the opening, a glorious picture of a half-illuminated planet below, dimpled with clouds and agleam against a black backdrop of deep space.

Alexandra felt some concern. She should have someone besides Semgee at her side, but not for fear of harm. There was little danger. Her personal safety was protected by Commander El-Hashem's diligence at the trigger of a host of weapons trained on the bay interior. Rather, she felt the occasion called for a more impressive welcoming contingent, an imposing host of the League's capable warriors, a show of might. Circumstances dictated otherwise. Still, she thought to reassure herself. Speaking into her intercom, she said quietly, "Commander, do you have their craft in your sights?"

"Aye, Honorable Captain, deflection field up and weapons trained."

"And the internal defenses?"

"Affirmative. I have the entire Lander Bay covered. If they twitch in the wrong direction, I'll bring them down before they can bring any weapon to bear."

Turning to Semgee, she continued the thought, "How many delegates have we agreed to allow onboard?"

"Only five. We can expect one of them at least to be experienced in defensive skills." Taking a moment to consider what other information his captain might wish to consider, Semgee eventually added, "The lead delegate is probably the only one of any importance. I'm sure the other four will be merely bodyguards."

At the instant the outer bay doors came together, a dull thud travelled through the ship's structure to announce the seal. A slight creak from the inner doors testified to the equalization of air pressure within the bay. One short moment later, a segment of the shuttlecraft's side swung out and down to meet the deck, sending a metallic clang through the restored atmosphere and forming a smooth exit ramp below the doorway now open in the side. A man appeared in the doorway. The bay's inner doors slid open. Nothing more than ship's air and a few steps stood between Alexandra and Semgee and the newly conquered aliens.

Alexandra took a few, but only a few, steps into the bay. It was more fitting that the aliens should do most of the walking. She watched them file down the ramp and re-order themselves at the bottom, crossing the open space as a small phalanx, shoulder to shoulder.

Noting the height of several delegates, Alexandra squared her shoulders. The idea rankled that they would look down on her. She touched the medals on her dress tunic. "*The two on the one end are certainly strange looking ... and what kind of dress is that?*"

Occupying one side of the approaching contingent, two very dark, nearly eyeless faces, one sharp and angular, one flat and round, peered back from atop tall bodies clad in shimmering white robes. On the opposite side of the group, strode two uniforms befitting starship officers, cleaner and less gaudy than Alexandra's, but decidedly handsome. Between them all walked a smaller man, wearing nothing extraordinary, a simple blue tunic, belted at the waist. As if synchronized, they all stopped in unison, leaving perhaps a three-meter gap between themselves and the two representatives of the League of Planets.

Semgee tried to take them all in at once without turning his head. Failing, he allowed his eyes to rest on the tall two in the shimmering robes. They were most interesting. He'd never seen anyone like them. They seemed human, but more exotic than any person he'd ever seen on any world within the League's reach. He found them marvelously beautiful.

For her part, Alexandra had a hard time concentrating on the details of the moment. "*Perhaps,*" she thought, "*I might find it quite rewarding to represent The League of Planets'* interests here. Think of it. I could be the governor of the Lesser Magellanic Cloud ... governor of an entire galaxy. That might be worth more than a seat on The People's Council."

When the small man in the middle stepped forward, Alexandra's thoughts fell suddenly quiet. What's the protocol here? Too engrossed in the grandeur of the impending event, she hadn't even consulted the ship's manual. No matter. When has this ever happened before? When the man stretched out his right arm holding open the palm of his hand, she could only think to emulate the action. She held out her right hand.

Then she blinked.

....

When next she blinked her eyes were confronted with the rears of two high-backed cockpit seats where a moment before she'd been looking into the faces of several alien representatives. Now she saw only the two seats and farther away, a restricted view through the windows of a vehicle, a view of the Lander Bay. It took her a moment to realize she was aboard the shuttlecraft.

What happened?

She turned her head left. What's wrong here?

Then she noticed the straps around her wrists, binding her arms to the seat beneath her—a well-padded seat; a tight-fitting seat. Turning her neck as far as she was able, she could see her weapons officer seated beside her. If she strained forward, she could look left to make out Semgee strapped into the seat beyond Commander El-Hashem. Where the others here as well? In much too loud a voice, she spoke toward the vacant seats at the front. "By duty station, sound off! ... Navigation!"

Her answer came from close behind, if a little less energetic, "Here, Honorable Captain."

That's one, she continued, "Systems?"

Young Thomas's voice sounded a bit muffled, farther away. "Here, Honorable Captain."

"Communications?"

"Present."

"Engineering?"

"Here, Captain."

"Maintenance?"

"Here, Honorable Captain."

"Galley watch?"

"Present, Honorable Captain."

Alexandra hesitated, unable to remember what station they'd formally assigned their jack-of-all-trades, "... and you, Mr. Fuhrmann?"

"I am present also, Captain."

Although she knew the answer before asking, she felt compelled to ask, "Is anyone free to move about?" A complete silence gave her the answer she expected. The same result followed her next question. "Does anyone have the slightest idea how we got here?" Hoping to perhaps encourage a freer discussion she began thinking aloud. "The last thing I can recall is holding out my hand to greet the alien representative. I touched his hand and then I think I blinked, and the next thing I saw was the inside of this vessel ... Commander El-Hashem, you were watching the scene from the bridge, through the bay's cameras. What did you see?"

"I am thinking, Honorable Captain ... I can remember the group approach. I remember you holding out your hand. Then I think I saw four of them vanish ... Before I could even be sure of that, I found myself here."

"Semgee, you were there with me. What did you see?"

"Honorable Captain, I've been searching my memory. I remember no more than you. The last thing I remember is thinking that you were being quite gracious to hold out your hand as you did. Then everything changed and I could see only the back of this seat."

CHAPTER 40
Reunion

Its sheer size evoked awe; a truly remarkable vessel, larger by far than any ever built in Haven. The League of Planets seemed to expect their ship to accomplish its mission by size alone. Standing in the ship's bridge, the entire group, seven world governors, a number of senators, and the four honorees, marveled at the openness and the gleaming new appearance of the large space. Angus tried to imagine the group stuffed into Raiju's bridge where they might have fit only if they pushed into every back corner.

Russell Four's quiet-spoken governor led the visiting contingent. Angus found difficulty dealing with the man's slow pattern of speech and frequent silences.

The ship's tour had left Angus subdued, thinking of what the destructive potential he'd seen might have done to the planet below. His quiet attitude signaled the end of his duties as tour guide, opening the floor to the Governor.

"I'm sure I speak for the entire contingent ... when I say, thank you, Captain Hirano ... for your hospitality ... in guiding us through this grand vessel ... Speaking for myself ... this is the first time ... I've ever seen ... an operational example of a League warship ... In fact ... this is the first time in quite a while ... that I've set foot off of Russell Four.

"It occurs to me, Captain ... that every person of Haven ... owes you a great deal ... Not only ... have you been instrumental ... in averting the greatest crisis our civilization has ever faced ... but you've also managed ... to deliver to us ... this magnificent vessel ... That makes three now ... does it not?"

Angus hesitated, considering the truth of the statement. It was, in fact, true. During his service he had piloted three League starships into the custody of Haven. "Yes, sir. I guess it does."

"Do you have any idea ... how much it costs ... to construct a starship, Captain?"

"No Governor. I've never thought of a ship in such terms."

"A great deal more ... I think ... than you or I will earn ... in our lifetimes." A longer pause fell onto the exchange. The governor took his time shifting onto another subject. Angus stood silent.

Although it remained soft, there was no mistaking the dramatic shift in the governor's voice. "I'm afraid ... our immediate future ... will see a large diversion of energy ... toward the production of warships ... At least ... we'll have some time ... You've given us that much."

The statement demanded no response but Angus realized the occasion might offer an opportunity for another idea he'd been forming. "Sir, it strikes me that there is time but it won't be enough." The observation hung unchallenged until Angus picked it up again, speaking slowly, sprinkling his words with pauses, as though taking a note from the Governor. "I may have an alternative for you to consider ... The League of Planets has thousands of warships ... already built and in service ... We've done it once. We might do it again ... Do you suppose the League would greatly mourn the disappearance of a few more of their ships?"

The last to leave, Angus and Eilen stood before the lift door awaiting their turn. The others had already ascended to the reception awaiting on the galley level. Angus let his eyes roam the bridge, drinking in its expanse.

Noting the faraway look, Eilen said, "Quite something, isn't it?"

"Yes, it is. Quite something."

"Think you'll be happy playing captain here?"

"Now that would be something!"

"And who else do you think they'd give it to?"

Angus smiled. She was probably right. "The thought reminds me of the ship's former League crew. How do you think they'll fare as farmers on Calivar?"

"I think that captain of theirs will have some trouble, but the others will figure out how to make themselves useful. I hope they can satisfy themselves with a limited view of the stars."

Angus continued to let his mind roam free. "Can you believe Wezi and La'ann, leaving us alone like that? When was the last time you can remember being without them?"

"They do learn quickly, don't they?"

"Yes, but they'll want to return home soon ... just as we will." Angus paused. Thoughts that had been forming for some time came back to him. "I've been thinking about just what 'returning' may mean and I've come to realize that it may not be all that simple."

Eilen face tightened. "I think I know what you mean. I've been a little worried myself about what our 'return' may mean for the people of Nahélé."

"And of Inyanga. And those issues are only a part of it. What we discovered there puts that planetary moon in the eye of a gathering storm and I don't know if we'll be able to ward off the damage that is likely to come along with it."

"At least, you'll have a new ship and a new crew to help

you manage it all. I wonder if Deshi would want to come with us?"

"That's a nice thought. But don't go thinking that a fully manned starship will make things all that easy. No one can know we're there. We'll need to establish a stealthy base of operations and a secure means of transport before we'll be able to allow anyone but the four of us who have already been there to descend onto that planet, or moon if you will."

Angus stopped speaking and his eyes drifted upward as thoughts suddenly turned down yet another road. "You know, we never gave that planet a name. The Nahélébato call the forest 'Nahélé', and, Wezi's people call their desert the 'Isihlabthikhulu', but neither have a name for the entire world. It seems to me that we're free to give it one. What should we call it? I was thinking: Uko's Child, 'Mwanaūko' in Batololému. How does that sound to you?'

"I kind of like it. I've come to love seeing Uko, in the sky and her moon feels like a new home." Eilen paused before completing the thought, surprising Angus with where she took it. "And maybe Wezi can teach me to ride jimi's."

"Yes, there are many good reasons to return to Mwanaūko. I took a number of hand-torches from the ship's stores. I think we have debts to pay ... What do you say? Do you think you can find it again?"

"I'm pretty sure I can."

"Good. I'd like to go home, too. We have much to tell Su'ban."

About Atmosphere Press

Atmosphere Press is an independent, full-service publisher for excellent books in all genres and for all audiences. Learn more about what we do at atmospherepress.com.

We encourage you to check out some of Atmosphere's latest releases, which are available at Amazon.com and via order from your local bookstore:

Saints and Martyrs: a Novel, by Aaron Roe

When I am Ashes, a novel by Amber Rose

Melancholy Vision: A Revolution Series novel, by L.C. Hamilton

The Recoleta Stories, by Bryon Esmond Butler

Voodoo Hideaway, a novel by Vance Cariaga

Hart Street and Main, a novel by Tabitha Sprunger

The Weed Lady, a novel by Shea R. Embry

A Book of Life, a novel by David Ellis

It Was Called A Home, a novel by Brian Nisun

Grace, a novel by Nancy Allen

Shifted, a novel by KristaLyn A. Vetovich

Because the Sky is a Thousand Soft Hurts, stories by Elizabeth Kirschner

Stronghold, a novel by Kesha Bakunin

Eyes Shut and Other Stories, by Danielle Epting

Unwinding the Serpent, a novel by Robert Paul Blumenstein

All or Nothing, a novel by Miriam Malach

About the Author

Rod was trained as a scientist and spent years writing stale technical reports. Along the way, he stole a few odd hours to write more colorful tales onto notepaper resting on the tray table before him while seated in coach at 33,000 feet. He now lives in California and manages to find somewhat more hours trying to coax a story or two into words.